KINGS
OF THE
PROMISED LAND

A NOVEL

ENDORSEMENTS

The way that Justin Gabriel describes the characters, the landscapes, the atmosphere surrounding the events that take place in this work of biblical proportion calls to mind the writings of J.R.R. Tolkien. The meticulous attention to detail and historical accuracy is refreshing in a niche of literature dominated by overuse of "artistic license", but the author still brilliantly succeeds in conveying a story so well known in such a new and vibrant way that the reader is left thirsting for more after finishing the last page, and the story remains present in the mind long after the book is closed.

—Laurel Chapman

The rich storytelling is gripping. Hard to put down. The characters that you think you know come to life in ways I never thought possible. I feel like I can relate to the characters even though their culture, time period, and geography are different. Highly recommend to anyone looking for the next book series to get into. Ready for Book Two!

—David Bentley

WHAT READERS ARE SAYING

"A Biblical Game of Thrones."

"Makes the scarlet thread that weaves all Scripture together come alive for me!"

"A masculine work of biblical fiction."

"I actually felt as if these events were unfolding right before me."

"Calls to mind the writings of J.R.R. Tolkien."

"Visceral and captivating."

KINGS
OF THE
PROMISED LAND

A NOVEL

JUSTIN GABRIEL

PUBLISHING THE POSITIVE
Plymouth, Massachusetts

COPYRIGHT

Requests for information should be addressed to: Elk Lake Publishing, 35 Dogwood Dr., Plymouth, MA 02360, 2022

Author Represented By Hartline Literary Agency

Library Cataloging Data

Names: Gabriel, Justin (Justin Gabriel) 1984-

Title: *Kings of the Promised Land; A Novel* / Justin Gabriel

392 p. 23cm × 15cm (9in × 6 in.)

Summary: Conflict is erupting again in ancient Israel.

Identifiers: ISBN-13: 978-1-944430-12-2 (trade) | 978-1-944430-13-9 (POD) | 978-1-944430-14-6 (e-book.)

Keywords: Christian History; God's Chosen People; Kings of Israel; Samuel the Prophet; Hearing the Holy Spirit; Saul; David

TABLE OF CONTENTS

FOREWORD

From the very beginning of time until the end is a *really* long time, and all that time is packed full of events. Right? Any historical record consists of selected events based on the writer's knowledge and purposes. That's as true for the Bible as for any other history book. So what avid Bible reader has not at some time said, "I wish Moses (or any other of the biblical writers) would have included more about the life of Abraham (or some other biblical character)?"

That, of course, is where biblical-fiction authors come in. Sadly, some of those fiction authors take undue liberties as they expand the stories and the characters. After reading the first installment in the *Kings of the Promised Land* series, which focuses on Israel's first king, Saul, I'm confident the author, Justin Gabriel, did well in staying true to the original author's intent. With an eye for detail, respect for the original narrative, and an insightful imagination, Justin Gabriel has filled in much of King Saul's back story. I'll be watching, with great anticipation, for the next book in the series.

—Jerry Gramckow

ACKNOWLEDGMENTS

I would like to especially thank the following individuals for their contributions and support:

- Jim Hart

- Deb Haggerty

- Jerry Gramckow

- Joelle Diepenbrock

- Kelly V Miller

- Jonathan Coon

The historian will tell you what happened.
The novelist will tell you what it felt like.
                                                    —E.L. Doctorow

Instruct me, for Thou know'st; Thou from the first
Wast present, and with mighty wings outspread
Dove-like satst brooding on the vast Abyss
And mad'st it pregnant: What in me is dark
Illumin, what is low raise and support;
That, to the highth of this great Argument,
I may assert Eternal Providence,
And justifie the wayes of God to men.
                                    —Milton, *Paradise Lost, Book 1*

I will sing a new song to Thee, O God;
Upon a harp of ten strings I will sing praises to Thee,
Who dost give salvation to kings;
Who dost rescue David His servant from the evil sword.
                                                    —Psalm 144:9-10

ACT ONE

RELUCTANCE

—I—

"The P'lishtim are again surging at our borders, threatening to invade! Not to mention the 'Amoni. We will be powerless to defend ourselves this time."

The crowd stirred and murmured in agreement.

Another man spoke up, "Even the lowliest P'lishtim soldier carries weapons of iron, training constantly for war. We are just peasants with plowshares with no one to lead us in battle."

The murmurs grew louder. Then another voice, "Our enemies laugh at us! With their right hand they strike us at will from their outposts throughout our land, while with their left hand they take our money as our people go to them to beg for their services. They play tribe against tribe!"

The seer, Shemu'el, rubbed his face tiredly with his wrinkled hand as he sat before the throng of elders, representatives of every tribe. The men were growing bolder and began raising their concerns all at once. He started to lose track of who was saying what.

They had come to him as they had many times before, chief elders of the Twelve Tribes and their entourages arriving in sequence: Efrayim, Dan, Binyamin, M'nasheh, Gad, Re'uven, Y'hudah, Yissakhar, Z'vulun, Naftali, Shim'on, and Asher.

Here, in Ramatayim, Shemu'el resided in his ancestral home amid forest and limestone crevice in a corner of these fertile highlands. This was the place of the seer's withdrawal, as it were, from public life. The region, the district of the Tzufites, was named after his great-great-great-grandfather, and gave the now aged man a sense of place—a feeling of rootedness—to know both the location of his birth and the tomb of his wife were scarcely more than a hundred paces from him at this moment. But withdrawal was not retirement. In recent years, Ramatayim had swollen to over one hundred persons with the formation of the seer's special school.

Amid the bleating of penned goats and the dust from hoof and sandal swirling in the warm air, the townsfolk and students shared hushed rumors as the prestigious procession had made their way up to the high place for this gathering. A long time had elapsed since the whole house of Yisra'el together had come before Shemu'el. Something was different about this visit.

The seer had begun with sarcasm, "So now, what brings you all, respected men from every tribe, to my humble home? Is it my birthday and you have come to throw a feast in my honor? Or perhaps there is a dispute among you your judges cannot work out in your own gates? Or, is it that you all, at the same time, have come up with some question about the Law, which your own scribes and the Levites living among you cannot answer? Which of these bring you to me?"

The elders responded with flattery. "Shemu'el. Truly you are a man of Yahweh, the one true God," an elder from the tribe of Binyamin said, "a more righteous judge is not to be found in the land."

"It is safe to say," an elder from Asher added, "there is no more respected man in all of Yisra'el than you."

Shemu'el waved his hand dismissively.

"If I wanted to hear flattering words all day, I could have remained in town with some of my insufferable students. Speak plainly!"

He impatiently scratched in the dirt with his staff as the men argued among themselves in rising tones. One by one they began unloading their multitude of complaints until all of the elders reached their present state. The cacophony rose to a fever pitch until the wizened seer could bear it no more. He raised his staff for silence.

"What are all these bitter words? You weary my heart. And still you have yet to ask anything of me."

A respected elder from the tribe of Y'hudah, near in age to Shemu'el, stood and cleared his throat.

"Shemu'el, you have counseled us justly and judged for us at Beit-El, Gilgal, Mitzpah, and even here, for as long as I care to remember—as long as some here today have been alive. Furthermore, when the P'lishtim advanced on us at Mitzpah, you led us to great victory."

Shemu'el interrupted, "Yahweh gave you victory. Prayer, sacrifice, and repentance gave you victory."

"As you say," the elder continued, "Yahweh. Yet it was you who chastened us to repent and to offer up unceasing cries. You drove us to remove the idols from the land. You offered the burnt sacrifice. You erected the Stone of Help after we had routed the enemy. I myself remember in those days single-handedly chasing away three P'lishtim with one of their own swords. But I was a young man then, full of strength. Now I have grown old. You too have grown old. You don't travel the circuit to settle our disputes anymore. As you desired, we have let Yo'el and Aviyah judge for us in Beit-El and Be'er-Sheva. But ..."

An awkward, knowing silence spread through the crowd.

Then, someone near the back said in a loud voice, "Your sons are nothing like you."

Shemu'el winced at the words and lowered his gaze to the ground. The gathering rippled with tension. At length, the elder from Y'hudah exhaled resignedly and resumed his speech. "Shemu'el, please. You have heard reports. Your sons have not been walking as you walk. And now, fewer and fewer trust them, but what other choice do we have? If we continue in this way, the tribes will disperse, with every man doing what is right in his own eyes."

"It's true!" another yelled out. "We are growing weaker when we need strength and unity!"

The elder from Y'hudah quieted the bustling crowd and turned to again fix his gaze on Shemu'el.

"I will put it plainly, as you asked. 'Eli is dead. The priesthood is in disarray. The Mishkan has long since been dismantled and removed from Shiloh. The once mighty hero Shimshon has perished in Gaza. And you ... you have turned your attentions on your Nevi'im. Your sons whom you appointed cannot take your place. When you go to sleep with your fathers, there will be none to lead us."

Then came the request.

"We want you to appoint a king."

The staff slipped from Shemu'el's grasp and clattered down the small ridge where he sat.

"A king?"

"We are surrounded on every side by wealthy and strong nations. All led by kings!" said an elder from the tribe of Dan. "We need a king to unite us. To fight our wars. To judge for us."

"Yes! We beg you. Choose a man to rule over our nation. Someone who can protect our cities and storehouses from our foes and who can avenge us against all the wrongs of the P'lishtim!"

"A king! A king!"

The elders cried out in hearty support and entreated the wise man again and again.

"A king! A king!"

They would not be dissuaded. Shemu'el felt his tongue turn dry in his mouth and could make no more response seeing that they were all in perfect agreement. Finally, after their shouts and exclamations drew quiet, he mustered the breath to answer.

"Leave this for today. I have heard all you have come to speak. I will take this matter before Yahweh." He could not hide the disappointment in his voice.

That evening, Shemu'el paced the floor of his home distractedly waiting for his students to finish their evening prayers before ushering them out and extinguishing the oil lamp. Immediately, he turned and went into his inner chamber.

A king. Why? The fools! The arrogance of it all.

His breath felt hot in his throat, and there was a dull ache in his chest. And their remarks about his sons ... whispers of corruption ... accusations of bribery. The truth cut to his very core, and he could not help but think of Hofni and Pinchas and their failures ... and their deaths. He pushed these thoughts down and sunk slowly to his knees on the hard floor. Seldom before had he ever felt this old.

"Here I am," he groaned in prayer. "Your servant is listening. What shall I say to these hardheaded people? What answer can I give them for their evil request? These men who desire to be like all the other nations."

Shemu'el continued in fervent prayer, being able to find neither comfort nor rest. Well past the midnight hour, the still, small voice of Yahweh came to him.

Shemu'el.

"Yes, my lord ..."

You feel rejected by this people, but it is not you they have rejected. They have rejected Me as their king. Their desire is to rely on the power of man.

The seer exhaled slowly, bringing all of his attention to focus on the voice.

Truly, the people are only doing what they have always done—from the very day that I brought them out of slavery in Egypt. Their hearts are so eager to turn to any alternative to Me, toward their own destruction. Now then, in this request, you will listen to them and do what they have asked of you. You will appoint a king, but you shall first give them a solemn warning of all that I instruct you to say.

Early in the morning, Shemu'el arose and walked through his home. The sun was just beginning to rise, and the horizon was slowly being flooded with gray light. He detected movement out of the corner of his eye and was startled to see the form of a person loitering in the hall.

"Who is there?" he asked, squinting in the dimness.

"Master. It's me," answered Gad, a student barely twelve years of age.

"Gad? Is that you? What are you doing here? You were not on prayer duty last night. Why are you not at home?"

"I ... I traded places. Manoach was ... he has a sore throat."

Shemu'el grunted and shook his head.

"Well, I give you leave. Your watch is over."

Gad hesitated.

"Master, I ... I have some food for you if you would like. I noticed you didn't eat anything at dinner last night. You didn't even drink your water."

"Hmm?"

Sure enough, Gad was holding a platter in his hands. Shemu'el could smell bread and olives.

"Yes. I was not hungry."

"Are you well? I heard lots of noises in the night. Is something troubling you?"

Shemu'el sighed and placed a hand on Gad's shoulder, turning the boy around and moving him out into the main room with him.

"I think you are too young to understand this. But— people, the rulers of the tribes, every last one of them—they are not satisfied with their current form of government. That is what is happening now. That is why they are all here. As you should know, Yisra'el was called to be different from all the other nations, with Yahweh Himself as their leader. They are to be a chosen people, set apart. But their impulse is for a king, a human king to rule over them with human wisdom. Time and time again, Yahweh has provided for them and has rescued this people. And they want to turn their backs on Him."

Gad fell silent. Shemu'el took the platter from his hands and set it aside.

"And that, child, is why I have no appetite."

The seer thought Gad would say no more and was about to usher him out of the house when the youth added, "Didn't Moshe say this would happen? That the people would one day ask for a king? I believe it is written in the Law before the portion of the Levites is described."

Shemu'el was taken aback in surprise. "Well! Young Gad, I am impressed. You have certainly been studying your doctrine."

He reached down and ruffled the boy's hair. Gad's face flushed with pride, but this was hidden in the low light. Shemu'el let his mind go to the words of Moshe recorded in the D'varim, the five-fifths of the Law, words recorded almost four hundred years ago.

"So he did ... so he did."

"Listen here, men of Yisra'el," the seer addressed the assembled elders. "Ever since God brought your fathers out of Egypt with a mighty hand, this people has continually turned aside from following Him, even to this day. Now I have brought your petition for a king before Him, and He charged me to give you this warning regarding the manner in which a king will rule over you. Thus says Yahweh:

"He will take your sons. He will make them his horsemen and his charioteers and as infantry running before the chariots. He will assign for himself commanders of thousands and of fifties. Some of your sons he will make to plow his fields and to reap his harvest and to make weapons of war and equipment for the chariots. He will take your daughters. They will become perfumers in his service and bakers and cooks in his kitchens. Likewise, he will take the best you own—your fields and your vineyards and your olive groves. These he will give to his servants. Likewise, a tenth of your grain and a tenth of your vintage will go to his officers and attendants. He will take a tenth of your flocks. Your best male and female servants, your cattle, your donkeys, your young men ... these he will use to accomplish his work. And even you yourselves will become his slaves.

"In that day, you will cry out because of your king, whom you have chosen for yourselves, but Yahweh will not answer you."

Shemu'el allowed himself a wry smile after concluding. The gathered men turned and hurriedly began conversing with one another and discussing all he had told them. The seer could catch only bits and pieces.

"It only makes sense to give honor to a king and to give our sons for soldiers. Does it not?"

"We'll cry out because of our king, he says. Ha!"

"But which tribe will he be from?"

"It doesn't matter which tribe! We will turn twelve tribes into one kingdom!"

After some discussion, they one by one turned and unanimously declared ...

"There shall be a king over us! It must be!"

"A king! A king!"

Shemu'el gritted his teeth and with a sharp voice dispersed the gathering, instructing them he would once more take the matter before Yahweh. He had been told the people were not rejecting him, and he could make the choice to believe that. What made his heart fill with sorrow now was not about him—he was sad for the people. He was sad because he knew Yahweh was going to give them what they wanted.

That night in his inner chamber, in prayer, he repeated all the elders had said in reply to the warning, and he brought the whole matter once more before God.

Again, the quiet, steady voice of Yahweh answered, *Shemu'el. You will listen to their voice in this matter and appoint for them a king. Tomorrow morning, send every man back to his city and have them wait for the proper time.*

"I will do as you say. But who will be king over all of Yisra'el? Where will I find such a man?"

Don't worry. He will find you.

—II—

The late spring sun radiated down on the grassland, stretching out in the wide, cradling valley. Sha'ul knelt to untie and retie the leather strap of his sandal, which had been chafing against his ankle. He hesitated, low to the earth, and wiped a bead of sweat off his forehead. How far had he walked already today? And how much longer would he have to be out here searching?

"Master Sha'ul!" a distant voice rang out.

Sha'ul stood and shielded his eyes, trying to determine the origin of the sound.

"Master Sha'ul!" the voice cried again.

He turned and made out the dot of a man atop the crest of a gently rolling hill.

"Over here!" he yelled across the expanse.

Hamor, a family servant, waved his arms and hastened to make his way down toward him. He was nearly out of breath after crossing the field.

"Any luck?" Sha'ul asked, holding out his hand for Hamor's water skin.

"Nothing ... my lord. No sign of them," the servant panted. He handed over the skin. "Out of water again?"

Sha'ul shot Hamor a look as he raised the container to his mouth and drank deeply.

"Those asses," Sha'ul muttered, wiping his mouth and tossing the skin back. "We've been through Efrayim ... Shalishah ... Sha'alim. Where are those cursed animals?"

"Nobody in any of the towns has seen them. My lord, you must be more careful with your rations, especially in this heat."

Sha'ul grunted.

"We've been looking for three days," he said. "For all I know they could be three days in the opposite direction. What a headache!"

"Shall we split up again to cover more ground? Do you think we should head south, southwest, or back to the north? If we keep east, we will be in Binyamin once again."

"The last thing I want to do now is retrace my steps. My father needs those she-asses. Let's keep going the way we are."

Sha'ul and the servant Hamor continued their search, at length finding themselves in the land of the Tzufites. Still, there remained no sign of the prized donkeys. They made camp in the shelter of a small thicket of terebinth trees and tried their best to sleep through a night that was unusually chilly.

Sha'ul arose with the dawn and wandered about the camp, stretching his achy back and limbs and brushing stray blades of grass out of his night-black hair. Hamor opened his eyes and sat up sleepily. Without speaking, the two men ate a meager breakfast of dried figs. Sha'ul stared blankly into the space before him as he finished chewing.

"Master Sha'ul, you have a melancholy look about you."

"I didn't sleep well. Bad dream."

"What was it about?"

"I don't remember," Sha'ul sighed, pulling his cloak tighter around his shoulders.

Hamor looked at him expectantly in the growing silence, waiting for him to decide their next move. Their rations would need to be replenished soon. They were getting farther from Giv'ah, and the animals were nowhere to be found.

"If we stay out here much longer, my father is going to stop worrying about his lost herd and start worrying about us," Sha'ul reasoned. "Maybe we should pack up and go home."

Hamor nodded affirmative, and they began gathering their belongings. Then a thought came to the servant.

"You know, Master Sha'ul, it just occurred to me that we are close to Ramatayim. Do you know it?"

"What of it?"

"It is supposed to be that a man of God lives there. People call him a seer. They say everything he says comes true. Have you heard of him?"

"No, I don't think so."

"The place isn't far from here. I'm sure such a man could tell us about our journey, that we might not return to your father in vain."

Sha'ul considered this.

"Hmm. I see. But if we go, why should this seer bother with us? Who are we to him? And what can we even offer for his troubles? We're completely out of bread. We don't have anything valuable between us."

Hamor grinned and dug his hand into a concealed pocket of his garment.

"Well, Master, I just so happen to have in my hand here a fourth of a shekel of silver, for emergencies. Your father doesn't trust me to look after you for nothing."

Sha'ul began to smile for the first time in days.

"Well, what are we waiting for?"

The two men ascended toward the town of Ramatayim, tired, practically bare of all provisions, but with a renewed sense of purpose. What had Sha'ul to lose anyway? If this seer was all Hamor said he was, maybe a positive outcome could yet be salvaged from all this wandering.

They passed by a flowing spring. Ahead they saw a group of six young women walking down the footpath to draw water with their ceramic jars. They giggled among themselves when they saw the two strangers and were clearly eyeing Sha'ul as they drew nearer.

"Ah, perhaps your God had in mind for you to find a second wife through this ordeal," Hamor whispered playfully.

"Shush. The only females I'm looking for right now have four legs."

Sha'ul took a step toward the women and bowed his head in polite greeting, flashing a winning smile. The youngest girls in the group stifled giggles.

"Excuse me, ladies, could you help two travelers? We are looking for the seer. Where can we find him?"

The girl closest to Sha'ul batted her eyes shamelessly and held out her jar for him to take.

"If my lord would only be of some help to me and draw water from the spring, I'm sure I could be of some help to him."

The other women laughed uproariously. Sha'ul smiled again and obliged her. After easily filling the jar, he rested it on his hip, cradling it loosely in one muscular arm. Soon all the women were urging him to fill their jars as well.

Hamor stood to the side and observed the spectacle, shaking his head with a smile on his face. His master, the

Binyaminite, was a very handsome man—and he knew it. He stood a head and shoulders taller than the servant and just about every other man around. With his large, thick hands, broad shoulders, firm jaw, and a full head of dark black hair, he was accustomed to the flirtatious attentions of women. Hamor mused that if Sha'ul had lived in a more sophisticated and thriving city than what had become the relative backwater of Giv'ah, he may not have been so quick to marry Achino'am those sixteen years ago. Alas, Sha'ul was an uncomplicated man, and he took the duties of being his father's firstborn and tending to the family business in his hometown seriously. Still, he knew how to use his charms.

"It's been a pleasure to lend a hand to fine women like yourselves. Now I don't suppose you'll ask me and my companion to carry all your jars up the hill for you ... can you tell us if the seer is here?"

"It's a good thing you came today. He just returned from a journey," one of the women answered.

"So he's in town?" Hamor asked. "Great."

"Yes, he is. But hurry and go up. The people have a sacrifice today, and he's on his way up to the high place. Those invited won't begin to eat until he gets there because he has to bless the sacrifice. If you go quickly, you can probably catch him."

Sha'ul thanked the women, and the two hurried up to the entrance of Ramatayim on the lesser of the two hills. They passed through the gates and looked around. Sha'ul noticed a plainly dressed old man walking toward them as if to exit the town and decided to ask him for directions.

"Excuse me, could you please tell me where is the house of the seer who lives here?"

The old man looked up and met Sha'ul's gaze. The man's eyes were bright and his look intense in a way that troubled Sha'ul. His uncut shock of silver hair and full beard made him both startling and distinguished in appearance. The old man was studying him carefully.

"I am the seer, Shemu'el. I am the man you are looking for."

Standing before Shemu'el was the one Yahweh had spoken of. He certainly looked like he could be a king. He was tall, strong, and handsome, in the fullness of his young age. He looked like a man other men might follow.

"Oh! I ..." began Sha'ul.

"I am going up to the high place to bless and offer the sacrifice for the people. Go on up to the place of worship ahead of me. You will dine with us and rest tonight, you and your servant. Tomorrow morning, I will reveal to you all that is in your heart."

Sha'ul stuttered in reply, "B-but ... sir, I ... we ... we only need to ask of you about the welfare of my father's missing donkeys. We have tra—"

"Donkeys! Do not give a second thought to the donkeys that were lost three days ago. They have been found. You and I have much more important matters to discuss. Indeed, the desire and the hope of the whole nation of Yisra'el is upon you and your father's house, Sha'ul, son of Kish."

Sha'ul and Hamor exchanged a sideways glance.

"Me? I ..." Sha'ul replied, stunned. "Surely you must have me mistaken for somebody else. I am a Binyaminite, of the smallest tribe of Yisra'el, and my family is the least of the families in all of Binyamin!"

"No, but come with me to the offering and the feast. All will be made known to you tomorrow, as I said."

Sha'ul, in bewilderment, agreed. He and Hamor exchanged another look, and Hamor shrugged as they walked up to the place of offering ahead of Shemu'el. Hamor wondered if the seer was jesting with his enigmatic statement, but he knew who they were, and he knew about the donkeys.

A gathering of locals had assembled on the second hill in expectation. The weather was cool and the sky clear. A feasting hall was set up adjacent to the altar for prominent guests; the rest of the people would share their meal outside. Most of Shemu'el's students were in attendance, and playful children accompanying their mothers and fathers lent a festive air to the proceedings. Sha'ul and Hamor tried to blend in while they waited.

The crowd grew quiet as they saw Shemu'el approaching, leading beside him a young goat. He led the animal, a male without any visible blemish, up to the altar of uncut stones. A Levite from Efrayim had already kindled a fire that was steadily smoking.

Shemu'el placed his hand on the head of the goat and offered up a blessing to which all those gathered listened in solemn silence. Then, with the Levite holding a basin in which to catch the goat's blood, Shemu'el drew a knife from his robe with his free hand and slit the animal's throat.

After the sacrifice, Shemu'el located the visitors and brought them into the dining hall. Before them was a long table with about thirty seated guests. The seat of honor, at the head of the table, was vacant. Here Shemu'el led Sha'ul and encouraged him to sit. The servant Hamor was seated beside him.

Sha'ul swallowed hard and looked around at the faces of the guests. They stared back at him in curiosity. These were certainly distinguished men: the fathers of families throughout the district of the Tzufites, some Levites, and others personally invited to partake of this feast. Sha'ul had been deliberately placed at the head of the table as if he were of the highest rank. He suddenly became very conscious of himself—a man of no special standing, more or less unwashed, having sweated and slept under the stars for the past three nights. What must these strangers think of him?

Male and female servants began to pour wine and serve unleavened bread to the diners. Shemu'el, taking a seat beside Sha'ul, had milk brought for him, as he followed the diet of the Nazir. Others, not knowing exactly how to respond to Sha'ul, raised their cups politely and nodded in his direction. He did his best to smile and appear at ease.

Shemu'el beckoned one of the female servants near and murmured something to her. She quickly exited and returned with a middle-aged man who appeared to be the cook.

"Bring the special portion I told you to set aside and give it to this man seated beside me."

The cook nodded in agreement and left. He returned with a large portion of meat and set it before Sha'ul. His portion was the roasted leg and part of the thigh of the goat, and its aroma made Sha'ul's mouth water at once. No one else had been served with meat yet, and all eyes were aimed at the head of the table.

"Shemu'el, isn't this the part of the sacrifice reserved for you?" Sha'ul asked.

"This is what has been kept for you," the seer answered. "Eat, for it has been set aside especially for you from the very moment I invited the people to the sacrifice."

Without pause, the servants continued to serve food to Hamor, Shemu'el, and the other men at the table. As the rich meat and wine were consumed, the merriment of the guests increased. Their initial stares and whispers gave way to congenial fellowship as they partook of the meal together. No one questioned the seer about the unusual arrangement.

Sha'ul devoured his meal.

—III—

Sha'ul and Hamor lay on goat-hair blankets on Shemu'el's flat roof, hemmed in by parapet and walls. Cushioned and well fed, Sha'ul should have slept better than he had the past four nights. Instead, he tossed and turned, periodically starting awake before drifting back to sleep. He could not shake the surreal events from his mind.

The seer had kept him up late into the evening, talking to him about politics, tribal history, current events, and even religion. The mostly one-sided conversation went on well after the pleasant warmth of the wine wore off, and Sha'ul was eager to bid the old man goodnight.

Sha'ul opened his eyes to see the sun creeping over the horizon. Dawn. The remnants of a dream were quickly receding from his awareness. He had an image in his mind of himself sitting atop a palm tree.

"Sha'ul, son of Kish! Get up. I must send you away now," the voice of the seer rang out from below. The man had given him such baffling preferential treatment since his arrival in this place. He had honored him, but he had yet to give an explanation for anything.

The two travelers gathered their things and were given provisions for the return trip. They followed Shemu'el past the gate until they were at the outskirts of Ramatayim.

Reaching a small field of winter wheat, away from prying eyes, Shemu'el placed his hand on Sha'ul's shoulder.

"Tell your servant to go on ahead of us. Then stay with me a while longer, and I will make known to you the word of Yahweh."

Sha'ul gave Hamor a nod, and the servant began walking down the hill. Shemu'el watched him go and then turned his wizened eyes to the man standing before him. The seer reached into his robe and produced a small ceramic vial. Without another word he uncapped the vial and poured its contents over Sha'ul's head.

The younger man stood rigid as the liquid trickled down the contours of his hair, around his ear, and onto his neck. The oil was cool against his skin. He could smell the aroma—oil of balsam.

"But ... why?" Sha'ul managed.

Shemu'el gave him a reverent kiss, answering, "You ask why? Is it not because Yahweh Himself has anointed you as a ruler over His people and a prince over His inheritance? I tell you truly, Sha'ul son of Kish, you will reign over Yisra'el and even deliver them from their enemies that surround them."

Sha'ul's breath quickened, and he watched the old man carefully, not daring to speak. The slickness of the oil matted the dark curls of his hair and caused his skin to glisten. Shemu'el nodded in response to the unspoken questions.

"Yes, Sha'ul, and so you know I speak the truth and Yahweh has chosen you, I will tell you of the following three signs.

"You will soon depart from here and return to your own land. Near the border of Binyamin, you will pass by the Tomb of Rachel at Tzeltzah. There, you will encounter two men who will tell you what I have already made known to you—that your father's donkeys have been found, and he now worries about you instead.

"Then you will continue on and go as far as the great Oak of Tavor. There you will meet three men who are on their way to Beit-El to worship. One will have three young goats. The second will be carrying three loaves of bread. The third will have a jug of wine. They will offer, and you will accept two loaves for yourself.

"After this, you will come to Geva, past the P'lishtim garrison. When you approach the city of the Levites there, you will find a group of Nevi'im coming down from the high place with their instruments, and they will be making music and prophesying. Then, the Spirit of Yahweh will move upon you like a mighty wind, and you too shall prophesy with them, and I say you will be changed into another man."

Sha'ul shook his head in wonder. "What am I to do?" he asked, barely a whisper.

"When the power of Elohim is upon you, and these signs have been fulfilled, do what the occasion requires. Do whatever your hand finds to do, for He will be with you. Many things will need to happen before these tribes become a kingdom. We will speak again about these matters. Now, you must go."

"Right now? Back home? Isn't there anything else I need to know?"

"There is one last thing I will tell you—a final piece of advice. A warning. There will come a time, whether soon or in the distant future I do not know ... there will come a time when you go down before me to Gilgal. I will come down to meet you there and offer burnt offerings and peace offerings. At that time, you must wait for me seven days, and then I will reveal to you what you should do."

Sha'ul nodded.

"Remember this. When you go to Gilgal, you must wait for me seven days. Do you understand?" Shemu'el pressed. Sha'ul nodded again. "Of ... of course."

"Then may Yahweh be with you, King."

Sha'ul and Hamor journeyed toward Binyamin, navigating the turns of the hill country. Although he noted Sha'ul's distant expression and the strange perfume of the balsam oil, Hamor asked no questions, and Sha'ul volunteered no answers.

Sha'ul let the servant lead the way; he had a better sense of direction and more familiarity with this part of the country anyhow. They were making excellent time, and Sha'ul found himself longing to be home. Yet, he couldn't help but repeat in his mind every detail of the past two days: the revelations, the feast, the secretive anointing.

He thought of the seer's words concerning the "three signs" yet to be fulfilled. What if Sha'ul were to choose a different way home? What if he were to take a long, circuitous route, avoiding all the locations Shemu'el had spoken of? Would the vision cease to be? Did Sha'ul even have a choice in the matter?

"Where are we now?" Sha'ul asked.

"We're nearly at Tzeltzah, Master. We'll pass by the monument. It is the quickest way."

There, far ahead—the Tomb of Rachel. Twelve weatherworn stones piled atop one another on a raised area, covered with an ancient stone roof supported by four pillars. If the tomb was as old as the stories related, it was a miracle to still be standing.

No sooner had Sha'ul's eyes glimpsed the site than he saw two men heading in their direction, leading a donkey laden with bags and boxes. They were Binyaminites, merchants, and he recognized them from his father's business dealings.

"Is it the son of Kish?" one of the men asked, nudging the other on the arm.

"It is!" the other replied excitedly after his eyes had a chance to focus.

"Hello, there," Sha'ul replied. "Are you coming from Giv'ah?"

"Not directly, but we have been there. My friend and I actually had a wager that we'd encounter you wandering around out here," the first man said with a laugh.

"Which of you won then?"

"Oh, I don't mean the two of us. My friend back home. You see, your father ..."

"What news of Kish?" Hamor interrupted.

"Those donkeys you went after were found. Days ago. They were half a day toward the Yarden River."

Hamor and Sha'ul shared a meaningful look.

"Now all Kish can talk about is 'what shall I do about my son?'" the merchant continued. "He's offered a reward to anyone who can turn you back in his direction."

"Thank you. We were on our way back anyhow, so I guess my master can keep his money," Hamor replied.

The two merchants exchanged a glance and grumbled.

"Bah! Just as well. We've got better things to do than sit around in the city square at Giv'ah waiting to be paid."

The men parted company and Sha'ul and Hamor continued on. The encounter had been exactly as Shemu'el prophesied. Sha'ul kept silent.

Eventually, they approached the wide, flat plain of Tavor. Prominent and erect on the horizon was a mighty oak tree, locally known as D'vorah's Oak of Mourning. The hairs on the back of Sha'ul's neck stood up as he saw three figures crossing the plain before them. The first figure led three kids behind; the sound of their bleating carried on the breeze. Soon their paths crossed on the dirt road that cut through the plain.

"Shalom," the men said.

Sha'ul and Hamor returned their greeting. The second man was carrying a bundled package. The third had a jug in his possession.

"Where do you come from and where are you going?" asked the man with the jug.

"I'm returning to Giv'ah from Ramatayim and many more places before that," Sha'ul answered. "And yourselves?"

"North, to offer at Ya'akov's Altar and worship."

It was clear: the sacrifice, the thank-offering, and the libation. The second man began to unwrap his bundle.

"But, for two weary-looking creatures such as yourselves, who have come this distance, withholding bread from you would not be hospitable."

"Yahweh favors the compassionate," the first man noted approvingly.

"No, please," Sha'ul began. "You don't need to do that. Home is not much farther, and we ate well last night."

The kindly men disagreed.

"No, but there is more than enough. A loaf for each of you, and we still have one left to offer to the priests."

Sha'ul consented, and he and Hamor each received into their hands a loaf of unleavened bread made with fine flour. They thanked the men for their generosity and wished them well on their way up to the high place of Beit-El.

Sha'ul picked up the pace. Another accurate prediction. What was approaching next seemed inevitable. He felt himself driven forward to witness this series of foretold occurrences to the end.

They reached the land north of Geva, which was cut through with deep, winding canyons. They could ascend and follow a central ridge around to be closer to Giv'ah, but Sha'ul instead hurried with Hamor down into the wide canyon pass. Bypassing the city of Mikhmas, they descended into the deep gorge—the layered gray and brown contours of the cliff-like walls in shadow—and climbed the trail out the other side to the road that would take them past Geva.

Off on a high peak, the outlines of the P'lishtim military outpost could be seen defiantly entrenched, commanding a view of the surrounding land. Decades after they had been pushed out of Yisra'el's borders during the last major confrontation, outposts such as these, symbols of strength, remained to monitor, to harass, and to dare any foolish soul to go up against the superior military training and weaponry contained within.

Sha'ul saw only the minuscule movements of what were likely helmets over the garrison walls, but he imagined he could feel the dark eyes of soldiers watching him and his companion cross the land. For the first time, he felt within him a certain zeal, a sense of national pride he had not been accustomed to. A week ago, he would have listed the concerns of animal husbandry and providing for his children as his chief preoccupations. Now, he felt the insult that was the P'lishtim occupation on that hill. On Yisra'el's hill. On his hill.

"Come," Sha'ul said to the servant. "We'll turn aside and stay with my uncle tonight. Tomorrow, we'll go home."

Hamor nodded, his legs aching more than he would ever let on. They headed straight toward Geva, passing through the remaining hills onto the drier, rockier ground leading to the staggered walls and trees surrounding the Levitical city. Passing by the final hill, a hill of Elohim,

Sha'ul knew to expect exactly what Shemu'el had spoken. The sounds of music that reached his ears confirmed this.

"Hamor. Go ahead to my uncle's," Sha'ul said, scarcely being able to contain a quivering excitement. The servant obeyed, taking Sha'ul's belongings with him.

Coming down from the high place, a group of similarly clad men approached, each a Nabiy, singing and playing on instruments. One had a nebel, another a toph, another a chalil, and yet another was playing a kinnor. Their notes and melodies danced through the air, with the leader singing out and the others mirroring him in antiphon:

> "O my soul, march on with strength!
> Bless the God of Yisra'el.
> Hear O kings, rulers give ear.
> We praise Him with shout and cheer.
>
> "O my soul, march on with strength!
> Bless the God of Yisra'el.
> The kings they came and fought,
> The kings of Kena'an fought,
> At Ta'anakh near the waters of Megiddo."

Upon hearing the song, Sha'ul felt a warmth beginning to radiate within his body starting in the center of his chest and moving upward through his neck and head. He was sure his face was flush, but he couldn't care less. He could care about nothing at this moment except glorifying his deity. The rush was like the headiness of a strong wine without any of the drowsiness or disorienting effects.

He felt alive. The musicians, praising Yahweh, were in the throes of spiritual worship. They surrounded Sha'ul, singing and playing. He felt the warmth within him reacting, something deep in his inner man responding. Throwing his head back, he joined in the commotion with a giddy shout. He clapped and moved along with the procession, which incorporated him into the joyful accord. No one cared that he sang off key.

Prayers he didn't know, and words he didn't understand, and songs he hadn't learned seemed to reach his lips as his entire sense of self faded from his consciousness, or perhaps was replaced by a heightened awareness of something more real than himself.

The group continued on in their ecstatic exclamations until the sun was down.

Later, Sha'ul made his way to his uncle's dwelling by the light of the moon and the sparse remaining firelight in the city. A few other citizens regarded him curiously as he passed by them to reach the family compound.

"Sha'ul, there you are. Get in here," his first cousin Avner called from the front door.

Sha'ul was greeted with a warm hug from his aunt and a hearty pat on the arm from Avner but otherwise received an awkward reception from the other men of the household. After drinking some water to soothe his hoarse throat, he was ushered into a side room by his uncle, Ner. He sat down on a stool across from the other man.

Ner was somewhat taller than his brother, Kish, but retained the same thickness of build. Unlike Kish, he was nearly bald, and his face held a brightness of complexion that contrasted with the straw-like roughness of Kish's skin.

"My nephew," Ner began, placing a heavy hand on Sha'ul's knee. "What's all this talk that is coming to my ears?"

"What do you mean?" Sha'ul asked in reply.

"The whole city has been knocking on my door this night, telling me that they've seen you cavorting with those 'shouters' on the high place. I say 'No, no, my nephew among the Nevi'im? You must be mistaken,' I say."

"Uncle, I—"

"Is this not the son of Kish from Giv'ah? Is this not the same man we've known for over thirty years—having never shown any such devotion to the musical arts or to God before? This is what they tell me. To tell you the truth, I think my neighbor was a little embarrassed to speak of it. Your father—my brother—has been worried about you, waiting for you to return, and you go off on this ... diversion. I don't know if your father would understand your behavior."

"You see—"

"Now, don't get me wrong. A little religion is good for a man, especially one your age. I mean that. The servant has told me about your search for your father's animals. He said you were at Ramatayim and sought the counsel of the man of God there. Is that so?"

"Yes, that's right. After I couldn't find the donkeys and was at the point of giving up, I went to see Shemu'el to see if he could ask Yahweh about them."

Ner leaned forward in curiosity.

"Is that why you were with his Nevi'im on the hill? Please, tell me everything that Shemu'el said to you. I have never met him myself, but I know he is respected by all as a true oracle with great wisdom."

"I went up to see him at Hamor's suggestion. Shemu'el already knew about my search for the donkeys and when they had been found. He spoke the word to me about the herd and asked me to stay the night before returning."

"Very hospitable for such an important man to invite you to stay in his home," Ner mused, stroking the flesh under his chin thoughtfully.

"Yes, it was kind of him."

"Maybe it's an omen that our family has found favor with God!" Ner said with a boisterous laugh, suddenly in good spirits.

Sha'ul said nothing.

—IV—

Messengers carried the summons throughout the land, calling the elders and esteemed of the Twelve Tribes, representatives from every family, to gather at Mitzpah in national assembly. The sober weight of Shemu'el's proclamation spurred furtive talk as to the purpose of the meeting.

Despite his years of judging at Mitzpah and elsewhere, the last time this man of Yahweh had called all the people to come before their God at this location was when they had once stood to be overrun by the P'lishtim, an event of penitence and prayer preceding a mighty deliverance. Long before that, the tribes had assembled at this five-hundred-foot shaft of a hill just before the devastating civil war that had cost the lives of so many. The rumor was that even Achituv, the high priest by lineage, would be present. Maybe even the Ark itself.

So they came to the Watchtower, so-called, which lay between the boundaries of Y'hudah and Binyamin. The tower was surrounded on all sides by flat, flower-dotted grassland. From the peak on a clear day, one could even make out the ocean far to the west.

Kish and Ner both came representing the clan of the Matrites, along with their eldest sons and choice servants. Many other relatives from their thousand-strong division also made the journey. Pitched tents dotted the land around the base of the high, rounded hill, with more travelers converging on the location by the hour.

The atmosphere buzzed with anticipation. A group within the group, the elders who had approached Shemu'el before with their wish for monarchy, traded knowing remarks.

"Can this be so?" Kish mused to his brother, well aware of the talk that was going around. "Will a king be placed over us in my lifetime?"

Ner shrugged his thick shoulders, gesturing at the hill. "The sooner we get up there, the sooner we'll find out."

"Wouldn't that be something?"

Kish, Ner, and Avner ascended to the meeting place, while Sha'ul hesitated, lagging behind his family.

"Sha'ul, why do you tarry?" Kish asked impatiently.

"I ... I feel like I should check again and make sure our belongings are secured."

"Bah," Kish said with a dismissive wave. "Let the servants tend to that."

"No, I ... you go ahead. With so many families making camp, some things are sure to get mixed up. Look at all the people just now arriving. I won't be long."

With that, Sha'ul turned and scuttled back down to the camp. Hamor was there with the other servants, working to organize the beasts and belongings on their ever-shrinking portion of land.

Upon the summit, Achituv, in full priestly garb and with a retinue of subordinate priests, presided over the convening sacrifices. Silhouetted by sun and the curling smoke of the altar, Shemu'el addressed the mass of influential men gathered before him. This time, they were meeting on his terms.

"Children of Yisra'el. Thus says Yahweh, the God of Yisra'el," the seer began in a loud voice. "It is I that brought you up from the land of Egypt, and I who delivered you from the hand of the Egyptians and from the power of all the kingdoms that were against you.

"But today, you have rejected your God, who delivers you from your calamities and distresses. You have said, both with your mouths and in your hearts, 'No. We want a king to rule over us.' You have hungered for a human ruler instead of a divine one. Well, the request of this people will now be granted. Present yourselves now before Yahweh by your tribes and by your clans. The God of Avraham, Yitz'chak, and Ya'akov ... the God of Moshe, will show you who is to be your king."

The assembly displayed a turbulent mixture of reactions, some apprehensive, but the excitement of what was happening was indeed contagious. Every one of them was now present for and witnessing an event that would forever change their nation and even dictate their future. History was being made before their very eyes.

"Your high priest will draw the Urim and Tumim, but the answer of the lot is from Yahweh. Now draw near," Shemu'el ordered.

Achituv withdrew the two oval stones from the hoshen, the sacred breast piece of judgment, which was fastened to his priestly ephod with gold chains and blue ribbons threaded through golden rings.

Urim and Tumim. The Lights and Perfections. The Guilt and Innocence. The Yes and No. Each large precious stone, lighter in hue on one polished side and dark on the other, had engraved upon them six of the tribal names in order of eldest to youngest of the sons of the patriarch Yisra'el.

As directed by Shemu'el, Achituv began the process, whispering yet another prayer at this momentous occasion. He cast the stones inside the hosen.

"Tumim," he declared.

Shemu'el nodded. That quickly, six of the twelve tribes were out of contention for the kingship.

Achituv cast and drew lots for each tribe that drew near. Not Asher. Not Yissakhar. Not Z'vulun. Not M'nasheh. Not Efrayim.

The lot fell on the tribe of Binyamin.

The crowd shifted, allowing representatives from the clans of Binyamin to approach.

More lots, more selections, the clans by their divisions of thousands were parsed until the lot fell on the clan of Matri.

The fathers of the families presented themselves amid the growing excitement. The lot fell upon the family of Kish.

Kish, quivering, turned to locate his son in the crowd but could not see him.

Achituv faced Kish somberly as the other families melted away into the throng of onlookers. Every eye was on him. The lot was cast.

No.

"Present the other members of your family," Achituv instructed.

"I have a firstborn son and only daughters after him," Kish answered.

"Very well, we will cast the lot for him. What is his name?"

"Sha'ul."

Kish looked behind him again, waving for his relatives. Ner was in a reverie at the proceedings and seemed to pay no notice. Avner had long ago gone in search of Sha'ul and, not able to find him, had returned to the summit without his cousin.

Achituv once again threw the sacred stones into the breast piece and reached, feeling his fingers grasp the cool surfaces and withdrawing his hand for all to witness. The gray-headed seer Shemu'el looked on.

"Tumim."

Yes.

The crowd erupted in a frenzy of excited shouts. A king was about to be crowned! They could scarcely believe the result. All clamored to catch a glimpse of this man. A king! Yet, no man came forth, and the tide of exclamations softened to a hush. Kish went to Ner and Avner at the edge of the crowd.

"Where is my son?" he asked urgently. "Where is he?"

"I haven't seen him for hours now," Avner answered.

Shemu'el strode to the center of the gathering and swept his gaze back and forth.

"Bring Sha'ul the son of Kish forward!"

The crowd shuffled and pushed, looking throughout all their midst for this Sha'ul. He was nowhere to be found.

Shemu'el grimaced deeply.

Arguments began breaking out among the people. Kish felt himself standing over the very precipice of history, dumbfounded, as members of the Matri clan began to adjure him, pushing and pulling on his arms as if his son were hidden up his sleeve and just as easy to produce.

At the far edge of the gathering, a lawyer from the tribe of Y'hudah turned to a prosperous friend, a Danite, and remarked with a snort,

"Is this 'great king' to come from the lowest of people?"

"You said it. Has the shame of Binyamin really been forgotten?"

"I've heard this Sha'ul is nothing but a glorified farm hand. He has no knowledge of civil or military matters!"

"Ya'akov's blessing said that the scepter would be in the tribe of Y'hudah."

And they weren't alone in expressing their unease in the selection, although hopeful voices were carrying the day, eager to lay sight on this man God had chosen.

"Enough!" Shemu'el bellowed, quieting the confused assembly.

He turned his back to them and knelt before the still-hot altar, lifting his arms toward heaven. He prayed aloud, "All-knowing Yahweh, tell us: has this man arrived here yet, and where may he be found?"

After some time Shemu'el stood, turning to the congregation once more.

"Behold, he is hiding with the baggage," he said to the priests.

Hearing that, a mob of able-bodied men rushed down the hill in search of Kish's tents and luggage. Avner ran after them, reaching the family's camp just in time to see Hamor knocked aside by the zealous crowd, who ran into all the tents, searching eagerly. They found Sha'ul, carefully arranging and rearranging supplies as if oblivious to all else. They hoisted him in the air, carrying him like a champion back to the summit, building in a thunderous chant of his name. "Sha'ul! Sha'ul! Sha'ul!"

The mob set him on his feet before all, between Shemu'el and Achituv. He stood, taller than both esteemed men, with a look of strength and purpose in his features. And he was so handsome, with the tan of his skin and a beard covering a blushing face. He certainly looked like royalty.

"Do you see the man Yahweh has chosen?" Shemu'el asked the people. "There is no one like him among all of you."

"Long live the king!" they shouted and shouted.

Shemu'el dictated all the rules, laws, and statutes of this new form of government in the hearing of the people. The scribes worked furiously to record everything the seer spoke, as he received from God. Later, the writings would be placed along with the Book of the Law beside the Ark in the safekeeping of the priesthood.

Elders of Binyamin, as well as from other tribes, had thrown their cloaks to the ground to create a seat of honor for Sha'ul. With patriotic accord, heads of households brought forth precious things from their cargo or presented ornaments from their person—an impromptu and voluntary tax to honor their new king. Robes. Jewelry. Livestock. Gold. Ner assisted with tallying the motley treasure on his nephew's behalf.

Strong men, young and old alike, pledged their allegiance to Sha'ul, vowing to accompany him wherever he went as royal escort or bodyguard—although he hardly knew at this point where he might take them.

Not all were as enthusiastic. Entire families, swaths of clans, stood on the outskirts, regarding the scene coolly and bringing forth no offering to enrich this man who had seemingly transformed from simple agrarian to monarch in no time at all.

Avner helped to support a faint Kish with an arm around the shoulder as he appraised the situation.

"Those men pay no tribute to their anointed ruler," he remarked. "Will there be bloodshed here, even on this day? The ink hasn't even dried on the priests' scrolls declaring my cousin king, and yet, recognizing treason doesn't take long, does it, Uncle?"

Sha'ul seemed to pay no notice to the blatant disregard being shown him by some in the crowd. He sat—as regally as one unaccustomed to regality can— on a makeshift throne, head held high in decorous poise, listening to

Shemu'el articulate the duties and boundaries of his newly created office, ennobling them with his stillness, embodying them.

—V—

A month later, across the Yarden River, east beyond where the tributary of the Yabboq meets the Wadi Yabis, the threat of annihilation hung heavy.

The inhabitants of Yavesh-Gil'ad, in the tribal land of M'nasheh, gathered their goats, their baskets, and their belongings and fled for safety behind the city walls. Dust rose in the distance. The sounds of an approaching army echoed through the rugged canyon.

The 'Amoni had been campaigning fiercely to regain their ancient territory, subduing remnants of the Emori and wiping out scattered families of Gad and M'nasheh along the way. Success in those engagements now fueled the vision of the vigorous Nachash, dubbed the Serpent King, who had sworn an oath before his deity to push out the occupiers and make vacant all the Yisra'elite settlements east of the great river.

"Affix my helmet," Nachash growled to his Mo'avite armor bearers.

They hastened to attach the upper half of the bronze cobra's head, whose sculpted fangs rested above the king's forehead.

"Summon my commanders."

A horn was sounded, then another and the message was carried throughout the thousand cavalrymen and tens of thousands of foot soldiers. Nachash's commanders galloped forward from their positions, dismounting and kneeling as servants held their horses' reins.

"Balak, secure the high ground overlooking the city. Mesha, ride through the wadi with three cavalry patrols and clear it. Search for any wells or springs and kill anyone you find outside the walls, no exceptions. Afterward, rejoin Saraf; he will be stationing the rest of the army between the city and the Yabboq."

"Yes, King!"

The commanders obeyed immediately as Nachash mounted his decorated warhorse. 'Amaleki and Mo'avite observers accompanied his army on camelback, but they would have no share of the glory for victory today.

"Pay attention. I will show you how to bring a city to its knees," Nachash boasted. "From Aro'er to Avel-K'ramim and beyond, I will restore the boundaries of the land of my fathers."

"Were your fathers Emori?" one observer scoffed, wheeling his camel around and tapping a finger against his turban.

"Fool! Who do you think were here before the Emori? All the children of 'Amoni!"

The chief elder of Yavesh-Gil'ad peered over the top of the fortified inner wall, straining to observe the gathering menace. What he saw made him break into a cold sweat and duck down, making way for others to look. A mass of soldiers had filled the canyon like a dark lake, the glint of blades like the crests of waves.

The magistrates and principal men conferred behind the barricaded city gates. Too many among them were old or young or sick or inexperienced. They knew they could mount no formidable opposition. Their armaments, gathered from every home and storehouse, were little more than staves and farming implements laid out in a heap on the dusty ground.

Mothers tried to comfort their children, who sensed panic in the air.

"They have us beaten," an official wheezed as he descended from the observation post. "There are so many of them. Too many to count."

"'Amoni! What can they want with us? What have we to do with them?" the chief elder asked, wringing his hands.

"I'm afraid we have no access to fresh water; they've completely cut us off," said an official named Ammi'el, a middle-aged administrator.

"How long will our stores last us?" the first official asked.

"Unless we catch rainwater in the cisterns—not likely this time of year—I would estimate a week with rationing."

"And how long could we hold them off? Militarily?"

"A few days, maybe."

"Men, listen to me," the first official urged. "This is not a battle we can win! Our city is built strong, but a force like that can pull us down brick by brick."

"I have spent half of my life governing this city," the chief elder said, hanging his head. "Far be it from me to be the cause of its destruction. Ammi'el, you are the smoothest speaker among us. Ask what their terms are or what yearly tax we may pay so a treaty can be made. Give them what they want. I'll take that over being killed and looted any day."

Ammi'el, under a flag of truce, approached the opposing army. With him were a few select men carrying food and gifts. The party was met and escorted by 'Amoni soldiers and searched under the watchful eye of the commander, Saraf, whose face was a museum of battle scars. Finding no threat, Ammi'el was cuffed on the neck and brought roughly before Nachash, who sat astride his warhorse.

"What do you come here like a dog to beg for?" Nachash asked scornfully.

Ammi'el ignored the taunt, averting his eyes and speaking in a respectful tone.

"My lord, the elders of Yavesh-Gil'ad wish to make a covenant of peace with you. We only desire to know your terms, and we will be your servants."

"A covenant? With a Yisra'elite dog? Ha! Surely, I will make a covenant with you and spare your city from destruction ... on this one condition."

Ammi'el looked up and met the Serpent King's haughty gaze.

"Your servant is listening."

"The condition is that I gouge out the right eye of every man, woman, and child among you. On that condition and that condition only, you will save your lives and spare your city."

The 'Amoni soldiers burst into cruel laughter.

Ammi'el's face drained of its color. He had to be yanked to his feet by Saraf and shoved back into the supporting arms of his companions. The small company was driven back to the city, the sharp points of weapons prodding at their backs along the way.

"Go. Go and tell them the good news!" Nachash shouted after the men, earning more laughter from the ranks.

When all the inhabitants of the city heard the report of Nachash's response, a great shouting and wailing arose from among them. Some men tore their clothes in anger, others in disgust.

"What will we do?" one man pleaded, trying not to throw up.

The arguments went back and forth.

"We have to send for help. We have to send messengers to all the tribes."

"You're dreaming!"

"He's right. What portion do we have with the tribes of Yisra'el and why should they help us now? We're on our own."

"It's our only hope for deliverance."

"At least our kin of the tribe of Binyamin may respond. If only they of all Yisra'el have a care for what happens to us."

"My sons are the swiftest of anyone in Gil'ad," Ammi'el said, his formerly pale face now red with anger. "Have them slip out through the western walls, cross the river and get the word out."

"You'd risk the lives of your own sons on such a slim chance?" the chief elder asked.

"We don't need a chance. We need a miracle."

Nachash reclined on a cushion in his tent, giving audience to the Amaleki and Mo'avite observers accompanying his army. Slaves finished refilling their drinks and exited silently.

"Tell us, Nachash, why do you gouge the eye of all who surrender to you?" one of the Mo'avites asked.

"Not just the eye, the right eye. Isn't it obvious? When you hold a shield in battle, how do you hold it?"

The observers thought about this, envisioning the stance of a soldier advancing across a battlefield.

Nachash answered his own question, "You have your shield out with your left arm, protecting your head and face. You use your right eye to see. If I go through the trouble of sparing a people, I want to ensure they and their children will never rise to oppose me again. I make them unfit for war but still capable of carrying out the tasks one expects of slaves."

The Amaleki smiled broadly, showing yellowed teeth.

"You are very shrewd, King Nachash."

"All the more reason for the Amaleki to join my mission. And the Mo'avites," he said, raising his cup.

Just then, Saraf strode into the tent, bowing low before delivering his message.

"The Yisra'elite dogs are requesting seven days' reprieve. At the end of the week, they will then come out and surrender to you."

The foreign observers arched their eyebrows and nodded appreciatively.

"Go on," Nachash said, seeing that his commander had more to say.

"Balak has reported two men, no more than boys, have fled to the west from the city. Perhaps they are cowards, fleeing for their lives. Do you want us to run them down or take them alive?"

Nachash laughed, draining his cup and throwing it to the ground.

"Let them be. They mean to send messengers to raise help."

Saraf blinked, not comprehending.

"Don't you see? Now every tribe of these people will know my name and fear me. Oh, don't worry, my loyal scorpion. Yisra'el will sooner fight one another than stand up to our army. They couldn't muster a hundred fighting men between their petty squabbles and rivalries to risk their hides for a city this far east of the river. Yes, let those boys run and tell the world that Nachash and the sons of 'Amoni are liberating our homeland step-by-step. If anyone dares to oppose us, we will be happy to add their children to the sacrificial fires of Milkom."

—VI—

The yoke of oxen plodded along, dragging the heavy wooden plow behind them. Sha'ul followed, scrutinizing the straightness of the furrows as his eldest son Y'honatan led the beasts over their previous lines at right angles.

"You're doing well. Now keep it steady," Sha'ul said to the sweating teenager.

A piece of land adjacent to his father's field had been cleared, and Sha'ul hoped to plant lentils to diversify and supplement the family's barley crop. A servant of Kish led a yoke at the field's other end.

Through the air, the sound of hammering carried from the city. In Giv'ah, Sha'ul had begun to take the din for granted. Out here, the noise of construction caught his ear and brought an appreciative smile to his face. Workmen had been building an expansion onto Sha'ul's home for over a week now. They were volunteer laborers all, yet Sha'ul had urged his relatives to tip them from the treasury of gifts received at Mitzpah.

Completing their task, Y'honatan and the servant led their animals off the tilled ground and secured the vertical wooden spikes on the plow frames.

"How'd I do?" Y'honatan asked the other man, gesturing to the field.

"Wonderful, my prince. The oxen follow you without even having to use a goad."

Y'honatan scrunched up his face, but the servant didn't notice.

"I trust him to plow all on his own," Sha'ul said. "I was a lot younger when I learned, but he's picked the job up faster than anyone I've seen."

"Yes, my lord."

"We'll finish up here. Go home and have your lunch," Sha'ul instructed, working to detach the plows.

Y'honatan waited until the servant was out of earshot before speaking.

"I don't like when he calls me prince. I've known him my whole life! Why can't he just use my name?"

"Officially you are the prince. That's something you'll have to get used to. You and me both."

"How long do I have to be the prince?"

"I guess until you become the king."

"You really think I'll be a king someday? One day you were Sha'ul, son of Kish, and now everybody calls you King Sha'ul—"

"Not everybody. Believe me."

"—but what if, one day, they say you aren't a king anymore? Just as sudden?"

"Son. Being king is a gift from God. It's a gift and a responsibility. I admit that it feels more like an honorary title at the moment."

"So people will just keep acting strange around us and giving us free stuff, our whole lives?"

"What else is a king for?" Sha'ul said, throwing his arm around his son's shoulder with a laugh.

They began to lead the oxen back to the city.

"Dad. Do you hear something?"

"I don't hear the workmen anymore. Is that what you mean?"

"No. Something else."

Sha'ul strained to listen.

He heard the sound of weeping.

The streets of Giv'ah of Binyamin were filled with lamenting men and women in anguish over the news brought by the messengers. Sha'ul walked among them in bewilderment, finally catching Hamor near his father's home.

"What's wrong with the people? Why are they weeping?"

"Ah, Master, two Gil'adite youths arrived with grim tidings. They say the 'Amoni have put their city under siege. They have seven days to capitulate to slavery and mutilation—to have their right eyes put out—or be destroyed," the servant answered, shaking his head sadly.

A flame of anger burned in Sha'ul's eyes. "These messengers, where are they?"

Hamor quickly led Sha'ul to the western gates of the city. Y'honatan, left alone with the oxen, called in vain after his father to wait for him.

Hamor pointed out one of the messengers. The youth was tousled and caked with dirt and dried sweat, yet appeared both alert and strong. He was tightening his sandals, preparing to depart through the meadows toward his next destination. The other messenger, even younger, was resting against the wall and struggling to catch his breath.

"You there!" Sha'ul called, approaching the first. "What is this spiteful word about the 'Amoni? And who are you?"

The muscular youth stared back at him with sober eyes. " My name is Makhir, the son of Ammi'el. My father is an official of Yavesh-Gil'ad."

"Tell me what's going on."

"The king of the 'Amoni, called Nachash ... he surrounded us with his army. We have seven days—only six now—to submit to having our eyes gouged out and becoming his slaves. Nachash has been doing the same to towns and peoples east of us. My brother and I have sent others as messengers and are ourselves trying to find anyone who can save us from this evil ... before it is too late."

Sha'ul held his breath and balled his fists at his side, feeling a righteous anger welling up within him. His heart began to pound with terrible purpose. Every nerve tingled. The movement of the Spirit was upon him.

"He means to bring disgrace on all of Yisra'el," Sha'ul growled through clenched teeth.

"We had hoped our people's kinship to the tribe of Binyamin would offer some hope. But we can't afford to wait; we must continue on."

"No! Look no further. Yahweh has meant this moment for deliverance."

"You will help? I thank you, but know that Nachash commands an army, not a couple of—"

Hamor interjected, "Do you know whom you are speaking to, boy? This is Sha'ul, son of Kish, King of all Yisra'el."

Makhir's eyes widened.

"King ... of Yisra'el? Nobody in Yavesh-Gil'ad heard anything of a king placed over the Twelve Tribes."

"So it is. Stay with me, Makhir. Tell me everything you know about these 'Amoni. Men loyal to me will carry your message to all the corners of Yisra'el faster than you and your brother and whoever else you've hired. This tyrant will be punished for his evil."

Sha'ul wheeled and seized a yoke of oxen from his son, leading them straight toward the city square amid the distraught citizens. He barked orders to Hamor along the way as Y'honatan and the young messengers followed, mesmerized by the sudden command he possessed.

"Hamor, gather the men. Send for my cousin Avner as well. Now!"

Hamor rushed off to do just that.

Sha'ul took a large blade and immediately butchered the oxen in the street, startling the populace out of their bitter mourning as he hewed the animals into pieces. His hands were soaked and dripping blood as his loyal followers pushed through the crowd to stand before him, ready to serve.

Still gripping the blade, he addressed them in a loud voice. "Each of you, take a piece of one of these slaughtered beasts and hurry, carry this word to every man in every city of every tribe: A great insult has been raised against our people by Nachash and the sons of 'Amon. Whoever does not come out to battle with Sha'ul their king and Shemu'el, this will be done to their oxen!"

A fearful hush fell over the observers, but the men loyal to Sha'ul came forward and began to wrap up the bloody ox pieces in cloth or place them in baskets and sacks.

"They have four days to come with weapons in hand to Bezek, or I swear an oath that they will not go unpunished."

Later, inside Sha'ul's home, he kissed his two younger sons, Avinadav and Malkishua, and his very pregnant wife, Achino'am. He had washed his hands, eaten a meal and dressed himself for the journey ahead. The workmen had been sent off to prepare; no man of fighting age in Yisra'el was exempt.

"I want to come with you," Y'honatan said, lingering by the door.

Sha'ul placed his hands on the shoulders of his firstborn; he seemed to be growing taller by the day.

"I know you do, my son. You are very brave."

"Why can't I go?" he asked.

"While I'm gone, you are the man of the house. Your brothers have to be looked after. Your mother—with your new brother or sister on the way—the family needs you."

Y'honatan frowned and scuffed his feet against the ground.

"Listen to me, my son. Princes have responsibilities. Your duty is to stay here and protect this family. God willing, I'll be home soon."

At that moment, Avner walked through the door, greeting Achino'am and the children briefly before turning to Sha'ul.

"My cousin. My King. Are you ready to go to war?"

Sha'ul nodded sharply, and Avner tossed him a sheathed sword of bronze.

—VII—

The fear of Yahweh fell upon the people of Yisra'el. All the fighting men came to Bezek to join Sha'ul, leaving little more than a home guard to defend the lands left behind. Reverence mixed with vengeance in their hearts and many lips vowed to repay the insult of Nachash and the 'Amoni army.

Over four days, they gathered west of the great river and were organized into formations, tribe by tribe. On the final day of the summons, Shemu'el himself arrived with a small traveling company, instantly lending an air of legitimacy to the proceedings.

"I'm so glad you came," Sha'ul said, clasping the seer's hand.

The king stood outside his tent, positioned to survey the multitude at the head of the camp. He was accompanied by loyalists and the two sons of Ammi'el.

"Of course I came," the seer answered. "I see you have your army."

"They received my message. Tell me, is there anything else I should be doing?"

"As I said to you before, do whatever your hand finds to do. Yahweh has meant you for a moment such as this."

"Will you speak to the people, keep their courage up?"

"Me? No. I do not speak for the king. I will offer sacrifices and prayers for the people, but today I leave you to your task. Ah, here comes your man with news."

Avner approached. "The men number the people at three hundred thousand," he reported.

Sha'ul nodded, impressed. The multitude may have been untested by warfare, but one could not argue with the turnout. This was really happening.

"May Yahweh be with you," Shemu'el said, departing to tend to spiritual matters.

"Tell me," Sha'ul asked, turning to the young messengers by his side, "can you make it back safely to Yavesh-Gil'ad?"

"Yes. Under the cover of darkness, I am confident we can, King." Makhir answered.

"Good. I want you to return and tell the men of your city this: 'By the time the sun is hot tomorrow, you will be delivered.'"

"Yes!" Makhir said, invigorated. "We will get ready to leave at once."

When the boys had gone, Sha'ul convened a council of war with Avner and other loyal men.

"As soon as the sun is down, we move. We'll cross the Yarden at one of the fords by moonlight and march all night long, keeping a steady pace. Yavesh-Gil'ad is … sixteen or seventeen miles. We'll form up against the 'Amoni and attack at the first sliver of daylight."

"My lord, we don't need three hundred thousand men to fight. These are not soldiers. Let some of them return home," urged 'Uzi, a fellow Binyaminite from a family with combat experience.

"The bigger the force, the better, I say," Ehud, another loyalist, rejoined.

"We will use what Yahweh has provided for us. Prepare the march."

The army traveled for hours through the darkness. Sha'ul and Avner led the way with other capable men familiar with the route through the Yarden valley. From the front of the column, the night was tranquil with the ethereal forms of poplar, tamarisk, and wild oak passing in moonlight. At the rear, dust raised by the hundreds of thousands of footfalls obscured the stars. Under strict orders to refrain from conversation, the thoughts of every man drifted to the impending confrontation.

With each passing hour, the tension within Sha'ul grew—a sweet mixture of fear and zeal. At one point, he jumped as a family of gazelles startled and fled before them. He walked for another half mile before his grip on the handle of his sword relaxed.

The army trifurcated as they drew near the junction of the Wadi Yabis, and the fighting men assembled into three companies. Sha'ul crept forward to a rocky ledge to survey the enemy. He squinted hard but could see nothing beyond a shadowy sea in the bowl-like expanse below and faint flickering lamplight from somewhere beyond stone city walls.

Now was the morning watch. Early. Adrenaline countered any fatigue from the midnight march. They waited for the light to break.

Nachash slept soundly in his tent. Today was the day the besieged city would surrender to him. This conquest was so easy, like plucking a ripened apple from a low-hanging branch. Gouging out all those eyeballs would take quite a while, but a little sport was good to break up the rigors of military campaigning.

Nachash's eyes snapped open.

The ground was shaking.

The Serpent King sat up straight in his bedding.

"Guards!" he yelled.

A sound was building, ever louder—a chorus of shouts approaching from multiple sides, surrounding the encampment. Nachash got to his feet. He hastened to fasten his garments and gird himself.

"Guards!" he yelled again, louder.

Two soldiers stumbled into the royal tent, and even in the dim light, Nachash could read the terror on their faces.

"What's going on?" he demanded.

"We're under attack! We're surrounded!" one soldier answered, clutching a spear.

"What? Impossible!" Nachash sputtered with less confidence in his voice than he would have liked.

The trembling earth and bellowing war cries preceded the assault like invisible arrows closing in around the tents and soldiers. Horses whinnied, and a great clamor arose as the 'Amoni grabbed for their weapons in the confusion.

Three companies of Yisra'elites broke into the camp from three directions—hacking at the enemy with farming tools and short swords, stabbing with makeshift spears, bludgeoning with stones and clubs.

Bodies of half-dressed and unarmed soldiers littered the ground among collapsed tents and scattered belongings. One of the Mo'avite observers, tripping over a fallen comrade, screamed in agony as his hand was trampled under the hoof of an 'Amoni horse running rampant. Soldiers who attempted to stand their ground were outnumbered threefold by attackers. Those who tried to mount a coordinated defense, standing back to back in twos or threes, were soon overwhelmed by nearly a dozen Yisra'elites.

Sha'ul and Avner entered the fray, swords drawn and urging their men forward.

"The horses!" Avner yelled.

The Yisra'elites stabbed at the hindquarters of horses to send them fleeing from the camp and slashed others at their legs, dragging off the riders and finishing them on the ground.

Saraf and the personal guard of Nachash surrounded the Serpent King in a protective circle. Nachash had managed to attach his helmet and a few pieces of armor and now wielded a borrowed blade.

"King," Saraf began, "we need to get you out of here."

"No! We stand and fight. Where are Mesha and Balak?"

"Mesha is dead. Balak ... I do not know."

"By Milkom, these can't be Yisra'elites, can they?"

"We will fight them, King, to the last man, but you have to go right now!"

Saraf and the guardsmen forcefully led Nachash away from the tent, maintaining their defensive formation as they moved toward some waiting horses.

A middle-aged Yisra'elite man charged at the group swinging an 'Amoni sword above his head. Saraf dropped low and with lightning speed thrust upward with his spear, puncturing the attacker's abdomen then delivering a swift punch to the attacker's wrist, causing the sword to fall harmlessly backward out of his grasp.

"Don't just stand there; keep going!" Saraf barked at the guardsmen.

The tumult was clearly heard in Yavesh-Gil'ad, and the rising sun exposed the battle.

"We're delivered!"

"Praise be to God!"

A mighty cheer went up from the city.

"Throw open the gates!" the chief elder cried out. Ammi'el repeated the order enthusiastically. A few hundred men of the city, emboldened, were lined up in the courtyard, ready to rush out and join the fight.

Sha'ul jumped to avoid the hissing tip of a blade and answered by swinging his own. Metal clanged on metal, and Sha'ul's brute strength was enough to knock his opponent's weapon to the ground. Sha'ul quickly killed him, turning to face the next challenge.

"For Yisra'el!" Sha'ul shouted.

'Uzi and a band of men from the tribe of Gad mounted horses and camels and tried to circle the battle, blocking off potential routes of escape, which was too late for some. Lone enemy soldiers on horseback and on foot had scattered and fled in fear while their more courageous or unlucky comrades fought on against the overwhelming opposition.

Saraf, Nachash, and the guardsmen wheeled their horses around, running into wave after wave of Yisra'elites everywhere they turned.

"We'll have to fight our way through," Nachash said.

"Not yet. We should keep trying for an opening," Saraf replied, sweat glistening on his scarred visage. To illustrate the commander's concern, a hurled rock hit one of the guardsmen below the line of his helmet, opening a bloody gash on the side of his face.

"Hurry, King, this way!"

They turned and prodded their horses on, galloping through the camp debris.

A Gil'adite, one who had come out before as part of Ammi'el's procession, spotted the fleeing group. He turned to the fighting men close to him and sounded the call. "There he is! That's their king! Get after him!"

Chasing on foot, the men were unable to pursue for long, but the cries carried to Avner, who leaped into action, mounting a captured horse and racing after the enemies. Sha'ul watched him go and rallied others nearby to join the pursuit. Several of Sha'ul's loyal men joined the hunt alongside embittered residents of the city eager for revenge.

Seeing the enemy was gaining on them, Saraf pivoted and stood his ground, ordering two guardsmen to do the same, creating a barrier for Nachash. He swung his spear hard, knocking a Gil'adite backward off his horse. The two guardsmen advanced, clanging swords with the other men on horseback.

Just then, Avner appeared out of the blue, charging Saraf's flank. The 'Amoni commander turned and barely had time to raise his spear in defense. Avner's short sword cut through the shaft of the spear and made a slanting laceration on Saraf's arm as he roared by.

As blood poured down his bicep, Saraf gritted his teeth and turned, kicking his horse furiously and riding away from the battle weaponless, leaving the guardsmen to their fate. His horse was faster than any possessed by the Yisra'elites, and he was quickly out of reach.

Nachash, however, had not made nearly as much progress in his attempt to escape and found himself bogged down between groups of soldiers engaged in hand-to-hand combat, piles of corpses and the wreckage of the 'Amoni camp.

Scooping up the top half of Saraf's broken weapon from the ground, Avner rode on, closing the gap between himself and the enemy king. When he was within range, he gave a full-throated shout, "King Nachash!"

The Serpent King turned to look, exposing his face through the opening of his helmet. Avner hurled the broken spear with all his strength.

The sun burned bright in the sky before the battle ended. The shattered remnant of Nachash's army fled to the hills and wilderness, not two of them being left together. The air was tinged with the metallic scent of blood, and the field of battle was covered with the consequences of war. Soldiers picked over the spoils for valuables, armor, weapons, and souvenirs.

There were relatively few Yisra'elite bodies among the dead. Sha'ul surveyed the grisly scene of the victory only briefly from the high walls of Yavesh-Gil'ad. He had been given a hero's welcome and a jug of cool water, of which he drank generously before splashing the rest over his face and neck.

Shemu'el had been sent for from Bezek and arrived on a donkey just as Sha'ul's commanders and the city elders convened amid the jubilant inhabitants.

Sha'ul stepped away from the others to embrace the seer. "Shemu'el, it's done!" he said, relief in his voice.

"It is, it is. The victory belongs to Yahweh," Shemu'el said softly, patting the large man on the back.

"Yes, thank you, God. Praise be to Yahweh!" Sha'ul cried out in triumph toward heaven.

The city's residents were mingled with increasing numbers of soldiers—just yesterday only men—who entered the city and were joining in a chant of, "Sha'ul! Sha'ul! Sha'ul!"

Sha'ul couldn't help but break into a huge grin. Never before in his life had he been treated with such warmth from so many people. He unsheathed his sword and held it high in the air.

"Victory! Our God has destroyed our enemies!"

The crowd cheered and cheered, a revolutionary zeal running through them like a fever. One man at the front of the crowd called out to Sha'ul and Shemu'el, "Where now are those fools who said to Shemu'el, 'Who is Sha'ul that he should be a king over us?' Where are those who dared not give tribute to the king?"

Others quickly took up the theme.

"Bring them out so we may put them to death!"

"Yes! Stone the traitors!"

"Stone them!"

Shemu'el looked at the king to gauge his response. Sha'ul tensed. The thing was unthinkable to him; he felt his very soul reacting against it.

"No, brothers, no," Sha'ul urged, trying to calm the crowd before they got out of control. "No one will be put to death today for this is the day Yahweh has worked a great deliverance for Yisra'el!"

His command seemed to temporarily appease the people, but their fiery energy needed an outlet. Sha'ul turned to the seer, seeking guidance. Shemu'el nodded knowingly and stepped forward, raising his hands until all were silent.

"Come now; bury your dead and let us depart from this place of bloodshed. Gather all Yisra'el to Gilgal—men, women, and children—where we will reaffirm the kingship of Sha'ul and hold a royal coronation. I will confirm Yahweh's anointing of our leader, and there will be no doubt he is truly king. All those who murmured and were dissatisfied before can have a second chance to pledge their loyalty to Yahweh's choice."

—VIII—

The solemn ritual with its peace offerings, thank offerings, and a second anointing quickly gave way to the biggest celebration the people of Yisra'el had ever seen. Spirits rode high on the twin blessings of military victory and a kingship they could boast in. Not a coarse word against the rejuvenated monarchy was on the lips of anyone present as wine flowed and fine foods were enjoyed, followed by music and dancing.

Sha'ul, dressed in a new robe, sat at a stately table under the open sky, his son Y'honatan seated proudly by his side taking in the festivities. Father and son laughed and talked freely of the sights of the celebrating crowd.

Gilgal. The site of the first Pesach held in the land of Kena'an, west of the great river. Families of every tribe—young and old, male and female—all beheld the crowning of Sha'ul, son of Kish, as ruler of Yisra'el.

Sha'ul's young children were present, as was his pregnant wife, his father, his uncle, his cousins—seemingly everyone he had ever known. Jubilation surrounded the family, and the feast showed no sign of ending.

Yet, Shemu'el alone sat with a troubled expression at the end of the table, having not even touched the food set before him. His mood seemed to deteriorate with every passing hour. The new king couldn't help but notice. Try as he might to ignore the seer, Shemu'el was always, distractingly there in his peripheral vision. Then, slowly, Shemu'el rose to his feet and turned to look out over the revelers.

Bit by bit, ripples of quiet passed through the rowdy celebration as more and more noticed the esteemed man preparing to address them. When all were completely silent, Shemu'el spoke.

"Children of Yisra'el!" he began. "I have listened to your voice in all that you petitioned and behold, a king has been appointed over you. Here sits your leader, Sha'ul, the son of Kish.

"As for me, I am old and gray. Look and see, my adult sons sit among you now, private citizens of this nation … subjects of the king … just as all of you are. You know me. I have walked before you since I was just a boy under the tutelage of 'Eli, and my life has been open to your observation until this very day. Here I am. If I have wronged any of you during my time as a judge over you, or committed any injustice, bear witness against me now before Yahweh."

The seer made deliberate eye contact with many in the crowd as he continued, "Whose ox or donkey have I taken? Whom have I defrauded? Whom have I oppressed or from whose hand have I accepted a bribe to turn a blind eye to justice? If I have taken any such thing from any of you, I will restore it."

Shemu'el paused expectantly. The people thoughtfully replied he had taken nothing from them nor cheated them nor oppressed them in any way.

"Then Yahweh is witness against you, and His anointed king stands witness you have found nothing in my hand," he said, holding his palms out, asserting his innocence and his integrity before all.

The people shouted in agreement, "He is witness!"

Sha'ul nodded along, wondering where this was going.

"Yahweh was who appointed Moshe and Aharon and brought your fathers up out of the land of Egypt and into this Promised Land. So now, stand still and listen as I plead with you before Yahweh as to the many righteous deeds He has done for you and your ancestors.

"When Ya'akov went into Egypt, and your fathers cried out to Yahweh, then Yahweh sent Moshe and Aharon to deliver them and bring them to this place. But they forgot Yahweh their God, so He sold them into the hand of Sisra, captain of the army of Hatzor and into the hand of the P'lishtim and into the hand of the king of Mo'av, and they fell into bondage.

"And in their distress, they cried out to Yahweh and said, 'We have sinned because we have forsaken Yahweh and have served the Ba'alim and the 'ashtarot. But now, deliver us from the hands of our enemies, and we will serve You.'

"Then Yahweh sent champions such as Yeruba'al and Barak and Yiftach and Shimshon ... and He delivered you from the hands of your enemies all around, so you lived in security. Yet, you feared the P'lishtim and, when Nachash the king of the 'Amoni was making war in the east, you said to me: 'No, but a king shall reign over us,' even though Yahweh your God was already your divine and perfect ruler.

"Now here he sits," Shemu'el said, gesturing toward Sha'ul's table. "You rejected your God and asked for a human king ... and Yahweh has given you such a man. If you will fear Yahweh and serve Him and listen to His voice and not rebel against His command, then both you and also the king who reigns over you will follow Yahweh your God. And if you will not listen to His voice, but instead rebel against His words, then the hand of Yahweh will be against you as He was against your fathers before."

The people were dumbstruck at these words. Half-empty cups of wine were set down. Unfinished portions of food were set aside. Musicians held their instruments by their sides, unsure when or if the merrymaking would begin again.

Y'honatan looked intently at the old man and strained to make sense of the words while his father sat stone-faced, fixing his gaze on a point on the table in front of him.

"Now then," Shemu'el continued. "Stand still and see this great thing that Yahweh will do before your eyes! Is now not the time for the wheat harvest to begin? Is not the autumn rain still a way off? I will call upon Yahweh that He may send thunder and rain. Then you will know that your wickedness is great in which you have provoked Yahweh by asking for yourselves a king!"

Shemu'el began to pray and almost immediately peals of thunder could be heard in the near distance. The people, startled, turned to behold dark clouds over the western mountains, moving their way. Avner leaped to his feet and stood behind Sha'ul, staring at the sky in disbelief.

Kish and Ner, seated together, gaped as raindrops began to fall and the sky grew increasingly dark. Sha'ul made no effort to move from his seat, not even as the rain began to spatter against the table. A massive thunderclap sounded directly overhead.

The people began to panic and feel the fear of Yahweh. As the rain began to mix with light hailstones, they began crying out to Shemu'el in unison.

"Pray for your servants that we may not die!"

"We have added to all our sins and the sins of our ancestors by doing this evil thing and asking for a king!"

"Help your servants! Pray to Yahweh your God for our deliverance and forgiveness!"

Shemu'el held up his rain-soaked hands to calm the crowds.

"Do not fear! Yes, you have committed all this evil, true. But do not turn aside from following Yahweh. Serve Him with all your heart! You must not turn aside and chase after futile things and idolatry, which can neither profit nor deliver.

"Yahweh will not abandon His people on account of His great name because He has been pleased to make you a special people for Himself. Moreover, as for me, far be it from me I should sin against Yahweh by ceasing to pray for you. But listen to me ... and I will instruct you in the way that is good and right. Only fear Yahweh and serve Him in truth with all of your heart. Consider what great things He has done for you.

"But, if you still do wickedly, both you and your king shall be swept away."

With these closing remarks, Shemu'el made preparations to return to Ramatayim.

Servants hastened to clear the tables of food spoiled by the falling rain and hail. Cooking fires burst into plumes of steam, and children tried to hide under their mothers. The party was over for today. The crowds, struggling to stay dry, murmured among themselves by family and tribe.

King Sha'ul, sitting at the head of his table, looked on and said nothing, betraying no emotion.

—IX—

"I call to order the Council of the Seranim," said Azzuhath, ruler of Ashdod, dressed in his finery with multiple gold rings weighing down his hand.

The Five P'lishtim lords met at Ashkelon, a wealthy seaport and one of the five city-states comprising the P'lishtim Pentapolis. They sat at a banquet table in a great open-air hall, overlooking the Great Sea where they could see the white sails of ships and listen to the churn of the tide against the shore below.

Young female servants with braided hair and tanned, clean-shaven young males in crisp linen tunics brought forth red and black painted ceramic platters of rich foods to set before the men. Roast pork, roast pheasant, fresh fish and eels, whole bunches of grapes and salted cucumbers, all accompanied by new wine imported from across the ocean.

"What's the first item of the agenda?" Ma'okh, Lord of Gat, asked, yawning.

"We want a report on the doings of the Hebrews and what they are up to," said the Lord of Gaza, plucking grapes from their stems and popping them into his mouth as he spoke. "Reports are tickling my ears that they have been fortifying cities. Is this the doing of this ... this so-called 'king' of theirs?"

Azzuhath unrolled a small parchment scroll and squinted at its contents.

"Hmmm, Ma'okh, be a dear friend and try to make sense of this chicken scratch, would you?"

Ma'okh reached down the table and took the scroll, staining the edges with grease from his fingers.

Azzuhath continued: "Indeed. It seems that their experiment in having a king for themselves has lasted well on two years now, despite the fact that he is, in essence, a nobody—a garish farmer's son with his own litter of piglets ... no offense to you," Azzuhath said with a shrill laugh, saluting with his cup of wine at the pig's head staring back at him on the table. "These Hebrews, as you know, have no real lineage ... no royal blood to speak of. They are but field rats, scampering out of the wilderness and digging holes in the hills in which to nest."

Ma'okh cleared his throat to read from the scroll, "Ahem. The word from our outposts is that this Sha'ul has kept a core of three thousand trained soldiers—"

"An army of only three thousand?" Ashkelon's ruler sputtered incredulously.

"—as it says, three thousand trained men as a personal or 'royal' guard. Reports indicate that the force has been moving between Mikhmas and Giv'ah of Binyamin."

Ma'okh looked up from reading to comment. "Ah, the Hebrews who come to have their tools sharpened in Gat have taken to calling it Giv'ah of Sha'ul now."

"Their capital! That little dung pile?" Ashkelon's ruler hooted, pounding the table with the flat of his hand.

"The population has more than tripled over the past few years in that city. That is the main site of the fortifications ... stronger walls it would appear and some sort of soldiers' quarters in the works."

"Thank you. My instinct, and my instincts are usually pretty good," Azzuhath began, "is all this hubbub is for internal purposes only—protect the king, tax the people, avoid civil war. A few walls and a gang of goons is of no concern for us."

"So our intelligence is trustworthy?" the lord of 'Ekron asked, concern in his voice.

"Relax, brother! We've had those Hebrew hill-dwellers right where we've wanted them for years. They wouldn't dare cross us now. We have outposts everywhere. A Hebrew can't even empty his bowels in the forest without our spies knowing about it."

"I believe you. But we were surprised a couple years ago when they fought with the 'Amoni. I don't like surprises."

"That ... that was a flash of lightning, never to happen in such a way again, I assure you. And what should we care if those hill-dwellers chased off a few desert inbreeds one time? It's meaningless."

"That being said, I feel it would be wise to have a contingency plan to kill this king and his firstborn."

"The son is not of the Hebrew age for military conscription, but the people say he is well regarded, tall like his father, and courageous," Ma'okh added. "Alas, dramatic as he is, Azzuhath is right. We have nothing to fear. Our iron chariots would ride over their army like ... well ..."

"Analogies are not your strong suit, Ma'okh. More wine?" Azzuhath snapped his fingers for the servants to refill Ma'okh's cup.

The Lord of Gaza was ready to move on to the next topic: "Perhaps we should talk about increasing our export of olive oil to Egypt while all members of the council are still relatively sober."

Y'honatan paced the hall of his family home in Giv'ah.

"What worries you, my son?" Achino'am called from the other room where she sat bouncing young Eshba'al on her knee.

"I wonder what Father is doing," he replied, looking out the narrow window at the end of the hallway before walking toward his mother. "He's out there somewhere with all his men."

"Not all his men, son. There are plenty here in Giv'ah with us!"

"Oh yes, he has two battalions of soldiers with him in the field and has left me home with a thousand babysitters."

"Oh Y'honatan, you sound so grown up when you talk about these things."

"I am grown up!"

"You have become quite a young man, but you aren't yet of fighting age."

"Mother, you don't have to be twenty to swing a sword or shoot a bow. I could be helping Father right now."

Achino'am shook her head and turned her attention back to her youngest child. This was not a discussion that pleased her.

Y'honatan decided to go find one of the officers to see if he could get a status report or any new tidbit of information. He went downstairs and located 'Uzi, the trusted commander and acting head over the stables. True to form, 'Uzi was brushing the mane of his favorite colt, a remaining spoil of war from the Battle of Yavesh-Gil'ad.

"'Uzi!"

"Prince," 'Uzi responded respectfully. "If you're looking for news, I can only tell you the same thing I told you last time you asked."

"But 'Uzi, surely you must know something about my father's plans! He left for Mikhmas days ago."

"The king is a careful man. And I know he is with Commander Ehud, who also does not take war lightly. To him, it's a game of strategy."

"It seems that all they do is march from place to place, making camp, looking at maps, and debating over plans. Do we really want to drive the P'lishtim from our land, or do we just want to dream about it?"

"Prince Y'honatan, my sympathies are with you. Like this fine animal here, I am built to charge into the glory of battle. But the commanders do not want to be rash. Picking a fight with the P'lishtim is a serious thing."

"Is it rash to obey God? He said my father was made king in part to deliver this nation from the P'lishtim. Is it foolhardy to believe His word and achieve it?"

'Uzi stopped brushing.

"My father declared that we would drive the P'lishtim out of our land, starting with their garrisons right here in Binyamin. I'm tired of waiting. The king and Yahweh both have decreed the P'lishtim must leave. These uncircumcised squatters are beyond due to be kicked off our property!"

"What would you propose?" 'Uzi asked, with a glint in his eye.

"My kinsman ... my grandfather's brother ... dwells in Geva. I know those nearby hills well, right where the P'lishtim garrison is. They have swords ... spears ... horses. They have a treasure of silver our people have paid to have their mattocks and axes sharpened. For far too long our enemies have been allowed to oppress us, sitting there like a tumor on this land that God Himself gave to our people! My father has stated that we will attack the garrisons. I only propose that we obey the king's order. I propose a surprise attack."

King Sha'ul and two thousand soldiers waited in their rugged encampment on the mount of Beit'el. Below their position in the heights and to the east was Mikhmas, which was too small to accommodate them and would negate the purpose of their surveying the land and remaining mobile. Beyond Mikhmas lay the pass, a pathway cut out of rock with two jutting crags, one on each side of the gorge.

The days of inaction grew monotonous, and boredom had set in for many of the soldiers. Little entertainment was to be found in these hills, and even less comfort.

That changed when a breathless messenger arrived to tell Sha'ul the news. He found the king crouched by the smoldering embers of a campfire with Avner and Ehud. "Prince Y'honatan has sacked the P'lishtim garrison near Geva! He has killed the governing officer!" he announced.

Sha'ul removed the barley stock from his mouth and looked at his astonished cousin.

"Why, that's got to be less than nine miles from where we are!" Avner remarked.

Sha'ul rose and tried to look out in the direction of Geva, to no avail. "Yahweh, help us," Sha'ul whispered. At once he felt a swelling of great pride and great fear.

Ehud turned pale. "My king, your son has thrown a rock at the hornet's nest."

"We should dispatch scouts to keep watch and inform us of any P'lishtim activity," Avner answered, assessing the situation.

"Any P'lishtim activity?" Ehud replied. "Of course there will be P'lishtim activity. This is open war!"

"Be quiet, Ehud," Sha'ul barked, scratching his facial hair thoughtfully.

"Yes, my king."

"I want you to gather the messengers. Have the men sound the horns and let every Yisra'elite hear. We need to summon the fighting men. Every last one."

Ehud went to make arrangements, and Avner drew close to the king.

"Sha'ul, this won't be like picking a fight with the sons of 'Amon."

"I know."

"The P'lishtim ... some of their military advisors are descended from veterans of the Trojan Wars. That is what my father told me."

"I don't know anything about such wars. But I believe that if God will be with us, we can survive this. I think we are meant to survive it. Maybe at long last we can be free from the oppression of these enemies."

"You'll want me to send for the seer," Avner said, anticipating.

"Yes, we'll need him. We will need God's favor. Send our fastest man to Ramatayim and then prepare the men to march. First, we'll join my son at Geva, then we'll all go east ... to Gilgal. Perhaps there we can mount a defense against what's sure to come."

Avner nodded gravely.

—X—

The P'lishtim responded swiftly. Three thousand chariots, six thousand horsemen, and foot soldiers too numerous to count marched straight from P'leshet to the site of their sacked outpost. They were coming for revenge, and they knew exactly who was responsible.

Yisra'elites fled from the P'lishtim warpath, abandoning their homes, their belongings, and even their livestock. Families ran for their lives to get out of the way of the swath of warriors cutting through their country, a sharpened sword aiming at the heart of the Hebrew uprising.

With their foes melting away before them, the P'lishtim reached their destination unopposed and meticulously combed over the smoking heap of the outpost near Geva, salvaging what little of use was left and reclaiming their dead.

Ner was stuffing jewelry and family valuables into a bag while his wife, children, and servants hurriedly gathered garments and rugs and anything else they could bear to add to their already heavily loaded beasts.

Hamor was present, having already helped his master, Kish, depart to the east and been sent back to support the extended family's flight to safety.

"Master Ner, the P'lishtim are on the outskirts of the city. We need to leave right now," he urged.

"I heard you the first time!" Ner growled, swinging his bulk through the house in a desperate attempt to leave behind nothing of real worth. "I need to get the family idols. Help me carry them!"

"Master, please. There is no time. We have to go."

The plan was to cross the river into the tribal territory of Gad. Less mobile neighbors had already hid themselves in nearby cisterns, ditches, pits, thickets of thorns, and all manner of humiliating abodes. Ner was too proud to crawl into any of the caves in the gorge. Beyond that, being the king's uncle made him an appealing target, and he could not fully trust that a fellow man of Binyamin wouldn't inform on his location under duress or for a sizeable reward.

Sha'ul's army waited anxiously in Gilgal. The summoned reinforcements hadn't materialized in sufficient numbers. Shemu'el was nowhere to be found. Rumors of desertion shook the ranks of the core of three thousand soldiers.

Yisra'el had become odious to the P'lishtim.

Sha'ul paced inside his tent. Y'honatan sat close by on a wooden stool.

"Tell the truth, are you angry with me, Father?" Y'honatan asked.

"Angry? I'm not angry. No. No. What you did was dangerous—very dangerous—but brave. You did with a few what I was scared to do with many. You aren't even of age yet, but already you make a great warrior."

"Then do I get my own armor bearer?" A mischievous grin crossed Y'honatan's face.

"Consider it done. I'm proud of you, but please be careful. I assigned those soldiers to protect you, not help get you killed!"

"Are you glad I did it?"

"I wish it were that simple," Sha'ul answered. "As king, I'm responsible for the people, and they are trembling with fear right now ... fear for their lives. This army of ours is no match for the P'lishtim."

"But if Yahweh fights for us, who can stand against us? Remember when you fought the 'Amoni and defeated them?"

"My son, we outnumbered Nachash and his army tenfold. This is a very different situation," Sha'ul argued. He stopped pacing and sighed, "But yes, of course you are right. With Yahweh's favor, we can succeed. But without it ..."

Avner entered the tent. "Our scouts report that the P'lishtim have encamped at Mikhmas. Their strength is even greater than we feared. They are sending out raiding parties through all the surrounding territories to find you. By the grace of God, they don't know quite where we are yet."

"Have any more men come to join us?"

Avner shook his head.

"What about Shemu'el? Has he arrived?"

Avner shook his head again.

"Shemu'el told our messenger he was coming, but he isn't here yet. I hope he hasn't fallen into the hands of the P'lishtim."

Sha'ul chewed his bottom lip. "Without him here to give the burnt offering for us ... without his blessing, I fear for the hearts of our men. Do we have any Levites with us at all?"

"The priests from Geva have crossed the Yarden or have otherwise hidden themselves. I believe Achiyah was to be with us, but I heard a report that he is hiding in the wilderness. I will scour the camp again and see if any remain with us."

"We can't go into battle without first offering a sacrifice!"

"Then let us hope that the old man gets here soon."

Days passed. The soldiers felt as if a crest of P'lishtim chariots would appear on the horizon at any moment. Sha'ul tried to stay close by his men to bolster their courage, retiring to his tent only to sleep, but this did little to relieve the fear of the people. Shemu'el had not yet arrived. The altar remained bare.

Looking at the uncut stones, strangely, Sha'ul felt the words Shemu'el had once cryptically spoken to him coming back to his memory. *"There will come a time when you go down before me to Gilgal. I will come down to meet you there and offer burnt offerings and sacrifice peace offerings. At that time, you must wait for me seven days, and then I will reveal to you what you should do."*

Sha'ul grunted. Was this some sort of test? Shemu'el was four days late by his calculation. That left the seer just three days.

The king balanced an iron sword in his hand. Despite the successful overthrow of the P'lishtim outpost, Y'honatan had been able to recover only two swords, now carried by Sha'ul and himself, the only two in the hands of any Yisra'elite. Sha'ul kept the weapon by his side at all times. The blade felt lighter, yet somehow stronger. In a fair fight, he would be eager to test it on the field.

Commander Ehud cautiously approached the king.

"Yes, Ehud, what is it?"

"My king, the men desire to know what the plan is. What can I tell them?"

"They do, or you do? Tell them that I said, 'The seer, Shemu'el, is on his way. He will be here within three days to give the offering and ask after Yahweh for us.' Then we will know how best to proceed. But tell the men to rest when they can. I think there will be a lot of fighting ahead."

On the seventh day, soldiers began to abandon their posts in droves. Sha'ul doubted he had the ability to compel or punish any deserters just then, and he urged Avner not to strike out against anyone. What had grown by a couple of thousand patriotic bodies now shrunk just as quickly. Still, Shemu'el had not arrived.

Sha'ul walked to the camp's farthest observation point where sentries kept a constant lookout. He saw no one approaching.

"Where is that 'man of God'?" Sha'ul grumbled.

The sun was past its zenith, and he began to sense panic setting in with the remaining soldiers. The seer had said seven days, but he had not arrived. There would be no sacrifice, no blessing, no divine wisdom. Doubt plagued him. He turned and walked straight to the altar at the height of the camp.

"That's it," Sha'ul began. "Bring the animals to me and I'll offer the sacrifice myself."

Y'honatan shot his father a quizzical look.

Avner asked, "Are you certain?"

"Bring them here and tell the men to gather for the offering."

Sha'ul drew his sword. If night fell without taking any action, the people would abandon him completely.

The king killed the thin young bull while some of his men hurried to light the wood fire on the altar. Receiving assistance in skinning the animal, Sha'ul separated the portions as he had observed and laid them on the fire, voicing a prayer on behalf of the looming trouble. Fat and entrails crackled and popped into fragrant smoke as the soldiers stood observing, seeking solemnity to calm their treacherous nerves.

Next, Sha'ul called for the animal for the peace offering, and two men struggled to lead a reluctant cow toward the altar.

A call rang out and carried across the camp, "It's Shemu'el! He's coming!"

The king's face flushed, and he turned, wiping the blood off his iron sword and rushing to the observation point. Indeed, the seer and two of his students in their traveling cloaks were steadily crossing the plain toward their position, riding on their donkeys.

"Avner! Prepare my horse."

King Sha'ul, the prince, and a small retinue rode out to meet the travelers in the plain.

"Greetings and peace, Shemu'el," Sha'ul said, dismounting and walking briskly to greet the seer, who did not dismount. "Thanks to Yahweh you have arrived!"

The king unwound the cord connecting a water skin to his person, ready to offer it to the presumably thirsty travelers. Shemu'el held out his hand to stop him.

"What have you done?"

The seer was not pleased. He obviously knew about the sacrifice, somehow, and there was no point in avoiding it.

"I came here to Gilgal to summon all the people together to go to war, but instead, the people ran away. I saw that even the men I had with me were beginning to scatter. I waited for you these past seven days to arrive, and when I saw that you didn't come within the set time and the P'lishtim army is assembling at Mikhmas ..." Sha'ul faltered, then regrouped. "I thought, now the P'lishtim are going to come down and attack us here, and I haven't yet sought after Yahweh's favor. So I forced myself to offer the burnt offering."

Shemu'el shook his head.

"Sha'ul, you have acted foolishly. You have not obeyed the word of Yahweh your God, which He commanded you. Had you done so, Yahweh would have established your kingdom over Yisra'el forever. But now your kingdom shall not endure."

The two men stared at each other intensely: the wizened seer on his donkey and two young students opposite King Sha'ul, tall and muscular, dressed for war and surrounded by his loyal followers.

Shemu'el continued, "I tell you the truth, Yahweh has sought out for Himself a man after His own heart. Yahweh has appointed him as a ruler over His people, because you have not kept what was commanded you and, moreover, took it upon yourself to act as a priest over Yisra'el, a role which Yahweh has not granted you."

Sha'ul stood, clenching his jaw and resting his fists on his hips.

Shemu'el looked away—was there moisture in his eyes?

"Come, Gad, Nahum ... let's go." Shemu'el's students, one really only a youth, looked exhausted from their journey, but without audible complaint, they turned their donkeys and followed their master's lead.

"But you just got here, Shemu'el! Where are you going?" Sha'ul called out. "Where are you going? The P'lishtim are coming!"

"We are no threat to them," the seer said. "Yahweh will protect us."

"Shemu'el! Shemu'el!" Sha'ul shouted as the three departed. "SHEMU'EL! I am still your king! Am I not? Have you anointed me for nothing?"

Shemu'el halted.

"Come back here! Finish the sacrifice, for the sake of the people at least. Please. Then you can go on your way."

The old man slowly turned around.

"Yes, you are still the king."

They all returned to the camp, and Shemu'el set about completing the sacrifice and saying a prayer for the remaining people. More men seemed to have left in the interim. When finished, Shemu'el too would depart.

Sha'ul pulled his cousin aside.

"Avner, how many remain with us?"

"Only about six hundred."

−XI−

Stalemate.

Sha'ul and his six hundred played cat and mouse, constantly on the move to avoid detection by the three companies of P'lishtim raiders, scouring the land for the upstart king. There were sightings of such marauding bands near 'Ofrah in the hilly land of Sha'ul within the tribal territory of M'nasheh to the north. Another band was sighted near the caverns of Beit-Horon on the border of Efrayim to the west; another on the edge of the valley of Tzvo'im in the east, overlooking the wilderness inhabited by hyenas.

As information trickled in, the ragtag Yisra'elite army decamped and scurried from place to place, avoiding major roads, attempting to conceal evidence of their travels. When there was no news, they simply had to guess. They could take comfort in the belief that the enemy did not know where they were, the evidence of which was that they were still alive.

They found themselves on the outskirts of Migron, an abandoned farm plot north of Giv'ah. Sha'ul sat under the splotchy shade of a pomegranate tree not yet in fruit, while Achiyah the priest said prayers for the soldiers as they dug trenches in the shelter of the semicircular outcrop of stone.

Achiyah's father, Achituv, had disappeared without a trace.

The most disheartening news came from reports the P'lishtim had begun setting fire to villages suspected of harboring Sha'ul's soldiers and planning public executions of uncooperative citizens. In contrast, collaborators were to be granted amnesty and paid labor.

Many of the six hundred felt sick to their stomachs at how helpless they were to intervene. Avner did his best to console the men, convincing them that Yisra'el's best hope was to preserve the monarchy and that the wisest course of action was to wait it out, however dire the circumstances. Privately, he conferenced with Sha'ul and the remaining commanders about where the enemy might hunt them next.

Y'honatan sat apart. Resting his back against a large boulder, he stared off into the northeast distance, deep in thought. His armor bearer, a young man, approached him.

"Prince, are you all right?"

"Too much fear and speculation in camp right now. I needed some space to clear my head."

"What is on your mind?"

"I just wonder ... we hear reports of the raiding parties searching for us, but we don't know the strength of the remaining force at Mikhmas."

"You want to spy on the enemy's camp."

"I do. How else can we exploit an opportunity if we don't fully know the P'lishtim's strengths and weaknesses?"

"Should you tell the king about your idea?"

"My father would only burden me with more and more men for my protection, which would ruin our chance of making the trip unseen. The two of us, traveling lightly, can scout the P'lishtim and be back here by morning. Can I count on you?"

"Of course, you can. That is why you chose me to be your armor bearer."

Slipping away from the army, Y'honatan and his armor bearer carefully made their way beyond Geva and snuck up the southern ridge overlooking the great gorge. They rested behind one of the highest points, a sharp, thorn-shaped crag of rock towering over the rocky cliffs. Lying flat on the coal-colored earth amid occasional patches of grass, the prince spied out across the ravine.

Directly opposite their position was another steep crag, still catching sunlight that glinted off the white, chalky peak of the otherwise ruddy rock. A half dozen or so armed P'lishtim stood watch at this strategic point, guarding against any Yisra'elite movement across the pass. It was one of the few places soldiers could traverse from one side of the gorge to the other. However, at the time, the guards were disadvantaged by the position of the sun, which shone directly in their faces.

The two young men withdrew behind the protective shield of their rock. Y'honatan was breathing rapidly with excitement.

"The P'lishtim camp is just on the other side. Yahweh, we pray for your help."

The prince turned to his armor bearer and flashed a rictus grin.

"Let's cross over and pay a visit to the garrison of these ... uncircumcised. Perhaps Yahweh our God will work a miracle for us. He isn't restrained to save by many or by few. What do you say?"

"Do all that you have decided to do. I am with you, heart and soul!"

Y'honatan scratched his sandaled foot against the ground in twitchy, nervous energy. He closed and opened his eyes, mouthing silent prayers.

"Here, wrap my sword in cloth and tie it securely to my back. You have a dagger? Conceal it. This is what we will do. We're going to show ourselves to the guards across the pass. If they tell us to stay where we are, and they come for us, then we escape. If they tell us to come up to where they are, this will be the sign for us. We'll know that Yahweh has given our enemies into our hands."

"Okay. I trust you."

Without any sudden movements, the Yisra'elites circled to the bottom of the crag and carefully began to make their way down the steep, winding path of the pass. When they reached a spot in the open, they halted. Y'honatan waved his arms and called out across the ravine.

"Hello! Hellooo! We come peacefully!" he shouted.

On the other side, three P'lishtim soldiers snapped to attention and tightened their grips on their weapons, glaring suspiciously at the source of the sound.

"Looks like a couple of Hebrews."

"Only two?"

"Two more deserters … crawling out of their holes."

"Heh heh heh. Guess they can stand living like cowards for only so long, huddling in some dank cave, eating bugs, and drinking their own urine to survive."

"Ha ha! You're hilarious!"

"Be serious, you two. What should we do with them?"

"Take them into the camp to process them. They probably want to join the others as servants, but I don't think the welcome will be too warm for them. Looks like they're fighting men."

"Are they armed?"

"Don't look like it, but they are young men, strong too."

"Okay!" one of the P'lishtim shouted down to Y'honatan. "If you are surrendering, come on up here and we'll talk about it!"

Another soldier snickered under his breath, "Yeah ... heh heh ... we'll have a real nice discussion."

"Thank you! We'll come up the pass to you! Bless you!" Y'honatan called back. He turned to his armor bearer and said, "Follow me, for Yahweh has given them into the hands of Yisra'el!"

The prince and the armor bearer hurried down their side of the pass into the deep gorge, out of view of the posted guards, as the sun began its descent. Instead of continuing up the other side, Y'honatan traveled horizontally through the winding ravine, skirting the position of the guard post far above their heads.

"How are you at climbing?" Y'honatan asked.

"I ... as good as my prince needs me to be."

"Do as I do. We'll climb straight up the cliff and surprise them."

Y'honatan, sword fastened to his back, began to scale the crenelated, contoured gray cliff walls with his hands and feet.

His accomplice tried to keep up. Before long, his calf muscles burned under the exertion as he scrambled to find precarious footholds in the fading light.

"You okay? Keep coming," the prince encouraged.

"Yes," the armor bearer panted.

Y'honatan reached a small ledge and swung his leg over, hoisting the rest of his body up and scanning the cliff face above for the best route. The armor bearer strained to grip the edge with one hand ... then the other. He started to shift his weight. "Ahhh!" the young man gasped, his fingers slipping from the ledge as gravel dislodged and spattered his face. For a few terrifying moments, he hung over the precipice by a single hand, swiveling over open space.

Y'honatan was on his knees in an instant, seizing his forearm, pulling him upward. Scrambling, the young man's foot found purchase, and he thrust himself over.

Huddling on the ledge, panting, heart thudding in his chest, the armor bearer tried to compose himself. The palm of his hand was red with blood, but he quickly turned the hand down and away so as not to show the prince his injury.

Y'honatan rested his hand on the armor bearer's shoulder, waiting for the other to signal that he was ready to continue. The armor bearer nodded, and they scaled the steep rock wall until they reached the top, creeping over and lying prone.

Dusk was approaching. They were about one hundred and fifty feet or so from Bozez, the northern pinnacle. They could hear the murmur of conversation and stirrings of the P'lishtim soldiers guarding the mouth of the pass. Further north lay the encampment of the P'lishtim army, and the smoke from many small cooking fires curled upward. They struggled to catch their breath.

"A man returns from a voyage across the sea. He goes to see an incompetent fortune-teller. He asks about the well-being of his family, and the fortune-teller says, 'Everyone is perfectly fine, especially your father.' The man gets angry and says that his father has been dead for ten years. The fortune-teller says, 'You have no idea who your real father is!'"

The P'lishtim soldiers milling around the fire laughed.

"I've got a better one. A glutton gives his daughter to another glutton in marriage. When asked what he was giving her as a dowry, he replied, 'A house next to the bakery!'"

More laughter. Most of the guards were eating their evening ration of bread while a few watched the pass. The Hebrews still hadn't shown themselves.

Another P'lishtim snickered to himself, remembering a joke he had learned.

"Here's a good one. Listen. So three men—a barber, a bald Egyptian, and a philosopher—are on a journey to Tiryns for the yearly boar hunt. On the way, they stop to rest for a night, and each is given a shift to guard the baggage. The barber, not used to night watches, becomes bored—"

The soldier did not have time to finish the joke. Like a flash of lightning, Y'honatan swung at his neck with his iron sword. A gurgled cry escaped the man as he fell face first into the fire, sending a burst of sparks, ash and smoke into the air. In another instant, the prince pivoted and stabbed another soldier through the stomach, shouting a war cry.

The P'lishtim dropped their bread and grabbed their weapons, trying to mount a defense against the blindsiding attack. Too late. Y'honatan advanced, swinging and striking with deadly precision. Right on his heels, his armor bearer fell upon wounded men and finished them with a stab to the heart or a slice to the throat. One guard, trying to escape, plummeted into the gorge with a scream.

When the carnage was over, twenty men lay dead and bleeding within a space of about six square yards.

"Grab a sword and follow me; we're going to charge the main camp! Yahweh is with us!"

No sooner had they set foot in that direction than a deep rumbling was felt beneath their feet. The very earth seemed to be shaking with a terrible booming, grinding noise.

—XII—

The earthquake was felt all the way in Migron. Sha'ul and his six hundred arose as one and readied their weapons, bracing themselves against the moving ground.

"This is a trembling from God!" several soldiers shouted.

"It's coming from the direction of Mikhmas," Avner observed.

As the shaking subsided, the men worked to calm the spooked horses. Commander 'Uzi dispatched two of the most skillful riders on the strongest geldings to find out what was happening.

Under the moonlight, one rider returned with an exciting report.

"There is a mighty uproar and confusion in the P'lishtim camp! We saw several dead soldiers just beyond the pass. We heard many shouts and even the sounds of horses fleeing!"

Sha'ul was puzzled.

"Avner!" he barked authoritatively. "Number the men. See who has gone out from us."

The commanders rounded up and counted every man in the camp. Avner's face was ashen when he returned to answer the king.

"Sha'ul, your son is missing! Y'honatan, as well as his armor bearer, are gone."

"Oh, God."

"What do you want us to do?"

"I want the men to hold defensive positions. And ... the priest. Bring the priest to me!"

"Right away."

"And make sure he has the ephod with him!"

Achiyah, bleary-eyed, came forward in his full priestly garments with his father's ephod attached to his chest.

"Something must have happened to your father," Sha'ul said to him. "You must take the responsibilities of high priest now. I need you to inquire after Yahweh. What we should do—whether or not to go up to the P'lishtim camp."

As they were talking, the second scout returned. Avner led the messenger to the king, where he breathlessly described everything he had seen.

"My king, the enemy camp is in complete confusion. I even saw them fighting against one another! Their soldiers are running for their lives, this way and that! The P'lishtim are melting away!"

Sha'ul turned to Achiyah, who was about to cast the Urim and Tumim.

"Never mind, there's no time," the king said to the priest before turning to his soldiers. "Listen, all you men; we move! The P'lishtim are fleeing! They are defeated before us! And we are going after them!"

Y'honatan crouched in the shadows with his armor bearer and watched the chaotic scene, his body dripping with perspiration and the blood of enemy soldiers. Panic had spread like a contagion. In the paranoia and confusion, P'lishtim soldiers were falling on one another in mortal combat while many others fled.

"Traitors among us!" a P'lishtim commander shouted to his subordinates nearby. The foreign, mercenary elements of the P'lishtim army were instantly under suspicion, but could hardly be identified in the dark violence.

What the earthquake had not disrupted in the camp and city, the confusion did. Hot, scattered embers set ablaze a number of tents, casting the nearby struggles in flickering, shifting light. Shadowy forms and silhouettes fought for survival.

"Are you rested?" Y'honatan whispered to his armor bearer, conscious of his own aching muscles beneath the surge of adrenaline. The armor bearer gave a slight nod. "Good, let's go try to find ourselves some horses."

To the southwest, Sha'ul and his six hundred stormed into the battle, each man giving his own shout as they charged. Faced with this new assault, the P'lishtim began to flee en masse, retreating haphazardly. The stragglers who were unable to find horses or flee by chariot were quickly cut down.

The Yisra'elites who had surrendered themselves or had been pressed into service saw Sha'ul's army driving the P'lishtim away and turned to join in, striking against the P'lishtim with rocks, cooking implements, and even their bare hands until they could take more suitable weapons from the dead and the abandoned caches. Y'honatan rallied to these men and women and shouted encouragement, helping to organize the motley group and round up additional horses.

King Sha'ul caught sight of the prince and rode up beside him.

"Son!"

"Father."

"Are you hurt?"

"No, this isn't mine," Y'honatan said, indicating the blood.

"Good."

Just then the morning sun broke over the horizon.

"I'm clearing the camp, then Mikhmas, and then we're going after them," Sha'ul said.

"I'll be with you."

"I know you will."

Sha'ul galloped back toward the action. Y'honatan watched him go and then regarded the new recruits gathered before him. Some hugged each another and celebrated the turn of events. Others stared after the retreating P'lishtim with opportune anger. Even the collaborators among them seemed to have turned completely against their former masters without a hint of shame.

"You heard the king," Y'honatan urged. "Don't let a single of these uncircumcised remain!"

The P'lishtim fled to the north and west, and Sha'ul's army closely pursued them, engaging any soldiers they overtook. Word quickly spread, and many Yisra'elites who had concealed themselves in the hill country of Efrayim came out of hiding and joined in the chase.

Striding in front of the swollen ranks, Sha'ul held his sword aloft and bellowed a challenge, "Today is the day of settling scores. Today is the day we pay the P'lishtim back for all the years of torment they have caused us! They are running for their lives, and we will chase them all the way to the gates of Sh'ol! We will not rest! We will not let them escape! We will not eat until our enemies are cast out of our land! Hear this. Cursed be any man who tastes food before evening. Cursed be any man who eats before I have avenged myself on my enemies. Let's go!"

The Yisra'elites shouted in agreement and rushed onward.

Y'honatan lingered to ensure that Mikhmas was secure, then raced ahead to rejoin his father's men and took up a position with the rear units. The prince had taken several well-crafted bows and quivers of arrows to equip the men assigned to his personal guard. He had also acquired a fine staff for himself.

The P'lishtim were heading toward the Ayalon Valley and would soon be at Beit-Aven. The Yisra'elites pursued and slew whatever P'lishtim they could on the heels of the main force. But the day grew long and the sun hot. Having no sustenance to refresh themselves and having adhered to Sha'ul's oath with deadly seriousness, fatigue began to draw on the ranks, and their pace began to slow.

When they reached the forest, the weary men pressed on, drawing on reserves of energy. Y'honatan, himself exhausted, stalked forward on horseback at the back of the formation. The forest was dense but navigable, with many tall, thin-trunked trees and bursts of foliage and stone.

A luscious scent tickled the prince's nose, and he looked down. Wild honey was oozing from a hollowed tree trunk on the forest floor. Reaching with the end of his staff, the prince dipped into the wild honeycomb and brought a lathering of the viscous honey to his lips. It was sweet and bursting with an almost pungent, floral complexity. Y'honatan smiled wide, already sensing the sugar giving him a much-needed boost.

"Prince!" one of the six hundred sputtered in horror.

Y'honatan turned and looked across the woodsy patch at the soldier.

"Yes?"

"What ... what are you doing?"

Y'honatan stared blankly, then held up his hand to offer some of the honey. The man looked as if he were about to be sick.

"Your father put the people under an oath! Didn't you hear? He said 'Cursed be any man who eats food before evening.'"

Y'honatan's eyebrows shot up. He shook his head sorrowfully as the circumstances dawned on him.

"My father has brought trouble on us with these words. Just a taste of this wild honey has revived me. How much more strength the people would have if they had been able to eat freely of all the spoil of the P'lishtim! I fear now that our victory will not be as great."

—XIII—

The Yisra'elites returned to Mikhmas, having pursued the P'lishtim army and killed many until their foes escaped into the plains beyond Ayalon. The weary mass, now numbered in the thousands, needed to regroup. And they needed to eat.

As the deadline for Sha'ul's oath had passed, the filthy, exhausted men fell upon the enemy spoil—sheep, cattle, calves, and whatever else they could get their hands on—slaughtering the animals on the ground and either making hasty cooking fires or partaking of the flesh raw.

Elders and scribes among the civilians who had rallied to the Yisra'elite army, taking great offense, approached Sha'ul with dire words of warning.

"King Sha'ul! You must do something. The people are sinning greatly against Yahweh by violating the Law. Look, they're eating meat that still has the blood in it! Do something or we'll all be defiled!"

Sha'ul's brow furrowed as his gaze swept across the field where, indeed, every man seemed to be desperately gorging himself without any regard for the laws recorded in the Vayikra. The king's face burned red, and he shouted for his commanders.

"I want a great stone rolled here before me right now! Then go and spread the word among all these treacherous people. Tell them to bring their cattle and sheep here, to slaughter the animals in front of me on the stone and eat. Tell them that they must not sin against Yahweh! They can't eat with the blood!"

Sha'ul stabbed his sword into the ground in frustration as his men carried out the order. He called for his eighteen-year-old son, who had been washing his hands in a basin.

"Yes, Father?"

"Can you find Achiyah and ask him to gather the Levites who are here?"

"Yes, I think he's still in the city. I'll find him."

"He's probably sleeping," Sha'ul muttered.

"Then I'll wake him."

"Thank you," the king said, and then added almost as an afterthought, "You fought bravely today."

Y'honatan smiled broadly at the acknowledgment.

When the priests were accounted for, Sha'ul ordered that an altar be built on the spot, commemorating their victory. The people also complied with his edict and brought their animals to be killed on the rock and for the blood to drain out before the king. Afterward, the priests offered sacrifices. The army ate and rested with the others, mingling tribe-to-tribe and family-to-family.

Sha'ul, Avner, Ehud, 'Uzi, and other advisors discussed strategy as they dined.

"My king, we should prepare ourselves immediately for a counterattack," Ehud advised cautiously. "They still have many chariots at their disposal."

"Chariots are worthless in the forests and the mountains!" 'Uzi snorted.

"We go after them again tonight." Sha'ul's eyes shone with fervor. "We'll catch up to them and fall on them before the morning light!" He did not appear the least bit tired.

"Do you think the men have the strength for more marching and fighting this very night?" Avner asked, even toned.

"Now is our opportunity! We need to strike while we have the taste of victory in our mouths and the men have courage."

The advisors mulled it over noncommittally.

"In fact," Sha'ul continued, "I want you to get them ready—everyone who can still fight. They've had their break."

When the men and elders were assembled, the king stood atop his promontory.

"Who is ready to go with me after the P'lishtim this very night? I tell you, we will not leave a man of them alive!"

The people cheered. As it stood, the only good P'lishtim was a dead P'lishtim.

"We will follow our king."

"Whatever seems good to you, we will do!"

"Then prepare yourselves," Sha'ul said.

"King Sha'ul," Achiyah, the priest, said stepping forward to address him respectfully. "Perhaps now is the time to draw near to Yahweh at this place to pray, and seek His guidance."

Sha'ul nodded emphatically.

"Yes, I hear your wise words," he said, then, turning to the people, "Prepare yourselves and remain ready as we will seek Yahweh's favor and wisdom for the battle ahead. May He grant us total destruction of our enemies this night!"

"Should I go down after the P'lishtim tonight?" Sha'ul asked, providing the query before Yahweh to Achiyah and the priests. "Will You give them into the hands of Yisra'el?"

The altar smoldered. Prayers were offered. The Urim and Tumim were cast.

Yahweh did not respond.

The prayers went seemingly into the void. The Urim and Tumim were inconclusive, time and time again. Sha'ul paced anxiously, pressuring the priests to continue asking. There was nothing.

Hours passed. Restlessness turned to boredom turned to slumber. Soldiers lay in the field, or crawled into tents, or slept sitting up. Youths, elders, and women took shelter in Mikhmas. Humiliation crept into Sha'ul's heart like a sickness.

"Why? Why won't He answer?" Sha'ul demanded.

Achiyah replied with some fatigue, "Maybe there is some sin among the people, and Yahweh has turned His face from us and covered His ear."

"Keep trying!"

At morning light, Sha'ul, not having slept a wink, called for all the men to assemble before him, grouped roughly by tribe with whatever leaders were among them at the forefront. As they stood in helpless array, the king harangued them.

"There is sin among the people! This is why Yahweh will not answer us in this time of need. What is the sin? And who is responsible? I charge you to find the answer! We will not leave this place until this evil is avenged. I swear it, as Yahweh lives who delivers Yisra'el, even if this sin be found in my son Y'honatan, he shall surely die!"

The people murmured uneasily while Sha'ul paced back and forth, his fingers grasping the hilt of his sword. Y'honatan stood nobly beside his father, watching the crowd.

"Tell me; which of you has done this detestable thing? Point out the man!"

Nobody said a word. Confused, fearful, guilty, and uncomfortable looks flickered through the sea of faces.

"Not one of you cowards dares to speak out," Sha'ul growled through gritted teeth. "Fine!"

Sha'ul took his sword and drew a line in the ground dramatically.

"Y'honatan and I will stand on this side, and everybody else will stand on the other. Achiyah, bring forth the Urim and Tumim!"

The people reluctantly accepted this plan, and the separation was made, with Avner, Y'honatan's armor bearer, and all others crossing to join with the crowd as the king had commanded them. The priest dutifully came forward with the ephod.

"Oh, Yahweh, our God, I pray that you give the perfect lot," Sha'ul pleaded to the sky. "Achiyah, cast the lot for my son and me."

Achiyah cast the Urim and Tumim and his eyes shot up to Sha'ul.

"The ... the lot has taken you. The people have been cleared."

Sha'ul blanched and felt his breath catch in his throat. In a blur, he nodded slowly and took a few conscious paces away from his firstborn. He indicated to Achiyah to continue.

"Cast lots between me ... and my son."

Achiyah held his breath and took hold of the polished stones, throwing them again into the hoshen with a prayer.

"The lot has taken Y'honatan."

Avner and the other commanders gasped in astonishment. The crowd began stirring. Sha'ul staggered away from his son as if struck. A vein bulged on his forehead, and with shaking hands he tried to draw his blade once again from its scabbard.

"Y-you? What have you done?" he moaned, mournfully.

"It is true. The fault is mine," Y'honatan replied in a loud, clear voice. He stood his ground but looked at his feet ashamedly. "In the forest yesterday, sometime after you had made the oath for all the people, I tasted a little honey with the end of the staff that was in my hand."

Y'honatan unfastened his leather breastplate and let it fall to the ground. He stepped over it and approached his father, hands resting at his side, gaze averted.

"Here I am, Father. I have done wrongly, and you cannot break your oath. I must die."

The king was nearly apoplectic. A single tear sprung from his eye. It trickled through the black curls of his facial hair and ran down the snarling ridge of his upper lip. He slowly drew the remaining length of his blade and clenched the weapon in both hands.

"Y'honatan, may God do this to me and more also if I do not carry out my vow, for you shall surely die."

In an instant, everyone began to protest loudly and crowd in on Sha'ul and Y'honatan, their sandals scraping and obscuring the line in the ground. Avner and Sha'ul's personal guard could not hold back the frenzied people as they pushed and shoved their way in, shouting for mercy.

"No! No!"

"Y'honatan must not die!"

"Why should you kill him, when he has worked this great deliverance for Yisra'el?"

"It shall not be!"

"Save the prince!"

The people threw their arms around Y'honatan protectively, placing their own bodies in front of any harm that would come to him.

"Y'honatan is our hero. He overturned the enemy camp with just two men!"

"As Yahweh lives, not one hair of his head will fall to the ground!"

"Y'honatan has worked with God on this day of deliverance!"

Sha'ul relented, carefully sheathing his sword as he was bumped and jostled by the shifting crowds. His officers moved in to create a buffer around him until the tumult was finally calmed.

"Surely by now what's left of the P'lishtim army has returned to their land," the king said, feeling his lack of sleep rapidly catching up with him. "Let every man return to his own tent. It's time to rebuild our homes and strengthen Yisra'el. I declare it ... we will no longer be a people who lie down before the P'lishtim ... or any of our enemies. We will not be slaves to any nation."

—XIV—

Time passed. Sha'ul's first priority was to build his army. Never again would he allow himself to be outnumbered and outmatched. He appointed his cousin Avner as head over the entire military. Divisions were made for chariots, horsemen, and foot soldiers. Y'honatan, young though he was, made it a special project to promote and organize archery as a military discipline.

The second priority followed. Sha'ul would need the means to keep a large army fed, compensated, and content. This meant taxation.

Sha'ul initially appointed his Uncle Ner to be overseer of the treasury and storehouses, but when his health began to fail from the years of his excessive appetites, Sha'ul promoted Ehud as a replacement, finding him to be better suited to protect material possessions than the lives of men.

The king's home in Giv'ah of Sha'ul, no longer commonly called Giv'ah of Binyamin, became a fortress, an increasingly powerful center from which to conduct the king's business. Sha'ul could provide his wife with fine things he had never before been able to give her, and she and their four sons adjusted quickly to the changes and improvements in their lifestyle. Sha'ul's widower father would never have to work again, living in his own residence within the family compound, attended to day and night by servants.

Still, this experiment of monarchy was complicated work. It wasn't enough for Sha'ul to plot warfare against the villainous Mo'avites, Edomites, 'Amoni, P'lishtim, as well as other foes that lurked beyond and sometimes even within the borders of Yisra'el. No, Sha'ul was suddenly faced with demands to make decisions regarding all manner of logistical, governmental, and outright mundane concerns. Half of his advisors, many of whom were blood relatives, advised him to refer these questions back to the tribal leaders, while the other half encouraged him to respond to all and, thereby, further consolidate his authority and rule.

During one such exchange with his inner circle on the need to delegate overseers to supervise the king's vineyards and fields, an attendant came to inform Sha'ul that he had a surprise visitor in the foyer.

The visitor was the seer Shemu'el. Sha'ul was struck anew by how ancient the man of Yahweh looked, and yet, somehow, not any older than at their last meeting, as if he remained in the same state of aged agelessness. Shemu'el's cool eyes stared penetratingly out between the wrinkles of his face and the wild mane of white hair and his overgrown Nazir beard. Sha'ul, no matter how familiar he became with the old man, was always discomfited by this gaze. He could never shake the lurking suspicion that Shemu'el could see straight through him.

"Shemu'el! I'm glad that at last you get to see our new home. Giv'ah has changed a lot, hasn't it?"

"You are doing well for yourself," was the curt reply.

"It is a work in progress. Being a king is ... not a simple thing. But I don't think you came down here just to chat or sightsee."

"No. I serve at Yahweh's pleasure, and I come on His business. All that you have here is because He commanded me to anoint you as king over His people, Yisra'el. He has once again commanded me, this time, to bring you a message. Are you ready to hear the words your God has to tell you?"

"Yes, of course."

"Thus declares Yahweh of Hosts, 'I will punish 'Amalek for the evil he did to Yisra'el when he set himself against the children of Yisra'el on their way up from Egypt. When they were exhausted and weary, the 'Amaleki attacked and killed the weak, the elderly, and the slow ones lagging behind, showing no fear of Me. The measure of 'Amalek's evil is full. Now go, strike the 'Amaleki and utterly devote them and all that they have to destruction. Do not spare or pity them. They will be made cherem. You must put to death both man and woman, child and infant, ox and sheep, camel and donkey.' This is the will of Yahweh."

Sha'ul informed Avner of their next target and asked for his assessment.

"The 'Amaleki are nomadic people. Skilled fighters on camel or horseback. They roam from the Negev to the Red Sea and strike where they want. They make their home in the plains and the deserts. They prefer the curved blade. Their chieftain or king is called Agag, I think. But, shouldn't we be strengthening our forces against the P'lishtim?"

"The 'Amaleki have been a thorn in Yisra'el's side for too long. It is the will of our God that we destroy them."

So the king's army went south and staged their campaign from T'la'im. The fighting men of Yisra'el were numbered at two hundred thousand foot soldiers. Spears and javelins, as many could be had, would be used to deal with the camel-riding irregular cavalry.

Scouts spied out the enemy's main camp, a day's journey into the desert.

"Their capital is like an endless city of tents," Avner reported. "We think they have wells there that they protect—jealously. Beyond that is a giant stretch of sand with smaller settlements. In that desert and the wilderness beyond, that is their turf, and I don't doubt that they are familiar with every inch of it."

"So we don't want to fight in that desert."

"No. Not in the open desert. The capital must be our priority. Cut off the head. Most interesting, there are communities of the Keni, descendants of Yitro, between our location and their main camp."

"And?"

"Some of these settlements are on a ridge overlooking a particular valley … a great location from which to stage an ambush."

"We have no fight with the Keni, do we?"

"Not at all. Historically they are friends of Yisra'el."

"We should send word to them. Tell them to leave from among the 'Amaleki, as we mean them no harm. Then we move our soldiers into that valley by night."

Yisra'el fell upon its foes in that dust and sand-colored wilderness. The fierce battle for the capital raged for six days. Then the smaller encampments were besieged, with Yisra'elite soldiers digging fortified positions and cutting off access to water. They pursued the 'Amaleki westward toward Egypt until their forces were decimated, although some managed to escape into the distant wilds on camelback.

Their camps were destroyed. Their possessions were burned and trampled. Families were not spared from the edge of the sword. Execution was the only option for those who dared surrender. On the order of Sha'ul, no prisoners were taken—except one.

Meanwhile, the men rounded up the livestock of the 'Amaleki, herding the sheep and cattle startled from the violence and unfamiliar people who now accosted them.

"Look at this one!" a young man shouted from the tribe of Shim'on, holding a fat, writhing lamb in his arms. "Have you ever seen such a beautiful lamb?"

"It'd be a shame to waste it," another soldier answered as he sifted through smoldering debris with a stick. "We have our orders."

"Yeah, but, even if we left any flocks for the 'Amaleki, we didn't leave any 'Amaleki for the flocks!" the younger man grunted as he put the lamb down in a makeshift pen he had constructed. It scampered about, bleating fearfully.

"But we have our orders."

"God has given them into our hands. 'Amalek has nothing left! My brothers found some cattle of the finest quality. They slaughtered most of the herds, but they couldn't bring themselves to hurt such beautiful cattle. Why shouldn't we keep them? Our families can use them. They can benefit our nation. We can breed them, or add them to our herds, or even present them as a tribute to Sha'ul the Conqueror!"

"You may have a point with that last one. This lamb would make a fine gift for the king."

Others had the same idea and spared the best of the flocks and herds, leading them back to the Yisra'elite camp and away from the wreckage of war and the stench of the dead.

Agag, the 'Amaleki king, dressed in a fine, dark robe and adorned with a royal headdress, was dragged before Sha'ul. The Yisra'elite, reclining in his tent, laughed heartily despite himself at the sight of the foreign ruler thrown defenseless before him, hands bound. Sha'ul's guards pressed spear tips against Agag's throat.

"I'm Sha'ul, king of Yisra'el," Sha'ul said, staring down at the captive. "You are Agag ... king of dirt."

Agag spat on the ground and cursed Sha'ul in his native tongue. Sha'ul's face was bright with excitement. He looked at the soldiers who had captured Agag.

"You are brave men. What are your names and where are you from? I am going to promote you for this."

After dismissing the soldiers, Sha'ul turned his attention back to his prisoner.

"How does it feel, I wonder, to rule a nation one day and to have nothing on the next? Nothing and nobody."

Sha'ul felt a pang of remorse in his heart. The alien sympathy caught him completely by surprise, and he turned away to conceal eyes that were suddenly misty.

"Guards, take this man unharmed to my commanders. Have them place him under constant watch."

"Yes, King," one of the guards answered, taking hold of Agag. "He'll make an excellent trophy for your victory."

—XV—

Shemu'el.

The seer's eyes opened in the darkness of his room.

Shemu'el.

The voice of Yahweh was calling to him, nudging him awake in his spirit.

"Yes, Lord," he responded, rousing slowly and rubbing his eyes.

Shemu'el.

The voice was barely a whisper, but it was certain. Shemu'el got out of bed and began to dress himself. This was a time to seek the will of Yahweh.

"Yes, Lord. Your servant is listening."

Shemu'el. I am changing my purpose for Sha'ul, for it has grieved Me that I have made him king. He has been disobedient, turning after his own way and not fulfilling My commandments. The scepter will depart from his family and will instead be given to a more righteous man.

Shemu'el was aghast. He himself had anointed Sha'ul as Yahweh's chosen one in front of all the people. Sha'ul, achieving victory in war. Sha'ul, growing in fame. Sha'ul, the years of his young reign could still be counted on one's fingers.

What humiliation would Yisra'el suffer? What suspicion and scrutiny would Shemu'el himself and his ministry be under? And how would Sha'ul, with his army, possibly react?

Shemu'el cried out to Yahweh, begging for mercy for the king, seeking to intercede on his behalf, asking for Yahweh to forgive and pardon the king's transgressions, known and unknown. Shemu'el got no sleep that night and, when the sun came up, his throat was hoarse from the supplication.

"Gad," the seer rasped, finding the adolescent beginning his morning chores at the students' residence. "I need you and Shlomit to accompany me to T'la'im."

"What do we need to do there?" Gad asked, noting Shemu'el's bloodshot eyes and haggard appearance.

"You need to help guide your teacher. I need to deliver a message to the king of Yisra'el."

"Another message? Is it a good word?"

"Not quite. Hurry up and get your things together."

"But Master," Gad started. "I may get in trouble with the brothers if I don't finish sweeping this place."

"Leave it! Come along now; this is important. Yahweh knows ... someday you may need to deliver bad news to a king yourself."

The three travelers made their journey into the arid region to the south, where they encountered stragglers from the Yisra'elite rearguard.

Shemu'el was informed that Sha'ul was no longer at T'la'im, nor to be found anywhere from the Negev to the Red Sea. The king and his army had left for Karmel, a fruitful habitation in the tribal land of Y'hudah.

Adjusting course, the seer and his companions headed for that mountainous region. Upon arriving, they again found they were too late; Sha'ul had already left, this time for Gilgal. The locals at Karmel attested to the grand victory parade they witnessed and the monument set up in honor of the conquering king. Shemu'el bristled but said nothing, taking leave yet again.

At last, they came to Gilgal.

Shemu'el was led to the main camp to meet with the king. On his way up he surveyed the scene. Everyone seemed to be in good spirits, and the camp was positively fat with spoil.

Sha'ul set down his wine goblet and burst out of his tent when he heard that Shemu'el was outside. He cheerfully opened his arms as if to embrace the old man.

"Shemu'el! Blessed are you of Yahweh! I'm so glad you got here. Now we can offer sacrifices of thanks for our victory!"

Shemu'el said nothing, but Sha'ul continued on. "Another great day for Yisra'el. I have carried out the command of Yahweh!"

"Have you?" Shemu'el retorted. "Then what is this bleating of sheep in my ears and this lowing of cattle?"

"Oh! The people ... they spared the very best of the sheep and oxen to sacrifice to Yahweh your God. Everything else was completely devoted to destruction, as you said. I saw to that. We want to glorify—"

"Stop!" Shemu'el said, raising his hand in emphasis. "Let us go inside and let me tell you what Yahweh said to me last night."

Sha'ul nodded cautiously, leading the seer into his private tent and sending his guards away. The two men stood facing one another.

"Speak!"

"Isn't it true, though you were once little in your own eyes, that you have become the head of all the tribes of

Yisra'el? Yahweh anointed you king, and Yahweh sent you on a mission. He said to you, 'Make cherem and devote to destruction the sinners, the 'Amaleki, and make war against them until they are exterminated.'"

Sha'ul said nothing as he held Shemu'el's stare, but tilted his head ever so slightly in confirmation of what had been said so far.

"Why then did you not obey the voice of Yahweh? Why did you pounce on the plunder and do what is evil in His eyes? Why—"

"But I have obeyed the voice of Yahweh!" Sha'ul broke in. "I went on the mission Yahweh assigned me. I completely wiped out the 'Amaleki and brought back Agag, their king. He is my captive. But the people, they took some of the spoil—the sheep, the oxen, the pl-plunder. They took the very best portions of what was devoted to destruction to bring it here to sacrifice to your God, right here in Gilgal!"

"Tell me. Does Yahweh delight in burnt offerings and sacrifices as much as He delights in obeying His voice? Truly, to obey is better than sacrifice, and to listen is better than the fat of rams. Rebellion is like the sin of divination and witchcraft, and your arrogance is like the evil of idolatry. Because you have rejected the word of Yahweh, so has He rejected you as king!"

Sha'ul's jaw jutted open as if surprised by a slap to the face. His eyes went wide, and he sputtered, wrestling with the temper rising from within. He clenched and unclenched his fists at his sides. His eyes progressively narrowed to slits, and then he dropped his head to stare at the ground, his mouth working over invisible words.

"Y-yes," he managed to say.

"Yes, what?" Shemu'el asked.

"You're right. I have sinned. I have ... transgressed the command of Yahweh and your instructions. I feared the people. I listened to their voice. They ... they didn't understand, to have such a victory without any spoil ... it ... I ..."

The king trailed off, then began again with renewed purpose: "I have made a mistake and have acted foolishly. Now I beg of you, forgive me for my sin. Return with me to the camp so that I can worship Yahweh!"

"No," Shemu'el answered with sadness in his eyes. "I will not return with you. Since you have rejected the command of Yahweh, He has rejected you as king of Yisra'el."

Shemu'el turned and began to leave the tent. Desperately, Sha'ul leaped forward, falling to the ground and grabbing for the hem of the seer's robe. It tore loudly. Shemu'el turned his head and looked coldly at the groveling man.

"So has Yahweh torn the kingdom of Yisra'el from you this day and has given it into the hands of one of your neighbors, a man who is better than you. And you should know that the Glorious One of Yisra'el will not lie or change His mind, for He is not like man, who is fickle."

Shemu'el wrenched his robe from Sha'ul's hand and walked out, looking for his traveling companions and their donkeys. He was surprised when Sha'ul pursued him still farther, falling to his knees in the dirt in front of the seer, his eyes welling with tears. The guards and commanders nearby gaped at the spectacle.

"I have sinned! I have sinned. Yet please honor me now before the elders of my people, and before Yisra'el. I beg you to turn back and come with me to offer sacrifice so that I may bow before Yahweh your God and worship. At this moment, I am still king, as you anointed me to be, am I not? I am still king ... I am still king."

Shemu'el gradually relented, and, without stopping to replace or repair his damaged robe, he and the king walked to the altar in the midst of the gathered people. Gad and Shlomit watched with the crowd. Sacrifices were made, and Sha'ul openly worshiped Yahweh in the sight of all, with his son Y'honatan close by his side.

After offering a prayer for the people, Shemu'el said, "Bring me Agag, the king of the 'Amaleki."

Two commanders went to fetch Agag and brought him before Shemu'el. Agag walked as one accustomed to being treated deferentially and still wore his royal garments. His face appeared thick and full, retaining its color as if he had been well fed and looked after on this march to Gilgal.

The 'Amaleki king's eyes shone with optimism. What treatment was this? Or what strange Yisra'elite custom? What could this old man do to him? Or perhaps he should wonder what this old man might do for him? Agag smiled cheerfully, even as he was forced to his knees before this strange individual.

"Agag!" Shemu'el said with rumbling authority, not a hint of pleasure or satisfaction on his wrinkled face. "As your sword has made many women childless, so shall your mother be childless among women."

Shemu'el took hold of Y'honatan's sword, drawing it from its sheath in one smooth motion. From the crowd, Gad covered his eyes with both hands. The seer raised the weapon high above his head and then brought it down, hacking Agag into pieces.

ACT TWO

THE GIANT
AND
THE DEMON

—XVI—

Shemu'el sat in the shade and watched as workers laid the foundations for the dormitories. Alternating ashlar blocks of limestone were laid in the shallow trenches dug by the volunteer crew, many of them the students who would benefit from the completed construction.

The location was ideal, only a few miles from Ramatayim, isolated yet accessible, offering pleasant vistas of the surrounding hills and woods.

Gad, shining with sweat and short-winded from the exertion, came over to sit beside to the man he once called Master.

"I think it's coming together," he said between gulps of air.

Shemu'el smiled faintly as he looked over the building plans drawn on the writing tablet in his hand. Yahweh willing, this would be his legacy, a culmination of his career.

"Have you decided on a name yet?" Gad asked.

"I am going to call this place Naioth, for it will be a place for living. Not just physical life, but spiritual life."

"I'm excited. I mean, I know it won't be completed for a while ... but, we've come a long way."

"Buildings are just buildings. It is the spiritual fruit and the ministry that determine success. As for this School of the Prophets, I suspect the real work has yet to begin."

"But, how can you say that? All these years, your pupils ..."

"You, Gad. I will agree you have come a long way. I remember when you were first brought to us, still a babe in every sense of the word. You did not even know who God was. And you had never before heard the Law."

Gad began to color and turned away, squinting in the sunlight.

"Say," Shemu'el continued, "you must be at least thirty-five by now. You are a man. Why do you not get married and have some children?"

"I ... I feel that Yahweh has called me to serve Him. You know that."

"Serving Yahweh and marrying are not mutually exclusive. I married. I even have great-grandchildren; can you believe it? Not that I ever see them."

"I don't think I'm ready to be a father."

Shemu'el nodded soberly.

"Fatherhood is the most difficult task Yahweh gave to mankind; I believe that. Difficult but so important."

"What was your father like?"

"Oh, my natural father was one of the elders in Ramatayim. He was fairly well off. He married twice ... you met some of my sisters and one of my half-brothers when they still lived. Just about everybody in the city is at least distantly related somehow, and I have other siblings still living in Efrayim someplace. After my father passed, the family split. Anyhow, I haven't kept in communication with them.

"My father, Elkanah, had a very nice singing voice—I do remember that. That's one of the few things I remember about him. You see, I grew up in Shiloh, at the sanctuary. I was placed under the tutelage of 'Eli, the high priest in those days. You could say that he was more of a father to me."

Gad stared at the ground and thought that Shemu'el, too, had been more of a father than his own, and he thought to say this. Instead, he said, "But I know to live at the school, to be a part of the daily life here in Naioth, I am not to be married. You expect your students to keep themselves from women for a season, to remain celibate for the initial period of training."

"Gad, you are more than a student! You have proven yourself to be spiritually mature. You can have your family in Ramatayim and come here during the day."

"But you said the purpose of building this habitation is to be separate from the people, removed from the distractions and mixture and temptations and problems of life in the cities. I want to be part of that. I want to be able to take the full measure of disciplines expected of any student."

"Then I pray that Yahweh blesses you for your heart."

The two sat side by side in silence for a time, observing the laborers. The workers from Efrayim and some of Shemu'el's adult students discussed news of the kingdom as they toiled.

"Did you hear? The army has made war on the Giv'onim."

"In Yisra'el? But we are at peace."

"I tell you the truth. The king has declared them enemies of Yisra'el."

"They don't stand a chance against us."

"Huh! I bet you weren't complaining when the king hunted down all the witches and occultists. Why should Emori be allowed to dwell in our land?"

"The first was a matter of righteousness. But this is a matter of oath; to break that covenant is wrong!"

Shemu'el, overhearing, grew deeply agitated. It had been many years since he had had any contact with Sha'ul. Had the man gone so far as to now violate the covenant their forefathers had sworn to with the Giv'onim? What had this kingship come to? His disturbance was evident, and Gad gently tugged the sleeve of his robe.

"Shemu'el, are you all right?"

"It is time for me to head home and rest," he replied, leaning on his staff as he struggled to his feet.

"Is it the talk of the king that troubles you?"

"Bah! Do not speak to me about the House of Sha'ul. It only makes me sick to my stomach."

Elsewhere, in the pasturelands outside Beit-Lechem, a fifteen-year-old boy watched over his family's ewes and their nursing young. His hair was all ruddy curls, and his eyes were a shade of hazel-green. His skin was smooth and lightly tanned, holding the youthful subtlety of sparse, mottled freckles.

Perched on a rock in full sunlight, his shepherd's staff resting beside him, the boy unfastened a small kinnor from the outside of his shepherd's bag. What a beautiful day it was. The air was sweet with the scents of grass and spring flowers, and all creation seemed to hum with peaceful music.

The boy tucked one curved wooden edge of the harp into the crook of his left arm and let his fingers brush over the strings, feeling their tautness. The sheep grazed nearby, paying him no notice.

"My heart is not proud ..." he sang out in a soft, testing voice.

The strings were in tune. The boy adjusted the position of his fingers on the instrument and began again,

"My heart is not proud ... O, Lord ... my eyes ... my eyes are not ..."

The boy continued playing the notes while he whistled a melody, considering the words of the song he was composing.

This shepherd boy in Yisra'el, whose mother was a remarried widow, whose great-grandmother was a foreigner from Mo'av, whose great-great-grandmother was a prostitute in the Kena'anim city of Yericho ...

He sang:

> "My heart is not proud, O Yahweh,
> My eyes are not haughty.
> I don't concern myself with matters too great,
> Or things too wonderful for me.
> I have calmed and quieted my soul ..."

Again he paused, closing his eyes to savor the feel of a breeze across his face. He opened his eyes and watched as one of the lambs playfully scampered up to its mother, indifferent to the ewe's determination to continue grazing. He smiled.

"A weaned child with its mother."

The boy again took up the kinnor and cleared his throat, taking the song from the top:

> "My heart is not proud, O Yahweh,
> My eyes are not haughty.
> I don't concern myself with matters too great,
> Or things too wonderful for me.

I have calmed and quieted my soul,
Like a weaned child resting against its mother.
Like a weaned child is my soul ..."

That night, Yahweh spoke to Shemu'el.

How long will you keep grieving over Sha'ul, since I have rejected him from being king over Yisra'el? Fill your horn with oil for anointing and go, for I am sending you to Yishai of Beit-Lechem. I have provided for Myself a king from among his sons.

"But ... how my Lord? If Sha'ul hears of it, he will kill me!"

I will show you what to do.

—XVII—

In the little town of Beit-Lechem, the family patriarch, Yishai, sat on a bench in the courtyard, watching his stepdaughter's child, 'Amasa, explore. The toddler gurgled with delight as he took his wobbly steps, his mother following close behind to catch him when he inevitably stumbled.

"He's so precious," Yishai said to Avigayil through a wide smile. Then he called to the child, "Your grandma and I wish you could stay with us forever!"

"And I'm sure my husband wishes we were back home already!" Avigayil retorted with a laugh.

Two of the town elders walked briskly in Yishai's direction, drawing his attention. The first bent low and whispered in his ear. Yishai's joyful expression flattened, and he pushed himself up to a standing position.

"Right now, you say?" he asked.

"Yes."

Avigayil scooped up 'Amasa and cradled him. As usual, Yishai had many obligations that tended to interrupt family life.

"Oh, do pardon me. I am needed. Maybe you can help your mother in the kitchen and give her more time to be around her grandchild?"

She nodded dutifully while Yishai followed the men to the well by the gate, where the remaining elders of the town waited anxiously.

"It's Shemu'el, the seer."

"Coming to Beit-Lechem? To our small town?"

"He's walking right toward us. He'll be here in mere minutes!"

"Alone?"

"If there were others, he has gone on ahead of them."

"What could it mean?"

"It makes me uneasy. You know the House of Sha'ul has ordered that all Shemu'el's movements are to be reported."

"You're saying this is political?"

"Either that or he has come to pass some supernatural judgment on our city. When has he ever had reason to come to Beit-Lechem? When does he ever leave his hometown anymore but rarely? Maybe he is to pronounce some curse upon us."

"So we're either in trouble with the king or in trouble with God."

"Will you all calm yourselves and take a breath?" Yishai pressed. "I have met Shemu'el once before, at Gilgal, when Sha'ul was made king. I don't know him personally, but he is a good man."

"You should be the one to speak to him. You are a Yahweh-fearing man and the eldest of us. We'll go out to meet him and find out what he wants with us."

"King Sha'ul is going to hear about this," one of them groaned.

With no little trepidation, the elders went out to meet the man of Yahweh as he approached on the road, flanked by fields of barley. Shemu'el led behind him a young heifer and regarded the elders as they presented themselves before him.

"Shalom, Shemu'el, welcome to Beit-Lechem. I am Yishai, son of 'Oved. Is it peaceably that you come to our obscure town?"

"Yes, it is peace. I have come to offer sacrifice to Yahweh," the seer answered.

The elders visibly relaxed. There would be no scandal, no judgment this day.

"Please, I invite you to consecrate yourselves and come to the sacrifice with me," Shemu'el said to them.

Relieved and in agreement, the men turned and together they walked into town. Still, Yishai's instincts told him something else was afoot.

"I must ask further hospitality of you," Shemu'el said to Yishai along the way.

"Yes, of course," Yishai replied.

"If you would have the feast at your home, I would ask that you, as well as your sons, be consecrated and partake of the meal with me."

"I would be honored."

"It is good of you to be hospitable, for he who receives a prophet will receive a prophet's reward. Now be sure that your sons change their clothes, wash themselves, and prepare their hearts to receive the offering."

After the ceremony of the sacrifice, Shemu'el sat at Yishai's table while the women finished preparing the meal in the other room.

"Yishai, tell me, do you revere and worship Yahweh?"

"Yes. Everything I have has come from Him."

"It is good of you to say so. Now let me disclose to you the will of Yahweh that has brought me to your dining table. Yahweh has selected a king for Himself from among your sons, for He has rejected Sha'ul. I am to anoint the one whom Yahweh designates for this chosen purpose."

Yishai folded his hands over his belly and gave a slow exhale. Ah. So there it was. He let the words sink in. This was momentous. Seismic. Was this a sentence of death for his child—for his entire family? This was treason. But how could Yahweh and His spokesman be denied? And how dare Yishai disbelieve?

"Okay," was all he could answer.

"I know what you're thinking. You must put your trust in Yahweh."

"Just so you know, three of my sons fight in the king's army."

"That is irrelevant. I have here with me a horn of oil to anoint the future king of Yisra'el, as Yahweh directs. As He speaks, so I obey. So now, I will ask you to bring forth and introduce your sons to me, one by one. Yahweh will make known His choice."

"I will. Of course. Yes."

Yishai went to gather his sons who lived close by and those still within the family home, assembling them in the next room. Shemu'el stood to appraise those who would be brought before him. After muted discussion, Yishai returned with another man.

"This is my firstborn son, Eli'av."

Eli'av gave a smart nod and looked at Shemu'el confidently. He was tall, handsome, and strong, appearing to be in his early thirties. Impressive. Inside, Shemu'el immediately thought this man must be Yahweh's anointed, the chosen king to replace Sha'ul.

Don't look on his face, or on the height of his stature, because I have rejected him. For Yahweh does not see as a man sees; man looks at the outward appearance, but Yahweh looks at the heart.

Shemu'el turned to Yishai and slowly shook his head. No. Eli'av was a bit perplexed, but Yishai beckoned for his son to stand to one side while he went to fetch another.

"Here is my second-born, Avinadav."

Like his brother, he was striking in appearance.

"Yahweh has not chosen this one either," Shemu'el said matter-of-factly, shaking his head. Avinadav was bid to stand beside his older brother.

Next was Shammah, the third eldest.

"Neither has Yahweh chosen this one."

Next came N'tan'el, then Radai, then Otzem, and lastly Amnon. The answer was the same for each.

"Yahweh has not chosen these," Shemu'el announced, furrowing his brow. "Are these all of your sons?"

"Well, there remains yet the littlest, my youngest son. He is out tending the sheep and won't be back until sunset. He's only fifteen years old."

"Send for him and bring him back, for we will not sit down to eat until he gets here."

It took more than two hours for the youth to be summoned by the family servant and brought home. In the meantime, Yishai, Shemu'el, and the brothers waited as the food grew cold. When at last the youth arrived, his father instructed him to wash up and change his clothes before coming to the meal.

He stepped through the door, unaware of what was taking place, and instantly noticed the stranger—an old man he did not recognize—sitting with his family. Shemu'el, in turn, looked at the shepherd: a boyishly handsome face with a kind, agreeable expression, a head of ruddy curls, and the naturally muscular arms and tanned skin of an outdoorsman. He was truly youthful in every sense.

Arise. Anoint him, for this is he.

Shemu'el rose and signaled to Yishai, who beckoned his youngest son close to stand before the seer.

"What is your name?"

"David."

"I am Shemu'el."

Shemu'el leaned in and said something that only David could hear. He took the horn of oil and poured some of it over David's head, beginning to pronounce a blessing. As the seer prayed, David felt his heart strangely warmed.

—XVIII—

All was dark within the royal fortress of the House of Sha'ul. Avner slept soundly in his private chamber, having finally drifted off to sleep after reviewing over and over in his head the conflicting reports of P'lishtim troop movements. They were strengthening their forces on their eastern border and were no doubt contemplating some maneuver against Yisra'el ... but where? Or was it just a feint?

There came an urgent rap of knuckles against his door.

Avner snorted and sat upright. The knocking continued incessantly. With a grunt, the commander threw his legs over the side of the bed and rubbed his face with the palms of his rough hands. This had better be important. Shuffling to the door, he noticed the faint light of a flickering candle at the cracks. He reached for the knob.

"Ritzpah!"

It was the king's concubine, and she was alone. The shock of finding her outside his door at this late hour, in her gown, her soft features illuminated and made even more lovely in the candle's glow, caused Avner to at first fail to notice the fear in her eyes.

"Avner, oh ... I didn't know who else to turn to," she spoke in low tones.

"W-what is it?" Avner asked, snapping out of his reverie.

"It's the king, my lord. He's ... he's not ... can you just come with me?"

"Sha'ul? Just let me get ... uh ... fully dressed, and I'll be out."

Avner gently closed the door and tried to get his bearings in the darkness, groping for more appropriate attire. Soon they crossed the courtyard and walked through the hallways until they were outside Ritzpah's chambers. So, Sha'ul had spent the evening with her tonight.

Slipping inside, the concubine lit another candle. Avner blinked as his eyes adjusted, trying to make sense of what he was seeing. There was the bed in the center of the room with the blankets in disarray, but no Sha'ul.

Ritzpah motioned with her hand, and Avner followed her around to the side of the bed. There he was, lying on the floor in a fetal position, naked, shivering despite the warm night. Avner reflexively averted his eyes, grabbing a blanket off the bed to cover the king's lower half.

Sha'ul did not seem to be aware of Avner's presence. Instead, he stared straight ahead with a panic-stricken look and clenched teeth, his pale arms hugging his knees.

Avner looked accusingly at Ritzpah.

"What happened to him?" he growled.

"My lord! We were asleep, and then, suddenly, he was like this. I was so afraid; I didn't know what to do."

"How long?" Avner asked.

"Maybe ten, fifteen minutes. I don't know. I tried to comfort him, thinking maybe he had a bad dream ... but ..."

"Stay here with him for a while longer. I'm going to wake the physician and the attendants, then you can wait in my room until ... no, it would be better for you to go to your maidservant's room. Tell her to sleep with the other servants for the rest of the night."

Then Avner added, "And don't speak of this to anyone!"

"Yes, my lord."

Sha'ul's closest attendants and the royal physician were woken and led clandestinely into the concubine's room. Avner also summoned one of Sha'ul's most trusted advisors, Bela.

The king was moved onto the bed and lay there unresponsively for a time, groaning quietly with half-open, hollow eyes. The physician touched his forehead, expecting to find it hot with fever, but it wasn't. There were no signs of cuts, bruises, rashes, or discolorations on his body. Inquiries were made about his food and drink for the day, but his attendants vouched that nothing had been amiss.

"What ..." Sha'ul groaned.

Everyone snapped to attention at the sound of his voice and leaned closer to listen.

"Yes, my lord? Can my lord hear us?" Bela asked intently.

Sha'ul nodded weakly and rolled his head, as if unsure of where he was.

"My lord, are you in pain? Do you hurt anywhere?" the physician inquired.

Sha'ul looked up at the man in confusion.

"Breathe ..." he managed. "Felt ... something sitting ... chest ... couldn't ..."

The physician poured some wine into a cup and urged Sha'ul to sit up and take a drink. "Here, my lord, this will help ease you."

Sha'ul sipped weakly as the physician held the cup to his lips, then began to sputter and cough, spitting the red wine onto the blankets. It dribbled over his beard and mingled with his chest hair.

Avner touched Sha'ul's bare shoulder reassuringly. At this, the king visibly relaxed, slumping back onto the bed and breathing heavily. The physician could feel the king's heart pounding within his chest.

"Come to think of it," Avner said to the others quietly, "the king hasn't been himself lately. I didn't think much of it at the time, but I have found him sitting alone in the middle of the day, just staring at the wall. He seemed almost worried, fearful. Each time it passed, and I didn't say anything about it."

They all looked upon their weakened leader, each privately processing the uncomfortable reality before them. Sha'ul's labored breathing gradually, gradually became more regular. The physician rose slowly from the bedside.

"I think our best hope is for him to sleep through the night. Tomorrow morning we—"

Sha'ul bolted upright in bed, screaming. His eyes were wide, staring at a fixed point on the ceiling. Veins bulged on his forehead, and his face turned bright red. Sha'ul's entire body began to writhe spasmodically. It was all Avner and the others could do to restrain him as he thrashed violently. His screams of terror echoed through the entire fortress.

"What do you want with my son?" Yishai asked.

Three soldiers were standing in his house, as well as a man claiming to be a personal attendant of the king. If word had somehow leaked out about the secret anointing ... well, Yishai didn't even want to think of the consequences.

"It has been said that David, son of Yishai from Beit-Lechem, is a talented musician, both in singing and playing. Is this report true?"

"It absolutely is. He has a gift. But I'm not sure how you have heard of it."

This was unexpected. Perhaps the father's worst fears were not coming true after all. Not today.

"His reputation precedes him. He has been spoken of even in Giv'ah of Sha'ul."

"Three of his brothers are in the army and have been to Giv'ah. They must have spoken of his skill, for he doesn't perform before any audience," Yishai said, thinking out loud.

"That is about to change. My lord, the king, desires music. We have no court musicians, and I am offering your family the great honor of having your son personally play in the presence of the king and his courtiers."

"That is an honor indeed. When does my lord the king desire it?"

"King Sha'ul wants you to send your son as soon as possible if you can spare him. I have it that he is with the sheep."

"We can find somebody else to watch the sheep for a time. Who can delay the request of the king?"

Yishai had David dress in his finest clothes while David's mother gathered some provisions for their son to take on the road. David was also given gifts to take for the king: a donkey loaded with bread, a jug of wine, and their best young goat. Yishai and Nitzevet hugged their youngest tightly and sent him on his way, watching him and the soldiers from the city gates until they were out of sight.

"Who would have ever dreamt that my baby boy would be invited to entertain the king of Yisra'el?" Nitzevet mused with pride in her voice. Yishai smiled and clasped his wife's hand.

David marveled as he was led through the fortified walls of Giv'ah and into the royal stronghold. After being searched for concealed weapons, he was led into an ornately furnished room and seated while male servants offered to serve him food and drink. David politely declined, and once he was left alone, he removed his kinnor and made sure it was properly tuned.

He should be nervous. He should have butterflies in his stomach. Anybody in his situation would be. Instead, he was excited. Yahweh had blessed him with a gift, and now he would have a chance to use this gift in such a high form of service. It gave him joy to sing and play for Yahweh, and now he could share this joy with Yahweh's anointed king.

A balding, rail-thin man with a serious expression entered the room and immediately addressed David in a flat tone.

"I am Bela, a servant of the king. You must be our young musician from Beit-Lechem."

"Yes, sir, I am."

"How old are you?"

"Sixteen."

"Is that a nebel?"

"No sir, a kinnor."

"Are you as good as they say you are?"

"If you would like me to play a song for you right now, I—"

"No, that won't be necessary. King Sha'ul is a wise and noble man. He is a great man. We sent for you because we heard you were one of the best. Apparently all who have heard your music commend your ability."

"Yes, sir, um, you flatter me, sir."

"Do you realize what an honor it is to be able to play for the king?"

"Yes, sir, I do."

"I have to tell you that the king is not feeling well. He has been deeply troubled lately, within his very soul. He has not fully been himself."

"Oh."

"The concerns of a king are manifold. He has called for a musician to play for him and help ease his anxious mind. Do you understand?"

"Yes, sir."

"If he is feeling particularly ill today, he may not even acknowledge your presence. You are not to speak to him unless he asks you a direct question. You are not to come within ten feet of him at any time. Do you understand?"

"Yes, I do."

"And about this, about this ... sickness which troubles our great king, we must have full confidence in you. We must trust that you will honor and obey your king and keep any knowledge of this sickness to yourself. The enemies of the king do not need to know that he is feeling ill, nor do the people need to lose any confidence in him. Do I make myself clear?"

"Yes, sir. Far be it from me to break the trust of Yahweh's anointed. I only want to do my best and play for him, as you said. If Yahweh is willing, I will play a song that is pleasing and can soothe my lord the king. I pray he may recover soon from his ailment!"

"Hmmm. You see, the king is under attack from an evil spirit."

"Oh no!" David said, startled and deeply concerned. "May Yahweh deliver him!"

"This foul thing comes upon him and torments him day and night. The physician, the priests, and even the court prophet have not been able to help. Nothing under the sun has given him any solace or reprieve when under such a spell, except for music—and that only fleetingly. Do you understand?"

"Yes, sir."

"What will you be playing?"

"I have some original songs that I have composed. I usually just play whatever I feel at the time, whatever I feel led to play in my heart."

"Hmmm. Fine. Do you need time to practice? You mustn't go before the king unprepared."

"Sir, I was tuning my kinnor before you came in, but now I am ready."

Sha'ul sat slouched on his throne, gripping the armrests.

Bela ushered David in and seated him to one side of the king. Other servants in attendance quietly took their seats at the edge of the chamber. Two armed guards remained standing at attention at the entrance.

"My lord, here is the musician," Bela spoke loudly, trying to register Sha'ul's responsiveness.

Sha'ul grunted, not looking at David. The king's face was ashen.

Bela waited a moment then gestured to David, backing away from the throne obsequiously and taking a position at the perimeter.

David took up his kinnor and cleared his throat, taking in his surroundings. He had seen the king once before from a distance in previous years. But being here, mere feet away from the king of Yisra'el, in his very throne room ... this was an experience unlike any other in his life.

The young shepherd strummed a chord that rang out in the stillness of the room. His fingers began to move over the strings, plucking the individual notes, and he leaned in with eyes closed, beginning to feel the music. Almost instantly the tension in the room eased, and those in attendance sat up and took notice of the pleasing melody, played with a level of skill that could not be ignored.

Sha'ul's large hands relaxed their hold on the throne's armrests. He sighed.

As David played he felt the warmth growing and expanding within his chest. He began improvising, and the inspiration for new lyrics came to him.

"Peace, Yahweh. Peace, Yahweh. I pray for your heavenly peace, Yahweh. For You alone make me to dwell in safety ..."

As the clear, sweet voice sang out, Sha'ul's hands clenched tight, his fingernails digging into the painted wood of the throne. He began grinding his teeth, audibly, his eyes flitting back and forth in his head, chasing nothings in the air in front of his face.

David was disturbed by this reaction but did not break his pace for an instant. The attendants tensed. David shut his eyes tightly and began to sing again,

"Peace, Yahweh. Peace, Yahweh.
I pray for your heavenly peace, Yahweh.
For You alone make me to dwell in safety.
I will lie down and sleep, Elohim,
And search in my heart and be silent.
For You can give relief from distress,
And fill my heart with joy."

Little by little, King Sha'ul's raging began to diminish. David continued to play and sing as the king's private, inner war was slowly stilled. After an hour, the shadow that lay across Sha'ul's heart lifted, and he was resting in his seat, snoring gently, his face refreshed.

Bela was pleased with the result. He set David up in a small room with a bed, where he was asked to stay for a time. Servants brought David food at regular intervals, and he was allowed to walk through Giv'ah once a day for exercise.

Returning once from such a stroll through the city, David encountered a pretty girl being escorted through the hallway by two adults of unknown station. David flattened himself against the wall to allow them to pass. The girl was tall, slender, with a narrow face and straight black hair falling over her shoulders. She carried herself with an icy calm that almost made David believe she hadn't seen him in the corridor at all. Who was this girl? She was gone around the corner before he knew it, and he did not encounter her again, to his disappointment.

David would have loved to have access to the fortress's fledgling library, but it was not to be. Instead, he spent much of his time composing music and praying. Over the next several days, he was brought before the king to perform. Bela assured David that the king was very pleased with him and his music, although their interactions remained superficial. Bela even had David named as an honorary armor bearer.

When at last it seemed the king's soul was sufficiently quieted, David was allowed to return home to his family until such a time that he might be called on once more to serve.

—XIX—

Again it was the season for war. The P'lishtim amassed their armies and struck east from Gat, rapidly breaking through into the tribal lands of Y'hudah and overwhelming Sokhoh, a town standing on the mountainous boundary between the coastal plain of P'leshet and the fertile Sh'felah lowlands.

Yisra'el responded in kind, mobilizing their armies and racing to cut off the P'lishtim advance. With the Yisra'elite soldiers forming up in battle array in the Valley of Elah, the P'lishtim also drew up fortifications between Sokhoh and 'Azekah. This was a familiar battleground for the two nations. Soldiers on both sides had taken to calling it "The Boundary of Blood."

Sha'ul and Avner set up camp on a hill overlooking the valley, while the men provided a protective barrier below the king and his officers. Likewise, the P'lishtim command drew up camp opposite their foes. It was a standoff, neither side making the first move. Yisra'el had become a disciplined and powerful fighting force, but their weapons were still inferior to P'lishtim ironsmithing.

Crouched behind their shields in the tall grass were David's three eldest brothers, Eli'av, Avinadav, and Shammah. There they waited with their fellow men-at-arms, watching to see what the P'lishtim would do. Little noise was coming from the P'lishtim lines. It was too quiet. What could they be planning?

In the morning, they found out.

A loud, thunderous shout reverberated through the valley, sending birds scattering from the oak and terebinth trees and rousing every last man in the Yisra'elite camp.

"Hebrew cowards!"

Eli'av, Avinadav, and Shammah left the nearby creek where they had been drawing water and pressed up against the fortifications with the others to see who dared to call out such an insult against them. They could hardly believe their eyes.

Standing in the middle of the valley was the towering form of a man. He was easily nine feet tall, approaching ten, and massively built. An enormous helmet of bronze covered his head. Wiry black hair spilled out on either side of the helmet and framed his features: dark eyes, a large, flat nose, and a wide, sneering mouth. His cracked and yellowed teeth were surrounded by lips of equal thickness all the way around, more like the mouth of a fish than a man.

A heavy coat of bronze scale armor hung over the man's broad torso, weighing over one hundred and fifty pounds; each of his rock-chiseled arms burst out from either side, the bulging veins decorating his muscles looking more like tree roots than flesh and blood. This giant of a man wore bronze greaves over his shins, in the manner of the armor of the Sea Peoples and the Aegean lands across the ocean. A shield bearer walked before him, hoisting a large, rectangular shield emblazoned with the image of Dagon, the P'lishtim deity.

Fastened onto the warrior's back and worn between his shoulders was a bronze javelin. In one hand he held a thick spear with a large, sharpened iron head. The weapon hummed as he swung it casually about him, threatening instant death to anyone in its arc. Finally, a large, curved iron blade rested in a scabbard on his hip.

"I am Golyat! I stand before you as a champion of the P'lishtim armies!" the fearsome warrior roared.

His voice so sounded out that even King Sha'ul and his commanders high on the hill heard his words clearly and emerged from their tents. Avner stood and squinted at the field below. Surely his eyes were playing tricks on him.

"I see you all drawn up against me!" Golyat taunted. "I am but one man! Tell me; why should there be so much blood shed and lives lost here? Your blood! Your lives! You know our strength; you know our chariots; you know our weapons! Why die in battle for a hopeless cause? I offer this challenge! Servants of Sha'ul, pick your strongest man and send him down here to face me! Ha ha ha! If he is able to kill me, then we will all become your servants, but if I kill him, you can come serve us! Ah ha ha ha ha!"

Shammah, gripping his shield, began to tremble. Eli'av and Avinadav stared.

"What is this monster?" Shammah asked.

Eli'av bit his lip and looked on as the giant bellowed his challenges. The Yisra'elite commanders drew near to the battle lines and observed the P'lishtim champion with horror.

"Come on, you fools; the war can be over today! Ha ha! Fight me, men of Yisra'el! Ah ha ha ha!"

Who could stand against such a foe?

David herded the sheep into their pen and went indoors, leaning his staff against the wall. Yishai was sitting at the table alone, a bundle of provisions laid in front of him. His eyesight having begun to darken in his older age, he asked, "David, is that you?"

"Yes, father."

"Run into any trouble out there today?"

"No, everything was fine."

"Good! I believe this will be a prosperous year for our flock."

"How was the elders' meeting?"

"You can imagine; everyone's preoccupied with this war."

David rinsed his hands in a basin of water and sat down across from his father.

"Any word from my brothers?"

Yishai shifted on his seat.

"Only that they are with Sha'ul and the army is in the Valley of Elah, fighting the P'lishtim."

"On the front lines?" David asked with excitement in his voice. "Are you sending me?"

"Do you have to say it like that? Your mother's having a hard enough time as it is. First Amnon ... and now three sons away at war. Oh, a father should never have to outlive his child," Yishai said, saddened by the idea.

David reached out and touched his father's hand softly.

"Well, you fought against the P'lishtim once! And Yahweh gave us victory! He can do so again. So ... are you sending me?"

"David! Yes, I am sending you, but why must you be so eager to be around war? My son, you have the heart of a poet, not a soldier!"

"Why can't I have both?"

Yishai sighed. Had David's stints of service as an armor bearer in the House of Sha'ul made such an impression on him? Or was this just a case of boys being boys?

"Only three more years," David said. "I can't wait to be able to serve my country! I'm not afraid."

"I know you aren't. Come here. Give your father a hug. I've got a bushel of roasted grain and ten loaves for your brothers. And ... here, deliver these ten cheeses to the captain of their regiment as a gift. We'll leave the sheep with a hired shepherd until you get back."

"Yes, father!"

"And please hurry. Find out if your brothers need anything—anything at all! Bring back news of their well-being to your mother and me!"

Before first light the next morning, David left with the cart of supplies, heading to the Yisra'elite camp in the Valley of Elah as fast as he could manage.

Just as he arrived, he heard a great war cry ring out. With a ground-shaking rush, all the fighting men charged out from their camp and came to the battle lines in the valley, banging their weapons and shields together. The P'lishtim quickly formed up opposite the Yisra'elites but advanced no further.

David's heart beat faster.

He quickly located the officer in charge of keeping the supplies and left the baggage with him, running as fast as he could to find his brothers in the ranks.

"The sons of Yishai!" David shouted to whoever would listen. "Where can I find the sons of Yishai?"

Despite the commotion and vigilance, he was pointed in the right direction and hurried to the place where his brothers' troop stood ready.

"Shammah! Eli'av! Avinadav!" David cried joyfully, greeting his brothers.

"David, you rascal!" Avinadav responded, grateful for this momentary distraction. He put David in a headlock and ruffled his hair until David broke free of the hold with a laugh. Avinadav realized his little brother was getting too strong for him.

David shouted over the noise, and Shammah and Avinadav listened to news from Beit-Lechem and the family. Eli'av kept a stern eye on the enemy lines.

The vigor and energy around them began to dissipate, and David turned his head to see what had caused such a sudden deflation of the soldiers' spirits. He could sense a tension come over his siblings and strained to detect the source of this unease, peering between the shields and fortifications.

"Oh no. Not again," Eli'av groaned.

Golyat strode out onto the field, as brazen and bold as ever, his shield bearer, no weakling himself, dwarfed under the P'lishti's towering form.

"Hebrews!" Golyat bellowed. "I'm tired of this game! For forty mornings and forty nights I have come before you, and still you have not found a single man who dares to face me in a fair fight! Is my challenge not a good one? Would you rather all be broken under the wheels of our chariots and bleed to death under a thousand arrows? Dogs! Why are you wasting my time with your disgusting cowardice? Are there no men in Yisra'el? You bunch of women! Hebrew sodomites! Ah ha ha ha!"

The Yisra'elite soldiers slowly backed away, their battle lines receding as Golyat strode toward them, swinging his dastardly weapons, toying with them. David's mouth hung open. He couldn't believe what he was hearing.

"Pathetic! Look how you run like children! Come on! Who is man enough to challenge me? Kill me and this ends; we will all be your slaves this day! Redeem whatever shred of honor you have left, you disgusting cowards! I've killed many of you Hebrews in my time, ha ha ha. I'll be happy to do it again! Come out; have your skull crushed like a grape!"

David's face began to burn red with anger.

"What is this abomination?" he asked, baffled by everything he had seen.

Some of the disheartened soldiers standing nearby turned toward him.

"You don't know? This man is Golyat ... a P'lishti warrior from Gat," one of the men said.

"He's a P'lishti?"

"Rumors in the camp say he is descended of the N'filim," the man said with conspiratorial unease. Other soldiers grunted in agreement.

"The N'filim of the ancient world?" David asked.

Shammah butted into the conversation, feeling lost.

"What are you all talking about?"

"They say in the ancient world," the soldier began in a superstitious tone, "that fallen angels lay with human women ... birthing these giants ... these horrible men of violence."

"You're speaking of fables!" Shammah scoffed.

"Brother, it may be true," David wondered. "Haven't you heard of the Refa'im? Such brutes were fought against in this very land, by none other than Y'hoshua! But I thought Y'hoshua put them to death once and for all."

"If their cursed seed can somehow survive Yahweh's judgment over the whole earth, then why not survive Y'hoshua and the Shof'tim of Yisra'el?"

David stared hard at the figure in the field, feeling indignation growing as Golyat continued his insults and taunts. How could it be that not one man of Yisra'el had come forward to defend the honor of Yahweh's chosen people and their country?

"If Yisra'el had completed the work Yahweh had given them when taking hold of Kena'an and had completely destroyed the wicked nations in this land, then such evil would not have remained as thorns in our flesh!" he said.

Shammah shook his head and gripped his shield tighter. Conjecture and history lessons wouldn't save them. The menacing giant loomed on the horizon, a very present threat.

Two other soldiers nearby were conversing, and David overheard them.

"I can't stand much more of this. Did you hear what the king promised for the man who kills him? Sounds good, but it's hard to enjoy wealth and a nice young wife when you're dead," the first said.

"Answering this challenge is suicide for any man," the other agreed.

"Excuse me," David interjected, approaching them. "Tell me; what will be done for the man who kills this P'lishti and takes away the disgrace from Yisra'el?"

The soldiers looked at one another and laughed. This young man had guts!

"The king will make him rich! His family will be nobles, free from pledge and tax. Not only that, the king has promised to give his daughter, Merav, in marriage to any man who can overcome this Golyat! What, I suppose you're going to take him on?"

"Who is this uncircumcised pagan that he should defy the armies of the living God?" David answered boldly.

At that, David's eldest brother, Eli'av, stormed over and grabbed David by the shoulders, taking him aside.

"What did you come down here for, huh? Aren't you supposed to be looking after our father's little flock of sheep? What did you do, leave them alone out there in the wilderness or with some stranger?"

Avinadav tried to step in and mediate. Eli'av stopped him with a glare.

"I know your wicked and conceited heart, David," he continued. "You came out here just to watch the battle!"

"But—" David began to protest.

"Remember when we were younger?" Eli'av asked the other siblings. "We were all helping our cousins with the barley harvest, but David was at the other end of the field, playing make-believe war. 'Y'hoshua ambushing Ai!' he would shout, running around the little piles of rocks he made."

"Heh heh, yeah, I remember," Avinadav said.

"He thinks this is some game. We're out here risking our lives, and instead of taking care of his chores he sneaks over here to watch the action!"

David sloughed off his brother's grasp.

"Now what have I done? Was it not just a question?"

David turned away from his brothers and walked down the lines, asking other soldiers to confirm the information he had heard. Had the king really promised all that for the man who would kill the giant? The answers he got were the same.

An officer of the regiment who had been watching David's interactions with interest called for his messenger.

"I need you to get a message to the king."

—XX—

David stood before none other than King Sha'ul and Prince Y'honatan in the king's tent. His bravado had been noticed. The king, bags under his eyes from countless sleepless nights, leaned forward attentively. He carefully looked the youth over. The prince just stared quietly at the ground.

"You look familiar. What is your name?" the king asked.

"Your servant's name is David," came the humble reply.

"Well, do you have something to say to the king?" the officer who had summoned him prodded.

David stood up straight and cleared his throat.

"My lord, the king, let no man's heart fail because of this P'lishti. Your servant will go and fight him."

Y'honatan's eyes shot up in surprise.

"You against this Golyat in single combat?" King Sha'ul asked with a smirk. "You cannot fight him; you are just a youth, and this P'lishti has been a man of war since he was young. Are you one of the armor bearers? You aren't even of military age!"

David nodded as if to indicate that he agreed with all the factual information contained in the king's remarks.

"Your servant was tending his father's sheep," the shepherd began, "and once a lion came, and took one of the lambs from the flock. I chased after it, struck it, and rescued the lamb from its mouth. The lion then turned on me and attacked, but I grabbed hold of its mane and struck it again and killed it. Likewise, on another occasion, a bear came to steal a lamb from the flock. Your servant has killed both the lion and the bear. This uncircumcised pagan will be just like one of them, for he has taunted the armies of the living God!"

David's boldness grew with every word. His eyes blazed with confidence.

"Yahweh who delivered me from the mouth of the lion and the claws of the bear will deliver me from the hand of this P'lishti!"

King Sha'ul rose from his seat and stood before David, placing his hands on the youth's shoulders.

"So be it! And may Yahweh be with you," then turning to his attendants, the king added, "Send in my armor and my sword!"

The king felt reinvigorated. Out of the many thousands of men in his military, not even one had the courage to step forward ... until now. Two of the king's armor bearers entered the tent, carrying Sha'ul's battle tunic, helmet, coat of mail, and his iron sword.

"David, you will have my own weapon and my own armor at your disposal, and anything else you need. Servants, help him get dressed."

The attendants crowded around David and worked to put on the king's armor. The bronze mail was heavy, but not too heavy for David to bear. Due to the height difference between its owner and David, it felt oversized. The helmet as well fit more loosely than was ideal, but the attendants worked to position it just right on David's head.

Lastly, David strapped the sword over the armor and tried to take a turn around the inside of the tent. The armor felt clumsy and loose, making him sluggish.

The king eyed David expectantly.

"Your servant is sorry, but I cannot go in these. I haven't tested them; I'm not used to them."

Sha'ul's expression fell.

David began to unfasten the sword, and the armor bearers hurried close to help remove the pieces of armor instead of having David set them on the ground.

"What will you fight with?" Sha'ul asked.

"My lord, the king, I will find my own equipment."

King Sha'ul shook his head in amused disbelief. Whatever would happen would happen. How could the situation get any worse? But this kid had something— courage, at least.

"Boy, again I say ... may Yahweh be with you."

"Thank you."

David nodded to the officer and guards as he walked out of the tent. King Sha'ul dismissed the others and turned to his eldest son.

"Can you believe this?"

Y'honatan stared at the place where David had been standing as if remembering something important he had long forgotten.

"If the fighting men of Yisra'el could have only half his faith!" Y'honatan remarked. "That young man, he reminds me a lot of myself when I was his age. It makes me ashamed that—"

"You know I forbid you to face that P'lishti! I absolutely forbid it. If anything happens to me, this kingdom falls to you. You're too important. You have responsibilities to your family and to Yisra'el! Don't ever forget that."

"I know, father ... I know."

"Do you think he has a chance? I mean ... do you think he can really defeat that ... giant?" The king paced with nervous energy, rubbing his hands together.

"If Yahweh is truly with him, nothing will be impossible for him."

David took up his shepherd's staff that he had left lying outside in the grass along with his pack. He walked through the camp and down the hill toward the creek. Crouching at the edge, he peered through the shallow water at the stones beneath. He reached in and searched, selecting five smooth, rounded stones of roughly equal size and weight. He carefully wiped each stone dry on his cloak and tucked them into the pouch on his pack.

Growing up in Beit-Lechem and tending the flocks not far from the border of Binyamin, David had often come into contact with Binyamanite children. Some were so skilled with the sling that they could sling a stone at a single hair and not miss.

He headed to the barricades, where beyond Golyat continued his loud taunting and his raging.

Word spread through the camp like a wildfire, and soldiers everywhere began to turn and stare at David as he marched forward. They parted at his approach. Reaching the edge, he shed his cloak and slipped through the fortifications, stepping out onto the valley's grassy plain. He could see the giant and the shield carrier, and past them the P'lishtim lines.

All eyes were on David. Soon the only sound that he could hear was the beating of his heart as he continued on, presenting himself across from Golyat in answer to the challenge.

"What is he doing?" Avinadav gasped as he saw his youngest brother. Shammah squeezed his hand tight as others crowded around to get a good view.

King Sha'ul, dressed in his royal armor, stood with Y'honatan and the commanders.

"I've never seen anything like it," Avner said.

"Avner, whose son is this young man? Where does he come from?" Sha'ul asked.

"As your soul lives, O king, I do not know."

"Well find out! I've promised Merav to him if he succeeds."

Golyat stopped in his tracks when he saw David across the field, the insult catching in his mouth mid-sentence. His brow furrowed, and the P'lishti craned his bulging neck forward to observe his prey. Golyat's eyesight was not the greatest, and he squinted to decipher this strange vision.

Here stood some young Hebrew in tunic and sandals, not dressed as a soldier, holding a simple wooden staff. And what was that in his other hand?

Golyat growled with disdain and began walking forward, his shield bearer hurrying to stay in front of him. Each step Golyat took resonated under the thudding bulk of his form and armor as he approached David. He could see that this young boy was indeed no proper soldier. He appeared strong for his size, but utterly defenseless standing there. His face was smooth enough to be called effeminate. What was that little strap he was holding?

"What do you think I am, a dog that you come at me with a stick?" Golyat shouted thunderously. "You filthy little maggot! You mock me? Damn you! May the great god Dagon curse you and your family and all your coward Hebrew brethren! May you all go down to death together! You and your mountain god!"

David's hand tightened around the leather sling. His pack lay across him with his ammunition within easy reach. He felt the power of Yahweh's Spirit within him. This P'lishtim monster could not go unpunished.

"Come to me, if you dare! I'll tear you in half! I'll rip out your guts and feed them to the birds of the air! I'll feed your flesh to the beasts of the field! I'll pour out your blood and desecrate your bones!" Golyat was sneering, showing his large teeth. He swung his gigantic spear through the air and stabbed it menacingly into the earth, easily burying the tip at least two feet deep.

David stood his ground, feeling the still air and the hot rays of the sun shining on his bare arms and legs.

"I've heard you, now hear this!" David shouted back in a clear voice. "You come at me with a sword, a spear, and a javelin … but I come to you in the name of Yahweh of Hosts, the God of the armies of Yisra'el, whom you have taunted and defied!

"This day Yahweh will deliver you into my hands, and I will strike you down and remove your head. It will be the dead bodies of the P'lishtim that the birds of the sky and wild beasts of the earth with feast upon, so that all of the earth will know that there is a God in Yisra'el and all this assembly will know that Yahweh does not deliver by sword or spear. The battle belongs to Yahweh, and He will give you all into our hands!"

David never took his eyes off the P'lishti, looming tall across the grass. The Boundary of Blood yet between them was the dividing line of the valley.

Golyat's face turned blood red, a deeper shade than David had ever witnessed before. The giant was furious. He had no words to answer, only a primal, guttural roar that issued from the back of his throat.

Golyat ripped the javelin from off his back in a single motion and charged, his shield bearer having no chance of keeping up.

David reached into his pouch and grabbed a stone, fitting it into the thong of his sling and grasping the cords. He ran forward to meet the P'lishti, closing the distance between them. He raised his arm and began to whirl the sling.

Golyat raised his javelin above his head, hurtling toward David to pierce him straight through.

David hurled the stone with all his strength. It sailed through the air at an incredible speed, striking the P'lishti in the forehead, right below the line of his helmet.

The whiz of the flying stone was followed instantly by a crack as it broke through the front of the giant's thick skull, tearing into the frontal lobes of his brain.

Golyat toppled forward, his legs buckling beneath him, his face slamming into the earth before him. His collapse was like the felling of a large tree. The javelin slipped from the P'lishti's fingers and skidded across the grass.

David ran to his fallen foe and stood over him, seizing the handle of Golyat's massive sword and drawing it out of its scabbard. The shield bearer fell backward where he was, trying to scoot away in terror, the pagan shield clutched before him.

David turned and raised the sword high in the air. With a shout, he brought it down in a chopping motion onto the back of the P'lishti's thick neck. He broke through the skin and the top of the spinal column, bringing the giant's jerking spasms to a halt. He sawed deeper with the blade, through muscle and cartilage and esophagus until Golyat's head was cut free from his body. David kicked the helmet off and grasped the bleeding head of Golyat by the hair, raising it up high for all to see.

Anguished cries of disbelief could be heard all the way from the P'lishtim camp, and in a moment, the entire Yisra'elite army was storming the field, weapons raised and cries of war shattering the sky. The P'lishtim turned and fled for their lives with the Yisra'elites in close pursuit. Their champion was dead.

Avner rode out with a vanguard to meet David as he walked back to the Yisra'elite camp, still carrying the head of his vanquished foe—a trophy to present to the king. David had tied the giant's sword and scabbard around his own waist.

—XXI—

David sat on his mount as the victory parade, fat with plunder, weaved its way toward Giv'ah of Sha'ul, at last reaching the terminating point of their journey.

More than thirty thousand P'lishtim had lost their lives in their disastrous retreat, with twice as many wounded. The dead were strewn for miles upon miles, through the Sh'felah and lands of Y'hudah all the way to the very gates of the enemy cities of Gat and 'Ekron. David had been there for all of it.

Now, David smiled at Y'honatan riding alongside him. There was a twinkle in the prince's eye as if he knew of the celebration to come and could scarcely contain his eagerness for David to experience it. Y'honatan grinned and held his reins. How he wished he could kick his heels, gallop past his father's procession, and be home already!

David thought back to his defeat of Golyat. Sha'ul had been giddy with excitement, congratulating David, and himself, over and over again. Y'honatan's reaction had taken David by surprise; the prince had embraced the young man while tears of joy streamed down his face.

"David, son of Yishai," the king had said, "I know you have saved us and restored honor to Yisra'el today, and I am in your debt. Your valor and your courage will not go unrewarded! From this day, you will not only enter into my service but into my very home."

Y'honatan was pleased.

"Thanks be to Yahweh for sending you to us!" the prince had said. "If only there were ten such men with your faith in all the kingdom."

Y'honatan had stripped off his royal robe and draped it over David's shoulders. He took his finest tunic, his armor, his sword, his bow and his belt and laid them at David's feet.

"They are yours, David. Never again will you have to wear a common shepherd's cloak, but you will appear in the king's court dressed like a prince."

Y'honatan and David had clasped hands, and Y'honatan gripped his forearm tightly with his other hand. Sha'ul and Avner were already stirred up and ready to move.

"My king, let's give chase to our enemies!" Avner had urged.

"Come on then!" Sha'ul had called to his eldest son and the young hero.

David would now be living in Giv'ah of Sha'ul, likely within the very fortress of the House of Sha'ul. Apart from sleeping under the stars while tending sheep, and his times before staying in Giv'ah, which now seemed but a distant memory, David had never lived outside of Beit-Lechem. He had never called anywhere but his father's house his home.

On the journey back they had passed through Beit-Lechem. David and his brothers received heroes' welcomes in their hometown. Yishai and his family feasted with Sha'ul and the commanders and the town elders. The king honored Yishai in front of all the families of Y'hudah, who had come to see the victorious army. Yishai would now be the tribal representative to the House of Sha'ul and would receive a stipend and grain from the royal storehouses.

David had hugged his mother, his father, his brothers, and sisters goodbye. He could not guess the next chance he would have to visit them. Even though he expected to see them soon enough, things would never be the same. With the king's permission, David presented his family with Golyat's armor to display as a proud memorial to their boy who had irrevocably grown up.

As for the giant's sword, and even his very head, they were devoted to Yahweh to give Him full glory for the victory. At David's request, the penultimate stop on the celebratory march had been Nov, the priestly city in Binyamin that now served as the de facto center of Yisra'elite religious life under Sha'ul's rule. From this location, the city of Yerushalayim on its hill was clearly seen, and even Mount Tziyon, higher above, with the long-standing fortress of the Y'vusi. In the care of the Levites serving at the tabernacle, these P'lishtim artifacts would now stand as a continual witness of the great deliverance Yahweh had given Yisra'el.

Now, the fortified walls of Giv'ah were visible ahead on the road. An excited crowd of onlookers waited outside the gates as Sha'ul in his finery and all the king's men approached. David wore the garments given him by Y'honatan for this occasion. The cheers grew louder and louder.

King Sha'ul waved magnanimously to the throng of eager subjects, and many finely dressed women came out from the crowd and city and surrounded the returning soldiers, singing and dancing with joyous celebration, shaking tambourines, blowing flutes, and playing stringed instruments. No soldier could resist smiling and laughing at the pleasing sight.

Sha'ul caught a garland of flowers from one of the admiring women and beamed, pressing onward through the sea of cheering people as hands reached out to them. Catching sight of David and determining it was him, the crowd was even more beside themselves. Here was the champion, the hero whose exploits against the P'lishtim were already famous throughout the land!

The women sang to one another in call and response, "Sha'ul has killed his thousands, and David his tens of thousands!"

This chant of a song caught on quickly, and garlands were showered on David and Y'honatan as well.

"Sha'ul has killed his thousands, and David tens of thousands!"

David blushed and laughed as the women tried to reach out and playfully grab hold of him as he rode past. The prince, seeing his young friend given such admiration, gave a hearty laugh as well.

"Sha'ul has killed his thousands, and David tens of thousands!"

Sha'ul was significantly less pleased.

The call to dine was sounded, and the House of Sha'ul congregated around the massive banquet table within the fortress. Rich food and wine covered the expanse of the table—a feast literally fit for a king. The shepherd's mouth watered.

Y'honatan insisted that David sit beside him near Sha'ul, who sat at the head of the table, his back to a wall. David looked at the many faces around the table as Y'honatan introduced him to everyone. Some he had met already and some he had not during his breathless, whirlwind tour of the fortress.

Avner sat at Sha'ul's left hand. Y'honatan and the other princes, Avinadav, Malkishua, Eshba'al, all the sons of Achino'am, were there. Also present were Sha'ul's two youngest sons, Armoni and M'fivoshet, children of his concubine Ritzpah. Bela, who clearly remembered David from before, was there. In addition to the other advisors, scribes, counselors, ministers, friends of the king, and military commanders currently in favor, such a celebration allowed for the presence of Sha'ul's wife and concubine, as well as Sha'ul's two daughters. Y'honatan's wife and young child were also present, as were the family members of Sha'ul's second son.

David looked keenly at the two princesses. Merav, to whom he was presumably to be betrothed, was a handful of years older than he. It was not common for women to remain unmarried by such an age, but then again, what was common in a royal family? Her face had a square, plain quality to it. She sat and ate with a sort of simple dullness, interacting minimally with those around her. The tastes of her food and drink seemed to be all the stimulation she required. David thought about how he had not even spoken a word before to this woman.

Then David saw the other daughter, Mikhal. She was younger than Merav but still older than himself. David's eyes brightened with recognition. Could it be? Here was that girl, the one he had encountered in the hallway of the fortress during the time he had been called into service for the king! He hadn't known her family connection then, although it was obvious in hindsight. Catching his gaze, she gave a quick smile and looked away. She was exceedingly fairer than her older sister, at least in David's eyes.

The banquet progressed with boisterous stories of the war and the glories of victory over the hated P'lishtim. David was given a window into the workings of the kingdom, and Y'honatan would lean over and explain to him any references he didn't catch. Once the scraps were cleared away, the courtiers begged David to play for them with the kinnor, having heard of his great talent. After their persistence, David obliged to entertain them. He gave them a song, then another at their applauding request.

All were merry, except the king.

Sha'ul murmured vague responses when spoken to, and he raised his cup to toasts when prompted, but inside he wished this feast would hurry up and end. His mood had soured and was growing only darker.

"Sha'ul has killed his thousands, and David his tens of thousands."

What could it mean? What had possessed those people to sing such words? Had Sha'ul made a terrible error, inviting this newcomer, this shepherd boy, into his home, into his inner court, perhaps even into his family? Had he brought a poisonous snake to his dinner table?

Sha'ul took a heavy swig of wine and looked suspiciously over at David.

"Sha'ul has killed his thousands, and David his tens of thousands."

How could they sing such a thing? They didn't even call him king, but only Sha'ul. They credited this stranger with ten thousand kills and him with only a thousand. He was beloved by the crowds. Overnight he was famous, and his heroic deeds were being sung of. What more could David have but the kingdom?

As Sha'ul fixated on it, he became enraged. Holding his empty goblet beneath the table, he squeezed it until it began to crush.

—XXII—

Y'honatan nocked an arrow and pulled the drawstring taut, the muscles in his arms on display as he held the bow with perfect steadiness.

THWAP!

The string snapped forward, and the arrow sailed through the air in a fierce arc.

David shielded his eyes from the sun as he watched the trajectory. The arrow fell in the field beyond the Stone of the Way, which was actually a heap of stones on the outskirts of the fields of Giv'ah. David let out a low whistle.

"This is the future of war, my friend," the prince said, already selecting another arrow from his quiver.

"So I see."

"Yet you insist on still using a sword."

"I find that it suits me," David remarked with a laugh.

"It can be risky to be in such close combat all the time. Especially if you have responsibilities to lead others. You need to think about what's best."

"And what if I think it is best to lead from the front?" David added with a wink.

"Ah, well, Yahweh gives everyone different gifts, doesn't He? Ha! When I was your age, I always wanted to be in the thick of it. But I genuinely love archery."

Y'honatan punctuated his sentence by firing another shaft into the blue sky, this one also landing beyond the stones.

"Now it's your turn." Y'honatan held out the weapon for David. "If you can get an arrow past mine, I'll tell you a secret."

"And if I fail?"

"Then you must write a romantic poem that I can use to woo my wife!"

David laughed, nocking his arrow.

"How about ... your beauty pierces my heart more readily than a sharpened arrow."

Now they both were laughing as David squinted and pulled the drawstring. He tried inexpertly to judge the variables of distance, height and wind. At last, he let the arrow fly, and it hissed through the air.

It fell in the field, short of the target.

"Oh!"

"Your stance could use some work," Y'honatan counseled. "You need to make sure you have a stable base of support. Otherwise, you're leaning away from the target."

"Well, I guess I don't get to hear a secret then."

"I'll tell you what. You go retrieve those arrows, and I'll tell you the secret anyway."

David did just that, sprinting beyond the Stone of the Way and searching in the field for all the arrows that had been shot. He returned with a light film of sweat on his skin, but not the least bit winded.

"My arrows for your secret?" David offered.

"It's not much of a secret," Y'honatan began, taking the arrows and placing them one by one in their quiver. "You're going to be given command of a regiment."

"Really?"

"A thousand soldiers. My father already approved the order to Avner to promote you."

"Do you think that is too soon?" David asked with a note of concern.

"Nonsense. Everything you have been asked to do you have done well, and you have had success everywhere my father has sent you. The officers love you. All Yisra'el loves you!"

"Praise be to Yahweh for that, and thanks to the king ... but I worry that such a promotion might provoke jealousy. Many soldiers and officers are more seasoned than I am. The last thing I want to do is stir up strife."

"David, I will make it my business that no one speaks an ill word against you or raises a hand to trouble you. I know Yahweh is with you, my friend. Follow and honor Him, and He will prosper you in all you do. You are an inspiration to me, and I feel almost as if you are a kindred soul. More so, I will gladly pledge here and now before Yahweh my God, that you are to be my sworn brother and friend for life. May your blessings be my blessings, and may your hurts be my hurts. You have both my love and my loyalty."

David was deeply moved.

With eyes beginning to brim with tears, David clasped Y'honatan's hand firmly before the two embraced.

"My lord, my lord!" An urgent shout came from across the field.

A young servant of Y'honatan's came running in their direction. David recognized him as one who seemed to answer only to the prince, a loyal source of reliable information about all the goings-on of the House of Sha'ul.

"What is it?" Y'honatan asked.

"It is your fath—I mean, the king. He's ... he's not well," the servant said while eyeing David, wary of revealing too much.

Y'honatan's expression faltered, and David could read the anguish on his face.

"My lord, it is really bad this time," the servant added.

"T-thank you. Um … you may return," Y'honatan managed to reply, waving his hand in dismissal. The servant dutifully turned and hurried away.

David placed his hand reassuringly on Y'honatan's arm.

"Y'honatan, listen to me. I know about the king and how an evil spirit has tormented him. His pain is a burden on my own heart as well. You may not know this, but I have before played my kinnor for him when he was suffering in such a way, and by the grace of Yahweh have been able to bring him comfort and help. You can ask Bela if you like. Please, let me go to him with songs of peace and deliverance, that our God may see fit to lift this curse from your father."

Sha'ul was in a gloom. In his private chamber, the king slouched on his divan, the diadem hanging askew on his dark head of hair. He clutched a spear as if it were his last remaining pillar of support. His eyes alternated between deadened downcast vacancy and frantic searching.

His closest personal attendants had just about given up their attempt at ministration. The king would jerk his head spasmodically and spew unpredictable eruptions of bizarre words. These outbursts would be followed by a sustained trembling of the king's body. At least he was no longer pacing around the room, arms flailing, liable to hurt himself or others in the madness.

The attendants turned to see David and the prince standing in the doorframe, David with his kinnor under his arm.

"You can leave us," Y'honatan said quietly.

The attendants gratefully obeyed.

"It pains me so to see him this way …" Y'honatan's voice caught in his throat.

David slowly approached the divan and took a seat across from the king, looking at him with deep compassion.

"My lord. It is your servant, David. I wish to play a song for you. May I?"

Sha'ul gave a sputter, followed by another involuntary twitch.

David nodded to Y'honatan. The prince returned the gesture and quietly backed out of the room, closing the door behind him.

David prayed for Yahweh's mercy and raised his instrument, beginning in his sweet voice

"You are my hiding place, O God.
I find shelter in your presence.
You preserve me in times of trouble,
And surround me with songs of deliverance."

Sha'ul began to writhe and seethe as the music played. His raving heightened. Then, the gibberish made way to shouts of foul curse words, and the king's face contorted into a hateful mask. David kept playing.

"May we pray, while there's still time,
And not be reached by the rushing flood.
For many sorrows will drown the wicked,
But You surround those who trust with Your unfailing love."

Sha'ul gripped the shaft of the spear and pressed the butt of the weapon into the floor, feeling a wave of nausea rise up within him, choking him, gagging him. A thick stream of saliva dripped to the floor from his slack jaws, but his body ceased its jerking movements.

Kill him!

Sha'ul stared hard at David. Had he spoken? No. He kept playing that instrument of his ... kept singing ...

Kill him!

Had David heard that voice? No.

Kill him or your kingdom belongs to him. He has come to take it from you.

David kept playing. That young ... handsome ... smug face.

Usurper!

Sha'ul felt the weight of the spear in his hand.

Traitor!

David began a new chorus, "You are my hiding place, O God ..."

Deceiver!

How easy it would be to ...

Kill him!

Kill him!

KILL HIM!

Sha'ul lurched forward and flung the spear at David.

David dove out of the way. The spear pierced the wall where David had been sitting. David scrambled up off the floor, clutching his kinnor. He had no armor, no shield, nothing at all with which to defend himself.

Sha'ul glared with burning hatred at David and wrenched the spear free of the plaster, turning to point it threateningly at the young man.

"You don't think I know what you're up to?" the king shouted.

He lunged and threw the spear again. David dodged nimbly out of the way. The spear flew and crashed into a table setting, knocking dishes over and breaking a large jug. Sha'ul slipped and tumbled forward onto the ground, the diadem falling from his head, his bracelet scraping against the floor.

David stood, heart racing, not sure what to do as the king groveled before him.

"My lord," David whispered, keeping his distance.

Slowly, Sha'ul got to his hands and knees. He was obviously disoriented.

"My lord," David began again. "Are you all right? Yahweh, help him."

Sha'ul turned himself over and sat on the floor with his back against the wall. His face was red and glistening, and his head throbbed terribly.

"My lord ... King ..."

Sha'ul looked at David as if greatly inconvenienced by his insistence on communicating. He ran a hand through his sweat-damp hair and noticed the missing diadem, then found it lying on the floor beside him.

"Huh, what do you want? Leave me," Sha'ul muttered.

"My king ..."

"I said leave me!"

David bowed his head and made his way to the door, taking his instrument.

"Where are my attendants?" Sha'ul called out. "Where's Bela? Send in Bela!"

—XXIII—

David patrolled with his thousand-strong regiment, fighting P'lishtim scouts and raiding parties that skirted the porous borders. As he rode past, the inhabitants of the towns and villages would come out to catch a glimpse of the young hero they had heard so much about. Knowing he was near gave a sense of security to those on the frontier—those who would be first to suffer from P'lishtim incursion.

One day, after returning from a successful skirmish, David and his men stopped to rest.

"You like being out here with us?" Yashov'am asked. Yashov'am was a career soldier. More experienced than many, but unambitious to a fault, Yashov'am had gained promotion at a glacial pace, always deferring to others and showing no striving aspiration of his own. David valued his insight and plainspoken nature. "It is different from being in the king's palace, no?"

"What are you getting at?" David asked.

Yashov'am's habit of rarely making eye contact when speaking was something David had to get used to. This was not disrespect or false modesty, but rather he always seemed to be preoccupied with carving marks onto the shaft of his spear. One mark for every kill in battle. There were a lot of marks.

"I thought you would be made the king's personal guard, his armor bearer for life, never leaving his side for an instant," Yashov'am said.

"I serve at the king's pleasure, and I would much rather be out here than sitting in Giv'ah every day."

"And we are fortunate to have you."

"Still, there are some benefits to living in the fortress." David's thoughts went to Sha'ul's daughter. The younger one, slender and dark. Mikhal. He had caught her staring at him from across the king's table during his last visit to Giv'ah. Or had he?

Yashov'am seemed to know what was on his mind and grinned, looking up from his work.

"The king once promised you his daughter in marriage, no?"

David colored.

"I haven't pursued that; all things in time."

"You've come of age now."

"Hmm."

Yashov'am resumed his carving.

"The P'lishtim already have a target on your back. David—the boy who slew Golyat. If you are to marry into the royal family, you'll be a hunted man. They will stop at nothing to kill you."

"Exactly," Sha'ul said.

"My lord?" Bela asked.

"How can I let somebody into my family, to marry my own virgin daughter, if he is not proven to be courageous and steadfast? Let the P'lishtim know his worth and hunt for him! If he is the man we all think he is, this should not be a problem."

Sha'ul watched from the fortress ramparts as David and his company approached the city. From where he stood, Bela couldn't tell what expression was on the king's face.

"Besides," Sha'ul continued, "how would it look in front of the people if I failed to keep the oath I swore to the man who delivered us from the giant?"

"Hmmm. Of course, my lord. Very wise."

Below, David was getting another warm welcome as he entered the city. No doubt he had another victory under his belt. No doubt he would be showered with even more admiration.

David was glad to be back. He regaled Y'honatan and Prince Eshba'al with stories of his latest exploits as they waited outside the dining hall for the king to arrive.

In the corner, Sha'ul's daughters were conversing quietly with Sha'ul's youngest children and a maidservant. David noticed Mikhal glancing over at him. He met the princess's eyes and she quickly looked away, then looked back and smiled. David felt his body growing warm.

Just then King Sha'ul arrived. Everyone straightened and acknowledged him, then entered the hall to take their customary seats while servers began loading the table with rich, aromatic food.

"Welcome back, Commander David, hero of Yisra'el!" Sha'ul said abruptly in way of salutation.

"Thank you, my king," David answered. "It is good to be home again, even for a short visit."

"I would have thought you'd have a full beard by now!" Avner said, then roared with laughter at his own joke.

David laughed, touching his fingertips to the light scruff forming on his face.

"The sting of battle hasn't hardened those fair looks yet," Y'honatan added, elbowing David playfully in the ribs.

They ate, and the mood was lighthearted all around. It wasn't until Sha'ul had finished eating that he addressed David in a serious tone.

"David ..."

All those in attendance hushed and waited to hear what the king would say.

"David. My dear David. You have grown before our eyes. You are a man and a warrior of Yisra'el. You have obtained rank. You command a thousand men on the battlefield. Once I made a promise to give my daughter in marriage to the man who would rescue us from Golyat. You did. I have waited, but the time has come."

David instinctively looked at Y'honatan, then over at Mikhal for a fraction of a second. Everyone seemed to hold their breath.

"Here sits my eldest daughter, Merav," King Sha'ul said with a gesture. "As I have promised, I will give her to you as a wife. I only ask that you be a valiant man for me and my house and that you continue to fight Yahweh's battles."

David looked down at the table before him, then down at his hands, concentrating on them. His head was bowed low, and he wore an expression of supreme humility.

"My king ... I am flattered, but ... who am I ... and what is my life or what is my father's family is Yisra'el ... that I should become the king's son-in-law? I have no desire to disappoint the king or his family, but I do not deserve this honor."

Everybody was speechless, not least Sha'ul himself. An uncomfortable silence descended on the table.

"Now I am afraid that I have caused embarrassment to my lord the king's family, and to his daughter in particular.

That was not my intention, and I apologize. I must ask that I excuse myself."

David slowly got up from his seat and bowed, turning and quietly leaving the room.

As soon as he was gone, Merav, on the verge of tears, stood and hurriedly excused herself. Mikhal, and then her mother, followed after her.

Later that night, Achino'am sat close to her husband inside his chambers.

"Don't worry, my husband," Achino'am said softly, rubbing his hunched shoulders.

"I don't understand ... I practically offered him the keys to the kingdom. Why would he refuse our Merav? That ungrateful ..."

"What will you do?"

"I know what I'll do; I'll give Merav to Adri'el the Mecholati! Yes ... and we'll throw the most lavish feast ever seen in the kingdom in honor of their wedding!"

Adri'el had a connection and friendship to Sha'ul's family, and he owned many flocks. The marriage would be both politically and economically advantageous.

"And what of your word, that you would give your daughter to the man who killed the giant?"

Sha'ul grunted and shook off her hands. She persisted. "Maybe there is still a way to honor your word. And maybe you misread David's intentions. Don't you think David is too young for Merav anyway?"

"What are you saying, woman?"

"Haven't you noticed ... the way Mikhal and David look at one another?"

Sha'ul stared blankly at his wife.

"Sha'ul, our youngest daughter is in love with David! She mostly keeps quiet about it, but I have often noticed her asking after David's welfare and his comings and goings. I have seen how she strains to listen anytime his name is mentioned. I tell you, Mikhal loves him."

"Really," Sha'ul mused.

"Yes, you haven't seen it on her face? I guess a mother knows these things."

"Mikhal and David?" he asked, clarifying.

"Yes! That is why he declines Merav!"

"Huh!" The wheels were turning. "I suppose one daughter is just as good as another." Sha'ul practically leaped off the bed and rang for his servants.

"Where are you going? It's the middle of the night!" Achino'am protested.

David was awakened by loud knocking on his bedroom door. Sleepily, he made sure he was covered and opened the door to find the king himself standing there with two attendants. David was startled and almost tripped over himself as he wondered if inviting the king into his diminutive room would be insulting or the polite thing to do.

Sha'ul spared him the decision and pushed past him, taking a seat while David hesitantly sat on the edge of his bed.

"What is it, my lord? Is everything all right?"

"I wanted to talk about what happened earlier."

David looked down at his hands.

"I've decided to give Merav in marriage to another man."

David flinched but remained silent.

"That offer has passed," the king said. "However, I will be willing to give you Mikhal, my youngest."

David's eyes darted up to read the king's expression.

"That's right, for the second time this day ... you may be my son-in-law."

David momentarily felt a surge of joyous excitement. But then, he began to visibly deflate once more, his head hanging.

"My lord, you are too kind to your servant. Your offers are beyond gracious; they are humbling to the depths of my heart. Still, my lord—and do not be angry with your servant for speaking like this—I am not yet deserving of your daughter. The joining of your servant to your family through marriage will be of little value to the House of Sha'ul."

Sha'ul couldn't believe what he was hearing. He felt the anger and venom boiling up inside of him. Before his temper got the better of him, he abruptly left the room without another word, leaving David alone with his conflicted heart.

The next morning the young hero readied himself to depart. He packed his belongings and rode out through the gates, reuniting with Yashov'am and several others under his command.

Before they got far from Giv'ah, two riders gave chase and caught up to the group. It was Bela and another of King Sha'ul's attendants. Bela's thin frame looked unnatural on the steed, and he appeared almost pale from the exertion.

"David!" Bela called. "Wait a moment. I had to speak to you before you left."

"What is it?" David asked, signaling to his men not to pay any mind to the interruption.

Bela continued in a confidential tone. "The king doesn't know we're speaking to you, but I and others feel we have to make our thoughts known to you. Listen, the king delights in you, even though you have rejected the offer of marriage to his daughter twice. And all of the king's servants love you. Everybody in the royal court speaks highly of you! So why won't you accept his offer? Why won't you become the king's son-in-law? It makes no sense."

David's face reddened, and his response was snappier than he intended.

"Tell me, is it so trivial in your sight ... is it such a small thing to become the king's son-in-law? Do you not know that I am a poor man? I was a shepherd before, and now I am but a soldier. How shall somebody lightly esteemed and so situated as myself wed a princess?"

In frustration, David gripped the reins and pulled away, galloping to rejoin his men.

This action didn't bother Bela one bit, for he suddenly understood. This was about the dowry. There was no way that David could afford to pay a dowry expected of one for marrying the daughter of a king. Perhaps David did love Mikhal. Even if David had every intention of marrying one of the girls, how could he expose himself to such shame and dishonor and to have the royal household affected?

"Hmmm," Bela murmured. Then he and the other servant returned to the fortress and reported everything to Sha'ul, just as planned.

—XXIV—

David and his thousand camped at 'Azekah while they waited for the latest reports on P'lishtim troop movements.

In the downtime, David found himself pining for Mikhal. So few words had passed between them, and yet it was only the thought of the act's impertinence that restrained him from penning her love letters. To distract his mind, he busied himself with inspecting the walls and fortifications. There had once begun an effort of digging out underground chambers of refuge beneath the city, but this project had been abandoned some time ago. David made mental notes to make a recommendation up the proper chain of command that this effort be restarted. Places like this would always be vulnerable to P'lishtim invasion unless 'Azekah could become a solid rock for the P'lishtim to break their teeth against.

What a shame it was that the Yisra'elites had not finished the task that Yahweh had given them to do upon entering the Promised Land! Now there appeared no end in sight to the harassment of these unrighteous, idolatrous nations that surrounded them like so many thorns in their sides.

Daily, David dined with his men, accepting no special treatment for himself, not for the sake of admiration of the heroic deeds he had performed nor for his perceived special position within the House of Sha'ul. Increasingly he would lead his fellow soldiers in prayers for protection, guidance, and victory.

Privately, he had other prayers. One day an answer of sorts presented itself. Messengers from Giv'ah, riding in the name of Bela, came with words from the king's mouth. They met with David privately.

"The king does not desire any dowry except one hundred foreskins of the P'lishtim, to take vengeance on the king's enemies. Now Bela states that you should hasten to do this thing, and therefore accept the marriage to Mikhal. If you delay, the king will interpret your lack of interest as a final rejection of the offer, and Mikhal will be given to another, just as Merav was."

David was pleased. The next day he organized a daring raid into enemy territory.

The royal court was in session. The king sat on his throne with his princes on either side. Avner, royal advisors, officers, commanders, scribes, friends, attendants, guards, entertainers, and esteemed guests from several tribes were present, seeking an audience.

The business of the House of Sha'ul, of the tribe of Binyamin and of the kingdom of Yisra'el, was being carried out. The court was about to hear a report from Do'eg, an Edomi by birth, who oversaw all who cared for the king's mules.

There was an interruption.

"My lord, it is the young commander David!"

Conversation ceased, and all eyes turned to behold David, dressed smartly in his soldier's uniform, confidently striding forward with a wooden box in his arms. Sha'ul tensed.

"My lord," David began, kneeling and placing the box before him. "Your servant brings a gift."

Sha'ul nodded to his attendants who came forward and tentatively opened the box. One attendant gasped as the lid came off. The box appeared to be full of small pieces of human skin caked with dried blood.

"If my lord's servants wish to count, they may, but I present to the king two hundred foreskins of his enemies."

The stunned onlookers slowly began to applaud, crescendoing in enthusiastic cheers.

"Wait, wait. He's got something to say!" Y'honatan called out, silencing the crowd. The applause abated and David raised his eyes to the king who regarded him coolly but expectantly.

"My lord, if it pleases you," David began, "your servant would ask for your daughter's hand in marriage."

Y'honatan, no longer able to contain his excitement, leaped from his seat and hugged David roughly.

"Ha ha! Now we really are going to be brothers!"

The court was again filled with applause and cheering.

By the king's decree, announcements were made throughout Yisra'el that the hero David was betrothed to marry the princess Mikhal. Even to the furthest corners of the kingdom, and consequently into the ears of P'lishtim spies and informants, the royal wedding was proclaimed.

When the number of months had passed, a feast and ceremony were held. Mikhal was bathed, oiled, and perfumed by her maidservants, then clothed in a dress of embroidered cloth, fine linen, and silk. She was bejeweled with a golden bracelet and earrings, and a necklace beaded with precious stones. Finally, veiled, she was escorted with much singing and dancing to the house in Giv'ah that King Sha'ul had given to the couple as a wedding present.

David awaited her. Inside, the wedding chamber had been prepared as a luxurious sanctuary of love. David was eager. He coaxed the veil away from the face of his coy young bride for want of kissing her lips, and he fell into the tangle of her long limbs.

There they would remain for seven days. After love had been given its time, an even larger feast and celebration was held lasting another week. David's aged father and the rest of his family were present to join in the merrymaking.

King Sha'ul realized with sinking certainty that his daughter did indeed love this David—wholeheartedly. She was devoted to him, enamored with him, fulfilled by him. The princess had her hero, had her nice new home, had her title, and had no need for her father. In his strategic use of his own daughter, moving her like a piece on a game board, had he made the biggest mistake of all? Letting the wolf into the sheep's pen? Everybody else was so blind to David's treachery.

David and Mikhal, for their part, were swept up in the moment and with one another. The people of Yisra'el were thrilled with the match. They showered the young couple with wedding gifts, with joyful expressions and blessings. David couldn't have been happier.

But such pleasures could not last forever.

The Five P'lishtim lords again organized their armies to attack Yisra'el. They were well aware of the Hebrew tradition for men in their first year of marriage to abstain from war and other such weighty commitments. What better time to seek vengeance on their foes than when their hero was removed from the field of battle? And the P'lishtim had no shortage of soldiers, with immigrants from across the Great Sea pressed into service to bolster their ranks.

But they underestimated David's zeal and his sense of duty to his God, to his men, and to his country.

David so distinguished himself that Avner unilaterally promoted him, and then urged Sha'ul to approve of even further military promotions. A regiment of a thousand men was not nearly worthy enough for the man who continued to prove himself more successful, braver, and wiser than all the rest of Sha'ul's officers.

This remark from Avner lingered and replayed in Sha'ul's mind, and finally pushed the king over the edge. In a raging fit, he barricaded himself in his inner chambers, destroying furniture, ripping apart curtains and linens, and smashing objects with surprising ferocity.

Once the anger and adrenaline subsided, Sha'ul sank to the floor in the corner of the room. He was in a pitiful, trembling state. Fury had been replaced by terror. At length, Sha'ul's attendants cleaned up his mess. They went about acquiring and installing replacements for all that had been destroyed, refurnished the room, tended to their ruler's cuts and scrapes, and otherwise hushed up the entire incident.

—XXV—

"I want you to kill David."

Sha'ul's inner circle stood in the throne room in private conference.

"My lord?" Bela asked, straining to hide his incredulity.

"I have it on high authority ... that David is planning to assassinate me and seize the throne. Therefore, I demand his life."

Y'honatan gaped in disbelief. His father could not have been speaking with a more neutral, even tone or with a straighter face. This was no sick joke. This was no mad whim. He was serious. Deadly serious.

"What are you talking about?" the prince managed. "What authority? Where does this rumor come from?"

"Oh, my son, you are not privy to all my sources of information. I am still king after all. I have heard from a trusted informant very close to me that this is the sad truth."

"I don't believe it for one second! This is madness."

"Watch your tongue!"

"Father, I can't believe David would do anything to betray you. This has to be a mistake. You must take back this command you have given for his life before something happens that you will regret!"

"Y'honatan, have you not sat in this court long enough to learn the ways of the world? After I'm dead, David will come after you. Don't you see what you have to lose? Yisra'el is yours after I'm gone! He understands that even if you don't. Disturbing as it is, I know that he is plotting treachery against this family, even as he lies with your own sister."

"Father!" Y'honatan shouted.

"I will not let this evil come to pass. David must be stopped, for the good of this family and for the good of this kingdom. I want him dead before the sun has risen tomorrow morning. But it must be done quietly, for we do not want to cause a panic; and it must be done carefully, for I know how this David is like a serpent in the grass, full of cunning. Now go and see it done."

Sha'ul waved his hand to dismiss the others.

"Father, hear me out. Bela, all of you, stop! Don't you dare leave this room until I have spoken my piece."

"I said we are finished. Everyone out! Leave my sight or face death yourselves!"

The king's order prevailed. Y'honatan crumpled to his knees, tears of frustration and confusion welling in his eyes while the others hastily retreated. The king turned his back on his eldest son.

Y'honatan started as if to plead the point with his father, but then realized the jeopardy his dear friend faced. David was due to return home today. He would be tired and ready for the warm embrace of Mikhal. He would not have his guard up. Why should he fear his own countrymen, his own father-in-law? If the prince didn't somehow intervene, David would be dead within less than twenty-four hours. He had to act fast.

Around noon the next day, Y'honatan waited under an overcast sky by the Stone of the Way in the midst of the intersecting fields and roads outside of Giv'ah. The prince watched as his father rode out to him alone for the requested meeting, leaving behind his burly escorts. The men were armed and vigilant, ready for anything.

"What do you have to tell me?" Sha'ul asked.

"Please, father, can you not alight and have a face-to-face conversation with your own son?"

Sha'ul grunted and climbed off his horse, leading it behind him as he stalked closer to the prince and the large rock pile serving as his backdrop. He looked Y'honatan over with a keen, knowing gaze.

"It seems David never came home last night," the king said. "Reports say he left his camp, he was seen more than once on the road, and he was even spotted near Giv'ah. Yet, he is nowhere to be found. Now you wouldn't know anything about that, would you?"

"Father, all I ask is for you to hear me out. Allow me this once to just say everything that is on my heart, and then you must do whatever you decide."

Sha'ul fought down his anger and reminded himself to breathe.

"As you wish."

"You are the king of Yisra'el, anointed by Yahweh. David is your servant. He has always been your servant. Let it not be that you sin against your own servant by taking his life, as he has not sinned against you in any way. Such an act would break the commandment against murder in killing an innocent man, an act not worthy of you! Why put him to death without cause? I cannot believe any report about David thinking to conspire against you. Hear me.

"David has been nothing but loyal, and his deeds have only brought prosperity to you. He took his life in his hand and struck down the P'lishtim giant, and Yahweh brought a great deliverance for all Yisra'el. You yourself saw it, and you rejoiced, as did I. Furthermore, with service and sacrifice, he has served our God, our country, and our family. He is your own son-in-law. Would you make your own daughter, my beloved sister, a widow on an unproven report? David has played his music for you in your inner chambers on many occasions, even when you have not been well. If he had ever sought to harm you, he had the opportunity. But I know that such evil is not within his heart to do.

"I beg of you to reconsider your order against his life. Please, vow to me that you will not have David put to death. And let him be in your presence once again as he was before. Think no more of these false, slanderous reports of conspiracy!"

At the persistent words, Sha'ul felt his heart soften. Perhaps he had overreacted. Perhaps he had acted rashly. His son obviously had a real love for this man, shortsighted though it must be. Sha'ul certainly did not want to scandalize his reign nor drive a wedge between his own flesh and blood. What harm could this David really do? And wasn't it true that David had been courageous when no one else dared to oppose the giant, and he continued to rout the P'lishtim at every turn?

Sha'ul's resolve disintegrated, and he hung his head, feeling very tired.

"As Yahweh lives, he shall not be put to death," he sighed.

Y'honatan smiled, tears forming at the corners of his eyes.

"David! Come out," the prince called.

King Sha'ul looked up to see David emerge from behind the rocks, unarmed, and meekly approaching the two royals. Sha'ul felt conflicting pangs of emotion as David sank to his knees in the field with bowed head. Had he a sword or dagger in his hand, Sha'ul could strike David down with one blow.

"My lord," David spoke. "Your servant is grateful for your mercy and a second chance. The king must know that his servant would never do anything to harm the king or his family, and whatever my lord has heard cannot be the truth. Your servant only wishes to serve Yisra'el and Yahweh's anointed faithfully."

King Sha'ul unclenched his fist and slowly reached out his hand to rest it on David's head.

"Come now and return home. I'm sure your wife misses you."

—XXVI—

Other military regiments of Yisra'el had faced embarrassing setbacks and defeats under their commanders, while David appeared to be able to do no wrong. Orders came for such regiments to be brought under David in the form of a brigade, but with their original commanders still in place over each regiment. The soldiers were glad to align their fortunes with that of the war hero. The pride of the commanders, some of whom were political appointees by Sha'ul, did not fare as well.

Avner encouraged David's proposals of shoring up the fortifications of the western frontier towns and cities. The endless harassment of P'lishtim troops dwindled the morale, the production, and even the population of the fertile Sh'felah region. David sought to end this.

'Azekah was as good a place to start as any, situated so near the Boundary of Blood. Improving on what fortifications were already in place would ensure a lasting base of support for the citizens of the territory and would allow for the defense of the Valley of Elah. Under the right guidance, 'Azekah could be a very strategic site.

"Waste of time!" grumbled Hi'el, one of the reassigned commanders.

David had called a meeting of the officers.

"What's the problem?" David asked.

"We're officers in the king's army, not laborers, not masons," Hi'el complained.

The disagreement stemmed from David's directive for all the men in 'Azekah, whether civilian, soldier, or officer, to share equally in the burden of building up the walls and digging out the passageways.

"And while your men sweat and toil, what would you be doing?" David inquired calmly.

"Why should any of my men do peasant work? I should be leading them in combat against the P'lishtim. That is what we are best at."

Yashov'am interjected, "Lead? The only leading we've seen from you is first to the dinner table!"

David raised his hand to silence Yashov'am as Hi'el bristled at the rebuke, his hand instinctively dropping to the hilt of his weapon. Just then a soldier ran up and whispered urgently in David's ear.

"Okay, listen. There have been reports that a band of P'lishtim spies has been hiding out in some caves near Eitam."

The subordinate commanders stirred. David continued, "The height of Lechi is rocky, and a spring of water flows there. No doubt these men are sustaining themselves at this source. Besides uprooting these malefactors, I am concerned for Eitam. It is an unwalled village, is it not? Very vulnerable."

The men grunted in affirmation. Some were eager to act on this information and wash away the stains on their service records. A few P'lishtim spies cornered in a cave sounded like easy prey.

"Hi'el! You say you want to lead your regiment against Yisra'el's enemies. So be it. Here is your chance," David said. "But I'm going to ride with you. It will help me become better acquainted with you and your men."

"Fine, but we certainly won't need a thousand soldiers. A few hundred will do the trick. My men are tired from being relocated all the way out here, and the majority should save their strength for when we face real combat."

"If you as their commanding officer believe this is the wisest course, and you are willing to take responsibility, then I will not argue with your decision."

Hi'el bit his tongue.

"You want some of our men to come along?" Yashov'am asked David.

"No, stay here with them. The last thing I want is to give our foes any opportunity to exploit a weakness here at 'Azekah. You are in charge until I return. Get the men to work!"

David accompanied Hi'el and his men as they marched northeast through the terrain, navigating the narrow, rock-strewn mountain footpaths. They eventually approached the village of Eitam and saw the rocky height beyond it. The village was quiet. David could not detect anybody outside their homes. Had word been sent to the villagers to expect violence?

"Okay, boys!" Hi'el shouted, thrusting his sword in the direction of the supposed hideout. "Let's go get 'em!"

David shook his head but said nothing, following and observing on horseback. The transplanted commander seemed oblivious to his own character defects. Why was that always the case? This wasn't bravery; it was bluster. Would David yet be able to win over Hi'el and earn his respect? A fractious and divided brigade was no good to him or to Yisra'el.

The few hundred men positioned themselves at the base of the incline in a semicircle. The spring could be heard trickling between rocks and the spring's hollow basin, and shadowy indentations in the cliff above suggested the presence of caverns. Any P'lishtim inside would have heard or spotted the troops long ago. They would be cornered, trapped. They would know that they were—

Just then, a lone figure emerged on the height above the spring. It was a man dressed in the garb of a traveler. Was it a P'lishti? Was it a villager drawing water? Under the man's cloak, David could make out the edge of a scabbard.

"Ha ha! P'lishtim spies, huh? Come on down here, you and your friends!" taunted Hi'el. "We want to give you a warm welcome in the name of King Sha'ul."

The man steadily looked down at the Yisra'elites below, unfazed. Then he brought a horn to his lips and blew.

The ground vibrated and dust and gravel scattered down the rocks as a wave of P'lishtim soldiers appeared at the top of the height, readying bows and javelins.

"Oh, no," Hi'el murmured.

The Yisra'elites cried out in shock. How? Where had they come from? The ominous figures above stood like grotesque statues, silhouetted by the sun at their backs.

Then more commotion and the sound of soldiers' feet arose behind the Yisra'elites. David swiveled on his horse and saw P'lishtim soldiers pouring out of the village. Had they been hiding in the houses? Did that mean all the villagers were dead?

It was a trap, and soon they would be surrounded.

A shout of command in a harsh Kena'ani dialect was issued from above, and javelins began to rain down. Men screamed in agony as they were skewered.

"Shields!" David yelled. "Shields!"

The men who heard him or who were not overcome by blind panic desperately tried to protect themselves as javelins gave way to whizzing arrows. David threw his shield up just in time to catch an arrow flying straight at his face. Two more buried themselves in his horse's backside, sending the animal bucking wildly.

David slid off his frantic horse and rolled away, ducking low for cover and holding the shield above his head.

"Retreat! Retreat!" Hi'el screamed hysterically, fleeing on his horse.

"No!" David shouted in countermand.

His voice was lost in the hubbub and in a momentary break in the onslaught of arrows, many of the soldiers turned and ran.

"Stop!" David cried. "We need to get out of range and regroup!"

The majority were fleeing, but a few were still pinned down. Some were backing away from the height, uncertain whether or not to abandon David, whom they respected. David ran to each of them, shouting instructions.

"The riverbed!" David yelled. "Follow it, now!"

The men turned and ran for the nearly dried up riverbed issuing from below the spring. One fell with an arrow to his shoulder, but David stopped and hoisted him up. Another soldier helped, and they quickly dragged the wounded man out of range of the arrows.

The P'lishtim on foot were close now, weapons drawn and charging.

"Hurry!" David urged. "We can't let them surround us."

Meanwhile at 'Azekah, the surprise attack had begun as quickly as a flash flood. An army of P'lishtim surged across the open ground toward the city.

"Sound the alarm!" Yashov'am ordered, slapping men on the back to hasten them into action. With horns blowing, they ran across the ramparts, mobilizing a hasty response. "Every man, grab a weapon. I don't care if you are a soldier or citizen!"

The alarm wasn't necessary; the P'lishtim assault was unmistakable and massive. A thought occurred to Yashov'am: the city could not be defended. The walls were breached all over due to the repairs and reconstruction. The soldiers would fall. The old men, the women, the children of the city would be taken captive or killed. And the city itself ... if the P'lishtim were to seize this stronghold ...

"We have to go out to meet them," Yashov'am said under his breath. He picked up his spear off the stone-paved ground. He ran his fingertips across the carved grooves in the shaft. More would die today. Many more. But it didn't need to be him. What had David called them? The armies of the living God. Yes, they were the armies of the living God.

"Yahweh," Yashov'am breathed.

He turned to face the men who were forming up to await his orders. They were nervous and jittery, caught off guard by the attack.

"We are going out to meet them in battle," Yashov'am declared. "This city belongs to Yahweh! If we are on His side, He will be on our side!"

The men, especially those who had spent the most time with David, shouted in agreement. Yashov'am raised his spear high, then turned and pointed it at the city gates.

"For Yahweh! For the king! For Yisra'el!" he urged.

As the gates were opened, the men picked up the chant. And they added, "For David!"

David and the remaining men had backed themselves into a patch of farmland outside Eitam. They stood at the ready, weapons drawn, as their enemies rolled toward them like a crashing wave. They were so few in comparison.

"What are your names?" David asked, alert.

"Sh-shammah," the nearest soldier answered.

"That's my brother's name," David said with a smile.

"I'm El'azar, the son of Dodo," another answered. "I never expected to die in a barley field ... or are these lentils?"

The P'lishtim had reached the edge of the fields and weren't stopping.

"Do you trust me?" David asked the men, none of whom he had fought with before.

"Y-yes," Shammah stuttered.

"Do you trust Yahweh?"

"Yes!" El'azar said, gripping his sword and bracing for impact. He had been there when David toppled the giant. He had seen the miracle with his own eyes. He had tasted that victory firsthand. Others shouted in agreement.

"Do you not know that near this very spot, the hero Shimshon struck down a thousand P'lishtim with the jawbone of an ass?" David asked.

The men turned from their approaching enemies and stared in surprise.

"It is the truth. It happened right here at Lechi. If the Spirit of Yahweh can do that with one man and an animal's bone, think of what He can do with us!"

The Yisra'elite forces were completely outnumbered as they faced the P'lishtim army on the field of battle before 'Azekah. This assault had taken careful planning and coordination on the part of the P'lishtim. And cunning. Without a miracle Yashov'am and the men would all die this very day.

"Attack!" Yashov'am shouted as he ran headlong into the rushing P'lishtim lines with his countrymen following at his heels. The bronze head of his spear reached out to claim its prize. In this moment, he was unafraid of death. He felt a growing strength within. For the first time in his life, he knew that Yahweh was with him.

Three hundred P'lishtim fell before him. The men fighting beside him killed five hundred more.

The blood of the slain ran in rivulets between the rows of the fields. The survivors staggered away and scattered like dust in the wind. It was over.

El'azar panted with exhaustion, his eyes giant saucers of disbelief. His legs buckled and he fell to his knees in the death-spackled soil, the bloodstained sword frozen in the clutch of his cramped hand. He couldn't find the strength to utter a word.

"Yahweh has brought a great victory today ..." David whispered.

He removed his armor piece by piece and let it drop beside his shield and sword in the field where they had taken their stand. He stalked several paces away and fell to the ground, bowing before Yahweh and quietly glorifying Him with tears of gratitude on his cheeks.

The Yisra'elite soldiers who had run away slowly returned, one by one, and began stripping the dead.

—XXVII—

The dinner was notable for who was absent—King Sha'ul himself, who had been confined to his bedchamber all evening. Avner, Y'honatan, David and all the others dined and conversed while an undercurrent of concern for the king's well-being remained. After the dishes were cleared, David prepared to return home with his wife.

One of Sha'ul's attendants approached David and said, "The king wants to see you in his room. He requests that you play for him."

"Yes, of course," David answered. He kissed Mikhal, saying to her, "I'll be home right after. Have one of the guards escort you back."

David collected his kinnor and followed the attendant to Sha'ul's chamber.

"David, my son ... come in," the king rasped. He was lying in bed with the covers pulled up to his torso. David could see wrinkled folds of skin on the bare chest, betraying the king's age. He remained physically strong and vigorous, more so than many men, but the reality was that Sha'ul was a grandfather many times over. If David had to estimate, he would say Sha'ul was well into his sixties.

David closed the door behind him. He could not see the spear that Sha'ul held at his side beneath the blanket.

"Your servant is sorry to hear of my lord the king's poor health."

"Oh ... how can you feel so sorry when you have performed another wonderful military miracle?" the king asked.

"Your servant did nothing ... except trust in Yahweh." David took a seat near the bed and readied his instrument. "Would my lord the king like a song?"

"Oh, yes, play for me. Any old song will do. Something to calm my nerves."

Snake!

King Sha'ul gave a weak smile of approval as David began to pluck the strings.

"Yes ... that's it. Just what I need, my son. Keep playing like that."

***Betrayer*!**

Sha'ul's fingers tightened around the concealed weapon. He could see it all quite easily now. He could see the plot. The treason in David's heart was as clear as day.

Backstabber!

David sang words of prayer and healing, of peace and rest.

Liar!

David closed his eyes as he played.

Your foolish charms will not work on me!

Sha'ul swung the spear out from under the blanket and leaped out of the bed. David opened his eyes. The spear flung forward from the king's hand. The tip brushed David's clothing as he dodged the attack at the last possible instant. The spear stuck into the wall. Sha'ul grunted and tried to pull the spear free but could not.

David escaped from the room, slamming the door behind him. Panting, he looked around. The hall was empty: no guards, no servants. Clutching his kinnor,

David took the opportunity and slunk away, seeking to make a hasty exit from the fortress, even as Sha'ul began to cry out in a loud voice from behind him, "You're a dead man! You're a dead man!"

Sha'ul's attendants found the king in a state of bitter vehemence and did their best to comfort him. He would not be comforted. What he wanted was unmistakable.

"Tell this to no one else. Send men from my personal guard to watch David's house. Have them lie in wait tonight and when he arises and tries to leave in the morning, kill him! Kill him before he takes a single step from his front door."

Mikhal embraced David as he entered their home, securing the door behind him. He was frazzled, breathing heavily, upset ... even tearful. Mikhal had never seen her husband like this.

"What is it? What's wrong?" she asked.

"I ... it's hard to say. Your father is angry with me."

"What did you do?"

"Nothing! I did nothing. Your father is not well. He is very angry with me for no cause. Oh, hold me, my love."

David hugged Mikhal tightly and buried his face against the crook of her slender neck. She felt his cool tears dampen her shoulder.

"It'll be okay. Don't cry. Please don't cry, my husband."

When they had married, Mikhal hadn't known that David was as emotional as he was. She had not experienced that side of him, except regarding his love for her. She relished his romantic nature ... but crying was different. She had never seen her father cry. Nor Avner. Nor any of the other men of war who stayed in the royal fortress.

Such displays made her uncomfortable. Still, she loved him. He was her husband. Her adored one. His distress was her distress.

"Tell me what's going on, I beg you," she urged.

"Your father believes things about me that are not true. He thinks me his enemy. And I am not! His heart is under bondage and tormented. He has attempted to kill me this very night."

Mikhal put her hand to her mouth.

"Yes," David continued. "I'm telling you the truth, and this isn't the first time he has sought my life."

Mikhal had to sit down. This was too much for her.

David reached out to comfort her. She stiffened at his touch, then slowly relaxed. There were so many different thoughts running through her head.

"What will you do?" she eventually asked, breaking the anxious silence.

"I don't know. This night was different. I don't know what is going to happen ... I thought we had resolved ... I ... I just don't know."

In the ensuing stillness, a conspicuous scraping noise was heard outside. Mikhal and David froze. There was something alien about that sound, something that made it stand out. Mikhal got up and extinguished the lamps, going to the window that overlooked the street.

Without moving the curtain, she peered out through the open sliver onto the city below. Giv'ah was quiet at this hour of the night and the moon bathed the paved streets in pale blue light. She thought she saw something.

In the alleyway across from their house, there was a bulge in the darkness, an extra shape in the shadow where there should not be one. She beckoned David over, and he too scanned the surroundings with the vigilance of a trained hunter. There were low shuffling noises coming from another section of the street, then a muffled cough, then all was quiet again.

David backed away from the window and led Mikhal into their bedroom.

"Who are they? Have they come for you?" Mikhal whispered.

David sat on the bed and held his head in his hands.

"They are your father's men ... his personal guard." David's mind wheeled. "Assassins."

"No! No! He can't do this!"

"They are waiting for something. They would have come after me already if that was their intention ... something restrains them."

David fell to his knees and began to cry out in prayer.

"Deliver me, O my God. Deliver me from my enemies. Save me from men of bloodshed! They are setting an ambush for me. Fierce men seek to take my life ... not for any sin or transgression of mine. Save me, Yahweh!"

David and Mikhal waited, holding each other and straining to listen to the sounds in the night. The assassins had not made a move, yet the shadowy figure in the alley remained. How many of them were out there?

"David, if you do not escape with your life tonight, you'll be dead by the morning."

"I believe you're right."

"You need to leave Giv'ah. Now!"

"Without you? How can I? You are my beloved wife, my other half. Where would I possibly go?"

"Just get out of the city! Get to safety! If what you say is true, my father's men won't stop. They'll come after you.

I will do what I can to stall them. If anything happens to you, what shall I become? I can't let it happen!"

David kissed her.

"Dearest, I don't know when I'll see you again, but I will put my trust in Yahweh. Contact Y'honatan. He will make sure you have everything you need until I can return."

David began moving about the house and gathering his belongings, wanting to strap on his armor and his weapons. Mikhal stopped him.

"There's no time, David. Take only what you need. Please hurry!"

David nodded. She was right. What was he going to do, fight against the king's men? Kill Yisra'elite soldiers? Become guilty to defend his innocence? His priority now was to survive, and he couldn't afford to be slowed down.

They went back to the bedroom, and David let a cord out the rear window. Mikhal secured the other end and helped David lower himself down the outside wall to the ground below. Mikhal drew up the cord. Her heart raced.

David crouched and surveyed his surroundings. Had he been too loud? He would have to creep behind the buildings, moving from shadow to shadow. He would have to make as little noise as possible and pray that he did not encounter any of Sha'ul's killers.

David stared up at his wife, and in the glimmer of the moonlight she could see the uncertainty in his eyes. He put on a brave face and blew her a final kiss.

The next morning there was heavy knocking on the door. It had been a sleepless night, and Mikhal's nerves were frayed. She found several stern, grizzled soldiers and an officer—seasoned and loyal men from Sha'ul's personal guard.

"David is wanted urgently on behalf of the king's business," the officer said.

"Please tell my father that my dear husband is sick," Mikhal said, brushing a loose strand of hair out of her face. "He cannot get out of bed. As you see, I've been up all night tending to him."

One of the men went to report this to the king while the others temporarily withdrew, keeping the house under observation. When the messenger returned, they again knocked.

"On order of the king, we are to come up and see David. Sick or not, we have urgent business with him!"

Mikhal protested as the men pushed past her forcibly, making their way through the home and heading for the bedroom. David did indeed appear to be in bed, sound asleep and bundled up. The first guard, a formidable dagger tucked in his belt, carefully approached the sleeping form and pulled back the covers.

He gave a startled grunt.

In the bed lay a large teraphim, one of the household idols Mikhal had been given by her Uncle Ner. It was covered with human clothes, some of David's garments, and upon its head sat a patch of goat's hair. The illusion was complete and now shattered.

"I think you'd better come with us ..." the officer said grimly to the young woman.

Soon she found herself before her father.

"Why have you deceived me?" Sha'ul bellowed. "Why did you let my enemy escape?"

Mikhal cringed. She had never before been the target of her father's anger. She hated it.

"You're my daughter! What has happened to this family that my own flesh and blood betrays me? How could you? David has been conspiring against this family from the very first day, and now he is in the wind! Do you care nothing for your future? Would you rather be disowned and cut off from this family? What would you have then?"

Mikhal began to cry. It was madness, but in a sense, her father's final point rang true. Her husband was gone. She was alone. She prayed he was not gone forever. She didn't understand this. But now he had a price on his head, and she had no guarantees. Without her family, what did she have? She was a princess. She too had to survive.

"Father, I had to. I had to. He told me that he'd kill me if I didn't let him go ... if I didn't lie for him and help him get away. I had no choice."

"Where is he going? Did he say? Is he running back to his family in Beit-Lechem?"

"I don't know, I swear. He told me nothing!"

—XXVIII—

Shemu'el found David huddled outside his front door in Ramatayim. He was exhausted, hungry, thirsty, and afraid.

"I didn't know where else to go," David said weakly.

Shemu'el felt great sympathy for the pathetic figure and took him inside. The old man's servants brought water and bread for the weary guest, and they sat in silence while David ate ravenously.

When he finished, David started to explain all that had happened to him and his narrow escapes from the hand of the king. Shemu'el sat quietly and listened while David related his experiences.

"Ah," Shemu'el replied simply.

"Does it not surprise you?"

"Very little that man could do would surprise me. It seems he harbors an unnatural hatred against you, no less the wicked spirit that plagues him. He is jealous of you. He hates what you stand for. He sees how Yahweh is with you while, at the same time, Yahweh has deserted him. Tell me, has he officially declared you to be an enemy of the kingdom?"

"No. Not yet. He sends his own men against me by stealth."

"And you believed he would hunt for you among your relatives?"

"Of course. Beit-Lechem would be the first place to look."

"But why come here? I do not believe you will be any safer in Ramatayim. Sha'ul's reach is long, and his eyes and ears are everywhere. He will inevitably track you here."

"Because I need your help. I need to know what I am supposed to do. It may only be a matter of time before the whole army is after me."

Shemu'el nodded gravely.

"Then we must remove at once and go to Naioth."

"What's that?"

"It is my prophetic school. It is in a secluded place, and my students live there. Perhaps we can shelter you there ... for now."

David was given a bed in a modest room shared with one of the students at Naioth. He adopted the plain dress of the others and sought to blend in, observing the routines that took place each day in the institution: shared meals of simple food, three daily sessions of prayer at regular intervals, musical worship tending to the ecstatic, careful reading and discussion of the Law, and so on.

When the seer was not preoccupied with overseeing the instruction and daily activities of the school, he met with David privately.

"I need you to make sense of this for me," David pleaded during one such meeting, feeling particularly distraught about his circumstances.

"Go on."

"In my father's house, years ago, you anointed my head with oil. You spoke over me then a word that Yahweh had chosen me to be a king. I believed that, and ... I believe it now. Never have I spoken of this to anyone, not even my own wife. I certainly have not sought to make it happen by my own power. I put my trust in Yahweh, believing His ability to make His word come to pass. And I have been faithful and loyal to the king already in place, Yahweh's anointed. I have not raised my hand against him in any way, Yahweh be the judge."

"Yes."

"And now am I to be a fugitive in the land when I have committed no crime? I don't understand it. How is this God's plan?"

Shemu'el sat in thoughtful silence for a full minute, eyes shut, hands clasped together in his lap. His posture was so relaxed that David began to wonder if the old man had drifted off to sleep. But then, he spoke.

"Have you not heard what happened when Yahweh spoke to Avraham and told him he would have a son? I tell you that twenty-five years passed before this word was fulfilled and Yitz'chak was born. Not only that, but Yahweh tested Avraham's obedience by asking him to sacrifice this child of promise, only to provide a substitute in his place when the time was right. Or do you not know that our people spent four hundred years in bondage in Egypt, although Yahweh had promised Yisra'el a hope and a future in this land? And have you not read that the heart of Pharaoh was hardened after Yahweh sent Moshe to him, and Pharaoh ordered that the burdens upon Yisra'el be increased? And did not Yisra'el, despite having come at last to the land promised to them, have to take possession of it battle by battle? Tell me then, did Yahweh fulfill or not fulfill His purposes?"

David was humbled. He had no argument.

"He fulfilled them. Praise be to Yahweh, He is faithful."

"Yes, that is the only correct response. David, I perceive you have a good heart, you trust in Yahweh, you pray and worship in sincerity, but you have further yet to go."

"What do you mean?"

"The Spirit of Yahweh has been upon you mightily, but have you actually met Him? Have you had a supernatural encounter ... a true entering into the presence of the Living God? A dialogue with your Maker?"

"A dialogue? I ... I'm not sure."

"Then you have further yet to go. I would like for you to come and join in the worship tonight with the others. I have heard that you are quite talented with a kinnor."

"You want me to become one of the Shouters?"

"I want you to learn what it means to be a prophet. Yahweh formed you, He purposed you, and He numbered your days before you had lived even one of them. Now you need to be led by Him. If you are to be king, you need to be the best king you can be. You need to be instructed and trained by Yahweh Himself. If you have to shout, then shout; if you have to sing, then sing; if you have to dance, then dance. Do not hold anything back in your pursuit of Him!"

David remained at Naioth. He decided to learn all he could. He wanted to quiet his spirit, to let go of all his ambitions, and to meditate solely on Yahweh. Perhaps his days of being a soldier and a hero were over. He wanted to learn the Law backward and forward. He wanted to spend his days composing songs of worship. He began to understand how the priesthood had fallen under the control of the House of Sha'ul, not daring to speak out for what was right, but being subservient to the king's rule. It was the Nevi'im who stood in the gap, seeking to preserve the ways of Yahweh in the face of a declining culture. David wanted to abide in this spiritually nurturing environment indefinitely, waiting for Yahweh's direction for what step he should take next.

These idealistic plans were cut short when a band of armed men were spotted on the path to Naioth. One of the students ran and told Gad, who told Shemu'el, who told David.

"It's Sha'ul's men. They're coming to kill me," David said, rushing to ready himself for a hasty departure. The dreaded moment had arrived. The peace was shattered. "Somehow he's heard that I'm here."

"You are under our protection," Shemu'el assured him.

"I can't let harm befall any of you on account of me. I have to get away from here!"

"No. Stay hidden in your room. We'll meet these men with the power of Yahweh."

"But—"

"Now is the time to pray, not run away."

All of the students gathered outside and formed a human barricade at the edge of Naioth. The musicians among them started playing, and Shemu'el led the diverse group of men in worship.

As the king's men approached, weapons ready, the students began to pray loudly, their cries for help intermingling with the hymns of praise in a crescendo. As they continued they felt the Spirit of Yahweh descend upon them, illuminating their inmost being with holy fire.

The Presence was palpable. Sha'ul's men could not escape the power. One by one they dropped their weapons to the ground and stood, transfixed by the warm rush of the Spirit. Shemu'el pressed his prophets on. These villains would not take David. The strength of man would not prevail over the glory of God!

The students spoke prophetic words under the divine inspiration. Words about the future. Words about David and a kingdom to come. Overwhelmed, Sha'ul's men began to prophesy as well, uttering words not of their own making and babbling in unknown tongues.

Hours later they sat resting on the ground, humbled and dazed. The students graciously tended to their needs.

Sha'ul and a troop of his most loyal, elite guards arrived at the well of Sekhu. These men were trained warriors, mostly Binyaminites, who would follow orders without question.

Three times Sha'ul had sent contingents to apprehend David, and three times his men had failed in their one task. In fact, only one man out of all he sent had returned, and the report he gave made Sha'ul's heart sink. If he needed something done right, he had to do it himself. Apparently these incompetent men could not be trusted to do it alone.

Sha'ul himself would come and see to it. No so-called prophets would stand in his way. Not even the traitorous seer, who had shown his true colors by harboring the fugitive. The conspirators were in cahoots against his rightful kingship. Sha'ul had been clearly informed, "David is with Shemu'el." There would be a price to pay for giving asylum to the king's enemy.

Sha'ul's men interrogated the locals who were congregating at the busy well.

"Where are David and Shemu'el?"

One bystander knew the answer and readily gave it. They were both at Naioth, the prophets' dormitory near Ramatayim. They were there right now.

The bystander was pressed into service to lead them to the school straight away. There would be no escape this time.

As they rounded the hill on the narrow path, Sha'ul heard the growing sounds of men's voices up ahead. It sounded almost like singing. What was this? They pushed onward, drawing their weapons.

Little by little, Sha'ul began to feel a strange sensation in his chest. It grew stronger as they came closer to Naioth. Within him, a distant memory began to stir ... something he once knew but had forgotten, something he had not felt since half a lifetime ago. Warmth began to spread through his upper body, and he felt a lightness to his being, even as he was being drawn inevitably forward to Naioth.

There they were, the company of Nevi'im and Nevi'im-in-training, and the seer himself! They were worshiping boisterously, and the movement of the Spirit was strong upon them.

Sha'ul recognized faces in the crowd. His men! Some of his very own had joined these Shouters. They were no longer dressed as soldiers but wore the plain garments of the others, lost in the raptures of the divine. The men on either side of him began to lay their weapons down, they too caught under the power. Sha'ul knew he was caught as well, and he couldn't stop it. The Presence and glory had hold of him. The less he fought against it, the less he was concerned by it. This sensation was pure life, bubbling up from his heart. What wonderful clarity he felt! What freedom and abandon! It had been so long.

Sha'ul removed his armor as he walked. He dropped his sword. His lips began to move, and he was soon uttering inspired words along with the rest of them. Shemu'el, without ceasing his praying, looked straight at the approaching king.

Sha'ul stripped down to his undergarments and fell to the ground in front of Shemu'el. He couldn't help himself as songs and words formed in his mouth. He spoke of the future, of things to come. He spoke of the throne passing from him, and how the entire earth would one day be blessed through the line of David. Words he would never dare utter in normal life spilled out, and he was helpless to stop.

Hours later, only Sha'ul and Shemu'el remained outside. The seer sat on the ground, meditating and quietly watching over the king, who lay naked and prostrate in the dirt, prophesying all day and all through the night without rest.

−XXIX−

While Sha'ul lay in his trance, David disguised himself and fled from Naioth back to Giv'ah. He, at last, reached the royal fortress and threw himself before the mercy of Y'honatan, who was holding court in his father's absence.

"Prince! Tell me, what have I done? What is my sin? Why is your father seeking to kill me?" David pleaded on his knees.

"What?" Y'honatan asked, alarmed.

He had no idea why or where David had disappeared these past days, and now his young friend had reappeared in such a panicked state. The prince ordered everyone out of the throne room.

"I tell you, you can't be in danger! My father swore before you and me that he would not harm you, and now you say he is after your life?"

"It is the truth, my prince!"

"Stand up. Don't grovel before me. This is madness."

David stood and faced Y'honatan, who gripped him by the shoulders.

"Your father has been out hunting me. It is by the grace of Yahweh that I made it back here alive to see you."

Y'honatan shook his head in bewilderment.

"My father does nothing great or small without disclosing it to me first. I have heard nothing of this. Why should he hide such a thing from me? No ... no, it can't be. Didn't I warn you when my father believed that evil rumor about you? But that's long settled—a misunderstanding. Yahweh forbid if he means to harm you now!"

"Your father knows well that I have found favor with you," David responded. "He knows if he informs you of his true intentions against me, you will oppose it. I tell you, as Yahweh lives and as your own soul lives, there is but a step between me and death."

There was no guile, no confusion in the younger man's eyes. Y'honatan started to tremble ever so slightly as the implications began to sink in.

"Whatever you say, I will do."

"The new moon and the Festival of Trumpets start tomorrow. Everybody will expect me to be in attendance, sitting at the king's table. But I will go and hide myself in the field until the third night. If your father shows any concern about my absence, say this to him: 'David earnestly asked leave of me to run to Beit-Lechem, because of the yearly sacrifice there for his whole family.' If your father says this is good, then I will be safe, but if your father is very angry, you will know that he means to kill me."

Y'honatan chewed on his lower lip.

"Now please, O Prince, show kindness to your servant," David continued. "Remember the covenant you made with me before Yahweh. If there is any guilt in me, any guilt whatsoever, you should just kill me yourself. Why bother handing me over to your father?"

Y'honatan was aghast.

"Never! If I had even the smallest idea that my father meant you harm, would I not tell you?"

"Please Y'honatan, my life is in your hand. Will you help me?"

Y'honatan paused just then, straining to listen for any suspicious noises. Might any of his father's men be trying to eavesdrop? If what David was saying was true, this would not be a safe place to talk.

"Let's go out to the field."

Careful not to be followed, the two men exited the fortress through a back passage and made their way outside the city to the familiar meeting ground near the Stone of the Way.

"I will do as you ask, my friend," the prince continued, feeling secure in this location. "Yahweh, the God of Yisra'el, be witness! Around this time tomorrow, or at least by the end of the feast, once I have learned what is in my father's heart, I will surely make it known to you. If my father is pleased with you, I will send to you and make it known, or if he intends harm against you, may Yahweh do the same and more to me if I do not tell you everything and send you away to safety!"

David dropped his gaze.

"Y'honatan ... there is something I must confess to you."

Y'honatan looked at him quizzically. Confess? What could he mean?

"Years ago, the man of Yahweh, Shemu'el, came to my father's house in Beit-Lechem. He said he was sent by Yahweh to anoint the future king of Yisra'el ... and ... on that day he anointed my head with oil ... and blessed me. I have never sought to claim this for myself, nor have I done or plotted any evil against our king, yourself, or your family. I am your servant and the servant of your father. I hope you can believe me. I just felt that ... you deserved to hear it. I never knew how or even if to bring it up before."

Y'honatan slowly began to nod his head.

"My brother ... I knew in my heart that the hand of Yahweh was too strong upon you not to have some greater purpose. You have been steadfast and honorable in every way. I could not wish better of my own sons than for them to grow up to be like you."

Y'honatan sighed.

"If this kingdom is meant to change hands, I ... I know you'll be a good king—no, a great king. I pray that Yahweh may be with you as He has been with my father. The oath I made with you before our God stands. If I am still alive to see this come to pass, I ask that you show me the loving kindness of Yahweh, that I may not die. Do this one kindness for me—do not cut off your love from my house forever, not even when Yahweh cuts off every one of the enemies of David from the face of the earth. I again vow before Yahweh my commitment to you; He is witness of the agreement between us forever. May Yahweh take vengeance on the enemies of David, His anointed. Surely, I shall not be one of them."

The prince felt his throat constrict with emotion.

"I love you as I love my own life."

The annual festival was at hand, it being the beginning of Tishri, the seventh month, and the start of autumn. Giv'ah of Sha'ul buzzed and bustled with preparations and excitement for the multi-day celebration, even as buying and selling were forbidden by divine edict. Shofars were blown over the instituted peace offerings by the Levitical priests, and the entire city was filled with the majestic trumpeting of the rams' horns.

At the first day's meal, Y'honatan took his customary seat at the king's table, across from his father. Sha'ul sat, and Avner was at his side. David's seat was empty. Y'honatan acted like nothing was amiss, casually eating a pomegranate, waiting to see what his father's response might be. His father remained quiet on the matter, seeming to pay more attention to the festival itself.

Inside, Sha'ul contemplated the meaning of David's absence. Surely it was not in the young man's character to miss a religious feast. He would be expected by everyone to be at his usual place. It was not public that David had become the king's enemy, and no report indicated that David had told any of his fellow soldiers or relatives. Sha'ul could not fully reconcile the events that had transpired at Naioth, but he had never laid eyes on David at that place.

No, David had a wife. David had a rank. David would not disrespect his king and country by not attending this ceremony; he would at least have to save face. Sha'ul knew that Mikhal had received no word from David. So where was he? The only explanation that Sha'ul could determine was that David had become ceremonially unclean, perhaps by touching a dead body, or through some sexual occurrence. Yes, that had to be it. David had not yet completed the purification ritual required for participating in this holy feast. He would remain unclean until the evening. It would be just like him to uphold the letter of the Law. Best to wait and see. Nothing would hold him back from seeing to the divine ordinance of the feast tomorrow.

But the next day David was still absent. This was troubling. And Y'honatan made no mention or notice at all of the empty seat. Did that mean he knew something about where his companion might be? As they sat waiting for the food to be served, Sha'ul got his eldest son's attention.

"Why hasn't that son of Yishai come to the meal, either yesterday or today?"

"Oh. David earnestly asked leave of me to go to Beit-Lechem. He said, 'Please let me go since our family has a yearly sacrifice in the city and my brother demands that I have to be there. So if I have found favor in your sight, let me go and see my brothers.' So I granted him to leave. That's why he isn't here."

King Sha'ul erupted, slamming his fists on the table and knocking over cups of wine.

"You son of a whore! Are you against me too!? Have you chosen to side with the son of Yishai?"

Y'honatan leaped to his feet, backing away from his father's sudden wrath.

"Surely you are not my son! How else can you shame yourself and your family like this? Don't you understand?" Sha'ul raged. "As long as the son of Yishai lives on this earth, you will never be established. You will never be king. You would tear down the House of Sha'ul and replace our royal line with that scheming rival! Now where are you hiding him? Bring him to me so he may die!"

"Why father? What has he done to deserve death?"

Sha'ul screamed and ripped a spear from the hands of a nearby guard. He threw the spear forcefully at Y'honatan, who moved out of the way and caught the weapon in midair. Avner too had vacated his seat, and he watched the confrontation with astonished horror.

Y'honatan glared at his father, furious. Taking the spear, he broke the shaft over his knee and let the pieces drop to the floor. He turned to leave, seething.

"That's right. Get out of here! I don't want to see your face at my table!"

After the sun had risen the next day, Y'honatan went out into the field with a young servant and his bow and quiver of arrows. He had not eaten a thing since the day before. He had no appetite.

"Look over there," Y'honatan said to the servant, pointing. "That is the spot I am aiming for, you see? Now run, boy; retrieve the arrows I shoot."

Eagerly, the boy ran into the field while Y'honatan pulled the bowstring back and released, sending a volley over the boy's head and beyond the mark he had designated. When the servant reached the spot, he searched in vain for the arrow.

"Keep going. Isn't the arrow beyond you?" Y'honatan called loudly, using the coded signal he had agreed upon with David. It meant bad news. "Hurry! Be quick! Don't stay!"

The servant found the arrow and raced back to his master.

"Thank you, boy," the prince said. "You know what? I don't feel like target practice anymore. Carry these back to the fortress."

The servant took the weapons and returned to Giv'ah without comment while Y'honatan stood alone in the field, unable to hide his dejection. David emerged from behind the large heap of stones.

David approached and bowed down before the prince three times with his face to the ground. Y'honatan knew David was taking a risk by showing himself. He wished his companion had just fled as instructed, and yet, at the same time, Y'honatan was glad he had not.

The two friends embraced and kissed one another on the face. Y'honatan wept. David wept harder. They both knew where things stood. They both understood the danger David was in.

"David, my brother, you were right. You are not safe here. My father will kill you," Y'honatan managed to say. "I can't protect you, but I shall never harm you. We have sworn to each other in the name of Yahweh, saying He will be between you and me, and between my descendants and your descendants forever. Now save yourself. Run. Get out of here."

David hugged him even more tightly, his streaming tears staining Y'honatan's tunic. David felt as if he was losing everything and everyone.

"Where will you go?" Y'honatan asked between sobs. "Where will you go?"

—XXX—

David traveled alone, on foot, with only the clothes on his back. He had no money. He had no food. He had no armor. He had no sword.

He didn't know what his destination would be, only that he had to leave, had to get away. On order of the king, his life was forfeit. Kill, don't capture. Dead, not alive. It was only a matter of time before the entire military would be sent after him. There wasn't a village in the kingdom where he could hide.

David stayed off the roads and kept moving. Stopping to rest meant certain death. His only advantage was that he had the smallest fraction of a head start. But a head start to where?

He would have to leave Yisra'el. The thought sickened him. This was his home. This was the Promised Land. These were the chosen people. These were his friends and family. Where else to the ends of the earth could he find solace, find purpose?

If he were to leave or even to die, there was one final place he had to visit. It wasn't far. It was on the way to the unknown.

Nov, the city of priests.

Here was the Mishkan, the holy tabernacle that Sha'ul had decreed be relocated within the tribal lands of

Binyamin, only twelve miles from Giv'ah. Many Levites and their families called Nov home, including Achimelekh, who had succeeded his now deceased brother, Achiyah, as high priest. Here they carried on the rituals and traditions outlined in the Law, serving before Yahweh.

So, David's last act as a resident of Yisra'el would be this pilgrimage. To see the tabernacle one last time. To seek some word for his future. To offer a prayer. To worship Yahweh at the center of His religious observances, in the very Tent of Meeting where His glory had once regularly descended during the great exodus.

David covered his face and kept his head down as he approached the city. As he entered the house of God, watchful eyes were drawn to the famous hero. Among those watching was Do'eg the Edomi, an official of the House of Sha'ul, who was undergoing a purification ritual for a sexual sin. As David rose from prayer, their eyes met. David pretended not to notice the other man and carried on.

As different Levites began to discern the identity of the young man in their midst, they conferred together, and word reached the high priest, who had been overseeing the offering of the holy incense.

Achimelekh found the situation deeply disturbing. David, son-in-law of the king, the beloved hero of the people, the high-ranking military officer. What was he doing here so suddenly and unannounced? Why was he dressed in unkempt, plain clothes? Why was he alone? That was the biggest mystery of all. One of the most powerful men in the kingdom did not travel unaccompanied. It was unheard of.

Achimelekh's stomach tightened into a knot. This did not bode well. Was David here on some errand from the king? Had Achimelekh inadvertently done something to offend the House of Sha'ul? The high priest broke into a cold sweat thinking about it. He didn't trust the king. He had heard too many stories, seen too many unrighteous actions performed in his name. More than a few political enemies had been liquidated over the years, and the king had often made edicts that seemed contrary to the rules that governed the priesthood and guided religious life. Now here was, by all accounts, the king's right hand man, an experienced killer, showing up with no notice, with no witnesses.

Achimelekh went into a private chamber and paced, trying to think of anything he may have said or done recently that could be interpreted as dishonoring the House of Sha'ul. He startled when he heard his name called. Another priest was saying David was here and urgently wished an audience.

David was let in and left alone with the high priest.

"Achimelekh, thank you for seeing me," David said graciously.

"Y-yes. What brings you to Nov? W-why are you alone? Why is no one with you?"

David noticed the priest's trembling. Had word already spread that David had become an enemy of the kingdom? This was not going as he had hoped.

"I am on a secret mission, by order of the king," he lied. "I can speak to no one about the matter. Not even you. As for my men, there is a small but elite group waiting for me nearby, in a hidden place."

"I see ... I see ... And what can I do for you?"

"What sort of provisions do you have on hand? Something I can take to my men. Can you supply me with five loaves of bread, or whatever you have available?"

Achimelekh was caught off guard.

"I'm sorry, I don't have any ordinary bread on hand."

"No bread?" David asked, surprise and concern in his voice.

"Not right now. There is only ... well, there is only the holy, consecrated bread here."

The Bread of the Presence, unleavened cakes made with fine flour, set among other items on a golden table before Yahweh and replaced with fresh bread each Shabbat. The preparation was the responsibility of the K'hat clan. The week-old bread, once removed, was meant for consumption only by the priests.

"I suppose I can give it to you since you are on important business from Yahweh's anointed king. But I can only do this if your men have kept themselves pure, not being with women."

David nodded with deep seriousness.

"All my men and I abstain from women whenever we are on a mission, even the ordinary missions. Not just ourselves but our clothing and belongings are kept from uncleanness as a rule. How much more so on an assignment such as this!"

"Very well then."

Achimelekh gave him the consecrated bread, and David carefully wrapped the pieces in a bundle. These few loaves would have to sustain him on his journey. He turned to leave, but then abruptly stopped.

"One more thing ..."

"Yes?" Achimelekh asked uneasily.

"Do you have a spear or a sword here I can take? I brought neither my own sword nor any weapon because the king's matter was so urgent."

The high priest raised his eyebrows.

Corre"I'm sure there may be a few weapons to be found in the city, but not in the tabernacle," Achimelekh answered, then remembered something. "Well ... there is one sword ..."

"What sword?"

"The sword of Golyat the P'lishti, the man you killed in the Valley of Elah. I believe you dedicated the sword to Yahweh. It is here, kept as a monument. We have it wrapped in a cloth where we keep the sacred things. If you want it, take it. But we have no other weapons here."

David's eyes glinted. "There is none like it. Give it to me."

David took a moment to admire the large, curved, iron blade. It still had a sharp edge. It had been years since he had laid eyes on the sword, and with that came a flood of memories. But those memories would have to wait.

The young man tied a belt around his waist and secured the giant's scabbard at his side. He wrapped his head around with a long strip of cloth. He fastened his leather sandals. He secured the bundle of provisions on his back.

It was time to go. The man Do'eg had surely recognized him; that was unfortunate. It wouldn't be long before Do'eg was due back in the king's court. David's branding as an enemy of the kingdom would soon be known to all.

David felt as if a rope was tightening around his neck. Where could he go? Even disguising himself and going to the house of Yahweh had become a perilous exercise. So David ran, heading eastward, avoiding the roads and major footpaths.

Where could he go to escape the wrath of the king and his armies? Where could he hide? Where would be the last place on earth that Sha'ul would look for him?

ACT THREE

_____

BEYOND THE BORDERS

—XXXI—

Gat—a pillar of the P'lishtim Pentapolis. The city was immense. It towered three hundred feet above the coastal plain to the west and stood in defiance against the foothills of Y'hudah to the east. Perched on its high hill between precipices of white rock, it resembled nothing less than an enormous insect hive.

The interior of the walled city-state was as intricate as a woven tapestry and dense with history and culture. Architecture of Aegean origin lay beneath Kena'ani-influenced structures, with entire neighborhoods accented by Egyptian trends.

Grand, two-story meeting halls, supported by columns, sat next to elaborate temples of pagan worship. Government buildings abutted residential sectors, which sat adjacent to bustling marketplaces, which lay next to busy industrial zones. Men across the city labored long days, pressing grapes and olives, and the streets practically flowed with wine and oil. Some worked in breweries, others at dye vats, others at tanneries, others at forges.

A young man walked through the labyrinth of city avenues. His neck ached, and his muscles were sore from sleeping on the streets again last night. He passed a large open-air yard filled with grimy workers, toiling over pottery kilns that spewed acrid smoke as they mass produced new containers for storing wine.

He turned down a series of back alleys, trying to wind his way back to the marketplace. He stepped over a drunk passed out in a pool of his own vomit. Orphan children hounded after him until they realized he had nothing to offer. Down another alleyway, two prostitutes called halfheartedly for his business as he brushed past. The man was certain he was lost when suddenly he made a turn and found his destination.

The central markets were an assault on the senses: colorful fabrics, exotic foods, diverse goods, and strange dialects. Vendors hawked their wares as residents, travelers, refugees, soldiers, and animals crowded among the stalls, shops, and booths. Fortune-tellers mingled throughout, trawling for customers.

The young man entered a blacksmith's workshop, clearing his throat to announce his presence. The blacksmith plunged a piece of hot metal into water, and the room filled with hissing steam.

"You again?" the blacksmith asked, irritated.

"Just seeing if you have any work today."

"I already told you, I've got nothing for you!"

"I can do anything you need ... anything at all."

"What use could a blacksmith have with a Hebrew exile? You people know nothing about this kind of work! I couldn't afford to pay you anyway."

"Sir, you can pay me whatever you want ... you can pay me in bread, or give me something to drink. I'll do anything you need me to do."

"I need you to get out of here and let me work!"

"Of course. I'll come back tomorrow, just in case. Thank you."

The blacksmith sighed, removing the metal from the water and clanging it down dramatically on his workspace.

"Fine!" he grunted resignedly. "My son Ittai is late ... as usual. I don't know why I keep that lazy fool around."

The young man grinned in anticipation.

"I'll do anything you need me to do. I'm a good worker, reliable, strong..."

"Whatever. I have one task and one task only that I maybe could use you for, then I don't want to see your face hanging around here again! Is that clear?"

"Of course, sir! What do you need me to do?"

"Go to Warati, the metal-worker, in the M'konah district. You know where that is, right?"

"Yes," the young man bluffed. He would have to ask around, but he didn't want to lose this opportunity.

"He has a package of copper ingots for me. Very heavy. If you bring those to me, I'll pay you a little something and give you some food."

"Thank you! I'll do it right now!"

"Not so fast. You'll need to take my seal along to prove that I sent you. And I'll need something of yours to make sure you don't run off with my package."

"I can leave my cloak with you—"

"No! Those ingots are worth more than many of your cloaks. You'll have to do better than that if you can. Otherwise, no deal."

The young man hesitated. "Well, I can leave this sword with you."

He opened his cloak and pulled the scabbard from his belt, placing the sword on the table. The blacksmith's interest was piqued.

"What have we here?"

The blacksmith walked over and wiped his hands on a cloth before picking up the weapon. He carefully unsheathed the sword and held it to the light, looking down the edge of the blade and feeling the balance in his hands.

"This is some sword!" he marveled to himself; then he asked, "Where did you get this?"

"I won it in a contest. Where it originally comes from, I do not know."

The blacksmith frowned as he inspected the craftsmanship.

"This is a fine weapon. I recognize the work; no doubt it is P'lishtim. A very skilled hand made this sword. A custom job. And I would wager my forge that this is meteoric iron."

"Meteoric?"

"A star that fell to earth. Some of the best iron blades are made from such materials. You said you won this in a contest?"

"That's right. You could say it was a wrestling match of sorts."

"It will do. Bring me my copper and you'll get your sword back."

The young man completed the assignment, returning with the package to find the blacksmith and his son arguing. The dispute put on hold, the blacksmith shared a morsel with the young man and put a third of a shekel's weight of silver in his hand. The son, Ittai, recommended a cheap inn where the young man could lodge for the night and showed him the way.

The young man was discomfited to discover that the lodging place was next door to a brothel, but after having a mug of barley beer with the blacksmith's son in the inn, he retired to his room, having paid for two nights in advance with the last of his money. He had told Ittai that his primary experience had been as a shepherd, but that he also was a musician. Ittai couldn't do much with that, but said that if the young man came by the workshop the next day, he might have some leads for other work in the area. Jobs were scarce, but Hebrew expatriates were viewed as cheap, exploitable labor.

The young man took off his sword and outer garments and arranged them in a pile beside the tiny bed. He noticed an occult charm in the shape of an eye hanging on the wall, apparently meant to ward off misfortune. He hid it in the cupboard. The bed was uncomfortable, the city was cacophonous, but it was the anxiety roiling within his breast that kept the young man from sound sleep.

The next morning, he arose groggily and tore off a piece of bread from his rationed provisions. He then ventured out into the chaotic melting pot of Gat once more.

Walking down a street, the young man passed by a few P'lishtim soldiers on patrol. One of the soldiers stared at him as he went by. There was a barked order from behind him in a dialect the young man didn't understand. He hesitated for a fraction of a second and then kept walking, calmly. Maybe it had nothing to do with him. Maybe he could just ignore it.

"Stop!" came the order again, this time in his own tongue.

The young man froze in his tracks, and the soldiers quickly surrounded him. The first soldier peered at his face intently while another held him firmly by the arm. The young man adopted a confused, offended expression.

"No ... no ... it can't be," the first soldier said, shaking his head in amused disbelief. He bared his teeth in a cruel grin. "Take him!"

The young man protested as he was hauled off into a large royal compound in the center of the city. He was taken past the prison and the army barracks and thrown into a holding cell adjacent to what appeared to be the palace. This must have been an office of the palace guardsmen.

Sitting on the filthy floor of his cell in isolation while a soldier stood guard outside, he prayed, "Be merciful to me, Yahweh! My enemies plot against me, eager to take my life. You have taken account of my wanderings. You have collected my tears in Your bottle. O, Yahweh, are not my troubles recorded in Your book? When I am afraid, help me to put my trust in You, whose word I praise. Yes, what can man do to me?"

There was a loud commotion as somebody arrived and began debating hotly with the soldiers. The young man strained to listen. He could decipher bits and pieces of their dialect. The situation became clear.

"I tell you this is David! This is the famous Hebrew!"

"You're delusional!"

"I recognize him. I tell you it is David! I'd stake my life on it."

"Here? In Gat?"

"This is the one the Hebrews sing songs about: Sha'ul has killed his thousands, and David tens of thousands."

The young man's blood ran cold.

The official, or whoever he was, came in and looked at the figure crouching in the cell. Could it be? The soldier kept swearing that the Hebrew captive was indeed the famed David, a mortal enemy of the P'lishtim.

"There is a resemblance, from how I've heard the man described. I'll inform King Akhish. He'll want to see this," the official said.

David was stripped and searched for weapons. Was he a spy or assassin? The P'lishtim would take no chances.

He was dragged into the palace and locked in an empty, windowless room on the main floor. A dozen or more armed men stood guard outside.

What a prize. What a ransom. What a valuable prisoner. What a political boon. Somewhere in the city there still stood a statue in memory of Golyat, the mighty hero of Gat. The attendants nearly tripped over themselves in bringing the news to the young King Akhish, who had taken over rulership from his father, Ma'okh.

The P'lishtim lord roused himself and came down with a retinue of attendants and even more armed men to examine this Hebrew specimen. Standing at the ready, they opened the door. They were unprepared for what they found.

Inside, the disheveled man hunched against the wall, scrawling nonsensical doodles in the plaster with a small rock. The door itself was similarly marked with vandalistic scribbling.

"You!" a soldier yelled, pointing a spear at him.

The man turned and looked with a slack-jawed expression of idiocy on his face. He showed no regard for the weapon or the man holding it. His eyes rolled about in his head, crossing and uncrossing as he let out a guffaw.

"Stop that! Stand up!" the soldier screamed. Two others ran in and dragged the man to his feet.

King Akhish looked at his attendants skeptically.

"You say this is the famous warrior, the son-in-law of King Sha'ul?"

"Speak! You are David, the Hebrew commander! Confess!" the official ordered, slapping the young man across the face.

The captive laughed, head lolling, tottering unsteadily.

"I'm David! King of the Hebrews! Bow before me! I can beat you all with my hands tied behind my back!" he said, laughing hysterically while spittle ran out of his mouth and down his beard. "I'm David! King of the Hebrews! How did you get into my castle? Where is my royal fishing boat?"

The official and the first soldier both reddened with anger and embarrassment. King Akhish turned on his attendants with vehemence.

"Look at this man! He is insane! And you thought it wise to bring this man to me?"

The attendants appeared nervous. Some members of Akhish's own family suffered from madness; it was a sensitive subject, to say the least. Their hearts sank as they began to realize the full implications of the situation they were in.

"Tell me! Do I lack madmen that you had to bring this one into my presence, into my own house? Do you find it amusing to have this Hebrew, cursed in his mind by the gods, to rave against me?" Akhish asked with a mixture of disgust and pity. "Get him out of here!"

David was thrown outside the city gates and told to stay away. To his surprise, Ittai, the blacksmith's son, met him outside the city an hour later with his sword and bundle of remaining provisions. Ittai related that he had felt strangely inspired to search for the young man at the inn and had learned, in a roundabout way, what had happened. Ittai did not know David's true identity but explained that he was secretly a believer in the Hebrew God and, therefore, sympathetic. As David departed, Ittai wished the young man better luck at his next destination.

—XXXII—

David wandered through Y'hudah's western foothills. He was in a remote no man's land between the warring nations, and he dare not travel any farther to the east or west. Where can one go when everyone is against him? He felt parched, dehydrated, and if he didn't find water soon, he might collapse. But he knew what he was looking for.

In the vicinity of 'Adulam, a few miles south of the Valley of Elah, were a series of caverns embedded in some out-of-the-way limestone cliffs. David begged Yahweh to direct his steps to this place he had seen only once before, that he might find some refuge within the rock's shadowy, hollow interiors.

The sun beat down mercilessly. David's mind began to drift—thoughts of his family, thoughts of his friends. Thoughts of Y'honatan. Thoughts of his wife. Would he ever again feel her touch?

Exhausted, he forced himself to walk on. Step-by-step. One foot in front of the other. The heat was suffocating him.

And then there it was. The shrub-speckled crevice dividing the limestone heights. And, praise Yahweh, he could just barely detect the white turbulence of the smallest of waterfalls, a trickling stream running down between the rocks.

David stripped off his head wrap and tunic, casting them aside with his few remaining belongings. He plunged his head under the flow of water, spattering the dust and dirt off his face and throat, rinsing grainy pebbles out of his hair. He gasped at the shock, then parted his chapped lips and drank greedily. Water had never tasted so good.

Once quenched he crawled into the largest cavern he could find and collapsed in its shade. He checked his bundle; two pieces of the consecrated bread remained. They were hard, stale. He broke off a corner and gnawed on it until he fell asleep with his back against the rock wall.

David sat in the mouth of the cave in meditative silence, watching the outstretched land from his vantage point. He contemplated the calm of a world without man's busyness and striving. Yet life did go on. Across the expanse, a bird of prey swooped down to pluck a rodent off the ground with its talons. Some time later, a deer wandered past in the near distance.

Later still came the sound of horses' hooves, unmistakable in the stillness. Two riders came into view. They were soldiers of Yisra'el by the look of them. And they were approaching, riding fast in the direction of the caves.

David tensed and withdrew, watching from the shadows. The soldiers rode up. They came as far as the trickling waterfall until the terrain blocked their horses. One of the soldiers murmured something and dismounted, leaving the other to watch his horse as the first man explored further, climbing over the rocks and shrubs as he ascended beyond the stream, searching.

Then David saw the soldier's face. He couldn't believe his eyes.

"Yashov'am!" David called, stepping into the sunlight. His words echoed loudly, and the soldier looked up in astonishment.

"David! It really is David!" the man shouted with joy. He turned and called to his companion, "It's him! It's David! We found him!"

David climbed down and clasped hands with Yashov'am. David peered over the ledge to try and determine the other man's identity.

"It's El'azar," Yashov'am said.

David led the men into a large, airy chamber where sunlight filtered in through various cracks and crevices. David offered to share his remaining stale bread with his companions. They brought in their own limited supplies and made a meager meal out of it, discussing everything that had taken place.

"I remembered that you said this place would make a great hideout. After you weren't found anywhere else, I thought it wouldn't hurt to check," Yashov'am explained.

"How will you explain your absence?" David asked in concern.

"I can't speak for El'azar, but I won't explain it. I'm done."

"Yashov'am!"

"After we heard what Sha'ul did to you? I couldn't stand it. That's just wrong! It's idiotic! He's a coward and a fool, no? I'm with you now, Commander."

"And what about you?" David asked El'azar.

"Yahweh is with you. I know it. I've seen it with my own eyes. That day in the field ... I owe you my life."

"I am thankful for your friendship and your trust, both of you. But I can't let you do this. You can't desert. You'll be branded as traitors and hunted as I am hunted. You shouldn't have to suffer because of me."

"You don't get it, David. Who else would we follow?" Yashov'am retorted.

El'azar nodded in agreement.

David sighed, humbled.

"What about my family? Have you heard anything about them?"

"Your family, your brothers, your parents, your sisters … they were all interrogated harshly. But they didn't know anything, so Sha'ul left them alone—for now. Probably waiting to see if you'll try to contact them, use them as bait," Yashov'am said with disgust.

"And my wife?" David asked.

Yashov'am just shook his head and shrugged. The conversation lapsed into silence. David sat, staring off into space.

"One other thing …" Yashov'am said. He reached for his pack. "I brought this along just in case we did find you out here."

Yashov'am pulled out a kinnor, battered and weathered, but intact.

"I know it's not as nice as your old one, but I thought you could make use of it."

David received the instrument as one is handed an infant. Without another word he rose, taking the kinnor and walking to another section of the caverns. He sat on a stone and looked out on the open land, feeling the strings. He began to sing softly,

"I will bless Yahweh at all times,
His praise will always be in my mouth.
My soul makes its boast in Him,
Let the humble hear and rejoice.

"Oh, magnify Yahweh with me,
Let us exalt His name together.

"I sought Yahweh, and He answered me,
And delivered me from all my fears.
Those who look at Him are radiant,
Their faces will never be covered with shame.
This poor man cried, Yahweh heard him,
And saved him out of all his troubles.
The angel of Yahweh encamps around,
Those who fear Him, and He delivers.

"Oh, magnify Yahweh with me,
Let us exalt His name together.

"Oh, taste and see that Yahweh is good,
Blessed is the man who takes refuge in Him.
Oh, fear Yahweh, you His saints,
For those who fear Him lack nothing.
Young lions may grow weak and hungry,
But those who seek Yahweh lack no good thing.
Come O children, and listen to me,
I will teach you the fear of Yahweh.

"Oh, magnify Yahweh with me,
Let us exalt His name together.

"Whoever among you loves life
And desires to see many good days,
Keep your tongue from evil
And your lips from speaking lies.
Turn away from evil, and do good,
Seek peace and pursue it.

"The eyes of Yahweh are on the righteous,
And His ears are attentive to their cry.

The face of Yahweh is against evildoers,
To cut off their memory from the earth.
The righteous cry out, and He hears them,
He delivers them from all their troubles.

"Oh, magnify Yahweh with me,
Let us exalt His name together.

"Yahweh is close to the brokenhearted,
And saves those who are crushed in spirit.
A righteous man may have many troubles,
But Yahweh delivers him from them all.
He protects all of his bones,
Not a single one of them will be broken.

"Evil will slay the wicked.
The foes of righteousness will be condemned.
But Yahweh redeems His servants.
No one will be condemned who takes refuge in Him."

Word was sent covertly to Yishai. All his household, including David's brothers and their families, stole away from Beit-Lechem in the middle of the night. They traveled through to the dawn and arrived at the network of caves. Despite his brothers' years of loyal military service, they were now suspect and ostracized by their blood relation to the so-called traitor. David greeted them all with an embrace and a kiss.

The knowledge of the break between David and Sha'ul was now known throughout the kingdom, and others who were disgruntled or disillusioned with the House of Sha'ul began to seek out a new allegiance, tracking down whispered rumors and chasing phantoms until they too wound up in the wilderness embrace of 'Adulam. A steady stream of outcasts, refugees, exiles, fugitives, the distressed, the indebted, and the discontented threw in their lot and pledged loyalty to the hero of the people, all affirming that they had no portion left in Yisra'el under Sha'ul's reign.

A society of misfits formed in that hideout, totaling about four hundred men.

But David grew concerned. Women and children of all ages—his nephews and nieces and others too young to defend themselves—also had arrived. His parents were with him, and a few other aged men and relatives. This was no place for such people to live, but now David was responsible for what happened to them. If Sha'ul discovered their location, they would be nearly impossible to evacuate with any speed. And there was no doubt that Sha'ul's men were searching.

While David was pondering this dilemma one night, Yishai found his youngest son sitting by the fire and sat with him, speaking into the late hours. Yishai reminded David that his grandmother Rut, David's great-grandmother, was from Mo'av. They had a legitimate family connection to that foreign country, and perhaps one they could exploit. The Mo'avites were no friends of Sha'ul.

"Sha'ul, the king of Yisra'el, has declared me his mortal enemy. He has turned against me. He has tried to kill me. I have no inheritance in his kingdom. I, my family, and all these with me have fled from that country."

David and his men stood before the king of Mo'av. The small group had made contact after stealthily crossing

Y'hudah, the parched wilderness, and the Sea of Salt. They had waited under guard at a Mo'avite hold overlooking the eastern shore while the king and his men came to them from their capital further inland.

Now, this king looked David over and listened as a court translator worked to bypass the peculiarities of the differing, but not wholly dissimilar, dialects. The king weighed David's words. A thousand armed men could strike this Hebrew and his companions down in an instant if the king commanded it. But the king of Mo'av had heard some very interesting rumors about this David and what had befallen him. Very interesting rumors indeed.

"My great-grandmother Rut was a Mo'avitess. Mo'av blood runs in my family's veins. Strange as it may sound, we are kinsmen, however distant."

"And what is it that you want me to do for you?" the king asked, waiting for the translation.

"Please allow Rut's grandson, my father, and his household to find refuge here in your land. My brothers, their wives, their children, and the men who are with me, we wish to dwell in Mo'av in safety from the hand of Sha'ul until I know what my God will do for me."

The king of Mo'av sat silently for a time.

"Yisra'el has been an enemy for many years now. Sha'ul has been a most hated enemy," the king said. "Yet there is an old saying, 'The enemy of my enemy is my friend.' Yes, you and your families and your people may stay in this land. I will give you this stronghold in honor of your great-grandmother. You may not know this, but tradition has it that she was a relative of one of our kings of old, Eglon, a man treacherously assassinated by a Hebrew. If it is the same woman we are speaking of, our genealogies indicate this. Yes, I've had my wise men do a lot of research on you, David. You are a dangerous man. Yet I believe you will be an asset to me, and a loss for my enemy. So, I say to you, welcome."

So began the daunting task of relocating the nearly five hundred men, women, and children from the cave of 'Adulam in western Y'hudah to their new home in Mo'av. They traveled many miles in secretive, nerve-wracking stages until each one was safely across the border and rejoined with the man they had left everything behind to follow.

—XXXIII—

King Sha'ul sat under the tamarisk tree on the height outside Giv'ah, dressed for war and clutching his spear. His commanders and advisors stood around him, as did prominent elders and other allies primarily represented by tribesmen from Binyamin. Three of his older sons, Avinadav, Malkishua, and Eshba'al, stood beside their father as he brooded. Y'honatan was notably absent.

The traitor David had been spotted. Somewhere in the southeast, in the wilderness. He had been on the move. Not just David, but others with him. Fellow defectors and usurpers. A whole cabal. A nest of snakes. David's relatives had vanished from Beit-Lechem into thin air, no doubt hiding with that runt. Avner, commander over the entire army, was out coordinating the maddeningly ineffective efforts to locate the fugitive.

Sha'ul's voice was thick with malice as he spoke.

"I, your king, have brought prosperity and security to Binyamin. And to Yisra'el. I have made you all rich! I put your enemies under the sword! I raised you out of the dust to become what you are today," he growled. "I did! Me! Listen, you men of Binyamin, what of this son of Yishai? What can he do for you? Is he going to reward you with vineyards and fields? Is he able to make you commanders of hundreds and commanders of thousands? Huh? Is he?"

The audience tried their best to avoid the king's searing gaze. They looked at the ground or at their feet or stared off solemnly into space, shifting uncomfortably.

"Is that why you have all conspired against me?" Sha'ul yelled, berating his followers. "My own son, my firstborn son, makes a covenant with that son of Yishai, and not one of you tells me about it! None of you care that my son has stirred up my servant to lie in ambush against me!"

That deceiver had seduced the people all right. He tricked them expertly. He had peasants of Y'hudah eating out of the palm of his hand, singing his praises. They would see. Everybody would see David's true colors. Then they would sing a different tune.

"Now I hear that David is here ... or he is over there. Or maybe he has fled the country with a small army! Or maybe he is preparing to attack Giv'ah with the help of traitors within my own house! And not one of you worthless men will open your mouths!"

The embarrassed silence hung like a heavy fog. There was no right answer to give. Everybody wished somebody else would just say something, anything, to relieve the tension.

A man cleared his throat. Sha'ul's eyes darted up to catch Do'eg coming forward through the small crowd. Yes, if not a fellow Binyaminite, if not a Yisra'elite, perhaps this Edomi would have something of value to say.

"I saw the son of Yishai when I was at Nov."

Sha'ul's fingers tightened around the shaft of the spear.

"Go on," the monarch said.

"He came to the priest Achimelekh. The priest inquired of Yahweh for him, and gave him provisions, and even gave him the sword of Golyat, the P'lishti."

Sha'ul's eyes narrowed into impenetrable slits. He spoke to a nearby servant.

"Bring him to me. Go to Nov and bring Achimelekh. And the priests. Bring them too."

"Uh, which priests, my king?" the servant asked.

"All of them!"

Achimelekh, the high priest, and all eighty-four fellow priests of Nov, dressed in their priestly garments, stood before Sha'ul and his followers. Unsure of why they had been summoned, Achimelekh knew that whatever the reason, it couldn't be good.

"Listen here, son of Achituv," Sha'ul said, looking the high priest directly in the eyes.

"Yes, my lord. I am here," Achimelekh answered.

"Why have you conspired against me? You and the son of Yishai together. Why have you given him bread, and a sword, and inquired after God for him so that he has risen against me and lies in ambush against me this very day?"

The high priest felt panic rise in his throat.

"B-but ... my lord, who among all your servants is as faithful as David? He is the king's son-in-law ... c-captain over your bodyguard ... honored among your household! Is today the first time I have inquired after Yahweh for David, your trusted servant? No! I have inquired after Yahweh for him and other of your servants often. How would I have known that I was not to assist him? I heard nothing of a disagreement between you and him. Far be it from me to raise my hand against my king!"

Achimelekh felt his knees beginning to buckle. He could see the irrational fury and suspicion on Sha'ul's face, and it scared him. The priest clasped his hands together in front of him, begging.

"P-please! Do not let the king impute any of these accusations to his servant or to any of the household of my father. Your servant knows nothing at all about any of this affair."

Sha'ul grimaced.

"You shall surely die, Achimelekh! You and all your father's household!"

The king turned to his guards.

"Kill them! Kill the priests of Yahweh. They too have joined sides with David. They knew he was fleeing, but they did not tell me."

The priests cried out in horror. The guards balked, looking at each other unsurely, hands hesitating near their weapons.

"What are you waiting for? Kill them!" Sha'ul demanded.

"My lord?" the guard nearest the king asked, beads of sweat appearing on his forehead.

"Do it!"

None of the guards could, or would. Their swords remained sheathed. Their spears remained upright. They could not bring themselves to carry out this evil task.

"The priests ... the priests of Yahweh? I can't," the guard murmured to himself, his head spinning.

Sha'ul turned back to Do'eg, who stood watching.

"You do it! Strike them down!"

Do'eg looked at the king and steadied himself. He drew his sword and walked over to Achimelekh, who was begging for his life. Do'eg breathed heavily as he raised the weapon.

"Kill them all!" Sha'ul ordered.

Do'eg struck down the high priest, crimson blood splashing on the white linen ephod. The others wailed and tried to flee, but were surrounded on all sides by Sha'ul's men. At least one priest soiled himself in his terror. Do'eg struck another, and another, and another, until he had murdered all eighty-five men.

With dark, wild eyes and a bitter smile of bared teeth, Sha'ul watched the spectacle from where he sat.

"Now … go down to Nov. Sack the city. Every man, every woman, every child, every ox, every donkey, every sheep, I want you to put to the sword. Obliterate it."

David shivered and pulled his cloak tighter around him, waiting for the patrol to return to the stronghold. The temperature had plummeted, and the stone walls had been dusted with frost in the morning.

Mo'av was a strange land. Despite their sanctuary, David and his men had to remain vigilant for thieves and brigands in the country, as well as wild animals that could threaten the little ones. Patrols also were useful for gathering news and information, and to watch for any possible incursion from Sha'ul, the P'lishtim, or hired hands of either of his opponents. David was a wanted man, after all. A price was on his head.

The patrol should have been back hours ago.

David turned and looked down over his followers as they went about their day: talking among themselves, sharpening weapons, tending to animals and other tasks. Children ran back and forth on the grounds of the keep, playing tag or hide-and-seek. For David and his men, it had become a waiting game, a time of idle exile. And some strange fellows indeed had come to join them. David wondered at the motley group.

Two relatives had come from the woodland town of Kiryat-Ye'arim, which lay on the border between Binyamin and Y'hudah and was famed for being the resting place of the Ark. 'Ira, owing lots of money, had fled rather than face debtor's prison. His cousin, Garev, whose skin was marred with severe eczema, had followed him. Helev, an overweight but strong man from a village near Beit-Lechem said he had joined for the sheer adventure of it. Other Yisra'elite soldiers had deserted to David, but not many. Some tribesman of Y'hudah had come.

Nachash II, King of 'Amon, descendant of the same Nachash killed in the Battle of Yavesh-Gil'ad, sent a caravan of goods to David to show favor and support in their dispute with the House of Sha'ul. A man called Elifelet, a Ma'akhati who had accompanied the caravan, stayed on, as did a dark-skinned 'Amoni named Tzelek.

The scent of roasting meat tantalized David's nostrils. It was almost dinner time, but he would not eat. He would stay on the wall and wait and see that the patrol returned safely. He prayed they would.

When at last the patrol came into view, David's fears were eased. They were in high spirits, shouting and joking with one another. A young man among them hoisted up what appeared to be a lion's pelt, freshly skinned. David and the others greeted the returning party, inquiring after the curious trophy.

"You should have seen it!" one of the men exclaimed, throwing his arm around the one with the pelt. "Look what B'nayah did!"

The young man glowed with pride and laughter as he clutched the animal skin. Touching the animal's carcass would make him ritually unclean and in need of washing, but in this moment he wasn't concerned with that.

"We were on our patrol in the north," B'nayah began eagerly. "Out of nowhere a snowstorm starts in, and it was cold. Really cold. So we decide to find some shelter."

"Yeah! We just ran for these big rocks," his companion added.

"Because I'm smaller than these guys, they want me to go down into this pit beneath the rocks first and check it out, make sure there is enough room," B'nayah continued. "And what do you know, this lion is in there! Scared me half to death."

The other men laughed loudly.

"And you killed it?" David asked, impressed.

"It was him or me, sir."

B'nayah pulled out a wooden club and held it for David to see.

"Nicely done. And please, just call me David. Whose son are you?"

"Y'hoyada, a priest."

"The son of a priest clubbed a roaring lion to death in a dark pit!" David exclaimed, slapping him on the arm. "Again I say, nicely done. Go and wash. You're late for dinner."

A few days later, a surprise visitor arrived at the stronghold. Traveling in disguise, the prophet Gad met with David privately in the outcast's sparse, lonesome chamber.

"It's good to see you," David said. "Do you bring word from Shemu'el? How is he?"

"He is okay, but he can no longer make long trips. His health has declined. And he is too high profile. Sha'ul would never let him get across the border to come to you, not that he would. His place is at Naioth, and he is happy in his work there."

"Yeah ... yeah. Well, we are managing out here. My parents are safe. The little ones have shelter. But I feel ... I don't know. I feel empty. Maybe empty isn't the right word. I feel useless, just surviving, just biding time for something to happen."

"I imagine there is a time and place for just surviving, but I have come to give you the word that you should return to Y'hudah and not remain in this stronghold any longer."

David nodded slowly as if expecting this. Gad continued,

"Mo'av is a wicked nation, full of false gods and detestable practices. They worship K'mosh ... Ashtar ... Ba'al. They even have gone so far as to offer human sacrifices to these abominations. Your place is not here. Yahweh has ordained you to be king over Yisra'el, and it is in the Promised Land that you are meant to dwell. So, I am here to tell you it is time to return."

David thought about this and scratched his cheek. Some of the men would follow him anywhere—to the ends of the earth if he asked them. The rest would probably agree with the decision, but would be fearful at the idea of going back into the den of lions.

"Ah, but we have overcome our share of lions, haven't we?" David mused aloud.

Gad gave him a puzzled look.

"Huh?"

"Nothing," David answered with a smile.

A substantial core of David's men pledged to return with him to Y'hudah. The families would remain behind, secure under the pledge of safety given by the king of

Mo'av to dwell in this land unmolested. David's aged parents, his brothers, and their families would stay and make a life in this foreign land, at least while the House of Sha'ul remained.

And so David was left with a lean band of fighting misfits, swearing loyalty to the hero even as they faced great personal risk by going back into Y'hudah.

David said his goodbyes. He hugged and kissed his father and mother, his brothers and their wives and children. They would be missed. David prayed Yahweh would watch over and protect them in his absence.

Before his departure, David's half-sister Tz'ruyah, much older than he, approached him. David smiled. This was to be another bittersweet parting, even though he had never been close with Tz'ruyah growing up, she living apart with her own family and he being the youngest in his father's house. She was strong and outspoken.

"Little brother, do me this kindness before you go."

"What is it?"

"Take my sons, your nephews, with you."

She was referring to Avishai, Yo'av, and 'Asah'el.

David was surprised. "I thought you would want them to remain here, to help you and your family settle in this land. If they go with me, they are going into certain danger."

"My sons will be an advantage for you. As you well know, Avishai is strong and brave. Yo'av, who has a mind like his? And my youngest, 'Asah'el ... there is no one faster than my 'Asah'el in a footrace. Brother, we all know that you are meant for great things. For Yahweh, for Yisra'el, for the family ... let your nephews be great with you. They deserve that rather than to be forgotten from history here in Mo'av with me."

David hugged his sister.

"If they truly wish to come with us, I welcome them."

—XXXIV—

Having quietly relocated to Y'hudah, David's band camped in the dense forest of pine and olive trees covering the hill of Heret, east of the Sh'felah valley. Gradually, more men rallied to their cause, somehow finding their way through, until the number of David's followers swelled to around six hundred. Shammah, the soldier who had also taken his stand alongside El'azar against the P'lishtim ambush, followed in the steps of his brother-in-arms and abandoned the army to follow the outcast hero.

One day a donkey carrying two riders approached their concealed position. The first tried to drive the tired beast forward with muscular determination, while the second bounced awkwardly and held on to avoid tumbling off the saddle.

The first rider pulled on the donkey's reins as several of David's men appeared from behind the trees like phantoms, surrounding the strangers with spears ready.

"I come peacefully!" the first rider said, raising his free hand above his head. "We must see the man David."

"We'll decide that," B'nayah answered.

The riders were searched and questioned repeatedly, and word was passed to the main camp farther in the forest. Finally, they were granted an audience before a heavily guarded David.

"David, this man says he's from Giv'ah. It is possible he could be a spy," his nephew Yo'av warned in an even tone. "Just give the order, and we'll take care of it."

"I don't like the look of them," Yashov'am grunted.

David inspected them. The first was strong and middle-aged, with sunburned cheeks above a thick beard. The second was practically hidden under the thick, brown cloak he was draped in.

"Tell me, who are you?" David addressed the first man.

"Ittai. I'm a farmer."

"From Giv'ah of Sha'ul?" Yashov'am demanded.

"From Giv'ah of Binyamin."

"Why did you want to see me?" David asked.

"The king has gone too far. I have no allegiance to him or his government. I rescued this one and brought him with me. He won't be safe anywhere but with you," Ittai said, indicating his shaken companion.

"Who did you say you were?" David asked the second man.

The stranger slowly removed his cloak, revealing white priestly garments beneath.

"I am Avyatar, son of the high priest."

"You are the son of Achimelekh?" David asked, startled.

"I was. I ... I am. My father is dead. Sha'ul had him murdered. Sha'ul ordered the murder of all of the priests of Yahweh."

David felt a chill run up his spine.

"Sha'ul ordered that Nov be destroyed. He accused the priests of conspiring with you. Everyone is dead. I alone have escaped with my life. This man rescued me."

Avyatar was pale, numb. The memory of the horror was so fresh as to remain unreal in his mind. Yet it was all too real to David, and his heart ached within him.

"My entire family is dead," Avyatar whispered. "I ... I managed to save this ephod. I grabbed the Urim and Tumim. I am all that's left."

David closed the distance between them in the forest clearing and grabbed hold of Avyatar.

"Avyatar, I knew on that day, when Do'eg the Edomi was there and saw me in the tabernacle, that he would surely tell Sha'ul. I realize now that I have brought about the death of every person in your father's household."

David choked back tears. All the priests murdered.

"It is my fault. I'm so sorry."

Avyatar stood, his body quivering with emotion but his mind still unable to process the tragedy. After a minute, David wiped the tears from his face and straightened.

"Stay here with me, and do not be afraid. The man who seeks your life seeks mine as well. You will be safe here. You also, Ittai. You are welcome, and I thank you. You have preserved the life of Yahweh's priest."

"High priest," Yo'av corrected quietly. "If Sha'ul has truly killed all the others, then that means that Avyatar is now the high priest by default."

Avyatar stared at Yo'av, wide-eyed.

They had not been hiding in the country long before a marauding company of P'lishtim breached the borders of Y'hudah and attacked the fortified city of Ke'ilah, hoping to plunder the corn and grain from the threshing floors of the agriculturally prosperous area. David and his men heard about it. Ke'ilah, called the Citadel, could not have been more than three miles west of their position.

David's heart was troubled, and his spirit stirred up within him. The uncircumcised P'lishtim once again dared to infiltrate the land Yahweh gave to Yisra'el, once again killing his countrymen and robbing their cities. And David and his six hundred men were within striking distance. It was within their power to help the people, to save the city. It was an agonizing dilemma.

David called for Avyatar and inquired after Yahweh, the high priest using the holy ephod and the Urim and Tumim.

"Should I go to Ke'ilah and attack these P'lishtim?" was David's question.

The answer was yes. Yes, go and attack them. Save Ke'ilah.

David was pleased, and he quickly convened a council for war.

"But David!" one of the men objected. "We are already in fear for our lives in this country, constantly hiding from the armies of Sha'ul! Now you want us to pick a fight with the P'lishtim too?"

"We put ourselves in danger, and we expose our position. I don't know."

There were murmurs of agreement all around.

"It is a risk," Yo'av added.

"Ke'ilah is a city in Sha'ul's kingdom. Let the P'lishtim make trouble for him. The more damage they do, the better for us," Tzelek the 'Amoni grunted.

David shook his head firmly.

"No. Ke'ilah belongs to Yahweh. Y'hudah belongs to Yahweh. Yisra'el belongs to Yahweh!" he answered. "Ittai, what do you think the likelihood is that Sha'ul can deliver Ke'ilah from this attack? You've been in Giv'ah more recently than any of us. What is your sense of the state of things?"

The farmer shrugged his large shoulders. "I don't know. The king's priorities are all mixed up."

"By the time his soldiers get there ... if they get there," Yashov'am added, "the men will be dead, the women will be raped, and the city will be a smoking heap, no?"

"I couldn't live with myself if I just let the sworn enemies of this nation pillage and murder our kinsmen when we could have intervened," David said.

"Please, David, make sure this is the right decision," Shammah asked. "You know we are with you either way, but be sure."

David went back before their high priest in residence and inquired again after Yahweh.

"Should I go down to Ke'ilah?"

The answer was still yes.

"Will you give the P'lishtim into my hand?"

The answer was yes. Yahweh would give them into David's hand. Victory.

David organized his followers into three bands of two hundred fighting men each. Yashov'am was placed in command over the first band, El'azar was placed over the second, and Shammah over the third. Beyond that, each band was sub-divided into ten units of twenty.

Armed, they descended into the lowland toward Ke'ilah. Each band was readied for assault. Their strategy was settled. One would circle around to cut off the supply line and escape route for the P'lishtim while the other two would attack in a pincer movement to crush the foes and drive them away from the city.

"Be courageous. Fight well. Trust in Yahweh!" David urged his men, brandishing the giant's sword at the front of the charging pack.

They battled ferociously against the P'lishtim, driving them away from Ke'ilah and smiting them with a great slaughter. They plundered the P'lishtim camp and carried off their animals and goods, bringing the spoil into the grateful, stunned city.

Sha'ul was in the royal court when the word arrived. An informant from Ke'ilah had stolen away to deliver the news rather than risk the entire city falling under the wrath of the king for harboring the wanted man. David was at the Citadel. He and his men had fought against the P'lishtim and were residing within the city.

The king leaped out of his throne and spoke to Avner with dark eyes gleaming.

"This is it! God has delivered my enemy into my hand. He is trapped in that city, walled up with double gates and bars. I will make it his tomb! We'll surround him. Seal him up in it. Lock him in!"

"How many shall we send?" Avner asked.

"Everyone. Every soldier in Yisra'el," the king replied with great eagerness. "We march for Ke'ilah!"

—XXXV—

A young boy approached David in the city square as the young hero sat with some of his men. The boy appeared to be in awe of David, but not shy. Without saying a word, his eyes moved from David to the enormous sword fastened at his side and back again. David met his gaze and smiled.

"You've got an admirer," Yashov'am said with a laugh.

The boy tentatively reached out his small hand to touch the hilt of the sword, looking up at David again as if for approval. Just then, the boy's mother called to him from across the square. Her voice was tense.

"Come along, son, no need to bother the man. We've got to be getting home now."

The boy swiveled to look at his mom. She strongly beckoned for him to come, and finally, he did, glancing back reluctantly at his object of interest.

David let out a sigh.

"They don't know what to do with us. They're nervous, having us here."

David scoured the faces of the inhabitants of Ke'ilah, most of them giving him and his men a wide berth. The words of the chiefs and magistrates had been favorable at first, speaking peace and gratitude. The citizens were overjoyed with their deliverance and buoyed by David's celebrity. His men had shared the spoil, repaired the fortifications, and treated the wounded. Yet the body language of the populace now told a different story, as if they were anticipating a dreadful consequence to fall upon them.

"Do you think somebody sent word to Sha'ul about you being here? After all we did for them?" Shammah asked.

"Yes, I'm afraid so. My nephew Yo'av tells me there has been talk of Sha'ul's army on the move in force. It can't be a coincidence."

"No good deed goes unpunished," Yashov'am growled.

"They think they will save themselves, but Sha'ul will torch the entire city to get to me. I know that now."

"What's the plan?" El'azar asked.

"I will inquire of Yahweh and see."

David and Avyatar, with the ephod, withdrew to a quiet place. David prayed earnestly and sought divine guidance.

"O Yahweh, God of Yisra'el, your servant has heard that Sha'ul is coming and will destroy Ke'ilah on my account. Will he, in fact, come down as your servant has heard?"

The answer was yes; he will come down.

"O Yahweh, will the men of Ke'ilah surrender me into his hand? Will they give my men and me into the hand of Sha'ul?"

Again, the answer was yes. They will surrender you.

Then there was no point in staying a minute longer. David hurried back to his commanders and gave the order to leave the city. The armies of Yisra'el, under the command of Avner and Sha'ul, were barreling down on Ke'ilah, ready to overrun them with sheer, overwhelming numbers. They would leave no stone unturned in the desperate race to uproot the outlaw and his followers.

The six hundred left the city and hustled the several miles to their forest hideout.

"Take whatever you can," David urged. "We can't stay here!"

Hundreds of thousands of soldiers were approaching. Heret would not conceal them for long, even if the inhabitants of Ke'ilah hadn't been ready and eager to point out the direction in which they had fled.

David's men grabbed their weapons, traveling clothes, water skins, and whatever food they could carry. Then they abandoned the camp.

There was no time for strategy or planning at this point; they would have to improvise. They ran. They ran from one place to the next. They needed to create a buffer, to put some distance between them and their pursuers. They had little way of knowing precisely where the forces that hunted them were, but rear guards and scouts bravely risked themselves to gain evidence of the army's movements. Their only goal was to avoid a confrontation they could not hope to survive.

Sha'ul pursued them with a single-minded obsession. Seemingly all of the military resources of the kingdom had been assigned to this end. The king was searching for David day after day: city by city, town by town, village by village, forest by forest, cave by cave. And he was not going to stop.

David's men continued to shed excess baggage to remain as nimble as possible. They scavenged food where they could find it and refilled on water at the streams, springs, and wells they came across. They ran for their lives. They hid. They prayed. And, despite their number, they became very skilled at breaking camp and withdrawing at a moment's notice, barely leaving behind a trace.

When the sound of their hunters' pursuit finally faded, David and his loyal followers found themselves in the wilderness, in the southern desert of Zif, between the mountains of Y'hudah and the Sea of Salt. There they camped in the hills. It was the first time in a long time that they remained in one place for more than a couple nights, and the exhausted men were grateful for the rest, however brief.

The swift 'Asah'el, one of the sons of Tz'ruyah, brought the message to David. An anonymous official from high up in the House of Sha'ul wanted a private meeting in the nearby wood of Horesh. The fact that no Yisra'elite soldiers had been seen in the area suggested that the invitation was trustworthy, although David's lieutenants had serious doubts. Almost to a man, they said it was a trap, that David would be a fool to go no matter how many bodyguards he took with him.

But then 'Asah'el opened his hand to reveal a small object. It was the seal of the prince. David's heart quickened. Y'honatan, faithful Y'honatan, had sent a messenger to meet with him in secret. Yahweh be praised!

David and a handful of trusted men went into Horesh at the appointed time the next morning. David was painfully aware of his surroundings, and his senses were keen for the slightest sign of treachery. He believed his old friend would never betray him, but if some fiend had taken hold of the prince's seal to mislead David ...

Several shadowy figures could be seen ahead in the early fog that permeated the woods. David and his men drew closer. The official, obviously in charge by the deference paid by his few companions, stood in the center with his back turned to the approaching outcasts. The horses were tethered nearby, with various bundles stacked on the ground beside them. David drew closer still.

"You can leave us now," a familiar voice said.

The official's companions melted into the fog, leaving the figure alone with David. The official slowly turned around.

"Y'honatan!" David cried out.

The two friends embraced.

"David, my brother. I barely recognized you! You've changed ... in so short a time," the prince said, sizing up the man before him.

"What are you doing here?"

"I've come to bring you these supplies and rations," Y'honatan said, gesturing to the packages behind him. "And I've come to encourage you."

"Y'honatan, I—"

"Don't be afraid. Stay strong, my brother, even as my father seeks your life. Sha'ul will not lay a hand on you. I know you've faced hardship, but I also know you will be king! Even my father knows this in his heart. One day you will rule Yisra'el, and I will be there at your side."

David clenched his jaw and gripped Y'honatan by the hand. He placed the prince's seal into the other man's palm.

"What would Sha'ul do if he knew you were here?"

"My father has frozen me out. I no longer sit in the royal court, I don't eat at the king's table, and I am not included in the decisions. And yet, my father swears that he is doing all of this for me. He says he is after you for my sake ... for our family, and our future, and our legacy. It's madness."

Y'honatan spat on the ground in disdain. "Don't worry, friend, my father will do nothing to harm me. But I'm here to strengthen you, not the other way around. Know that I am with you, as always before."

David nodded, grateful.

"And what of Mikhal?" he asked.

Y'honatan's expression faltered. "David ... I ..." The prince looked away.

"The only kindness would be to tell you straight away. My father has given her to another man to be his wife."

David's hands clenched instinctively into fists, and anger began to rise in his throat. His face felt hot. Mikhal. His wife. Given to another. Stolen from him. An image flashed in his mind—the last time she lay in his arms. The last time his fingers had beheld that smooth skin. How was he to have known it was to be his last? And had he known, would it have made a difference? Would his heart be any less shattered now? In the blink of an eye, she was irreparably, cruelly torn out of his life. Nothing he could say or do in this moment could change that.

Mikhal ...

"I am so sorry, David. There was nothing I could do."

David had to sit down on a nearby stump. He felt sick. Y'honatan stood by his side and patiently rested a hand on the younger man's shoulder.

"Who is it? Who's the man?" David asked through gritted teeth.

"A Binyaminite. Palti from Gallim. He's nobody."

David said nothing.

"I am so sorry. It is unforgivable," Y'honatan said.

David still said nothing.

After a long silence, David stood. The prince looked him in the eye and addressed him soberly.

"You will be king. Yahweh has ordained it. The covenant between us stands … even here in this strange wilderness. Our covenant stands. You will rule Yisra'el, and I will be by your side."

David firmly shook the hand of his best friend. Truly, despite the age difference, despite the geographic distance, and now despite the family and political divide, there was such a thing as a friend that is closer than a brother.

Soon, Y'honatan left and returned to Giv'ah. David remained behind.

Neither knew they would never see the other again.

—XXXVI—

It wasn't long before the men of Zif, who dwelt in the surrounding countryside, informed on David after traveling to Giv'ah and presenting themselves before the king.

"David is hiding in the strongholds of the woods of Horesh, on the hill of Hakhilah, south of the desert. Now then, may the king come down whenever your soul desires. Our part will be to surrender him into the hand of the king."

As promised to anyone with information concerning the fugitive's whereabouts, the messengers were handsomely rewarded. Bela counted out pieces of silver into their hands. But Sha'ul was feeling cautious. He had wasted far too much time and manpower seeking his slippery foe; he wanted to be prepared. This time would be different. No more embarrassments.

"May Yahweh bless you!" Sha'ul responded spiritedly. "There are at least some men left in this country with a sense of loyalty to their king. Now I'll tell you what, take that silver and return to your homes. There is more where that came from. I want you to go back and investigate. Gather some more information for me. See if you can discover exactly where the man's camp is, from where he comes and goes, who is with him, and what kind of routine he follows. They tell me that he is very crafty."

The Zifites prostrated themselves and agreed wholeheartedly. David was a fellow tribesman of Y'hudah in a time that Binyamin had been enlarged, more often than not at the perceived expense of the other tribes. But what Sha'ul had done to the priests at Nov had shaken the men of Zif to their very bones. If this king would not hesitate to brutally eradicate the men, women and children of the priestly family on a whim, what chance did they stand?

Sha'ul continued, "I want you to find all the hiding places in which he lurks in the area and the names of anybody who may be assisting or harboring him. Then, when you are absolutely certain, return to me with all that information. When you do this, your king and his armies will go down with you to uproot this criminal. You will lead me straight to him. Yes, and your reward will be even greater! But be sure to do what you have said, for, either way, I swear to you ... even if I have to search through every household and family in Y'hudah, I will find the one whose blood I seek."

David had withdrawn farther south into the wilderness of Ma'on on the border of the barren 'Aravah region. It wasn't a simple matter to conceal and sustain six hundred men, and David had been growing concerned about their visibility in Zif. Now they were on the edge of a region few would find habitable.

The hills to the north, despite bordering a wilderness, still allowed for prosperity and fertility, with Zif, lively

Karmel, and other settlements thriving. But the land had a burned quality beyond the wall of cliffs to the south and the east. It stretched out in a striking, deep-sunken valley beset with winding grooves and trenches woven through the desolate earth. The farther one got, the hotter the climate became. Rain was a rarity. Travel too far and you would end up in the land of the Edomi.

So David stayed near a conical mountain of rock that afforded a panoramic view of the surrounding territory. They would be able to detect any troop movement from a distance. They would have plenty of warning, either to conceal themselves or retreat down the back of the mountain. Or so they thought.

Two columns of Yisra'elite soldiers on horseback suddenly broke from a tree line and charged across the plain at their position. The soldiers knew exactly where to look, and they were in a hurry. At the heels of the riders came innumerable foot soldiers. The assault had begun as suddenly as a lightning strike. Only Avner could have coordinated such an effective surprise attack.

David's men rushed down the back of the mountain. The Yisra'elite horses would not make it up the steep rock straight away, but would sweep around like water flowing past an obstacle. If David's men weren't off the mountain in time, they would be trapped on it, having no avenue of escape.

"Save me, O God!" David cried loudly as he clambered down, scraping his hands against stone. "Violent men are seeking my life! Vindicate me by Your power!"

When they reached the bottom, they got their bearings. Beyond them was rocky, uneven ground that extended to the cliff wall. They would be exposed in the open stretch, and finding their way down the cliffs into the 'Aravah would take far too long. They had to somehow keep the mountain between them and Sha'ul's forces.

David led as they ran eastward, adrenaline surging. They ran until David and those nearest him skidded to an abrupt halt. David held up his hand for silence.

Ahead of them, the rumbling of hooves and the shouts of men echoed through the rocks. The army was circling the mountain and on a collision course with David. They could feel the vibrations in the ground growing stronger.

"Back! The other way!" David yelled, throwing his arm wildly in the opposite direction.

They fled to the west, losing precious time as they retraced their steps, trying desperately to keep out of sight of the approaching soldiers. The swift 'Asah'el now led the pack, flying over the undulating earth. One man tumbled forward, gashing the top of his foot and badly smashing his knee against a rock. Others helped him up, supporting him as they desperately pushed on.

"Wait!" 'Asah'el yelled. He stopped in his tracks.

The sounds of approaching soldiers were again up ahead, coming straight at them. The other column. Sha'ul's forces had split, each circling the mountain from opposite sides. David's men backed away, retreating to the place where they had begun.

Sha'ul and the princes waited with their chariots beside Avner as they watched the assault unfold. It was beautiful.

"We have them surrounded," Avner informed the king with a pleased smile. Everything was proceeding just as planned. "They can't outrun us, and they can't hide."

Sha'ul slapped the back of the chariot driver excitedly and gave a whoop.

"At last!"

The dust from the horses drifted upward in twin trails curving around either side of the mighty conical rock. Soldiers hurried in their wake, their orders clear: take no prisoners.

Just then the loud galloping of a horse came from behind the commanders. It was a messenger from Giv'ah, and he was absolutely frantic.

"My king! Avner!" the messenger cried, trying to get somebody's attention.

Sha'ul turned in irritation. The last thing he wanted was a distraction. His moment of victory over the rebels was so close he could taste it.

"What is it?!" he shouted.

"The P'lishtim, my lord! They have entered Yisra'el! They are raiding the land!"

"So what? I'm sure our men can—" Prince Eshba'al interrupted.

"Quiet!" Avner rebuked. "We have many of our forces here with us. How far have they come?"

"Advance units have been spotted only miles from Binyamin! This is a full-scale invasion!"

Sha'ul's heart sank. He glared at the mountain on the horizon.

David's men could go no further east or west. Fleeing to the cliffs would be suicide. Maybe a few would escape if they got there in time and scattered. Maybe a few escaping was preferable to total annihilation. They were surrounded and could hear the enemy forces closing in.

They huddled together, the men on each edge facing out. They would go down fighting, even if David stubbornly refused to draw the blood of Yisra'elite soldiers. After all, not all the men following David were Yisra'elites. And those who were would still protect David. They had made it their business to do so.

The end was on everybody's mind, even as they panted and dripped with sweat in the dusty heat. David continued to pray aloud in the midst of the six hundred, his eyes ever watchful. Any minute they would see the first of the soldiers, his own countrymen, coming around either bend. Avyatar, the priest, hugged the ephod and shut his eyes.

They braced themselves.

The sounds of death grew louder and louder in their ears.

And then there was a different sound. A long, piercing trumpet sound. It called out and was followed by another identical to it. Multiple instruments in unison, giving a signal. An order. The trumpets sounded a third time.

The approaching riders slowed. Then they stopped. They turned around. They galloped in the other direction. The sounds of death began to grow fainter.

David's men could not believe it. Young B'nayah and several others quickly climbed to the top of the mountain and confirmed that, yes, the entire army was withdrawing—heading north. It was impossible!

Truly, even the foreigners and newest recruits to have joined with David had to confess that the miraculous seemed to follow him wherever he went. The place ... this mountain ... was almost instantly nicknamed "The Rock of Escape."

They went east, straight into the desert leading to the Sea of Salt. A newcomer named Avi-'Albon, native to the region, told them of an oasis beyond the barren wastes, and he also spoke of caves and incredibly steep, craggy rocks, accessible only to the wild goats. It would be an ideal place for a hideout, far removed and sheltering, yet sustainable. But there were many miles of sun-scorched earth between them and the oasis.

When they finally reached their destination, they found it to be everything Avi-'Albon had advertised. 'Ein-Gedi, the oasis, was like a jewel emerging from the bleak rock, situated on the western shore, naturally decorated with palm, balsam, and blossoming henna. David's men refreshed themselves in a clear, blue pool beneath falling fresh water springs, explored beautiful caverns, and ate of sweet jujube fruit.

They dug in and carefully charted escape routes and cave systems useful for hiding. They were as far to the edge of the kingdom as they could be while still remaining within Yisra'el. And, at least for now, they seemed to be safe.

—XXXVII—

Yisra'el regrouped from their long battle with the P'lishtim. They had managed to repulse the invasion at the cost of heavy Yisra'elite casualties. The citizens affected by the destruction mourned. The widows and orphans of the dead grieved. But Sha'ul once more turned his thoughts to the man he viewed as the real threat to his rule.

It wasn't long before word reached him that David's men had been seen near 'Ein-Gedi. The army was stretched thin, exhausted from chasing David and fighting the P'lishtim. They needed to rest, nurse their wounds, bury their dead, and reorganize. And the territory of 'Ein-Gedi was no place for horses, chariots, and infantry columns. A large army would be completely ineffective in such an environment and nearly impossible to supply across the scorched expanse dividing here from there.

Avner advocated for a small, elite force of hand-picked loyalists to be organized for a mission. They could travel lightly, approach 'Ein-Gedi without drawing too much attention, and scour the area in a systematic fashion. Avner also urged that Sha'ul remain home at Giv'ah. In the king's repeated absences, more duties and decisions were falling to Prince Avinadav. Leave David to Avner.

Sha'ul dismissed the suggestion immediately. He would be there personally to oversee the demise of his most hated enemy, no matter what. And, in fact, Avner could stay behind. Sha'ul had had enough of his naysaying. Soon the king found himself in the hunt once more with three thousand men in the wilderness of 'Ein-Gedi.

Days passed as the most skilled trackers in the army were put to work, combing through the land and questioning the sheepherders and nomads they encountered. Sha'ul felt his age as the more agile warriors around him made their way efficiently through the precipitous terrain. Sha'ul had to be continually prompted to drink water so as not to faint in the heat. But he was not discouraged. In this isolated corner of the kingdom, they were narrowing in on their target.

David and his men withdrew into the deep recesses of a labyrinthine cave, one of the many hiding spots they had found. Yisra'elite soldiers had been detected in the vicinity, and it was time to disappear.

The cave had two entry points: one narrow and concealed, and the other larger and accessible, near a winding path that ran past empty sheepfolds. At first glance, the larger appeared to open to a spacious but shallow chamber. Once further inside, passageways, seemingly bottlenecked, led into darkness.

The innermost part of the cave was enormous. David felt he was in the very heart of the earth. All six hundred of his men were swallowed up in the thick blackness. They maintained absolute silence. Unless an enemy stumbled deep into the unknown passages, grasping a torch and groping like a blind man, and accidentally ran into one of their hidden number, they would be undetectable.

David crept toward the front of the cave, followed by Yo'av and El'azar. They came to a turn in the rock where they could look out while remaining covered. It was nearly evening from the look of the light. They could hear the sounds of men outside; their would-be executioners were near.

Two shadows appeared in the entrance. Then a third. Three alert soldiers entered the cave. One grunted and brushed away a large spider web that David's men had been careful to leave undisturbed. They circled the chamber, searching. One soldier with his spear walked to the back and peered into the darkness of a tight corridor, only feet from David, listening for any sound.

"What's that smell?" another soldier asked.

"Sheep dung, what do you think?"

"I hate caves."

"It's clear. Let's go."

Satisfied with their inspection, the three exited. Then another figure appeared at the mouth of the cave and came inside. The silhouette, the barrel-chested gait, the sound of the man breathing through his mouth—David recognized him instantly. It was King Sha'ul!

Sha'ul walked around the back of the chamber, nudging several piles of rocks with his foot. He cleared his throat and began to remove his outer robe, folding it and laying it on the ground next to his belt and sword. The king squatted over the edge of a rock, his back to a dark corridor. He adjusted his garments, pulled his tunic up and began to defecate loudly. A sharp stench filled the cave.

Concealed, El'azar turned to David in the dim light. David did not return the knowing gaze but only stared at the form in the cave ahead—his hunter, his pursuer, the man who gave his wife to another. Yo'av touched David's knee; he was holding a dagger out for David to take. With his free hand, Yo'av made a slow cutting motion across his throat.

David fidgeted. He licked his dry lips. Yo'av gave him a sharp nod as if to say, "You know what needs to be done."

David tentatively took the dagger while he untied his sandals and slipped them off. He pivoted in place, fixing his eyes on Sha'ul. The king was still busy relieving himself. David started creeping forward as silently as he could, his knees bent, his bare feet moving across the cave floor in the shadows. He passed the sharp dagger from one hand to the other and back again. It would be nothing to reach out, seize Sha'ul by his hair, and slash his throat. It would be easy.

David was within striking distance. Sha'ul grunted and strained, having some discomfort or difficulty with his bowels. All David had to do was reach out. The foul stench of excrement assaulted his nostrils. He held his breath and steadied himself, gripping the dagger ...

David reached down and took hold of the corner of Sha'ul's royal robe as it lay on the ground. With the edge of the dagger he quietly cut through the fabric, removing a triangular corner from the garment. He felt the material between his fingers and glanced up. Sha'ul hadn't detected him. Slowly, David began to retreat, step-by-step in his crouching posture, never taking his eyes off the king until at last he was again hidden behind the rock. At that moment, Sha'ul finished, stood, and began to gather his belongings.

El'azar and Yo'av stiffened in their hiding place, yearning to attack. But David held them back without a sound. Sha'ul left the cave, and David and his companions returned to the others. Many were incredulous when they heard what had happened.

"You let him get away?"

"Yahweh gave him into your hand!"

"You could have ended this once and for all."

David rubbed the cut fabric between his thumb and forefinger. He began to feel a heavy pang of guilt.

"He is still the king. He is still Yahweh's anointed. Who am I to stretch out my hand against him? Yahweh chose him, and only Yahweh should remove him if that is His will. What have I done? Sha'ul is still my master ... and I came so close to ..." David trailed off, grief evident in his voice.

How could he disrespect the king, let alone entertain the thought of murder? David waited in the darkness until he could stand it no more. His conscience burned within him.

"This is wrong."

Abruptly, David turned and hastened to the front of the cave, his men protesting in confusion. He walked out into the failing light. Sha'ul and the soldiers had already started on the winding path that led down and away. David ran after them. He shouted with a loud voice that echoed through the canyon.

"My lord the king!"

Sha'ul and the three thousand soldiers stopped. Sha'ul turned and looked behind him. He was astounded. David came closer and prostrated himself, bowing low with his face to the ground.

"O king, why do you listen to the voices of those who say to you, 'David is seeking to harm you'?" David pleaded loudly. "Today you can see proof with your own eyes, Yahweh had given you into my hand in the cave. You were alone and unprotected. I was not. Some said to kill you, but I refused. I said to them, 'I will not stretch out my hand against my master, Yahweh's anointed king.' Now look here, my father, see this in my hand! It is the corner of your robe."

David stood and waved the piece of cloth in the air for all to witness. Sha'ul immediately grabbed the edge of his robe and held it up. Part of it had been cut away! The king was dumbfounded. A couple Yisra'elite commanders raced over, and they too examined the robe.

David continued: "Yes, I cut off the edge of your robe in the cave just now but did not lay a finger on you to harm you. Can't you see that there is no evil or treason in me toward you? Even though you are here hunting my soul, lying in wait to take my life and spill my blood, I have not sinned against you. May Yahweh judge between you and me, and perhaps Yahweh will avenge the wrongs you have done to me, but I will never harm you. As the proverb of the ancients says, 'Wicked deeds reveal a wicked man,' but my hand will not be against you ... not to harm, not to do evil, not to conspire.

"Who has the king of Yisra'el come out after? Who are you chasing? I am but a dead dog. Worse, I am a single flea upon that dog! May Yahweh be the judge. May He plead my cause and rescue me from your hand!"

David stood, breathing heavily, alone and defenseless before three thousand soldiers and the king who had sworn an oath to kill him.

Sha'ul squinted up the path at the young man through eyes filling with stinging moisture.

"Is that your voice ... David, my son?" the king asked shakily.

Then Sha'ul broke. He began to weep loudly. Every soldier heard him.

"Truly, you are a better man than I am," the king cried, fighting through his trembling shame. "You have repaid me with good for all the evil I've done to you. What man, when he finds his enemy, will allow him to go away unharmed? Yahweh let me fall into your hand and yet you did not kill me. Oh, may Yahweh reward you with good for what you have done today."

An image flashed in Sha'ul's mind. He remembered the torn garment of Shemu'el, so many years ago in the tent. Now his own robe had been cut. The stinging rebuke of the seer echoed in his memory. He felt a sense of clarity.

The king wiped tears and snot from his face with his large, calloused hands.

"Now I know you will surely be king. The kingdom of Yisra'el will be established in your hand," Sha'ul said soberly, nodding at his own recognition of the inevitability of this truth. "Now swear to me, my son, swear to me by Yahweh that you will not cut off my offspring after me, that you will not wipe out my name from my father's house."

"I swear it," David answered. "You have my word."

—XXXVIII—

David and his men roamed the south of Y'hudah in a nomadic existence, away from Binyamin and all the areas fortified with Yisra'elite soldiers. Sha'ul had relented from his pursuit. The king and his army had left 'Ein-Gedi and returned to Giv'ah. But David would have to be a fool to let his guard down. Officially he was still an enemy of the state, an exile, and the six hundred with him had no legitimate place to call their home.

And yet, his popularity was growing. Tales of his early exploits, already famous, were becoming the stuff of legend. His daring rescue of Ke'ilah was a topic of debate around the dinner table. With his wild, ostensibly bandit lifestyle, David's unique allure took on a new quality. He represented an alternative to the disappointing reign of Sha'ul in every sense. He symbolized the opposition—a guerilla leader, a scapegoat, not capable of having done all the wrong that the government alleged about him.

Rumors about David's last encounter with Sha'ul had begun to spread. There were ever-increasing whispers in the gates and inner rooms. Had the king really said power would one day pass to David? A small group of the elders of Y'hudah had been meeting in secret for many years, debating what, if anything, could possibly be done about the House of Sha'ul and its tyrannies. They felt that Yisra'el had lost its way. And there was still the ancient prophecy that the scepter and ruler's staff would not depart from Y'hudah. What if this David held the answer?

For their part, David and his men patrolled the south of Y'hudah, the Negev, and the wilderness, doing good deeds and defending the oppressed among the people. Farms and villages were protected from thieves and brigands. David also sent word to the elders of each town in the vicinity that they were under his protection in the case of P'lishtim attack, or any other threat. Eventually, small gifts and donations would be quietly brought to the roving camp, wherever the men happened to be. These contributions were welcome, but still barely enough to get by on. Six hundred mouths were a lot to feed.

One day an elder of Y'hudah from the mountain town of Yizre'el summoned David to a meeting by nightfall. By low lamplight, they talked about David's activities in the region, his prospects, his plans for the future. David made it clear that he had no treasonous desires or schemes, his love and loyalty for Yisra'el were rock solid, and he was only caring for those whom Yahweh had sent to him.

"And are the rumors true? Were you really anointed to take over the kingship?"

On that point, David remained coy. He dodged the question and later tried to change the subject when the elder brought it up again. Eventually, with dawn approaching, the elder concluded their meeting.

"You have my support. Your cause is righteous. I am ready to pledge my allegiance to you, but I cannot do so publicly, for obvious reasons," the elder said. "There are more. There are others like me in Y'hudah who are ready for a change ... praying for a change. They might throw their support behind you too when the time is right. But the time has not yet come."

"I thank you for your words of support," David said.

"Here, take some of this wine and grain to your men. And come back whenever you are in the area. I would like to continue our discussions."

"May Yahweh bless you for your generosity."

The next time they met, the elder introduced David to his daughter. Her name was Achino'am, the same as Sha'ul's wife. She was fairly pretty, with long brown hair, a dark complexion, medium height and form, a full, shapely face and chin, a pointed nose, and a graceful smile. Achino'am was even tempered, and she responded to David with perfect submissiveness, as if he were some great person, although he held no title, position, or authority to speak of. She was several years younger than David and still maintained a childlike innocence.

The purpose behind the introduction became clear. The elder wished to forge an alliance, to give a sign of his support to David without doing anything on an official level or making any public declaration that would bring about dire consequences. The elder wanted David to marry his daughter. David decided to think about the offer. When he returned to Yizre'el again, he spent some time walking alone with Achino'am in a nearby orchard.

She was willing to obey her father's wishes and be given to David as a wife. She admired the man from all she had heard, and, of course, she found him to be handsome. The thought of wandering the land did not seem to trouble her greatly, perhaps because she believed David would soon come into some form of inheritance or position. He was a hero, after all. He had men who had sworn their lives to defend him.

David still thought about Mikhal, and the memories stung. To have a woman, to have love, to be able to return to the consolation of your own marriage bed each night and then to have that privilege yanked away ...

On the run, David had more pressing concerns and very few nights of comfort. But every so often a deep loneliness would settle on him. And here before him was this girl: young, pleasant, malleable, a bit naïve, respectful, and seeming to appear, in David's eyes, prettier by the day. Even if the painful dagger of Mikhal's absence remained in his heart, perhaps this was the decision he had to make. Perhaps graceful Achino'am here was another option, another path, instead of spending a lifetime alone.

And she really was quite pretty ... wasn't she?

David and Achino'am married in a small ceremony and spent their wedding night in a house in Yizre'el. Achino'am was new, shy, and inexperienced. The scent of her hair and skin was all spice, like rich and pungent sandalwood. In the morning, they arose and left to rejoin the rest of David's men.

The camp had grown. Because they weren't constantly fleeing for their lives, some of the men had sent for their wives and other relatives as well. Despite trying to keep a low profile, David and his men were becoming a regular fixture in the countryside, offering protection, engaging in trade, and remaining in communication with several of the towns and villages throughout the outskirts of the kingdom.

The roaming misfits were turning into a community.

Shemu'el lay on the bed in his private room at Naioth, breathing with slow, ragged breaths. Gad and several other students of the School of the Prophets crowded around the bedside. Some whispered prayers. One patted a cool, damp cloth on the seer's forehead. Gad held Shemu'el's hand, not wanting to let go of the man he considered his spiritual father. The old man's grasp was weak.

Shemu'el's eyes began to drift.

Gad felt his own throat tighten.

Shemu'el breathed a heavy, final breath, and then he died.

In the funeral procession, Gad and all the students of Naioth carried the seer to his home in Ramatayim with great solemnity. There they ensured that all the burial rites were carefully observed. His body was laid to rest in his family tomb, beside his wife, his father, and his mother.

All Yisra'el mourned.

King Sha'ul, Y'honatan, and elders from every tribe came to pay their respects to the man of Yahweh. A time of national mourning was declared. Men and women from every corner of the kingdom came in pilgrimage to honor Shemu'el and lament the death of the man who had been a judge over their nation for so long, lived his public life with true piety, and led them as one who truly heard the voice of Yahweh.

Few could agree on the exact age of the seer. Some said he was ninety-eight years old. Others repeated a rumor that he had died on his one-hundredth birthday, but this seemed unlikely. Most who personally knew the specifics of his birth were long gone, returned to the dust of the earth.

"Rest easy, Master," Gad said under his breath, steadying himself as the tomb was sealed. The burden of the prophetic school fell to him, at least for a time. He didn't know if he was ready. He didn't feel ready. But he would have to be.

The priesthood was in shambles. The nation was still picking up the bloodied and broken pieces from their last war. And now this figurehead, this rock of faithfulness had been removed from their midst. The people of Yisra'el could sense the spiritual vacuum left in his wake and were afraid. The loss of Shemu'el was felt more deeply than the behavior of the people toward him in his final years would indicate. Sometimes people truly don't know what they have until it's gone.

And then came the regrets. Yisra'el wept for Shemu'el a great many days.

When news of the seer's death reached David, he tore his clothes, poured ashes onto his head, and refused to eat or drink. The others followed his example and joined in the lamentation. David played a mournful dirge before the assembly.

The man who had anointed him in secret to be the future king of Yisra'el was dead. Here David was, wandering with this unusual crowd, without a city or home to call his own, his family members in a faraway land, his father's flocks confiscated, his wife and his title taken from him. Now the spiritual guide of Yisra'el was gone. How had life become so unrecognizable? It didn't seem too long ago that he was just a boy, tending his father's sheep in a gentle meadow near Beit-Lechem, composing music under a clear blue sky, inhaling the sweet scent of spring flowers on the breeze.

How did he get from there to here?

David yearned to go to Ramatayim to pay his respects to Shemu'el, but he knew it was impossible. A trip into Efrayim would be a trip he would not return from.

"Let's go south," David told his men. "I don't want to stay here. Not right now."

"Give the order, boss," Yashov'am said.

"South, then. Far south, into the wilderness of Pa'ran."

David wanted isolation. He wanted a barren place. A lonely place.

—XXXIX—

It wasn't long before David's hungry mouths began to run out of food. In the south, the exiled hero faced a dilemma. His was no longer a nimble band but a swelling, moveable city. That city needed sustenance. David had instituted strict rationing for the past few weeks, but he needed a solution, and fast. The stress wore on his nerves.

To be in the right, to be doing good works among a mostly ungrateful people, to be providing for his followers, to be self-sacrificing, to be waiting for a promised blessing, and still to struggle day-to-day ...

Hetzrai, a Karmelite, had an idea.

"David, I heard that Naval, the rich man, is getting ready to shear his sheep."

David perked up.

A couple of months ago, the shepherds of Naval had brought their flocks down the slopes of Karmel into the pasturelands of Ma'on. Naval was very wealthy and owned property in Karmel, a land lush with fields, gardens, and vineyards. He had to his name about three thousand sheep as well as a thousand goats, making the livestock of David's father seem insignificant by comparison.

The shepherds had encountered David and his men in the south and spent many days in fellowship with them. David had given the order for all to show kindness to them. No man was to lay so much as a finger on any of the animals or belongings. In his company were many rough men with shady, unscrupulous pasts, but David would allow no injustice to be committed under his watch. Instead, David's men were like a shield to the shepherds and the flocks all the time the flocks were grazing, offering free protection from robbers coming out of the deep desert and wild beasts tempted by such a large spoil.

Now it was shearing season, a festive time David recalled well from his own youth. Naval and all his household would be celebrating. It would be a time for hospitality, generosity, and good spirits. Perhaps, taking into account their previous discourse with his shepherds, Naval would show favor to David and his men during the great feast, which Hetzrai assured would be extravagant.

"Good thinking, Hetzrai," David said with not a little relief. They needed this.

David sent Hetzrai and nine other young men native to the region as his ambassadors. Surely the rich man would not deny his humble request.

Several male servants led Hetzrai and the nine up the path to Naval's estate. It was practically a small town, with multiple, interconnected structures of exceptional construction for family, visitors, servants, herdsmen, and other employees. The place was abuzz with the commotion of the annual shearing in the large sheepfolds adjacent to the residences.

Children, visiting guests, and members of the household crowded around the pens and watched as servants corralled the sheep, flipping them onto their rears and holding them as their wool was cut free. Hetzrai greeted one of the familiar head shepherds as they passed at the entrance to the main house.

Like many of the wealthiest families throughout the tribes of Yisra'el, Naval had maintained a uniquely businesslike relationship with the House of Sha'ul over the years. In exchange for financial tribute and regular gestures of fealty, Naval was allowed to run his small empire in relatively undisturbed autonomy, a de facto nobleman.

The messengers were led into the lavish interior where Naval was reclining, sampling from different vats of wine, as other servants busily went about the preparations for the feast. Naval, stocky beneath his fine linen and purple clothes, cocked his eyebrow and eyed the newcomers with imposing coldness.

Naval spat out a mouthful of wine into a silver bowl and asked, "What is it? I'm busy."

Hetzrai began to say all that David had instructed, "We come in the name of David, son of Yishai. Our master says this: May you be blessed with a long and healthy life. Peace be to you, peace be to your house, and peace be to all that you have! Our master, David, says, I have heard that you are shearing. You know that your shepherds have been with us in the south and that they were never mistreated, nor did anything of theirs go missing. Ask your shepherds and they will tell you of our kindness to them. So then, may my young men find favor in your eyes, for we come to you on a festive day. I ask that you please share with your servants and your son, David, whatever you can find for them so that we may also rejoice with you."

Naval ever so slowly lowered the ladle in his hand. He let out a whistle, and numerous personal guards entered the room and drew to either side of him, standing with arms folded across their chest in a show of intimidation.

"You come in the name of David, you say. Huh! David ... David ... who is this David? The son of Yishai? Who is that? These days there are many servants who are breaking away from their masters. How does that make David special?" Naval sneered. "He is a nobody, not worth my time. And I guess that makes all of you who pledge to a nobody less than nobodies. You come into my home uninvited, like a bunch of beggars, and presume to ask for a hand-out? Should I take my own bread and water and my own meat that I slaughtered for my shearers and give it to a bunch of men who come from ... who knows where? Some bastard children? Men of ill repute? Huh? Get out of here! I don't want you hanging around my home. Go back and join the rest of your pack of wild dogs!"

The head of Naval's shepherds overheard all that his master had said, and he watched David's messengers as they left, bristling with anger, to retrace their way back to their camp to report every word. This did not bode well.

The shepherd slipped away into the adjacent administration building and found Avigayil, his master's wife, sitting at a table and pouring over a business ledger with one of her female attendants seated nearby. Avigayil's eyes darted up briefly from her work as he entered. She could read his trepidation.

"What is it this time?" she asked with a worldly sigh, scrawling a notation. Then, suddenly, "Confound it! It'll take me all season to straighten out these numbers! I don't know what my husband was thinking with some of these orders!"

She tossed the ledger aside in disgust and fixed her gaze firmly on the man standing before her.

"Sorry, you have something to say?"

The shepherd cleared his throat.

"I thought you should know, Mistress, that the man David sent messengers out of the wilderness to greet our master, but our master grossly insulted them and threw them out. These men were good to us! The whole time we were in the fields with them, keeping the sheep, we were totally safe, and the property was secure. Actually, it was better having them around; they were like a wall of protection. They came up here in peace for the sheep-shearing and our master practically spat in their faces!"

Avigayil winced as her husband's surly behavior was described. It was very easy to believe that he had done all that and worse. She knew David's reputation well and could not help but admire him for all she had heard. In fact, she had quietly followed the news and gossip of his career with great fascination. Once she had even seen the young hero in the flesh during a military parade, some years ago during happier times. David was handsome, confident, brave, and zealous for God and country—everything that her husband was not.

But Avigayil also knew that David was a hardened soldier, with a veritable small army of warriors, made perhaps more hardened through their wanderings and frequent dangers. Such blatant disrespect and hostility as the kind her husband hurled upon the messengers would not be well received. How could it be? Life had somehow brought her and her family on a collision course with this force of a man she so greatly admired.

"Please, Mistress!" the shepherd urged. "You have to do something. I've got a really bad feeling about this. Harm is coming against our master and us too if we don't make this right. You know Naval won't listen to a word I say. Worthless man ..."

Avigayil ignored the comment about her husband's worth; she was already several steps ahead of the shepherd.

"Come," she told her maidservant. "Get the girls together. Hurry!"

"Every man strap on your sword!" David shouted.

He fastened Golyat's blade to his side while all his fighting men did the same with their weapons. He led four hundred toward Karmel while two hundred remained behind to protect the camp.

The hateful insults of Naval burned within David like a scorpion's sting. How dare that wealthy man treat him and his messengers with such blatant disrespect. How dare he deny the obligation of hospitality. David's empty stomach tightened into a knot. He could not recall ever being so furious before in his life.

"What a waste!" David said bitterly through clenched teeth as they rushed northward across the land. "I guarded that man's property in the wilderness so that not one thing of his was missing. And now he has repaid me with evil for the good I've done him."

The men beside him hardened their faces, anticipating the vengeance that lay ahead. They quickly made their way through the mountainous ravine lying between them and their target.

"May God do so to all the enemies of David, and worse, if by the morning, I have not slain everyone in Naval's household who passes water standing up!"

The men shouted in bloodthirsty agreement.

Just then, coming through the ravine, the four hundred saw the strangest sight: a procession of donkeys coming toward them laden with all kinds of parcels and goods, ridden by six lovely young women.

David strode ahead and stopped in front of the women. The one in front of the train dismounted, falling to the ground in front of David and bowing before him. She was finely dressed but cared nothing that her clothes were being dirtied. She appeared to be about the same in age as he.

"What is this?" David asked, taken aback.

The other young women stayed where they were, trying not to appear frightened in front of this horde of dangerous men.

"My lord, let all the blame fall on me and me alone," their mistress spoke without reserve, her voice at once melodious and husky. "Let your maidservant speak to you. Please, hear what she has to say."

"Speak," David said, surprised by his sudden feelings of attraction to this mysterious woman.

"Please, do not let my lord listen to that worthless, wicked man Naval. He is a fool. Do not regard his actions. When my lord's messengers came, I did not see them. Your maidservant did not even know they had come until it was too late."

"Please, get up," David urged softly, extending her his hand.

Her groveling made him uncomfortable and self-conscious. She allowed him to help her up, and her large, hazel eyes met his. She was beautiful. Even in her distress David sensed a well of strength within her. Her eyes shone as she spoke.

"Thank you, my lord," she said, breaking off the intimacy of his stare. "Your maidservant has come to remedy the rudeness of her husband."

Husband, David thought. How could such a boorish man have such a wife as this? What a joyful treasure in the hands of one so undeserving. She seemed so full of life, like a flower bursting open in the sunshine.

"As my lord can see, your maidservant and her servants have brought these gifts for you and your men."

The mistress beckoned for the other young women to come forward with the donkeys. David's men began to mingle among them, examining the goods as they were described. B'nayah winked flirtatiously at one of the maidservants, who blushed a bright red.

"You will find five sheep already prepared, two hundred loaves of bread, two skins of wine, about a bushel of roasted grain, a hundred clusters of raisins, and two hundred cakes of figs ... all for my lord and his young men."

The mistress turned from enumerating the gifts and looked once again into David's eyes, continuing her penitent petition.

"Now please, accept these gifts and forgive the sin of your maidservant. As Yahweh and your own soul lives, since Yahweh has kept you from taking revenge into your own hands and committing murder against he who treated you wrongly, I pray that all your enemies and those who plot evil against you would become as foolish and thwarted as Naval is. He is no threat to you."

Despite the commotion and movement of bodies and beasts all around them, David felt as if they were alone. He could not take his eyes off her rounded cheeks and the perfect rows of her teeth that he could imagine forming into an easy smile. She sensed his softening heart and spoke to him with growing boldness and confidence, even as her speech retained the indirect, submissive language required of her.

"Your maidservant believes Yahweh will surely bless you with an enduring dynasty because you are fighting His battles, and evil has not been found in you all of your days. Although you are chased by those who want to kill you, I know your life will be kept as a precious possession of Yahweh, bundled up in His living treasury. But as for your enemies, Yahweh will hurl them away like stones from a sling."

She wondered if he would catch the reference, indicating she was quite familiar with his adventures.

"When Yahweh has done for my lord every good thing He promised," she continued, "and has appointed you as ruler over Yisra'el, my lord will not have to have on his conscience the needless burden of guilt over avenging himself on a fool. And I pray that when that day comes, and Yahweh has blessed you with great success, please remember your maidservant and show her favor."

"What is your name?" was all that David could manage.

"Avigayil."

And then there was that easy smile on her face. It was just as pleasant to look upon as David had envisioned.

"Praise be to Yahweh, the God of Yisra'el, who sent you this day to meet me," David said, the ferocity drained from his body, replaced by a different sensation altogether. "May you be blessed for your wise discernment and for keeping me from bloodshed. I swear, as surely as Yahweh lives, who has by His grace restrained me from causing you hurt, if you had not come out quickly to meet me, not one male in all of Naval's house would be alive by tomorrow morning."

David welled up with deep gratitude. He had acted and spoken rashly, condemning strangers to death for the offensiveness of one man. The anger in his heart had dissipated by the actions and articulation of this amazing woman standing before him. David did not desire for their interview to be ended so soon. But she was married. She had her own life, a life that had nothing to do with David—a life he had almost destroyed.

"Thank you for your gifts and kindness," he said to her with a subtle sadness. "Return to your home in peace."

Avigayil and her maidservants arrived at the estate as night was falling. Bright light and boisterous noise emanated from the main building. Nobody was outside to even witness their return, and they quietly put the donkeys back in their stable.

Inside, a feast fit for a king was under way, with food, music, dancing, singing, and much alcohol. Avigayil strode into the main hall and saw Naval lounging at the head of the banquet table, wine sloshing from his goblet as he swayed back and forth in revelry, laughing loudly with his guests as young women cavorted about the room.

Naval was drunk. Avigayil took her seat near him. He half acknowledged her presence through a slurred greeting before turning back to his friends. He hadn't even noticed that she had been gone! She fought to disguise the disgust she so strongly felt at this moment. She had much practice with such disguises.

Her marriage to Naval had been arranged. As it goes, rich men so often get what they want, and although Avigayil was the much-beloved daughter of her father, in the end, she was handed over to Naval like a piece of property in a business transaction.

Every fiber of her being made Avigayil want to get up and leave the table, but she knew her husband would pass out soon enough at the rate he was downing his drinks, thereby freeing her of her obligation to be present.

The next morning, Avigayil stepped through the detritus of the feast and found Naval sprawled out in a spare bedroom with a nasty hangover. He cursed as she opened the drapes, letting sunlight and fresh air into the acrid-smelling space.

"Wha ... what are you doing?" he moaned, shielding his face.

"I have something to tell you," she answered patiently, walking over and sitting on the side of the bed.

"Eh?"

"Yesterday, after your disgraceful treatment of those messengers, I went out with my maidservants and met David not far from Karmel. We brought him varied gifts of food and wine, so as to stop him from seeking revenge for your insults. David had four hundred armed men on their way to kill you and every man here. You don't know how close you came to death last night."

When he heard these words, Naval's eyes bulged in his head and his breath caught in his throat, as if choking. He began to turn pale and struggled to raise himself up; his eyes were twitching. Avigayil quickly jumped off the bed. What was happening?

Naval clutched wildly at his chest and gasped. Avigayil slowly backed away, eyeing her husband carefully. He was growing slower in his movements, trying to speak but unable to make more than a gurgling noise. Avigayil turned and ran to find help.

Naval lay in the bed for ten days, catatonic, and then he died.

The head shepherd rode south to David's camp and told him what happened.

"Praise be to Yahweh, who has judged Naval for treating me with contempt, and who prevented His servant from doing an evil thing. Yahweh has returned Naval's evil on his own head."

David thought of Avigayil. She was now a widow, if not by his direct hand, then by circumstances related to him. The last thing David wanted was for her to suffer. He was indebted to her. David sent several of his men back to the estate in Karmel with the head shepherd, who led them before Avigayil and her five maidservants.

"David has sent us to you to bring you back to him as his wife."

Avigayil smiled broadly and bowed low to the ground.

"Your maidservant is here, happy to accept, even ready to wash the feet of the servants of my lord!"

She quickly changed out of her mourning clothes and gathered a few belongings. She and her maidservants mounted their donkeys.

"What are we waiting for? Let's go!"

—XL—

Sha'ul sat in council with Avner, his sons Avinadav, Malkishua, and Eshba'al, the promoted Do'eg, and several of the kingdom's top commanders and advisors. Avinadav facilitated the meeting, prompting reports on the state of Yisra'el's military and civic concerns.

The king shifted with discomfort, trying to relieve the chronic shooting pains he had been feeling in his legs as of late. These sessions dragged on far too long for his liking, and he drifted in and out of the conversation intermittently. At one point, the room grew silent as one hesitant advisor prepared to give his report. Knowing what the news was, everyone looked at Sha'ul expectantly.

"Yes?" the king asked, coming back to attention.

"Naval, the wealthy man from Ma'on, has passed away," the advisor said.

Sha'ul leaned over to Bela for clarification.

"He was a good friend of your government, most gracious lord," Bela whispered. "Very generous."

"Ah, yes, I remember him. A shame. Send our condolences to ... whoever survives him."

Some awkward shuffling all around.

"Well, you see ... it turns out that Naval's widow has married ... David."

"David?" the king erupted with surprise.

"I'm afraid so, my king."

Sha'ul covered his face with his large hands, letting them slide down slowly until the tips of his fingers rested on his lips. His thoughts went to his daughter. So, the son of Yishai had found a new bride. Interesting.

"I've always thought of David as a first-rate soldier. I can admire that about him," Avner began. "But this changes things, doesn't it?"

"Yes, Commander. Naval's possessions, wealth, and I suppose even his livestock are likely in the hand of the king's enemy now," the advisor responded.

"That fiend already fans the flames of rebellion throughout the southern reaches!" Do'eg added. "Now he has resources?"

"Yes, talk of revolt has been increasing in Y'hudah ..." Avinadav said hesitantly.

"We can't allow that!" Avner exclaimed, rising with animation. "That is treason! Sha'ul, we have to act!"

"I want to know where he is now," Sha'ul addressed the council with icy calm. "In Karmel? Where they once erected a statue in my honor?"

"No, most worthy king," Bela oozed. "The men of Zif tell us he has returned to the south of the wilderness, hiding by the hill of Hakhilah. His numbers have increased, as has his property and flocks. They say there are women ... even children who travel in his company now."

Sha'ul brooded, elbows resting on the table, hands folded in front of his face.

"I guess I have to kill him then."

David had learned his lesson. He and his lieutenants made a determination—no more surprises. Under the inspiration and direction of his nephew Yo'av, David seeded the countryside with paid informants, building a rudimentary intelligence network.

This was how David heard that Sha'ul and three thousand soldiers had entered the wilderness of Zif. David dispatched quick-footed 'Asah'el and a few others for confirmation and to spy out Sha'ul's position while he relocated his followers farther south. The king was indeed on the hunt again, camped beside the road next to Hakhilah. And Avner was with him.

"That's it," David told his men. "Enough is enough. It is time to turn the tables."

"How?" Yo'av asked.

"By making a preemptive strike."

This was music to Yo'av's ears.

Yashov'am, Shammah, and El'azar were left in charge of the camp while David himself secretly traveled north with a tiny group of his best fighters. After dark, David met up with his advance scouts on a rocky height that afforded a view of Sha'ul's encampment and the hill beyond. To avoid making a silhouette, David crawled on his stomach to the edge of the overlook. It was hard to make out the details in the darkness, but he could see that the camp was arrayed in a customary circular pattern, with baggage on the outside, several small tents as a secondary ring, and the centermost being a protected space for the highest rank. That is where Sha'ul and Avner would be. The supreme commander and the king, the two biggest threats to David in one place. And about three thousand elite soldiers.

David saw no movement or firelight, heard no noise. Sentries must be on duty. But David did not believe they would be on high alert this night. They wouldn't be expecting a surprise attack from the inferior force they were chasing.

"It's time to end this," David said to himself, pushing himself up to a low crouch and turning to his comrades. "Who wants to go down with me into the camp?"

One of the men, a Hitti, gasped.

"You're going down there?"

"Yes."

"That's a terribly big risk."

"I'm not afraid," David answered plainly. "Well? Who's got the guts to come with me?"

"I'll go with you," said Avishai, the eldest of the sons of Tz'ruyah.

David smiled and clasped Avishai's hand in gratitude. "Let's go."

David and Avishai crept down from the height, crossed a brook over partially submerged stones, and moved from cover to cover as they silently approached the encampment across the wide expanse. Sounds of light snoring carried through the night air. They waited, watched, and listened. No guards appeared to be on the path of approach immediately before them. They pushed forward with David leading the way.

As soon as they entered the perimeter of the camp, they ducked behind a pile of baggage. David took slow, deep breaths, trying to ease his pulse. The camp was eerily still, with only the sounds of men sleeping to break the calm. Besides the tents, many soldiers were lying on the ground in the open air. David could see the numerous shadowy shapes of the slumbering bodies. This was indeed a hastily assembled camp, not meant for a long stay but simply to get through a few hours of rest before pushing off again. How was it that they had seen no guards? David prayed for this deep sleep to remain.

David tapped Avishai gently on the knee, and they continued farther in, weaving their way through the tents and human obstacles. One false step in the darkness could prove fatal. They were but two surrounded by three thousand—odds that even David didn't like.

And there they were, Sha'ul and Avner both asleep in the dead center of the camp. They were not in tents, but under the stars with the regular soldiers. Next to Sha'ul's head was his familiar spear, protruding out of the ground from where he had stuck it.

Avishai tugged the back of David's shirt, signaling for him to get down. They lay in the grass and watched Sha'ul's chest, rising and falling, rising and falling. Avishai leaned in so close his mouth was practically touching David's ear and spoke in the slightest of whispers.

"This night, God has delivered your enemy into your hand. Please, let me take his spear and pin him to the ground with one stroke. One stroke is all it will take."

It was a simple solution. David's tremendously strong nephew could shove Sha'ul's own spear through his throat, killing the king at once with hardly a sound. The man who had sworn time and time again to kill David, who had chased him to the ends of the kingdom, would be vanquished.

But David couldn't go through with it. He just couldn't.

Turning his head, he whispered, "No. Don't kill him."

Avishai exhaled through his nostrils, and David could sense his disappointment.

"Listen. Despite everything, he is still the king Yahweh anointed. You can't assassinate such a man and be without guilt. Trust me, either Yahweh Himself will strike Sha'ul dead, or his final day of natural life will come upon him, or he will go into battle and perish that way. But Yahweh forbid that I be his executioner."

Avishai made no move or reply. Another perfect opportunity ruined. He was disappointed, even frustrated, but he would obey.

Just then Avner stirred. David and Avishai froze in place, flattening themselves to the earth. The commander snorted, then moved his shoulders side to side as he adjusted his sleeping posture. David held his breath. All was still again.

David leaned in once more to whisper to his nephew, heart pounding.

"Go take the spear that is by the king's head ... and that jug of water next to him."

Sha'ul opened his eyelids and blinked. It was still dark. He felt heavy with sleep and in a haze of confusion. What had woken him? He sensed something was amiss. Soldiers were rousing all around him, even Avner. Many of the soldiers were sitting up, then standing.

A voice was calling as if from a great distance, from out of the darkness of the night. The voice carried from its mysterious point of origin and echoed off the hill. Sha'ul shook his fuzzy head and strained to listen and make sense of the words.

"Hey! Soldiers of Yisra'el! Everyone! Sha'ul! King Sha'ul! Wake up!"

The disembodied voice continued persistently, disturbing the sleepers with its full-throated call. The soldiers were all on their feet, murmuring, trying to gauge the source and meaning of the voice.

"Avner! Oh, Avner! Aren't you going to answer me?" the voice called.

The voice was definitely coming from that rocky peak a ways off. Avner tried and failed to calculate the distance in his mind; he was still too disoriented. The commander stood and answered with a hoarse shout.

"Who are you who dares call to the king?" he challenged.

"Avner! It is you! The great general, the commander of Yisra'el's armies, the mighty right hand man of Sha'ul! You do call yourself a man, don't you?" the voice taunted. "Tell me, why haven't you protected your lord the king? Isn't that your sworn duty? You have failed in your task! One of the people came to destroy your lord tonight!"

Avner took several big steps in the direction of the voice, trying to make out the contours of the rocky height as his eyes adjusted to the darkness.

"What are you talking about? Identify yourself!" he demanded.

"You did a bad thing!" the voice continued. "I never thought you so careless! As Yahweh lives, you and all your men deserve to be put to death because you did not guard Yahweh's anointed! How negligent of you! Take a look, where are the king's spear and the jug of water that were by his head?"

Avner hurried back to Sha'ul's side. The king looked down at where he had been sleeping and then all around him. He couldn't see the spear. He groped on the ground with his fingers. Had his jug of water moved?

"I can't find them," the king said. "They're gone."

Avner's mouth hung open as the implications sunk in. "Sha'ul ..." he began.

The king held up a hand to silence his cousin. He slowly walked toward the edge of the camp, pushing through clumps of anxious soldiers standing at high alert and wanting desperately to know what was going on.

"David, my son, is that your voice?" Sha'ul asked into the night, hearing his own voice echoing out.

"Yes, it is, my lord the king!" David answered. "Tell me why! Why! Why is my lord chasing after his servant? What have I done? What am I guilty of?"

Sha'ul bit his lip and said nothing.

David continued, "Let my lord the king listen to the words of his servant. If it is Yahweh who has stirred you up against me, then may He accept a sin offering or any other sacrifice on my behalf to atone for whatever I have done to displease Him! But if it is mere men who have stirred you up, either Avner, or Do'eg, or anyone else, may they be cursed before Yahweh! For then such men have driven me from my home, away from the tabernacle of Yahweh, out of the inheritance of His people, out of the Promised Land … sending me into the idolatrous nations! Without cause!

"Please, do not let my blood stain the ground of a foreign land full of pagan gods, far from the presence of Yahweh. The king of Yisra'el is hunting me as one hunts a partridge in the mountains, and I am but an insignificant flea!"

David waited, looking down at the dim figure of the king, now standing alone in the field outside the camp. Sha'ul appeared to be completely motionless, as if frozen in place, arms hanging by his sides.

"I have sinned," Sha'ul said, just loudly enough for David to hear it.

Had those three words ever left Sha'ul's mouth before? David wondered.

There was an ensuing vacuum of silence as if the world was holding its breath.

"Return, David, my son," Sha'ul managed. "Come back with us to Giv'ah. Come back to the royal fortress. I will not hurt you. You've spared my life once again. I am … a fool, and I have made a horrible mistake."

David stood erect at the edge of the overlook, hoisting Sha'ul's spear high and waving it back and forth like a trophy.

"Behold, the king's spear! Let one of your young men come up here and get it!"

David stabbed the tip of the spear down and wedged it hard into a crevice of the rock he was standing on, leaving it sticking out like a splinter.

"Yahweh will repay every man for the righteousness and faithfulness in his life," David called. "Yahweh delivered you into my hand this night, but I refused to take the life of the king whom Yahweh anointed. As your life was deemed valuable in my sight, so may my own life be valuable in the sight of Yahweh. May He deliver me from every trouble!"

The sky was beginning to bleed a bluish hue as the earth rotated into the early morning. Sha'ul sighed and gave a hand signal to the incredulous Avner to begin packing up the camp. The king turned and took one more step out into the field, gazing up at his rival, clearly silhouetted on top of the peak.

"Blessed are you, David, my son. You will go far."

—XLI—

David, his commanders, and his bodyguards knelt in front of King Akhish of Gat. David placed before the P'lishtim leader a wooden chest, which Akhish opened to find brimming with silver pieces and other valuables.

Akhish smiled broadly, shut the chest, and motioned for David to rise.

"Please, please. You are my guest. No need for such displays of humility."

"Thank you," David said.

Akhish again motioned for David, this time to follow him, and they each took a seat in the throne room to converse more comfortably while everyone else looked on.

"From the moment you sent your entourage to me I have wanted so very desperately to meet you," the king said. "Your feud with Sha'ul has become legendary, even in P'leshet. Or, should I say, especially in P'leshet!"

Akhish showed no signs of recognition of the previous, ignominious meeting between the two men. David's circumstances, and by direct extension his presentation and demeanor, had so changed as to be thoroughly unrecognizable. He was no longer a grubby beggar feigning madness to escape wrath, but a tribal chieftain with money and manpower in tow. If the king thought once about his strange encounter with the "mad imposter," he made no mention of it now.

"Then you know full well that my people and I have no portion in Yisra'el," David answered. "We seek freedom from the oppression of Sha'ul's regime. Every one of us has chosen to cast off that yoke and start fresh."

"Yes, you said as much in your message. But what I want to know is … what are your plans? How do you envision me being able to help you?"

"It's quite simple, King Akhish. I want to be your ally. I want to be able to call your fine country my home and raise children here with my wives. Your hospitality to other Yisra'elites who have left their country is well known. But I offer more. Your enemies will become my enemies, and your battles will become my battles."

Akhish rubbed his hands together giddily and laughed.

"They say there is quite a price on your head! What fun! I can just imagine Sha'ul squirming when he hears that we welcomed you with open arms. Is it true that you once snuck into a cave while Sha'ul was relieving himself … stole all his clothes and made him walk all the way back to his camp completely naked?"

"Something like that …"

David, his six hundred, and their wives and children were given homes within the capital city of Gat. The remaining livestock they didn't offer to Akhish as tribute were kept nearby under the watch of Akhish's herdsmen.

Crossing into P'leshet and appealing to King Akhish was a bold move, but David knew Sha'ul would not relent from his pursuit, despite any promises made to the contrary. How many times had Sha'ul sworn not to harm

David? At least three. David did not want yet another broken promise to be the death of him. Fool me once ...

Within minutes of settling into his generous new residence, David summoned Yo'av to a secret meeting.

"I have a very important task for you, nephew. I need you to put that strategic mind of yours to work. You are going to be my spymaster here."

"Anything you say."

"I need you to locate a man, a son of a P'lishti blacksmith named Ittai."

"Okay. Why?"

"He once helped me, but that is of secondary importance. Why are the P'lishtim the most dominant military force in the whole region?"

"Iron," Yo'av answered without hesitation.

"That's right. From the tips of their arrows to the axles of their chariots, P'lishtim iron-smithing gives them a huge advantage over us. And by us, I mean Yisra'el. We have a rare opportunity. I am charging you with the task of learning everything you can about this technology. Everything."

"With pleasure," Yo'av said with a gleam in his eye.

David maintained a bond with King Akhish, having regular audiences with him as they toured the city, discussed Yisra'el, or as David regaled Akhish with carefully edited tales of his adventures. The P'lishtim king was delighted to have such a brave and proven warrior on his side.

After about four months passed, David approached King Akhish and asked that, if he had found favor in the king's sight, would Akhish allow David and his growing "family" to relocate to a new dwelling place somewhere in the P'lishtim countryside, no longer to live in the bustling royal city. David implied that his continued presence was unnecessarily expensive and a burden to the king, not to mention the potential friction of rubbing shoulders with so many P'lishtim and contributing to the envy of Akhish's courtiers, who were used to seeing Hebrew exiles confined to the slums. Of course, David's real motives were quite different.

Akhish graciously granted David's request, far and above what David had expected. As the vassal of Akhish, David and his men were given the entire city of Ziklag, about twelve miles south of Gat, which had once belonged to Yisra'el but had long ago been conquered and occupied by the P'lishtim. David and all that was his were unilaterally relocated to Ziklag by royal command.

Although David technically remained under P'lishtim protection, this outlying city may prove irresistible bait for Sha'ul. Akhish dared him to try. David could certainly defend himself. Regardless, David was to use this southern position to strike out against Yisra'el, the country that had betrayed him and he had so ferociously denounced.

"Wait ... we're actually going to fight against our own?" El'azar asked incredulously.

David and his chief commanders—Yashov'am, El'azar, Shammah, Avishai, 'Asah'el, Yo'av and the young B'nayah—were dining in their new home, passing platters of food around the table as they strategized.

"Of course not!" David replied. "What Akhish doesn't know won't hurt him. We will still fight Yahweh's battles against the enemies of Yisra'el. We will put to the edge of the sword all the ancient foes of our God-given land who have remained like stubborn splinters in our side, though they were to be devoted to destruction long ago. We will complete our forefathers' unfinished business."

"But David, surely Akhish will hear of this. Then all the armies of P'leshet will be against us!" Shammah worried. "How could we ever get away with such a scheme?"

"There is a way," Yo'av added coldly. "We leave no survivors. Not a man or woman can remain when we attack, and we leave nothing of their settlements behind as evidence."

"Yes ... this way, there are no witnesses who can tell the P'lishtim anything," David agreed, wiping his mouth.

They struck against the G'shuri, then later the Gizri, and finally the 'Amaleki. No prisoners. David's six hundred destroyed their enemies and plundered their sheep, their oxen, their donkeys, their camels, and even their very clothes in a series of daring raids. Whatever remained was burned or buried.

After recuperating from one such fierce battle, David, with an entourage, made his regular trip to Gat to meet with his patron. In an open palace courtyard, David ceremoniously presented the P'lishtim ruler with a generous gift of the finest of the animals his men had taken. And the king was pleased.

"David! So good to see you," Akhish gushed. "What marvelous gifts you bring me."

Akhish turned to his nobles and courtiers standing by in the courtyard and admonished them.

"You see this? When was the last time any P'lishti brought me such a rich offering? Tell me, David, my good man, where have you raided today?"

"Against the territory of the Keni in the south, my lord! What a fight! One day they will sing songs about it."

"Oh! How exciting! First, you attack the Negev of Y'hudah, and then last time it was the descendants of Yerachme'eli, and now the Keni! I wish I could go with you," Akhish swished his hand through the air, engaging in imaginary swordplay. "Ha! Take that!"

"I wouldn't dream of putting your majesty in harm's way," David said with a wry smile, pulling back one of his sleeves to reveal a large scar on his arm.

"Ouch," Akhish said, his eager bravado deflating. "My father was the real soldier in the family. Still ..."

Akhish strolled over to where the gift animals were being led away in orderly procession by his attendants. He brushed his fingers against the soft white wool of one of the large, handsome sheep. The king sighed.

"You know, the other P'lishtim lords are still quite skeptical of you. But I know your worth and your dedication. Their loss!"

David rested in Ziklag from his travels and violent excursions. The seasons were changing, and it would soon be time for the men to rest, to build upon what they already had in their new city. David ensured that all the belongings his followers had acquired by battle and blessing were diligently and justly divided.

David decided to begin composing and playing music again, which he had fallen out of the habit of doing. He replaced his former instrument with a brand new one, of the finest craft and artistry that money could buy. He intensified his prayer life, not as a desperate plea for rescue, but as a regular meditation, seeking out the presence of the Spirit of Yahweh. He didn't know exactly what Yahweh had in store for him, not step-by-step at least, but he trusted. David knew that Yahweh had a hope and a future for him.

Time passed.

Before David and his six hundred could mark the anniversary of living in Ziklag for one full year, Achino'am walked outside the city to find her husband sitting alone, gazing as dramatic white clouds drifted across an open, grassy field where sheep grazed.

She stood behind him and wrapped her arms around his chest. David sat up straight, pressing his shoulders more tightly into her embrace. Even in this peaceful scene, his wife could feel the tension in his muscles.

Achino'am bent low until her soft cheek pressed against David's ruddy beard.

The words she spoke made David's heart skip a beat.

"I'm pregnant."

—XLII—

Without warning, an imposing column of P'lishtim soldiers marched toward Ziklag, with King Akhish at the head. All who were on David's side tensed at the sight. David always went up to Gat to see the king, never vice versa. This was unexpected, unwanted—the reason, unknown.

David went out to meet the procession, careful to betray no hint of unease, even as his men silently took up defensive positions. Akhish greeted him as if nothing were amiss, and David ushered the P'lishtim through the city gates and into his own home.

"The P'lishtim lords are planning an invasion of Yisra'el," Akhish began. "David, this is the big one! All the forces of the Pentapolis and the camps in between are joining together for a massive campaign. I am sorry I didn't tell you about it sooner. I was sworn to secrecy until now."

"You sound confident about this," David spoke quickly, hoping to distract Akhish from whatever expression may have unconsciously played across his face.

"Yes! The Seranim have been planning this for a long time. We've been testing the weaknesses in Yisra'el's defenses, scouting out the geography, coordinating our troops. As it stands, we totally outmatch the armies of Sha'ul! You see, the king of Gaza has been getting a huge influx of immigrants who have been pushed out of the territories of Egypt, and they are all eager to enlist. With our total combined forces, our strength cannot be measured!"

David nodded politely as his mind raced.

"Besides all that," Akhish continued, "our intelligence verifies widespread dissatisfaction with Sha'ul. The Seranim believe the entire country is unstable! The Hebrew holy man is dead. And even you ... you are proof that the favor of the gods is against Yisra'el!"

"Ah ... yes."

"You and your men must come with me to the battle. You will be part of our camp, and go out with us when we fight against our mutual enemy. This will be your revenge, David! Yes, I've come to collect you. Tell your men we leave immediately to join with the rest of the P'lishtim forces. Are you ready for war?"

It was clear from the king's tone that this was not optional. David flashed a brave smile. "You'll finally get the chance to see just what your servant can do!"

Akhish was joyful. "David, I think I am going to make you my personal bodyguard for life!"

The P'lishtim readied themselves to leave for the front, and the horrible momentum was carrying David and his men along like a whirlwind. They were being forced into mortal combat against their own countrymen, against Yahweh's chosen people, against their own kin. Yet, to refuse or even hesitate now would be to reveal their sham loyalty to the powers who were so confident in their ability to completely overthrow David's homeland.

David kissed vibrant Avigayil and graceful, pregnant Achino'am. His followers also said goodbye to their wives and children. So many families were in Ziklag—so much life, and love, and hope for the future. So many fathers being led off to kill or be killed in a war they couldn't be more opposed to.

The long march to the undisclosed staging area began. David's six hundred marched in the middle of the split P'lishtim column as they headed to join with the rest of the soldiers from Gat. Externally, David was the image of total enthusiasm and resolve, while his insides churned. He begged Yahweh for some way out of this dilemma.

In Giv'ah, Avner pounded on the bedroom door until Sha'ul opened, a sheet draped around his body and a film of sweat over his leathery, age-spotted face.

"What is it?" Sha'ul demanded as Avner averted his eyes, having caught a glimpse of the feminine foot and ankle of the king's concubine, Ritzpah, jutting out from under a blanket on the large bed in the room beyond.

"You have to come at once," Avner said, suppressing the thoughts of Ritzpah that sprung up within him.

"I'm busy, can't you see that?"

"You're about to be a lot busier."

On top of Mount Gilboa, Sha'ul was filled with abject terror by what he saw.

In the great plain below, stretching out from the Yizre'el Valley in the tribal land of Yissakhar toward the coast, was an unimaginable sight. The effect was as if the sand of the seashore had, against all impossibility, been moved many miles inland. A curving swath of an uncountable multitude spread across the land.

It couldn't be. It couldn't be possible for there to be that many P'lishtim soldiers! It was the largest military array the king had ever witnessed. And so many chariots ... so, so many chariots. Avner worked furiously to direct the officers of the many regiments and divisions arriving to dig in and fortify their positions. Sha'ul stood transfixed.

"Useless! Get out!"

Sha'ul threw a sandal after the man fleeing the king's tent. Bela dutifully walked over and picked it up as if nothing had happened, returning it to Sha'ul.

"These so-called 'court prophets' are worthless!" Sha'ul shouted and cursed. "Where is that real prophet? I told you to bring me one!"

"Yes, wise king, I believe he has just arrived. One of the protégés of the seer."

Bela stuck his head out of the tent flap, calling for the guards to escort the visitor. The visitor was not alone. Gad had a young boy with him, dressed in the same modest garb.

"Mmmm?" Bela murmured. "What's this?"

"His name is Natan. He is with me," Gad explained simply, leaving the quiet boy to stand by his side as the prophet faced Sha'ul.

"Inquire of Yahweh for me!" Sha'ul said brusquely. "I need to know what to do! Yahweh won't speak to me. No dreams, no words. The priests with their silly ephods can't tell me anything. My prophets have become like ... like ... arrgggh! They are useless! Can you tell me what I need to know?"

Gad swallowed the lump forming in his throat. The boy looked up at the prophet with big, watchful eyes.

"I have come here as you ordered," Gad said, "but you will not be happy with what I have to tell you. As soon as your soldiers came for me, I began to pray and fast, but so far I have heard nothing. I have not heard one word from Yahweh about this matter. It is strange, almost as if the sky has turned hard as flint and no words from heaven can get through. I am sorry."

Sha'ul sat, fuming. This prophet was just like the rest of them. Another dead end. The king said nothing for a long time, retreating into the recesses of his mind. Gad looked at Bela, then slowly turned and excused himself and Natan.

Bela fiddled his fingers in the eerie silence. The advisor knew Sha'ul had not eaten a thing all day, so great was his anxiety.

"I want you to find a woman who is a medium," Sha'ul said in a near whisper.

"What was that, my king?" Bela asked.

"A medium, a spiritist, a witch, a necromancer ... whatever you call them."

"Uh ... most gracious king, by your own edict, all occult practitioners were put to death or driven from the land many years ago."

"Don't tell me about my own laws!" Sha'ul yelled, grabbing the sandal as if to throw it at Bela. "I am very well versed in them! I'm giving you a new order, and that order is to find me a medium!"

Sha'ul removed his jewelry, diadem, royal robe, weapons, and all finery that identified him as either royalty or military. He wrapped himself from head to toe in shabby peasant clothes. Outside his tent, Bela was waiting with three saddled donkeys and another of Sha'ul's advisors in the flickering torchlight. The hour was late.

"There is a medium not far from here, in the village of 'Ein-dor on the slope of Mount Hermon. He will lead us," Bela said, pointing to the other man.

Leaving the safety of the camp, they rode in silence down narrow goat paths under a full moon as they clandestinely navigated their way through the valley. After seven or so miles, they arrived at their destination.

The village of 'Ein-dor was a dirty enclave, a dozen or so makeshift buildings in a state of decay, laid out concentrically around a small well. The moonlight cast sepulchral shadows from the row of homes, and Sha'ul and his companions dismounted, hitching their donkeys by the well. The village was deathly quiet except for the background chirp and buzz of insects.

Oddly, light spilled from the cracks of a window and doorframe of one of the residences. At this late hour?

"That's the place," the other advisor whispered.

The three men approached the door of the shack, their footsteps sounding unnaturally loud to their ears. Bela reached out and rapped his knuckles on the creaky wood. The door slowly swung ajar, and Sha'ul was hit with a pungent aroma as a cloud of incense smoke swept out to greet him.

"Yes?" a hesitant voice inquired.

A woman's head came into the opening. Various candles were arranged and burning behind her, and Sha'ul could make out a broad nose, curled, wiry hair, and a face set deep with wrinkles that made the woman look much older than she really was.

"We've ... I've come to see you," Sha'ul said, digging in his unfamiliar clothing for a silver piece, which he held up between thumb and forefinger like a morsel of bread.

"Come in … come in," the woman said, grinning. Sha'ul noticed several chipped and blackened teeth.

She opened the door wider and moved aside so Sha'ul could squeeze his large body through. Bela and the other man attempted to follow, but she held up a thin hand, wagging her long fingernail back and forth.

"Just him."

"Wait outside," Sha'ul told them.

Inside, the odor of the incense was spicy and overpowering, mixed with some other unpleasant scent that made Sha'ul's eyes water. He squinted and registered a small kitchen area and a bed. Sha'ul also noticed a fattened calf tied up in a room off to the side and wondered if its excrement was contributing to the smell. Thick candles were burning everywhere and dripped their wax. Bunches of dried herbs tied with string hung upside down from the ceiling.

"Follow me, follow me. This way," the woman said, brushing past Sha'ul and ducking through hanging drapes into another, even smaller room. "Sit, sit."

Sha'ul struggled to cross his legs underneath his body in the tight space. The woman slid into a space across from him, a round fire pit with still-hot coals lying between them. Scrawled on the walls were various symbols that appeared nonsensical to Sha'ul, and all around were various containers and, of course, more candles.

The woman held the silver piece up and scrutinized it. Satisfied, she dropped it into a jar with a clink.

"What is it you want me to do?" the woman asked, scrunching her face in a look of uncertainty.

"Conjure up a spirit from the dead for me," Sha'ul answered. "Bring up whoever I name to you."

"What? I can't do that," she said, sounding offended. "Don't you know it is against the law? Are you trying to lay a trap for me and get me killed? You are a Hebrew, so you must know, Sha'ul has cut off all mediums and necromancers from the land."

Sha'ul raised his hands in a show of harmless innocence.

"I swear, as surely as Yahweh my God lives, no harm will come to you for this."

The woman nodded and relaxed. She picked up a stick and began to stir the coals with the blackened end. Then she reached for a branch of some sort of herb and tossed it on the coals, quickly drizzling it with a liquid from a small vial she kept nearby. The fire sizzled and popped, emanating unnaturally colored smoke that quickly filled the small room.

The woman closed her eyes and inhaled deeply. Despite the assault on his senses, Sha'ul leaned forward, observing the woman with equal parts fascination and anticipation.

"Whom do you want me to summon?" she croaked, her voice deep and raspy.

"Shemu'el, the man of Yahweh."

The woman nodded rhythmically, her glassy stare disappearing behind her eyelids. She began to whisper and mutter, making unintelligible chanting noises to herself as she blindly plucked ingredients from various open jars and added them to the fire.

She was calling to her familiar spirit, the dark force through which she divined knowledge, often astounding her customers by revealing the secrets of their hearts. The spirit would assume any form to deceive the ones seeking communion with the dead.

But something unexpected happened.

The woman jolted upright, her eyes shooting open. Sha'ul, too, was startled in response to her sudden violent motion. She was staring into the flame and smoke in a panic, recoiling from whatever it was that she saw.

"You deceived me!" she screamed. "You're Sha'ul!"

"Wait! Don't be afraid! I told you; you're safe!" Sha'ul shouted back in a vain attempt to calm her. "Tell me what you see!"

"I see a divine being coming up out of the ground!" she called in horror, unable to tear her eyes away from the fire pit.

"What does it look like?" Sha'ul urged with nervous energy.

"An old man is coming up. He is wrapped in a robe."

"It's him! It's Shemu'el!" the king gasped.

Sha'ul threw himself down on the ground, having to contort his body in the tight space to bow and avoid burning his head or hands. Then Sha'ul heard Shemu'el's voice, loud and stern.

"Why have you disturbed me by bringing me up?"

Sha'ul kept his face to the ground, his body shaking.

"Shemu'el! I am in great distress! The P'lishtim are at war with me. They are about to invade the entire country! And God has abandoned me. He won't speak or answer me by dreams or prophets. Shemu'el, help! I called you so that you can tell me what to do!"

The disembodied voice answered with crystal-clear, put-upon irritation.

"Yahweh has departed from you and has become your enemy, and you decide to ask me? What more could I say? Yahweh has done exactly what He spoke through me. He has torn the kingdom out of your hand and has given it to your neighbor David. You did not obey the voice of Yahweh when He told you to carry out His fierce wrath against the Amaleki. Now, Yahweh has done this to you. He will give Yisra'el over to the P'lishtim, the army will fall, and you will fall with them." Then came the coup de grace.

"Very soon you and your sons will be here with me in the land of the dead."

When he heard this, Sha'ul collapsed to the ground, the blood rushing out of his head and his strength leaving his body. The woman snapped out of her trance. She saw what was happening and scrambled to her feet, dumping a pot of dirt over the fire to extinguish it. Sha'ul crawled on his face and sobbed pathetically.

The woman hurried to his side, unsure of what to do. She tried to pull on his arm to get him to stand. But he just lay there, stretched out and shaken, paralyzed with despair.

"Can you hear me?" the woman cried. "Listen, your maidservant has obeyed you. I did exactly what you asked, even risking my own life! Now, please, get up. Get up!"

The woman threw open the drapes and ran outside, calling to Sha'ul's companions. They came in at the sound of her alarm and beheld their king groveling on the floor.

"Please, he won't listen to me," she said, vanishing around the corner and returning with some bread. "Eat this, it will give you strength."

"No," Sha'ul sobbed.

"You haven't eaten all day, my king," Bela said. "It may help."

"I won't eat!"

Bela looked at the other man and pantomimed lifting Sha'ul off the ground. Together they struggled with his large body but succeeded in getting him to a sitting position.

"Lay him on the bed," the woman said.

"Yes! Please. Let my lord, the king, lie down here. We will get you something to eat and drink."

The woman and his companions both begged until Sha'ul finally consented and dragged himself weakly onto the bed with help from the others. The woman quickly led her calf outside the shack and slaughtered it by candlelight. She took flour and water and kneaded unleavened cakes of bread to bake, preparing a quick meal. When ready, she carried the food to Sha'ul.

The men solemnly ate the meal in the dead of the night before they departed.

—XLIII—

Y'honatan walked across the dark soil as he coaxed the yoke of oxen forward. The beasts dragged behind them the metal-tipped plow, furrowing the field. The prince worked shirtless, and the sun warmed his bare torso. He was sweaty and dirty, and thoroughly enjoying himself.

Y'honatan's youngest son, five-year-old M'fivoshet, sat nearby with one of the prince's servants, watching his dad work while resting his chin in his pudgy hands.

"You see? If the oxen trust you and know your voice, they'll follow you without having to use a whip or a goad. Understand?"

"Yes, Daddy."

"What do you think we should plant?"

"Some breads!"

Y'honatan laughed, wiping the sweat off his forehead with the back of his forearm.

"It doesn't quite work like that ... but let's see what we can do."

They heard the noise of approaching horses. Y'honatan placed his hands on the snouts of the oxen, easing them to a stop as he vigilantly looked about.

"Who is it?" he called to his servant.

"It's your father."

"Take the oxen. My son can stay."

Sha'ul was dressed for battle in his heavy armor. His iron sword was strapped to his side. After being helped off his horse by one of his guards, he took several steps toward his eldest son, stopping at the edge of the field. The king and the prince assessed one another quietly.

"Y'honatan, my son, I need your help."

"What is it, Father?"

"The P'lishtim are readying an invasion. The biggest one I've ever seen in my lifetime. All the armies are gathered. I need your wisdom, your strength, your courage. If we fail ... Yisra'el will fall."

"That bad?"

"The worst. Your brothers have already joined me at the battlefield. They could use their big brother."

"What about your other children? The concubine's sons?"

"You know they aren't old enough for war! But don't think the P'lishtim will spare them, or your own children. This is victory or death. I need you, just like when we fought together in old times."

"Old times, huh?"

"You know that everything I have done has been for you and this family. Everything. You are my son, my firstborn. I love you. But now this kingdom I have fought so hard for ... it's slipping through my fingers. I will have nothing left. Nothing. Please, my son, I need you by my side once again."

Y'honatan looked at his father, still strong despite his old age, still ready to go into the heat of battle with his sword swinging stubbornly. Y'honatan stalked through the dirt to his own young child. He caressed the back of the boy's head with his dirty hand, not caring, and kissed the boy lovingly on the forehead.

"Blech!" M'fivoshet said, wiping the kiss off his forehead with a giggle.

"Yes, Father, I will join you," the prince said.

"Follow me."

The P'lishtim mobilized their forces, advancing across the great, wide plain by carefully ordered divisions with their officers of thousands and hundreds, infantry and chariots. King Akhish and his troops caught up to the rest of the armies and joined at the rear. David and his cohort marched beside Akhish until the king excused himself and went ahead to confer with the rest of the Seranim.

The remainder of the Five P'lishtim lords, the kings of Ashdod, Gaza, Ashkelon, and 'Ekron, observed the movement of the ranks from the shade of their portable tent covering as they poured over charts and maps. The fiercest, most elite soldiers in all of P'leshet guarded them.

"You're late!" the king of Ashdod chided Akhish.

"I'm here now," Akhish said, rubbing his hands together. "Everything looks like it is going smoothly."

"We're going to wipe Yisra'el off the map."

"The Lady of 'Ekron, Ba'al-Zibbul, and 'Ashtarot be praised!" 'Ekron's king added, making a superstitious gesture in the air.

"Wait!" Gaza's king said, peering toward the rear of the formations. "What is that I see?" The concern in his voice got the attention of the other P'lishtim lords.

"Are those ... Hebrews with the rear guard?" Gaza's king demanded, thrusting an accusing finger at Akhish's chest. "What are they doing there with your men?"

The other Seranim took up the outcry, demanding answers from their colleague.

"That's David, the former servant of Sha'ul, king of Yisra'el! Don't you know that he defected to me? He's been with me for over a year! He is completely reliable. I've never found a single fault in him."

The king of Ashdod shook his head sadly and groaned, "The apple has fallen far from the tree. Your father Ma'okh would never have let himself be duped like this."

"What?" Akhish was offended.

"You fool! Send him back. Send him back to wherever it is you keep him!"

"Certainly, the last thing we need is for him to turn on us in the middle of battle! How better for the Hebrew to win back his master Sha'ul's favor than by taking the heads of our men?"

"No, no, no. You've got it wrong. David has been raiding the settlements of Yisra'el for me this whole year past. He has made himself so odious to the other Hebrews, he couldn't return even if he wanted!"

"Isn't this the same David the Hebrew women sing and dance about, saying 'Sha'ul has killed thousands, but David tens of thousands?' Send him back! He will not go with us to battle!"

Having advanced to their next position at Afek, the P'lishtim again pitched their massive camp. Akhish sat with his attendants and fretted, putting it off and putting it off until he finally sent a messenger to summon David.

David followed the man through the multitude of tents to the king's, ignoring the glares of other P'lishtim soldiers. Akhish's face was red and his eyes downcast, embarrassed to be confronting his trusted vassal.

"David."

"What is it, my lord the king?"

"I'm so sorry to tell you this. As Yahweh your God lives, you have been honest and true to me all this time. It seems perfectly right to me that you should march by my side in the upcoming campaign."

"Did your servant do something wrong?" David asked.

"No! I have found nothing wrong in you from the day you first arrived until now! It's just that ... the other lords do not approve of you being here. They want me to send you back."

"But ..."

"Please. I hate to have to do this! Return in peace to Ziklag. Don't do anything that is going to get me in more trouble with the other lords."

"But your servant desires nothing more than to fight against the enemies of my lord the king! I don't understand. Why can't I help you? What have I done wrong?" David pleaded and prodded, keeping a straight face.

Akhish blushed brightly with shame.

"David, you are as blameless in my sight as an angel of God! But I can't overrule the others. They won't hear of it. Please, as soon as it is morning light, take your men and return home. Don't make this harder on me than it already is."

The next morning, David and his six hundred did just as they were told. David rejoiced and praised Yahweh all the way. They traveled south, hugging the border of Y'hudah. It would be a three-day journey back to Ziklag.

On the way, they encountered a group of Yisra'elites on foot who came out to meet them. They had the appearance of soldiers. Seven of the men came forward and bowed down before David and his apprehensive guards.

"Who are you?" David challenged.

"My name is Y'dia'el, from the tribe of M'nasheh. These with me are 'Adnach, Yozavad, another Yozavad, Mikha'el, Elihu and Tziltai."

"Do you come peacefully?"

"Yes, peacefully. We seven come from prominent families of M'nasheh, and we are all the captains of thousands in Sha'ul's army. But no more!"

"You're deserters?"

"This war with the P'lishtim, it is a lost cause! We have no more faith in Sha'ul to save us or lead our nation. We choose to join with you rather than to die for nothing!"

"Follow me."

—XLIV—

Sha'ul and his sons stood dressed for war in their royal armor and weaponry. The king's polished diadem shone on top of his head. Sha'ul's loyal guards were by his side, and each man had his personal armor bearer. The king and his princes, Y'honatan, Abinadav, Malkishua, and Eshba'al, watched from Mount Gilboa as the Yisra'elites took their positions in the valley—they on one side of the spring of Yizre'el and the ocean of P'lishtim on the other.

Eshba'al let out an involuntary gasp as, without warning, the uniformity of the opposing lines snapped with the suddenness and irreversibility of a twig breaking. The initial wave of P'lishtim swept forward with bloody intent, crashing against the Yisra'elites. The war had begun.

Nearing home, at last, David and his men were tired. They had traveled far. But as they saw black smoke on the horizon, adrenaline replaced weariness and, as a whole, they raced toward Ziklag.

It was a smoking heap. A wreck. A burned-out charred skeleton of a city.

The six hundred raised a stunned, anguished cry.

His heart pounding, David ran so fast that he almost outpaced 'Asah'el to be the first to reach the remains of their ruined home. The men threw their weapons and belongings aside in their desperation, running into the husks of their former houses, digging through still-hot rubble with bare hands.

"There aren't any bodies!" one of the men shouted.

"Gone! Everyone is gone!"

The livestock were all gone. Their wives, their sons, their daughters. All gone without a trace. Only ashes were left behind. Everything they had, everything that mattered was torn away or destroyed.

David fell to his knees in the ash while all around him began to weep and wail with all their strength. Avigayil was gone. Achino'am, and his unborn child. Gone! They could be dead. Or raped. Or both. David felt a bitter scream fighting to escape his throat and hot tears flowing from his eyes.

Avner shouted orders to the officers until he was beyond hoarse.

The P'lishtim archers in their feathered helmets were unleashing swells of arrows that darkened the sky, flying over the infantry engaged in brutal hand-to-hand fighting and raining down on the secondary and tertiary Yisra'elite positions. Men fell by the hundreds, like tattered pincushions. The arrows kept coming. It seemed the onslaught would never end.

Then, when the front lines broke, the P'lishtim troops pushed outward to make way for the rows upon rows of chariots, churning forward and running down retreating

Yisra'elites, crushing their bodies and bones under hoof and wheel.

David and his men hadn't a spare drop of moisture left in their bodies or breath in their lungs to cry as they surveyed the debris. They were drained of all strength, all hope. Their worst nightmare had come upon them.

"Was it the P'lishtim?" one man, in shock, asked nobody in particular.

"Maybe it was Sha'ul's men!" another said, turning to grab one of the new defectors from M'nasheh with violent intent.

"No! No! Never!" the man protested.

One of David's followers, a Hitti, and other men with him began to grumble bitterly as they glared at David on his knees.

"This is his fault."

"My daughters ... I left my daughters here, defenseless, to follow him up to the P'lishtim! He should die."

The Hitti stooped and picked up a stone in his shaky hand.

"I'll kill him myself!" one of the men said through stinging eyes and clenched teeth. He too picked up a rock.

Young B'nayah ran over to David and shook him by the shoulders. When that didn't work, he splashed water from his water skin in David's face.

"What are we going to do? David! Talk to me!"

David blinked heavily and registered the man in front of him. David rose to his feet, even as men with hatred in their heart drew closer to harm him. A voice called from the edge of the smoking city.

"Whoever did this came from the south, out of the deep desert. It was a raiding party. They took all our people with them."

It was Avishai speaking, carefully examining tracks leading away from Ziklag.

"Where's the priest? Avyatar!" David called, gathering his wits about him.

The high priest stepped out from the crowd and came before David with the sacred ephod.

"I need to inquire of Yahweh. Shall I pursue this band of raiders? Will I be able to overtake them? Can I rescue any of those that were taken?"

The lines were collapsing. The P'lishtim were too strong, too many. Avner speared enemy soldiers one after another as they charged him. He was in the very thick of the fighting as the Yisra'elites were pushed back. Several of the officers began to run away.

"Protect the king!" Avner tried to shout with his battered vocal chords. "Protect the king!"

The commander could see the single-minded concentration of the attackers to break through and rush the slopes of Mount Gilboa. The P'lishtim were after Sha'ul. They wanted him desperately, and they didn't care how many men they sacrificed to get to him.

The Yisra'elite army was being cut in half, divided. Avner backed his way up the mountain as men fell dead on either side of him. Was it too late to retreat? The enemy soldiers were on the slopes too, swarming everywhere, fighting toward the top.

David and his six hundred raced southwest, following the signs of the raiding party and their captives.

"Help, Yahweh. Help, Yahweh," was David's constant chant under his breath.

They reached the ravine of B'sor, where a brook cut through the land. The air was scorching hot. One of the men collapsed from fatigue. Several others stumbled as they tried to push onward, wheezing. Six days of travel, the devastation of Ziklag, and now this frantic chase had taken its toll.

"I don't know ... if ... I can go much ... further," one of the men gasped, lying down on the ground and clutching his chest.

David surveyed the group and saw many of the same symptoms. He made a decision.

"Anybody who is too tired to go on, stay here by the brook. Guard what little supplies we have left. I am pushing on, and whoever comes with me. Wait for us to return!"

About two hundred stayed behind, too exhausted to continue. David and four hundred pushed on.

Farther south, they stumbled on a young man, crawling weakly in the open country. They grabbed him and brought him to David. He was faint and sickly in appearance, his face heavily sunburned and chapped, and his ribs beginning to show. The man had nothing on his person, which was odd as he was in the middle of nowhere.

David ordered that some water and bread be given to the young man. When the stranger had managed with that, David provided a slice of a fig cake and some raisins. Slowly, the man's strength began to return.

"Who are you, and where do you come from?" David asked, dabbing the man's head with a wet cloth.

"I'm an Egyptian, but I became the servant of an 'Amaleki," the man explained. "My master left me out here to die three days ago because I fell sick."

"'Amaleki? What were you doing all the way out here?"

"We were raiding the south of the K'reti, and Kalev in Y'hudah," the Egyptian managed to say through a coughing fit. "And we burned the town of Ziklag."

David clenched his fists and then forced them to relax. He wanted to interrogate this Egyptian about his wives, about the other women and children. He wanted to shake this man until every last detail of the raid was spilled from his mouth. But he resisted the urge.

"Can you lead me to where these marauders are?"

"Sir, if you swear to God that you won't kill me or hand me over to my master, then, yes, I will lead you to them."

The command post was overrun with P'lishtim. The tents were torn down and shredded and the baggage scattered as enemy soldiers fought for every inch on the top of Mount Gilboa.

Sha'ul and his guards were running. Separated from their father, Y'honatan and the other princes were trying to get to safety as well. P'lishtim infantry sprinted after them, swords and spears raised. The royal guards turned to engage, and bloody fighting ensued until the guards were outnumbered.

"Go! Hurry!" Y'honatan yelled at his brothers. But he knew it was too late. P'lishtim were coming up around the other side, cutting off their escape.

The prince stood, putting himself between the first group of P'lishtim and his brothers. He shot off the last of the arrows in his quiver, expertly nailing his targets. Then he dropped his bow and drew his sword while he raised his other arm to block a swing that clattered hard against the small shield attached to his wrist. Y'honatan thrust with his blade, killing the assailant. Two more were on him in an instant, and he fought against them desperately.

"Get out of here!" Y'honatan shouted again.

But his brothers instead followed his lead, taking a brave stand against their foes. There was nowhere for them to run anyhow. The only other Yisra'elites in sight were corpses.

Y'honatan's armor began to break off in pieces and fall away as blows from sharp blades struck him. Avinadav and Malkishua shoved two P'lishtim off their older brother with their shields, letting him regain his balance. The prince was bloodied from many cuts but didn't stop.

A whizzing arrow struck Y'honatan in the chest.

Then another, piercing his heart.

Avinadav, Malkishua, and Eshba'al ran as more arrows flew, some hitting P'lishtim in the back by accident. More soldiers rushed forward, and Malkishua was speared in the thigh, then finished off. Avinadav threw himself into the attackers and flailed against them until he too was cut down and his life extinguished.

At that moment, a small band of counterattacking Yisra'elite soldiers charged in from the side, too late to save the princes and hopelessly outmatched. Eshba'al put his head down and ran for his life, ducking between the soldiers and aiming for the opposite slope down the mountain, where he caught a glimpse of Avner and other scattered men trying to retreat in the chaos.

The young Egyptian led David straight to the 'Amaleki raiders. They were spread out across the countryside, stuffing their faces with food and swigging alcohol, reveling in their plunder. There were at least a thousand of them, and just as many camels.

"Look there," Yo'av said, pointing out the herds and livestock as David and his men lay along the lip of a hill, spying out the opposition. These fiends must have raided far more than just Ziklag. "And over there, look."

There were the captives! Many women and children, bound at the wrists and strung together, were forced to sit on the ground as a train of slaves while their captors celebrated. They appeared to be unmolested at the moment, but hopeless and afraid. David tried to spot his wives in the multitude, but it was hard from such a distance.

The four hundred watched and waited while the 'Amaleki drank and danced as twilight fell. Each man was itching to satiate his sword with the blood of the villains. Sleep would soon fall on the accursed nomads. Then they would die.

The fighting was fierce all around Sha'ul. Yisra'elites fell by the second, and blood pooled gratuitously on the ground. Sha'ul cut the tip off a spear thrust at him and head-butted the enemy holding it.

"Retreat!" Sha'ul shouted.

The king and his armor bearer tried to put distance between them and the relentless P'lishtim. They were gaining fast. The heart-breaking realization hit him that his sons were in all likelihood dead by now.

Sha'ul heard an arrow whiz by his head. The enemy archers had arrived, and they had him in range! With horror he saw several P'lishtim with raised bows, aiming for him. He had nowhere to run. The volleys were released.

An arrow pierced his shin, striking bone. Sha'ul cried out and stumbled, forcing himself up and trying to hobble away while his armor bearer tried to deflect more arrows with his shield. The armor bearer yelped as several of the deadly missiles narrowly missed his own flesh.

Another arrow hit Sha'ul in the shoulder.

"Aaaagggh!" he shouted angrily, ripping the arrow out with his hand.

Immediately, an arrow clattered off a piece of his remaining armor and then another found purchase through a gap, burying itself in his left bicep with excruciating pain. That arm would be useless now, and he could do no more than limp. The archers were gaining ground, as were additional infantry.

Yet another arrow pierced the king's side, below his ribcage. Sha'ul collapsed to the ground, wincing with pain and dizzy with lost blood. It was hopeless. There was no escape.

"Kill me!" he yelled to his armor bearer.

"What? My lord, no!"

"I said kill me! Curse you! Draw your sword and thrust me through before these uncircumcised come and make sport of me!"

"N-no! My lord, I can't!" the armor bearer pleaded, quaking with fear.

Sha'ul gritted his teeth. With his good arm, he pushed himself up onto his knees, using his sword as support. He eyed his approaching executioners.

"AAAHHHHHH!!!" the king yelled with all his might, turning the point of the iron blade against his own stomach and falling on it until it came out the other side.

Seeing that Sha'ul was dead, and the P'lishtim were almost upon them, the armor bearer also killed himself.

—XLV—

David trudged back to the ravine of B'sor, leading his wives on the backs of two camels. His men were exhausted but overjoyed. Their women and their children and all their goods were with them. Miraculously, not one of them had been lost.

The two hundred who had remained behind at the brook, guarding the supplies, saw the welcome sight materializing out of the wilderness like a mirage and applauded with joy as David greeted them triumphantly.

Some of the four hundred began to grumble, saying, "Give those worthless men their wives and children and tell them to get lost! They didn't go down with us; they don't deserve any of the spoil!"

David abruptly put an end to such talk.

"No, my brothers! Yahweh has worked a great deliverance for us. He gave the raiders into our hands and gave us back all that we lost. The share of the one who went to battle will be the same as he who stayed with the baggage. They shall all share alike!"

The Five P'lishtim lords stood over the corpses of Sha'ul and his sons as their minions stripped the dead that lay strewn across Mount Gilboa and shooed carrion birds away from the piles.

"Here lies the king of the Hebrews and his whelps," Gaza's king said spitefully. "But where is his crown?"

"Bah! Some scavenger made off with it, or maybe one of the Hebrews," 'Ekron's king said.

"Cut off their heads!" Ashdod's king ordered the soldiers nearby, pointing at the dead bodies with his scepter.

"Sha'ul's armor will make a fine trophy in the temple of 'Ashtarot."

"As will his skull in the temple of Dagon!"

Sha'ul's concubine Ritzpah grabbed her sons by the hand, dragging them down the hallway. The royal fortress was in chaos, with servants stripping anything and everything of value that could be salvaged before they fled. Dust fell from the cracks of the shaking construction, and people fell over one another in their frantic attempts to escape.

Ritzpah burst into a room at the end of the hall to find Y'honatan's young son M'fivoshet clinging to his nurse, crying loudly. His father and his grandfather were dead. The nurse, who had been trying to console the child, was startled by the intrusion.

"Why are you still here?" Ritzpah demanded of the maidservant. "The P'lishtim are right outside!"

"What?"

"Everyone is evacuating their towns. The P'lishtim are occupying or destroying everything! They are going to burn Giv'ah to the ground any minute! If you can't escape across the river, you're dead!"

Without another moment's hesitation, the concubine whirled around and was gone, dragging her boys behind her.

In a panic, the nurse grabbed the five-year-old in her arms and ran into the hall. She had no idea where the boy's mother was. The shouts of men could be heard at the other end of the fortress. Were the P'lishtim already inside?

She ran, cradling the child. Suddenly her foot slipped, and M'fivoshet tumbled from her arms, his legs hitting the hard floor with a crack. The child screamed in pain.

"Oh no! Oh no! No! No!" the nurse cried, scooping the injured boy up and holding him tight to her chest. No time to examine the boy. She had to keep running.

Eshba'al sat on the back of the horse as Avner kicked it mercilessly with his heels, driving it over rocky terrain.

"They're dead," Eshba'al said through quivering lips, clutching Avner's waist for dear life.

"I know!" Avner shouted back.

"They're dead! They're dead! They're all dead!" Eshba'al kept blubbering.

"Shut up! Get hold of yourself!" the commander yelled, driving the horse even harder. "You are all that remains of the royal line. But that means nothing unless we can make it to the ford of the Yarden! I need you to keep it together!"

David and his men reached Ziklag and stared at the ruins. They would begin gradually clearing the rubble and rebuilding, but their hearts were not in it. Not at the moment. Instead, they pitched tents outside the city walls, and every man hugged his wife, or relative, or child, and didn't let go. They would eat. They would rest.

David stared off into the distance toward Yisra'el, toward the unknown wider world. He felt isolated here. All this time he had been chasing raiders in the desert, the greater happenings of the kingdoms completely escaped him. A war was going on out there, perhaps the largest confrontation that had ever occurred between the sworn enemy nations of Yisra'el and the P'lishtim.

Achino'am called to David from her tent flap.

"David, feel this," she said, placing the palm of his hand on her abdomen.

"I don't—" he began.

"There!"

David felt something. His heart skipped. His unborn child had just kicked in the womb! David knelt down and kissed his wife's pregnant belly.

On the third day, a lone man approached Ziklag, wearing tattered clothing and with the dust of mourning upon his head. He did not look like a Yisra'elite, nor a P'lishti. He fell to the ground before David and paid homage.

"David! Most wonderful hero and champion! I have come all this way to see you! Oh, I am so glad to have found you!"

"Where have you come from?" David asked.

"I have escaped from the Yisra'elite camp."

"Tell me everything that has happened!"

This man had David's full attention.

"Well, my lord, the people have fled from the battle, and many have fallen and have died. But I have good news for you. Sha'ul and his son Y'honatan are dead!"

David stiffened.

"How ... do you know this?" he asked cautiously.

"I happened to be on Mount Gilboa, and I saw Sha'ul. He was leaning on his spear, and the enemy chariots and horsemen were closing in all around him. Sha'ul turned around and saw me standing there behind him, and he called to me! I said to him, 'What can I do?' He asked me who I was, and I told him that I am an 'Amaleki. Then he called to me and said, 'Please come over here and kill me! I am wounded and in agony, but my life lingers on!' So I did as he asked. I stood over him and put him out of his misery because I knew he couldn't survive much longer. And look at this!"

The man reached into the small sack he was carrying, removing two objects. He held them up with eager, sparkling eyes.

"I took his crown and his bracelet and have brought them here to you, my lord! I rejoice with you! Your enemy is fallen! Take Sha'ul's crown for yourself!"

The man held out the bloodstained diadem and bracelet with an anticipating smile, expecting praise and a great reward. David recognized them as authentic. So it was true. The king was dead. And Y'honatan, David's most faithful friend in the whole world. Dead.

To the man's confusion, David abruptly turned and walked away, sinking to the ground in the yellow grass and tearing his clothes. David was overcome with the deepest of sorrows. His six hundred gathered around him, one by one tearing their own clothes just as their leader had done. David raised his voice in mourning, and his followers joined in the lamentation. They wept and fasted until the evening, letting no food or drink touch their lips.

Before the sun had set, David, barely able to conceal his anger and grief, pulled himself together enough to face the anxious messenger with the ill-gotten treasures.

"Who are you? Where do you come from?"

"I am the son of a sojourner in Yisra'el ... an 'Amaleki," the man replied nervously. "I was doing manual labor for the army."

"Tell me," David asked with cold fury, "how is it that you were not afraid to stretch out your hand and kill Yahweh's anointed king?"

The man began to stammer, searching desperately for words.

David turned to one of his young men. "Go strike him down!"

The man began to protest, begging for his life.

"Your blood be upon your own head!" David said, spitting on the ground. "Your own mouth has testified against you when you said, 'I have killed Yahweh's anointed.'"

David walked away as the man was quickly executed. He went straight into the center of the camp, digging in his tent for his kinnor. David took a seat at the gate of the burned-out city. He contemplated Yisra'el's deceased king, his own former father-in-law, and his dear friend, the prince.

David plucked the strings and sang in his sweet voice, composing this funeral dirge, which he taught to all his followers:

"Your glory, O Yisra'el, is slain on your high places!
How the mighty have fallen!
Tell it not in Gat,

KINGS OF THE PROMISED LAND

Proclaim it not in the streets of Ashkelon,
Lest the P'lishtim daughters rejoice,
And the uncircumcised pagans exult.

You mountains of Gilboa,
Let there be no dew or rain upon you,
Nor fruitful fields that yield offerings of grain!
For there the shield of the mighty was defiled,
The shield of Sha'ul, no longer made slick with oil.

From the blood of the slain,
From the fat of the mighty,
Y'honatan's bow did not turn back,
And the sword of Sha'ul did not return empty.

Sha'ul and Y'honatan, beloved and beautiful!
In their death, they were not parted;
They were swifter than eagles,
They were stronger than lions.

You daughters of Yisra'el, weep over Sha'ul,
Who clothed you with luxurious scarlet,
And put ornaments of gold on your apparel.
How the mighty have fallen in the midst of battle!

The Prince lies slain on your heights,
How I grieve for you, my brother Y'honatan!
Very pleasant have you been to me,
Your love to me was wonderful,
More wonderful than the love of women.

O, how the mighty have fallen,
And the weapons of war have perished!"

Across the Yarden River, the elders and citizens of Yavesh-Gil'ad met in the city square. Refugees were swarming across the river into the eastern tribal lands of M'nasheh, the lands of Gad, and the lands of Re'uven.

The chief elder of Yavesh-Gil'ad, Makhir, the son of 'Ammi'el, spoke to everybody assembled before him. They gave him their full attention as one long ago proven to deserve respect.

"The P'lishtim have fastened the bodies of King Sha'ul and his sons to the wall of Beit-Sh'an in the Yizre'el Valley. They mean this disgraceful action to be a shame to us all, to break our spirits! To deter us! We cannot let this dishonor stand."

"But Makhir ... sir ... what can we do? We are so few."

"Listen carefully. When I was young, in the days of my father, our city came under siege from Nachash and the sons of 'Amon. We faced certain destruction. None would help us. None! Nobody in all of Yisra'el cared to save us until that man, King Sha'ul, rose up with courage and zeal, uniting and leading all of the tribes to deliver us in our time of need. We owe our king the highest honor, even in his death."

All the valiant men of the city were gathered for a clandestine mission, journeying all through the night into enemy-occupied territory and bravely retrieving the bodies of the king and the princes from where they were cruelly on display. They brought the remains back to Yavesh-Gil'ad, and Makhir oversaw the burning of the headless bodies. With solemn, dignified ceremony, all the people gathered as the bones of the slain monarch and his family were buried under a tamarisk tree. Then they all fasted for seven days.

"It is finished, just as you requested," Yo'av reported to his uncle.

David sat, scratching in the dirt with the tip of Golyat's sword, deep in thought.

"Good. Thank you."

Emissaries had been sent bearing generous gifts to many of the cities throughout Y'hudah. They went to Beit-El, Ramot of the Negev, Yatir, 'Aro'er, Sifmot, Esht'moa, Rakhal, the cities of the Yerachme'eli, the cities of the Keni, those in Hormah, those in Kor-'Ashan, 'Atakh, and Hevron.

Many of those southern cities, not yet overthrown or occupied by the P'lishtim, were reeling for the economic damage, political instability, and loss of life from the catastrophic war. Those cities would now be provided with animals, with food, and with money. The elders of those places, including some connections that David had previously made, would be encouraged and sustained in their time of need. The people would be blessed from the hand of David and his heroic outcasts.

David looked around him at his diverse comrades, at his loyal commanders, at the many women and children ... all these people here because of him, following him, looking to him for direction. The world as he knew it had been turned upside down. His life had been transformed. Somehow, in all the drama, he had turned thirty years old. He was a man. He had gained property, allies, livestock, and even a measure of wealth. He had killed many men. He had been married three times and was about to become a father.

David waited until he was alone and bowed his head in prayer. He was at a crossroads, and he needed guidance. He needed wisdom from above. He needed Yahweh to speak into his life, to direct his steps, to make his path straight. David poured out his heart, all of his worries, all of his fears, all of his questions ... everything to his God above.

Go up to Hevron in Y'hudah.

David obeyed.

He left Ziklag and went to Hevron. It was an ancient city and a large center of an important district in the southeast, nestled in the mountains of Y'hudah and far enough removed to still be safe from the P'lishtim menace. David arrived in a grand caravan, riding on a donkey, and was welcomed with glad shouts by all the inhabitants who came out to greet him, ushering him through the city gates.

Wake up.

David opened his eyes.

Wake up.

He sat up in his bed. All seemed peaceful and quiet. It was morning. David swung his legs over the side of the bed and got up. He dressed himself, washing his face and hands with water from a basin. He went outside. Birds were singing.

Having nothing else to do, David decided to go for a walk, strolling through the cobblestone streets and then outside the city. He walked to the top of a small, nearby hill, hoping to get a decent view of the surrounding area, the towns in which many of his followers had settled in with their families.

He indeed got that panorama and more. From his vantage point, David saw what looked to be a great number of people approaching Hevron from all directions, riding and walking, converging on this central point. He wondered at the strange sight.

A sweet voice from behind surprised David, and he turned to see Avigayil, looking radiant in the soft morning light, reclining with her back against the trunk of a tree. David smiled at his wife.

"I didn't expect to find you here, darling."

"They're coming," she said, gesturing out toward the approaching multitude.

"Who is?" David asked.

"Everyone."

"Everyone who?"

"All the elders of Y'hudah!"

"But why?"

"They are coming to anoint you as king."

ABOUT THE AUTHOR:

JUSTIN GABRIEL was born in California in 1984. In addition to being a Christian author and screenwriter, Justin has degrees in Psychology and Pastoral Counseling and serves in the mental health field. He lives in Atlanta with his wife and children. *Kings of the Promised Land* is his first novel. Visit his author website at justingabriel.org